What the experts are saying about ***Living Lies.***

Gary Schroen, retired Senior CIA Officer, who led CIA forces into Afghanistan after 9/11 and author of *First In*

"Mr. Lawler has succeeded in crafting a taut, riveting story of the world of espionage, nuclear proliferation, and the duplicitous nature of Iran's current leadership. You feel as present in a fine restaurant in Geneva as sitting in a small boat off the coast of Iran with a small team of Special Operators waiting to pick-up an Iranian spy. The well-drawn characters, non-stop action, and a stunning climax will make putting this book down very difficult. This is a damn good read!"

Andy Weber, former Assistant Secretary of Defense for Nuclear, Chemical and Biological Defense Programs and CIA lead for Operation Sapphire

"*Living Lies* captures the CIA's sub rosa race against catastrophe with the authentic voice of legendary Case Officer turned author, Jim Lawler. This story of one man's quiet war to keep the world's worst weapons out of the hands of rogue states and terrorists rings true. It is told with the gripping and gritty details that only someone deeply practiced at the art of espionage would know. It should be required reading at The Farm."

Ambassador Henry Crumpton, former senior CIA officer and State Department Coordinator for Counterterrorism, author of *The Art of Intelligence*

"One of the most creative, bold, and successful CIA operatives of his generation, the author knows more about enemy WMD and did more to thwart its proliferation than anybody I know. His brilliance shines through in his first novel, a complex web of nasty intrigue that could be tomorrow's headline. He writes with unvarnished authenticity... because he's lived it."

Bill Harlow, former chief spokesman for the Central Intelligence Agency and bestselling author

"This fascinating fictional tale of espionage, high-stakes skullduggery, and nuclear brinksmanship is *nearly* as exciting as Jim Lawler's real-world career. But unless you have a top security clearance and a need-to-know, he won't describe the highlights of his past CIA assignments. So, settle for the next best thing and read: *Living Lies.* It is an eye-opening glimpse at the world of counterproliferation."

Valerie Plame, former CIA covert Ops Officer, author of *Fair Game, Blowback,* and *Burned*

"*Living Lies* is a terrifyingly realistic story of how the CIA truly functions, the ever-present nuclear threat, and the crucial role of integrity in the murky world of espionage. Legendary CIA officer, Jim Lawler, captures and beautifully explains the metaphysical nature of recruiting spies, and he should know - as he is one of the best."

Alma Katsu, former CIA and NSA analyst, author of *Red Widow, The Hunger, The Deep, The Taker Trilogy.*

"If you read spy novels for a peek inside the most secretive profession on earth, *Living Lies* won't disappoint. A sprawling, non-stop spy thriller written by someone who clearly knows the business."

Doug Frantz, author of *The Nuclear Jihadist* and *Fallout*, former U.S. Assistant Secretary of State for Public Affairs

"In the finest traditions of John le Carré and Jason Matthews, Jim Lawler mines his decades in the CIA to take readers deep inside the hidden world of espionage where legends, lies and little betrayals lead relentlessly to a heart-stopping climax."

Dr. David Charney, Forensic psychiatrist and consultant to the IC on motivations for espionage

"*Living Lies* by Jim Lawler is a gripping spy thriller that benefits from its author's insider knowledge. The plot is intricate and terrifying since the stakes are existential—real risk of a nuclear war—based on policymaker miscalculation. Lawler specialized in *non-proliferation*, a niche portfolio with the unenviable mission of trying to head off the very worst outcome for humanity when necessary tools are scattered between different agencies controlled by people with conflicting agendas. Espionage novels tend to cover the same predictable themes, but not this time! I am not aware of any other novel that takes on the problem of non-proliferation from so many angles, explaining not just the politics and personalities of this relatively hidden world but also the engineering and physics! And that's part of the fun of *Living Lies.* I suspect many readers of thriller novels enjoy not just the plot but also learning the gritty details of arcane technical threats and how intelligence agencies actually work. No disappointment here because Lawler knows CIA internal relationships and interpersonal dynamics to a degree that could only have come from his deep experience. Believable, intense and colorful characters come alive and their motivations ring true. Lawler also created characters on the enemy side who are richer and more complex than the usual cardboard cutout one-dimensional enemies of the genre, which brings balance to the unfolding plot line. You know you've enjoyed a good read when you're not just satisfied for the ride—but you also feel much smarter than you did before you started."

Marc Cameron, NYT Bestselling author of "Power & Empire"

"Jim Lawler is one to watch! His writing is smart and it is unique and it is real, with an air of truth that only someone who has lived the life can breathe into this kind a story. *Living Lies* simply crackles with authenticity."

LIVING LIES

A NOVEL OF THE IRANIAN NUCLEAR WEAPONS PROGRAM

JAMES LAWLER

"Before creation, God did just pure mathematics.
Then He thought it would be a pleasant change to do some applied."

—John Edensor Littlewood,
"A Mathematician's Miscellany" 1953

The Guild Library
McLean, VA 22101

Ordering Information:
For details, contact TheGuildLibrary@gmail.com

Print ISBN: 978-1-09839-167-6
eBook ISBN: 978-1-09839-168-3

Printed in the United States of America on SFI Certified paper.

First Edition

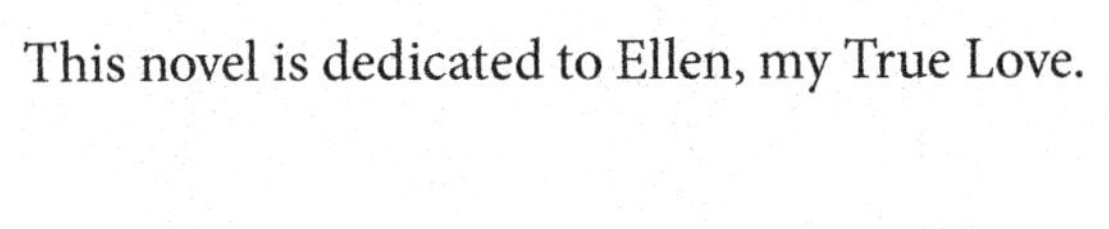

This novel is dedicated to Ellen, my True Love.

DISCLAIMER

“He was haunted by the image of the permanently etched shadows of three unfortunates near Ground Zero of that 13 kiloton bomb. They were. And then they were not.”

PROLOGUE

Langley

Lane Andrews hunched in his office at CIA headquarters, staring bleakly at his computer screen. Only five words. How could that be? He counted them for the tenth time: "I will write again soon." Did the word "I" count? Of course it did. There were only five innocuous sounding words rounding out the latest covert message from Leopard, his asset deep in the Iranian nuclear program. That meant that though Lane's world was falling apart, the guy on the other end of this message had it so much worse. Leopard literally had a gun to his head and was facing death. All of his previous messages over the past year ended in sentences of three, four, six, seven words but never exactly five. Five words were to be used only as a sign of duress – meaning quite clearly "They have discovered me and are forcing me to write you. Trust nothing I write."

Lane felt sick to his stomach. For more than a year, Dr. Ali Javadpour, codenamed "Leopard," had broadcast covert messages almost weekly from the heart of Iran, usually after Friday prayers. The messages were always eerie to read, emanating from the belly of the beast within the program. Lane could picture Leopard smiling at him across the table, lopsided grin and twinkling eyes, chatting easily about how much he hated the mullahs. The messages, his own small effort at peace between their countries.

Lane had turned these messages into top-quality intelligence reports on the status of the nuclear program. They provided significant verification that the Iranians were not cheating on their agreement with the United States – or were they? The agreement had essentially ended their nuclear weapons development efforts in exchange for a gradual relaxation of Western sanctions against the Islamic Republic of Iran. In essence, the U.S. had applied increasing trade and banking restrictions against the Islamic Republic, bankrupting the country until the mullahs blinked.

But had they? Leopard's last few messages indicated the contrary. This was basically a proxy message from the mullahs screaming, "Fuck you, Great Satan!"

PART 1

CHAPTER 1

◇◇◇

Through the Valley of the Shadow of Death

Samur Yalama National Park,
Azerbaijani-Russian Border

Stakeouts are so incredibly boring.

Lane Andrews remembered, not for the first time, why he had chosen to go into the CIA rather than the FBI. In his opinion, the Bureau's focus was mostly glorified police work, not that there was anything wrong with that. After all, his grandfather had been a cop. But the CIA…well the CIA had an air of mystery and flair. It was different and he liked that.

So, why was he now doing glorified police work?

An excellent question, but he knew the answer. He was seated next to Captain Aslan Aliyev, commander of the local Azerbaijani border guards, with two of his men, Yusif and Ilya, in the rear seat of their official four-wheel drive vehicle, a dented, forest-green UAZ Hunter SUV. It was ruggedly built to take the nasty ruts and bumps of the forestry road near where they were currently parked, concealed in a clump of thick trees in a lovely valley near the Russian border.

The surrounding Samur Forest consisted of serenely beautiful century-old chestnut oaks and Persian ironwood, but the most interesting feature, in Lane's opinion, was the profusion of liana, a type of woody climbing vine most often found in tropical forests. The dense forest straddled the border, and there were national parks on both sides to preserve the pristine natural beauty of this paradise.

But for the exotic location and the Russian language he was speaking to these liaison contacts, he could have been on a stakeout with his grandfather in the dense piney woods of East Texas. His granddad, however, would have been trying to ambush drug smugglers or bootleggers. Lane and his border guard contacts were after far more dangerous criminals: nuclear material traffickers.

As he sat in the SUV, Lane thought about his temporary duty assignment to assist the Azerbaijani authorities in preventing the illicit shipment of fissile material, highly enriched uranium (HEU) and plutonium, from numerous nuclear sites in Russia to a number of undesirable customers such as Iran, Syria and others with nuclear weapons aspirations. Azerbaijan, Armenia and Georgia were among the favored smuggling routes through which the criminal gangs tried to move this dangerous but highly lucrative fissile material. A shipment of even a few kilograms could mean many millions of dollars and afford a rogue country a shortcut to a nuclear weapon. So, this was righteous work in Lane's opinion.

But it could also be immensely boring.

Nevertheless, Lane liked Aslan and his "boys" in the border guards. It was silly, but Aslan's name reminded him of the lion in "The Lion, The Witch, and the Wardrobe," one his favorite childhood books. Aslan actually meant "lion" in the Turkic language that influenced names in this region. And true to his name, Aslan had a thick, grey beard that resembled a fierce lion's mane, but this was balanced with a gentle disposition and a gregarious nature. He liked Americans, and he especially valued the technical assistance he was receiving from Lane and his organization. This consisted of strategically-placed radiation detectors and upgraded radio equipment as well as some shared intelligence on proliferation threats of nuclear material movements in the region.

Lane happily provided the technical equipment to Aslan and his men, but he warned them not to become overly dependent on it. The detectors were expensive and thus could only be positioned on major traffic routes.

And frankly they had limited utility at detecting HEU if it were shielded. He hammered home the dictum that a single spy in a key trafficking gang could far outweigh all of the radiation detectors in central Eurasia.

Aslan agreed completely, and, to Lane's immense satisfaction, his men had recruited a well-placed source in one of the suspect gangs within the three months that Lane had been in-country. They had learned his lessons well. The source had reported that a major shipment of material would be going down tonight in this vicinity, using old forestry roads. Aslan had several units covering the possible routes.

A day ago, the source had gone mysteriously silent. This was troubling to Lane.

He looked over at Aslan and noticed that he had nodded off. He turned around and smiled at Yusif and Ilya. Both shrugged and grinned. It had been a long night.

A crystal-clear stream ran through the lush woods, about ten yards from their SUV, on its way to the Caspian Sea only a couple of miles away. The splashing sound was soothing through the open windows, however, it triggered an urge to pee. Too much coffee, but at least he wasn't asleep.

Lane cleared his throat. Aslan started and sat up straight, looking a little sheepish.

Lane chuckled. "Hey, I've got to go make a nature call and stretch my legs a bit."

"No, problem." Aslan turned and looked in the back seat. "Yusif, go with Mr. Andrews. Just in case."

Yusif was about twenty years old and barely shaving, but he had a cheerful disposition and was another of Lane's favorites among Aslan's "boys." He also carried an AK-47 with a forty-round magazine. Aslan and his men knew that the stakes tonight were potentially high.

Yusif and Lane left Aslan and Ilya, and walked up a trail into the forest. Yusif indicated that he too had to make a call of nature, albeit a more serious one due to the greasy food they'd had for supper in Yalama a few hours earlier.

Lane nodded. "Fine. I'll just walk a bit ahead and give you some privacy. Take your time. I'm not going far."

The boy smiled and looked relieved.

Lane walked on and found the forest enchanting but also a bit spooky. He wasn't frightened easily, but there was something off about his surroundings. Ordinarily, these woods teemed with wildlife -- Caspian red deer, otters, chamois, lynx, even brown bears. Tonight, however, the forest was deathly silent except for the distant sound of the stream. No birds, no other animals, nothing.

But something was there.

He didn't like the feeling and started to turn back to where Yusif was when his eyes caught a glimpse of a dark shape in the moonlight, about twenty yards through the trees, in the middle of the forestry road. He advanced toward it cautiously through the underbrush.

When he was about ten yards away, Lane saw it was a body, facedown. He approached. The back of the head was blown open by an obvious exit wound. He crouched next to it and, though he couldn't be sure, he had a terrible instinctive feeling that this was Aslan's missing source.

Lane ran back in Yusif's direction and arrived just as the young man was buttoning his pants. Yusif looked up at him from the clearing, startled to see the look of distress on his face. He started to say something to Lane. Just then, a small red dot settled in the middle of Yusif's forehead.

Lane screamed, "Get down!"

But it was too late. Something hit Yusif, and it snapped him back. He was surely dead before he hit the ground - the same ground that Lane was now hugging. If he hugged it any closer, he'd be burrowing underground.

In spite of, or perhaps because of, the nearness of death, Lane found his mind wonderfully focused. He thought he saw a metallic reflection in the moonlight, not far from Yusif's body. He scooted along the ground and retrieved the AK-47 from where Yusif had put it next to a large rock and crawled behind it among the thick liana vines. It wasn't huge, but the rock would have to suffice as cover.

He scanned his surroundings and saw at least eight dark shapes approaching, all of them carrying automatic weapons or rifles, at least one of them with the distinct outline of a sniper scope. Lane didn't think they knew he was armed, but they were cautiously approaching him in an encircling movement.

Lane took the small handheld radio from his belt and fixed it to transmit along with his GPS coordinates. He couldn't risk talking into it just yet, but he had to get word to Aslan and his other nearby units. He reattached it to his belt and thumbed it on.

He was badly outnumbered and outgunned. If he got up and ran the hundred or so yards to the SUV, he'd be shot in the back. If he stayed where he was, they'd soon surround him. He thought of his great-great-grandfather, who'd been a Union general in the Civil War and who'd been faced with a similar situation at Vicksburg. The old man said there was only one choice: charge.

Lane mentally recited the 23rd psalm. After a silent "amen," he flipped the AK-47 to fully automatic and kissed it.

He leaped up, screamed "Eat death and die!" and charged full speed, firing his weapon all the while. The brilliant flash and sound of its bursts were blinding and deafening in the quiet night.

Two of the men in front went down immediately, howling in pain. Two others on the flanks caught each other in their own cross-fire in the confusion and dropped. The remaining four panicked and ran into the forest as this banshee from hell charged them at point blank range firing his assault rifle and screaming at the top of his lungs.

Lane stopped upon seeing their lines break, threw the empty AK-47 down and beat a quick retreat to the SUV.

He couldn't believe it when he approached the vehicle and saw Aslan's head slumped over, sleeping again. How could he sleep through World War III, barely a hundred yards through the woods?

He went to Aslan's open window and jostled him. "Hey, are you deaf?"

Aslan toppled over onto the front seat and didn't move. Lane looked more closely and saw a blackness at the back of his neck. He turned on the SUV's dome light. A vicious sight assaulted him. And he thought he was past shock.

The back of Aslan's neck had been savaged, blood everywhere.

As he pulled his head out of the driver's side window, he heard a voice.

"Ah, Mr. Andrews. A pity you should return and see that."

A few yards behind him stood Ilya, one of the few ethnic Russians among Aslan's men, blond and athletic-looking, a long, wicked-looking combat knife in his hands. It was clear to Lane how they'd lost their penetration of the smuggling gang and how Aslan had died.

Spies aren't necessarily working only for us.

Ilya went into a knife-fighter's crouch and advanced, but Lane was tired and beyond fear. He was also pissed off at the loss of his friend, Aslan, the gentle lion. He dodged Ilya's first slash and hurled his handheld radio into his face with all his strength, catching Ilya on the bridge of his nose and causing blood to erupt. Ilya fell back a few steps, but he was soon preparing his next attack. Lane looked about for anything he could use as a weapon.

Nothing.

He backed up a few paces and quickly stripped off his windbreaker, never taking his eyes off of Ilya's steely-blue ones. He wrapped it around his left arm. He turned around as if to run, paused a second, then abruptly pivoted and charged, his left arm prepared to deflect the blade. Ilya's knife slashed down but barely penetrated the jacket. Lane kept going at full ramming speed, and his body and momentum knocked Ilya over on his ass. At that precise moment, a border guards car pulled up to the clearing, lights flashing.

Ilya sprang to his feet like a gymnast, saw the cavalry had arrived, and quickly ran into the forest. The night swallowed him.

Lane thought back over the evening later and concluded that perhaps he could do with a bit less flair in his life.

CHAPTER 2

◇◇◇

McBane

Baku

Conor McBane was perplexed. He sat in the hotel bar contemplating the troubled looking young Armenian man seated across from him. The man's jet black hair, brilliant with some kind of faintly sweet smelling hair tonic, was swept back in bold waves giving him the appearance of an Armenian James Dean. The white tee shirt, black motorcycle jacket and sharply cut black leather pants completed the look. He even had a slight sneer and a cigarette dangling from his lips, although his anxious twitching and constant watchfulness kept him just south of cool.

This kid was definitely uncool. In spite of the physical resemblance to the long dead movie star, this young twerp was more like a rebel without a clue. Nevertheless, McBane sat patiently trying to make sense of the story he was hearing. It had been his experience that some of the best information arises from the most unlikely of sources and at the most unexpected times. McBane had learned to trust his instincts early in his career and how to overcome his natural tendency towards abruptness, which seldom accomplished anything other than shutting up a potential lead.

Actually, the information itself was clear enough as he pieced it together, but the rationale for the young man passing this along to him was not yet firm in McBane's mind. He puzzled over this as he slowly sipped his glass of passable Malbec and waited for the punch line. He realized that this could take a while from the way this story was unfolding drip by drip. As he listened, McBane looked about the clubby hotel bar from time to time at his own pale reflection in the glass cases enclosing expensive Cuban cigars.

McBane's bespoke tweed suit and shirt were rumpled, his tie loose and hair disheveled. But McBane's mind was in perfect order. It worked every bit as well as it did when he took honors in history at Princeton at nineteen and completed his doctoral thesis three years later on a comparative analysis of narcotics smuggling and human trafficking organizations.

The thesis was expanded into an award-winning best seller that critics extolled for its fluid style and well documented research. *The New York Times* lavished praise for "McBane's uncanny ability to penetrate organized crime and recruit well placed stoolies, who confide in him as if he were their confessor." That was forty-five years and twelve books ago, but the old tiger still had claws. Despite his coming from considerable family money, McBane never wanted to rest on his trust fund and found his true life's meaning in his research and reportorial skills. His books were well respected in academic and government circles, and he had a considerable public following. He had since then branched out into scholarly investigative coverage of nuclear materials trafficking, and he considered this his chef-d'oeuvre. Certainly, he thought it the most meaningful.

Primarily, he was interested in tracking the dangerous fissile material – the guts of the bomb – itself. As he frequently said in his articles, "No material. No bomb." This was his mantra and his current life's focus – keeping fissile material such as plutonium and highly enriched uranium out of the hands of irresponsible parties. McBane lumped not only terrorists into this category but also all of the nuclear wannabes. That truly made a long list of sorry-ass countries in his own personal taxonomy. If McBane had anything to do with it, none of them would ever have a nuclear weapon. He couldn't do much about the idiots who possessed them already, but he could try to keep that club as small as possible.

Thirty minutes earlier, McBane had been seated in front of a crackling fire in the fireplace in his spacious suite at The Four Seasons Hotel in Baku, located on the waterfront promenade next to the Caspian Sea, writing an overdue submission on nuclear material smuggling for *Foreign Affairs*. He heard the slight whisper of a note being slipped under his door. Retrieving it, he read, "Dr. McBane, I have some important information to pass along to you which will help your research. Please to meet me in Bentley's Bar downstairs in the next thirty minutes."

McBane was not exactly surprised at such an unsolicited lead because he had been in Baku for a week now. He had made the rounds of various government ministries and consulted with some old contacts in the local press as well as among some academics and various prior collaborators. An American researcher sniffing around sensitive topics such as HEU smuggling was bound to attract some attention. McBane, who sometimes likened his tromping about in foreign cities to a jungle beater scaring out game in the bush, was pleased to have flushed something out of the Azerbaijani information bazaar. He could certainly spare some time in the hotel bar, and besides it was nigh on to five PM, and he could do with a glass or two of wine after writing all afternoon. Too much work and not enough good wine made McBane a boring boy.

The fidgety young man began by explaining that his family had extensive shipping interests in the Caspian Sea, although they suffered during the Armenian-Azerbaijani conflict in the 1990's. He noted that though Armenians are Christians and most Azerbaijanis are Muslim, his family had successfully steered clear of power politics and piety.

"Fortunately, business is more important than religion in Azerbaijan and now we know the right people in the right places. Things seem to be okay and business is good. Or it has been until now. Now we have a problem. We think you might help.

"Dr. McBane, we have learned that you are seeking information on some very dangerous material, material which should not be here at all but in fact is. I am talking about some weapons grade highly enriched uranium that is transiting Baku from a nuclear weapons lab in Russia. We understand there are currently four lots of such material – approximately fifteen kilograms each – which are being offered for sale to one of our competitors. And more in the pipeline. Maybe a lot more."

Startled, McBane interrupted, "Wait. You just said 'Fifteen kilos.' Did you mean fifteen grams each?"

"No sir. Fifteen kilos each. We have also heard that these four lots are just the first tranche in a series of three or four shipments. Our information is very precise about this first tranche because we were offered the material and we refused. We enjoy making money, but this type of business is insane." He shook his head. "*This* kind of business is actually dangerous to our overall interests. Extremely bad for business. If the authorities catch wind of it, all of our business will be scrutinized and suffer."

He paused a moment and added, "I know the contact who has the HEU and where he is staying. He is in touch with one of our competitors who's not as careful how he does business. The word on the street is that he and his friends have found a buyer in Iran. The transfer should happen very soon. The contact address we have is on this slip of paper. In case you have doubts, I can meet you there tomorrow at 3:00 in the afternoon. I will introduce you to my contact and then leave. I don't want the police involved because that is also bad for business." Having said this, he pushed the piece of paper under the drink menu and across the table to McBane, who palmed it after only a second's hesitation.

McBane sat back in shock, unconsciously sipping his wine. Sixty kilograms of HEU out in the wild…and possibly much more. If this were true, it would be a game-changer, particularly if headed to Iran. This shipment was about 25 times greater than any other trafficking scheme he had encountered in his years of chasing rumor and reality. Indeed, he recalled a sizable seizure of HEU in Prague in December 1994, but it was only 2.7 kilograms. And that tiny bit had scared him a great deal because it showed what could be moved. This amount, on the other hand, was terrifying. According to his sources, this was enough for a Hiroshima-type nuclear weapon. It would not take any more for a very bad day. A really very bad day.

The door to the apartment in the old city was slightly ajar as McBane rapped lightly on it the next day. Silence. He knocked again, this time more sharply. Nothing. He verified the address from the paper the young man had given him. No sign of the Armenian. He nudged the door open and looked inside. He heard a faint sound of a shower running from behind a far door. McBane stepped into the flat and edged past its shabby Soviet-era furnishings. Pausing to get his bearings, McBane suddenly noticed water seeping out from under the far door, presumably leading to the bathroom.

McBane hesitated and then thrust the bathroom door open. Steam wafted out. The water was already a half inch deep where it had overflowed from the bathtub. He sloshed into the room and reached his left hand past the shower curtain to shut the faucet off. It slightly burned his hand and he felt something stringy as he thrust his hand into the bathwater to cool it. He ripped the shower curtain back with his other hand and found himself staring down into the face of the young Armenian, eyes open but unseeing, his black hair floating around his face like a halo. The heavy porcelain lid from the toilet water tank sat on his chest, weighing him down in the water.

McBane froze for a split second and then began to backpedal out of the room in a hurry. For a large man in his early 70's with an artificial hip, he moved quickly.

CHAPTER 3

◇◇◇

En Garde!

Baku

McBane thought about how easily the young Armenian had found him the day before and wondered how common the knowledge of his whereabouts was on the street. Perhaps his jungle-beating had flushed out larger game than he cared to encounter. In a rare show of prudence, he decided not to go directly back to his hotel suite after finding the corpse of the young Armenian. Instead, he stopped by the front desk first and asked to see the head of security. Within a couple of minutes, a large beefy man with a crew cut named "Mr. Abdulov," who looked like he had stepped out of a 1950s cold war spy movie, presented himself and asked how he could be of service.

McBane thought it best not to tell him the entire story but instead said that he'd been threatened by an unscrupulous business associate and thought it wise to have someone accompany him to his room to verify that it was undisturbed. Abdulov looked at him briefly as if he were an old man afraid of his own shadow. He then nodded briskly and said, "But of course, sir. My pleasure. I can assure you that you are completely safe here at the Four Seasons. I will gladly accompany you to your suite and show you that all is in order."

They entered his sixth-floor suite with Abdulov in the lead. Nothing appeared to be disturbed in the anteroom of the large airy suite, and so they headed towards the living room area where he had been working the day before, so cozy in front of the marble fireplace. Again, nothing out of order. McBane was beginning to think he was indeed a silly old man as the house detective headed for the last room, the large bedroom adjoining the living area with its personal balcony overlooking the Caspian. The large man swung open the bedroom door, audibly sucked in his breath and just lingered there with his back to McBane as if he had been frozen. McBane stood four feet behind him, waiting.

Just as McBane began to ask him what he saw, Abdulov quietly toppled backwards towards McBane, a large knife with a military style grip protruding from his chest. McBane backed quickly towards the fireplace behind him as a lean and athletic looking man with close cropped blond hair emerged silently from the bedroom. The man, who had cold grey-blue eyes, distinctly Slavic features and an oddly discolored nose, stepped gracefully towards the corpse as if he were a large cat stalking prey and deftly retrieved the long-bladed knife. He never once broke eye contact with McBane who was now twenty feet away in front of the fireplace.

McBane eyed the front door of the suite but saw that it was at least thirty feet distant. The killer would be on him well before he was half that distance. Glancing to his side, he spied a three-foot metal poker in the set of fireplace tools just inches away. McBane grabbed it with his right hand, whipped it forward and up, and went up on the balls of his feet, his left hand upright and counterbalancing himself, his feet apart in a classic fencing pose, each one 90 degrees from the other. The look on McBane's face must have been intense because the blond man could not help but smile slightly and arch his eyebrows before moving steadily towards McBane with the long-bladed knife held in a similar pose, as if mocking him. Neither said a word.

To the man's obvious surprise, McBane did not retreat but advanced on him, the poker gently swaying like a rapier, the afternoon light glinting off it through the bedroom window. Both men moved their weapons slightly as they approached each other. The room remained totally silent. Even the traffic noises outside seemed miles away.

When they were about six feet apart, the blond man dipped and suddenly leaped forward with his knife slashing upwards, and McBane quickly parried it with his poker, and on the backward swing, snapped the sharp poker across the man's jaw. The blond man fell back as blood poured from a wicked gash. He struggled to keep his feet, backpedaling quickly. McBane never hesitated but pressed his advantage and scored another glancing blow across the man's left arm, which had been left undefended. The blond cursed in Russian and fell back farther.

Obviously, this was no longer amusing to the blond killer. And he appeared to be in considerable pain. He stepped forward again, his knife blade raised. His eyes narrowed, and he leaped forward again like a wounded lion, claws spread. The knife blade faked right, faked left and then went right again, slicing upwards toward McBane.

McBane suddenly dropped low before his startled opponent, placing his free hand on the ground for balance like a one-arm pushup. The stress of the pose on his back hurt like hell, but McBane managed to execute a perfect "passata soto," a defensive fencing movement with a counterattack – a furious upward twist and powerful stab of the poker directly into the man's body. He connected solidly, and the man staggered backwards into the bedroom bleeding profusely from a stab wound to his abdomen.

McBane struggled to his feet, his body roaring with aches and pain not felt in fifty years, and yet he knew he had to finish this here and now. He started towards the blond man with a determined look in his eyes, pain be damned. The man hunched in front of the open doors of the room's balcony, trying to marshal his strength into a defense. Everything depended on the next few seconds. McBane heard nothing except for their labored breathing.

The blond man darted forward, his blade slicing the air back and forth, his face contorted in a grimace as he approached. Suddenly, his blade arced up, but McBane's right arm was a blur as he swung the poker with all of his weight into the man's undefended neck. The man spun with the impact, banging into the balcony railing behind him. McBane charged into him, poker in both hands, like a hockey defenseman cross-checking his opponent, and the Russian assassin toppled over the balcony railing to the sidewalk six floors below. A few seconds later, there was a sickening wet thump on concrete. Then silence.

McBane stepped back, breathing hard, hands on his knees. He reflected on his two years as captain of the Princeton fencing team, thankful for the persistence of body memories even fifty years distant. With a weary sigh, he resolved to move into other possible areas of investigative journalism. Really any other type of smuggling might do. Perhaps orchids or rare birds.

After an interview with the police, McBane repaired to his upgraded suite, which was free of bloodstains and a dead security man and provided courtesy of the hotel with profuse apologies. He then quickly typed out an account of what had transpired over the last two days. He printed two copies and then asked the concierge for a taxi to the nearby U.S. Embassy.

McBane approached the Marine Guard at the inside security checkpoint, showed him his passport and asked to speak to a security officer or an intelligence officer. The young corporal immediately put a call through, and soon a tall man in his early thirties, using the name "Bill Rogers," appeared and escorted him to a nearby interview room. McBane presented his journalist credentials and gave him a quick summary of his background and his business in Baku as well as an account of what had happened over the past forty-eight hours. He then passed him the two envelopes and said that it was imperative that each letter get to the named recipients as quickly as possible, preferably by secure fax.

The first letter was addressed "Eyes Only" to Dr. Manuel Alvarez, Secretary of Energy, Forrestal Building, Washington DC. The second was similarly "Eyes Only" to Mr. Lane Andrews, Central Intelligence Agency, Langley.

McBane noted that he did not have the fax numbers for either gentleman but that he trusted that Rogers could see to that. Rogers accepted both letters and counseled McBane to leave Azerbaijan as quickly as possible, considering the body count that he was leaving in his wake. McBane assured him that he intended to do so the very next morning.

During his taxi ride back to the Four Seasons, McBane reflected upon his choice of addressees. His old friend Manny Alvarez seemed obvious. He had known Manny since long before the brilliant physicist had served as Lab Director at Lawrence Livermore National Lab, one of the two U.S. national nuclear weapons design laboratories. Now Dr. Alvarez was Secretary of Energy and engaged in nuclear negotiations with the Iranians. Manny needed this information urgently.

Lane Andrews was a less obvious choice. McBane had met him in a nuclear nonproliferation seminar only two years prior and thought Lane to be a serious and highly focused participant. Although Lane wore a badge that read "U.S. Department of State," he did not dodge and weave when McBane probed him on his background or his interest in the nuclear issue. In fact, McBane found Lane's candor refreshing and his grasp of the proliferation threat to be far and away superior to most of the State Department officers, National Security Council officials, and academics present. He also understood that Lane preferred action, even unilateral action, to endless discussion of this existential issue.

Indeed, Lane had endeared himself to McBane when he spoke up after a mind-numbing speech by a senior State Department official, who had droned on about the need for "multilateral engagement and IAEA involvement." Lane had stood, looked about the room for a moment, and said that the time for such discussion was over. He noted that it had ended fifteen years before when another mad dictator, Muammar Gaddafi, had acquired nuclear weapons technology for Libya from Pakistan's Dr. A.Q. Khan. "By choosing not to wait for multilateral action," Lane concluded, "we avoided a potentially cataclysmic disaster when Gaddafi was overthrown a few years later. In his desperation, he would have used them. Of this, I have no doubt."

He sat down and there was complete silence for a few moments. Then, McBane had stood and applauded, as had a few other brave souls. Afterward, as they filed out of the seminar, McBane had clapped Lane on the back and invited him for lunch at the Cosmos Club, where he had been a member for years. Soon, their luncheons had become regular – two comrades-in-arms, separated by generations but equally devoted to stopping the nuclear madness.

CHAPTER 4

If Iran Had a Nuclear Program...

CIA Headquarters, Langley

The letter from McBane sat in front of Lane Andrews in the middle of his desk. He tapped his fingers on it as he reread it. His description of the blond man with the discolored nose and preference for knives brought back memories of his stakeout in Azerbaijan a couple of weeks earlier. A chill went down the back of his neck.

Ilya. Aslan's murderer. Sixty kilograms of HEU.

It made sense. And McBane's comment that the word on the street was that Iran was the customer also made sense. Why go to all the trouble and expense of enriching uranium and having to conceal your centrifuge facility from the world if you can buy highly enriched uranium ready for weaponization? What's not to like, especially if you want an ace in the hole like a nuke?

Lane folded McBane's letter and decided he should take it to Pat McCabe, Chief of Near Eastern Division, who had recently re-absorbed Iranian ops into his division, several years after it had been hived off and become autonomous in an effort to focus on one of CIA's priorities; or so it was portrayed to Congress. Lane thought the original partition made no sense, but the "Persian Anschluss," as it was deemed by some, wasn't going to fix the problems, which were legion and had nothing to do with bureaucratic organization charts and everything to do with a lack of imagination and creativity. Still, duty compelled Lane to bring it to Pat's attention.

He knocked on McCabe's door after the secretary nodded that he was in and poked his head in his office, which was decorated in Middle Eastern kitsch and garish knickknacks, colorful prayer rugs and so-called objets d'art. The piece de resistance was a shining ceremonial sword from Yemen suspended in a metallic fixture over McCabe's desk that a former president-for-life had presented to McCabe when he was Chief of Station. Lane knew the irony behind the weapon on display because a similar one had decapitated the leader a year later in the Yemeni version of electoral Russian roulette.

McCabe looked up at him over his reading glasses, his gaze diverted from an Arabic-language newspaper. The distracted look was one that would be given a bothersome housefly that buzzed around interfering with serious contemplation. Lane knew that McCabe had native fluency in Arabic due to being the son of missionaries, who had served in a number of Middle Eastern countries. What he couldn't fathom was how he had ever risen to this exalted position on that sole virtue. Several million Arabs also spoke Arabic and were every bit as qualified in that respect as McCabe.

Before his anointing as "Emir" of Near East Division, a joke had circulated that the Director was searching for an NE Division Chief who was an Arabist with ruthless cunning, keen nerves, a predilection for action, and a complete understanding of the Middle East and its myriad diverse players. Sadly, because Saddam Hussein was long dead, he settled for McCabe.

Lane put McBane's letter in front of McCabe and said, "Pat, we've got indications that Iran is acquiring weapons grade uranium."

McCabe glanced briefly at the letter as if a wayward soiled toilet tissue had blown onto his desk and then stared over his glasses up at Lane with a look of ill-disguised contempt. "That's impossible. If Iran had a nuclear program, we'd know about it."

Lane started to argue, but McCabe's attention had already returned to one of his Arabic newspapers and had dismissed him as if he didn't exist. Lane stood there for a moment and then snatched the letter from the desk and strode out of his office without a word. He slammed the door shut as he exited and heard the sword clatter in its fixture. He wondered briefly if the Director would be looking for another Chief of Near Eastern Division soon.

CHAPTER 5

◇◇◇

The Magic of Tradecraft

CIA Headquarters, Langley

Still seething, Lane stalked into his office as his secure phone was ringing. He yanked it up and growled, "Yeah?"

"So 'yeah' is how you greet your friends and admirers these days?" breathed a sultry feminine voice on the other end of the line.

He recognized Betsy Wooten's soft voice on the line and instantly relaxed. Betsy was a study in refined elegance, someone his Grandpa would have described as a "classy dame" had she lived in the 1930's or 40's and been in black and white motion pictures. He could envision her as the sophisticated Myrna Loy playing Nora Charles in "The Thin Man."

On top of that, Bets, a case officer with a lot of moxie, was about three times smarter than most of her supervisors. This quality she attempted to conceal, however, due to an anti-intellectual bent in certain quarters of the Directorate of Operations, particularly among some of the male officers. Lane found her refreshing and stimulating nonetheless. In fact, he enjoyed watching her use her wits to slice and dice senior officers without their awareness, other than an occasional bemused expression as they realized belatedly that she had handed them their heads, smiling coquettishly all the while. A classy dame indeed.

"Oh, hi Bets. My apologies, but I'm kind of pissed off at someone."

"Not me I hope."

"Nah. Just some jackass up topside. So, what's up?" he asked.

"I just met a couple of cleared neuroscientists, some academics with an Agency contractor, who are doing a paper on the 'magic of tradecraft,' and I recommended they chat with you, because you're the best ops magician I know. Do you have time to talk to them?"

He tossed McBane's letter back into his in-box and smiled. "Bets, you do know how to win a guy's heart. Sure. Why not? Send'em my way. All I've been doing is contemplating the fate of the world." As he hung up, he thought that a trip to Geneva, where U.S. and Iranian nuclear negotiators were congregating could be in order.

A few minutes later, there was a rap on his door, and an owlish-looking middle age man and a young woman with purplish streaks in her coal-black hair and large red frame glasses stood before him. They introduced themselves as Dr. Timothy Wainwright and Dr. Tara O'Shaughnessy and explained that they were interested in studying the "magic techniques" that Lane employed in his operations.

Lane began, "I'm happy to discuss it because the Agency should be interested in anything that enables case officers to recruit more sources. I doubt that a study like this has ever been done...well, least not in recent years."

Wainwright replied, "Probably not. So tell us how you go about this 'magic.' What are your secrets?"

"It's kind of complicated to explain or even believe. Sometimes I'm just not sure what it is. But there aren't any real 'secrets' as you call them."

"No? So what are they then?"

"Okay, you asked for it. The mental link that I employ is metaphysical to a large extent but it exists. I can certainly feel the hookup with my target when I really focus and..." Lane stopped in mid-sentence as he saw the two scientists look at each other in confusion.

Wainwright said, "Actually, we wanted you to describe the tricks and illusions you use in your operations. You know like the sleight of hand employed by stage magicians...distractions, things like that, which conceal what's really happening. Trickery..."

Now it was Lane's turn to look confused. "Trickery? Illusions?"

O'Shaughnessy added, "Sure. Tell us how you trick people into working for you. What are the deceptions you employed in your many recruitments? According to Betsy Wooten, you have a recruitment record far superior to most case officers. What are your tricks?"

"But I don't trick anybody. I don't use illusions. When I heard you wanted to discuss the 'magic of tradecraft,' I thought you meant it literally."

The two scientists both said in unison, "*Literal magic*?"

"Okay, maybe not literal magic like something supernatural but something you can't explain scientifically...at least not yet. Maybe in forty or fifty years, you could explain scientifically the mental link that I can make with people if I concentrate hard enough. And how I can have them do what I want...well more or less."

Lane shrugged his shoulders and added, "Look, it doesn't always work, but it does if I try. I call it 'magic' because it probably isn't something you can measure in a laboratory or explain."

The two scientists looked at him as if he were out of his mind and were about to call the men in the white jackets for him.

Lane added, "Okay, listen. I know it sounds crazy, but it defies scientific explanation. For example, if you lived in the 1870's and saw an airplane, you might have called it 'magic' when in fact three decades later you could explain flight scientifically, right?"

Wainwright said, "Sure, but...but this isn't the same thing."

"I don't see why not," said Lane with a bit of exasperation.

O'Shaughnessy smiled patronizingly and said, "It's just not the same. We need to explain it in terms of neuroscience with scientific rigor in experiments that can be replicated time and again. Otherwise, it's just a fluke, a coincidence."

Lane shrugged. "Well, I doubt I can meet your criteria because sometimes I can do it...and sometimes not. It requires a force of will and immense concentration, plus I have to be motivated properly."

He sighed and then said, "Look, I can explain most of my success rate due to various factors: my patience, my persistence, my ability to read people and their needs." He shook his head and added, "Maybe my empathy, perhaps my soft voice modulation, not unlike Dr. Milton Erickson who developed hypnotherapy…all of these things help a lot. But there's a small portion that's a mystery to me except for the mental link I envision between myself and the target or subject or whatever you want to call it."

The scientists were quiet throughout Lane's soliloquy.

He smiled and said, "In the end, perhaps it's just the confidence edge it gives me. As long as I believe it, it works."

The two scientists looked at him with real skepticism.

Lane arched his eyebrows and said, "So you're telling me that the field of neuroscience is complete and that there's nothing new to be discovered… something which might explain in scientific terms in forty or fifty years why I can do this."

"Of course, neuroscience isn't complete but this…this…" sputtered O'Shaughnessy while taking off her red glasses and shaking her head. She looked over at Wainwright for support and then said in a conciliatory tone, "But I'd love to study you at a party and see you work a room."

"I'm sorry, but I don't do parlor tricks and I *usually* can't force it on demand or work multiple subjects at once. Maybe if you were willing to engage in a real study of what I call 'the magic of tradecraft'…then perhaps we could do something together." As he said these last words, he softened his voice almost to a whisper and looked into their eyes with a steady, unblinking gaze.

They seemed distracted for a moment as if tuned into another reality; then excused themselves, thanking him for his time.

Wainwright rose from his chair and remarked to his colleague as they were leaving Lane's office, "Perhaps we should look into this magic tradecraft phenomenon more closely."

She replied in a quiet voice, "I was thinking the same."

Lane grinned. *"Usually" may be too strong a word.*

CHAPTER 6

The White Giant

> "Oh, white giant with feet in chains,
> Oh, dome of the world, oh, Mount Damavand."
> —Mohammad-Taqi Bahar, Iranian poet, "Ode to Damavand"

Central Alborz Mountains, Northern Iran

The wind blew cool and dry across the mountainous moonscape, rounding twisted rock formations fashioned by a sculptor with a mind as tortured as his stone work. The snowfields were rapidly receding, yielding the floor to bright red and yellow wildflowers. Puffy white clouds scudded in the sky.

Towering in the distance, like the chief god in Valhalla, an enormous snowcapped mountain dominated the horizon. Its white peak pierced the scattered clouds. Usually, the huge mountain could be seen from Tehran, about forty-five miles distant. Mount Damavand, a semi-dormant stratovolcano about 18,400 feet high, was the tallest mountain in the Middle East and the highest volcano in all of Eurasia. It last erupted about seven thousand years ago, long before the glories of the Persian Empire.

A tall sliver of a man in his mid-forties picked his way along a meandering path. The path cut through a meadow where a gentle stream bubbled from under several large boulders and poured into a large pool of clear water. The water, icy cold from its origins in the mountain snowmelt, flowed bright and silvery past his feet. It had been a hard winter and the late-arriving spring had not brought much relief. Today, though, the man welcomed the bracing air as it sharpened his thoughts, a fine blade cutting away at deadfall and creeper vines in his grey matter.

Though he lived in bustling Tehran with its honking cars and milling crowds, Dr. Daoud Tabatabai escaped whenever possible to this idyllic land of his youth, especially when he needed to think. Only the day before, he had been hard at work in his office at the Atomic Energy Organization of Iran. Mathematical formulae and their related physics still floated in his mind like the brilliant white clouds above, their interlocking patterns breathtaking in their perfection. Numbers produced the harmonies of an exquisite piano concerto, each note irreplaceable, logically lending strength and beauty to the notes before and after.

It was as if God were whispering to him.

Yet, some pivotal piece still eluded him, just out of focus on the horizon of his thoughts. He could sense its fuzzy outline but not the finer specifics. It was agonizing to hover on the margins of a breakthrough. It hovered just beyond his grasp. He could sense it teasing him, flirting with his consciousness, insisting on a mental leap.

He had centered his career on contextualizing quantum mechanics within a mathematical framework. He had drawn inspiration from Dr. John Von Neumann's seminal 1932 treatise "Mathematical Foundations of Quantum Mechanics." Like Von Neumann, who went on to distinguish himself in the Manhattan Project, Daoud was a genius. And though the Nobel laureate Richard Feynman once dryly commented that "nobody understands quantum mechanics," Daoud thought he did.

Maybe. His mind worked on an entirely different plane from those of his colleagues and his latest challenge, if it came to fruition, would be his own version of a unified field theory. It combined quantum mechanics and a new, as-yet undefined, extension of quantum entanglement with a unique and novel approach to the concept of time and space as applied to nuclear particles. It would be as if he could cause a tiny ripple in space/time and manifest the previously impossible. No small feat.

There were perhaps two other scientists in Iran and maybe three dozen scientists in America who could follow Daoud's reasoning in the initial part of this new formulation – and then just barely. There were none anywhere, however, who could comprehend the full ramifications of where the theory was taking him. Not that he cared one way or another. He wasn't after adulation or praise, simply the gratification of solving one of the universe's secrets.

As a shadow passed overhead, he looked up at a large golden eagle soaring. It dived abruptly, having spotted its dinner. He wished his mind had that kind of acuity and certainty so that he could pounce upon the solution eluding him like a field mouse.

He rounded the bend in the path and approached the outskirts of a village near his old secondary school. This proximity triggered a memory from his teenage years. Daoud's family had lived an idyllic existence in the shadow of Mount Damavand. His father was a mining engineer at a sulfur mine on the mountain's eastern slope and his mother was a schoolteacher. Daoud's older brother Majid, whom he idolized, was a graduate student at the University of California at Berkeley pursuing a PhD in metallurgy.

Emulating his older brother, Daoud had been a diligent student who was constantly teased for his studious and shy nature. His outstanding grades made him the target of various bullies. The bullying was a torment in his teenage years, and probably would have continued had he not formed an unusual alliance with a sometime adversary, Masud Alborzi. While not a completely dedicated enemy, Masud hadn't really been a friend either. It was hard to say if Masud truly had friends. What he had were "followers and hangers-on" – other teenage boys who hung out with him, sensing a center of power.

Masud was both physically and socially powerful. Blessed with good looks, he also had an uncle who was a prominent local Islamic scholar and a newly proclaimed Ayatollah. Masud's rise in stature and influence paralleled his uncle's ascension in senior Shi'a religious circles, although Masud himself was hardly pious. Indeed, beyond adult supervision, he sometimes wore Rolling Stones tee shirts peeking from under his outer garments. Daoud had often wondered what the Ayatollah would say about Masud's "Sympathy for the Devil" tee.

Daoud and Masud had struck a deal one day after school as Daoud was trying to maneuver his way home. Masud appeared before him, arms crossed, blocking the path with his cohort. Daoud braced for a beating, although this was not Masud's style. He favored psychological coercion and implied violence.

"Well, here is the little professor Tabatabai. How're you doing, doctor?"

"Fine. And you?" Daoud managed meekly.

"Oh, cool. Couldn't be better, but I need to talk to you. Something came up today in school. Got a minute?"

This last question was hardly a request but more of a command, so Daoud shrugged warily and asked, "Sure, what do you need?"

Masud dismissed his minions while he chatted with "the professor." The other boys lounged about and smoked as Daoud followed Masud off the path to the shade of a nearby tree.

Masud was blunt. "You and I, we both have a problem and I think we can help each other. You're regularly getting the crap beat out of you and I'm failing algebra. My dad will raid my room and take all my music if that happens. But it doesn't have to happen. You see where I'm going with this?"

"I think so. If I help you with math, no one bothers me, right?"

"You're a bright boy. Very quick. You help me pass algebra and you live your days in peace. Fair deal?"

"Not bad, I guess. When do we start?"

"No time like the present, my friend. I'll swing by your place in an hour and you can explain my homework to me. See you soon, doc!"

As distasteful as this little protection racket was, Daoud patiently worked with Masud over the following months and the larger boy, far from stupid, managed a respectable grade. And though Daoud feared Masud's well-deserved reputation for self-serving treachery, the bigger boys in the school left him largely alone.

He'd heard that Masud had joined the Islamic Revolutionary Guard Corps after university and risen quickly due to his family connections. This was hardly a surprise; not that Masud harbored much revolutionary fervor or fervor about anything other than himself. But he was always the opportunist, so his joining the IRGC was almost a given. The Revolutionary Guard had their iron grip on virtually every industry in Iran, shipping, aircraft, automobiles, construction, telecommunications, petrochemicals etc. and milked them regularly for tribute and spoils. It was a perfect fit for him.

Had they been living in 1930s Germany, Masud would likely have joined the Nazi SS and thrived. Daoud could almost envision him sporting the twin lightening strokes and the silver death's-head emblem on a smartly tailored midnight black uniform. Ever the natty dresser, Masud would have worn it well. Daoud wondered where he was now.

CHAPTER 7

◇◇◇

Swiss Security

Zurich

The powerfully built man cut through downtown Zurich at an assured pace. Other pedestrians yielded easily to his brisk passage as his handmade Berluti shoes whispered along the Bahnhofstrasse. He was at once arresting and ephemeral, a good-looking man in his mid-40's with a vague, but untraceable scent of celebrity. He resembled a movie star whose name you couldn't quite summon. But rather than stare, most people averted their eyes and hurried away, unsettled.

The weather that day was cool and damp, but shoppers bustled in the tony boutiques. The staid Swiss banks stood unflappable and ageless along his route. He turned right on Borsenstrasse and then ducked deftly into the exclusive Club Bauer au Lac, adjunct to the Hotel Bauer au Lac. The hotel was the Grande Dame of the city, offering an unobstructed view of the gleaming lake and snow-kissed Zurich Alps in the distance.

As its doors closed quietly behind him, the club's manager greeted him with a warm nod and a deferential, "Ah, Herr Jafari, a pleasure as always. I hope you're well today. Your guest, Herr Dr. Mayer is already at your table."

With that, the manager ushered him past rich carpets and tapestries, dark wood paneling and shining leather, colorful Paul Klee, Marc Chagall and Joan Miró-signed prints. Lush and tasteful décor aside, it was the club's air of discretion and privacy and outstanding service that made for its three-year membership waitlist.

The balding man at Jafari's table, Dr. Hans-Ruedi Mayer, was Managing Director of Jacquard Privat Bank and its associated trading company Alpine Commodities. Mayer, cadaverous in his conservative three-piece wool suit, looked like a perched turkey vulture peering down upon Lake Zurich looking for something that had died and washed up on the shore. Mayer's bank held a sizeable number of dormant or "dead" accounts in his bank, opened in the 1930's by European Jews desperate to escape the Third Reich's clutches but never reclaimed. A fact that made his vulture resemblance all too apt.

And then there were the accounts of the war criminals (including more than a few senior Nazi SS officers who'd ensured the Jewish accounts would never be claimed), organized-crime syndicates from several continents, unsavory politicians of the left and right and several dictators whose love of the national patrimony was so great that they considered it their personal piggy bank. Finally, there were accounts owned by hard-looking men whose backgrounds and claims of "family money" were vague at best and whose eyes betrayed a thinly veiled penchant for violence. Some of these had shown up on nightly news programs about terrorists: Irish, French, Greek, German, Serbian, and, lately, Middle Eastern. Or at least they resembled the bank's clients, but one could never be sure, and was it a banker's business to draw unwarranted conclusions or to judge who was a terrorist and who a freedom fighter? In the end, money was money. It all spent the same.

Mayer had inherited many of these accounts from his father, who had preceded him as Managing Director and had judiciously married into the Jacquard family. But his own predilection for dealing with all manner of clientele ensured the continued financial health of the bank and the happiness of its key shareholders, especially himself.

Mayer stood, "Hello, my dear Herr Jafari. How is my most valued client?"

Jafari nodded as he shook Mayer's icy talon and sat. "It's always a pleasure to be in your fair city. And lunch with the man who has guarded and guided my investments these past years makes it all the more enjoyable."

Mayer responded that the pleasure was completely his and noted that Jafari's skill at making shrewd investments continued to astound him and his traders at the bank's Alpine Commodities. "For someone who only learned of derivatives and the commodities markets several years ago, you are a wunderkind – a prodigy of the first order. If I didn't know better, I would have thought you're clairvoyant," gushed Mayer. "How do you do it?"

Mayer's high praise was completely sincere. When Jafari had first asked Mayer to explain the ins and outs of commodities investments and how one could make a lot of money in either a rising or falling market, he had been a complete novice. Mayer carefully tutored Jafari and explained how he could leverage his investment war chest through options and more exotic financial instruments. He also cautioned Jafari initially that such investing was only for experienced and sophisticated traders, advising him to start small until he found the rhythm.

Or, better yet, Mayer suggested that Georg Kessler, the bank's most successful Alpine trader, make the trades on Jafari's behalf and save him the trouble and vicious learning curve. All for a most reasonable fee, of course. Would not this be the best solution for Herr Jafari?

It would not.

At the time, Jafari's bank account had been in the low seven figures – not shabby for Mayer's clients but hardly an eye-popping fortune. This changed and quickly.

On his first trade, Jafari authorized one million dollars – a sizable portion of his account - in "put" options in a rising oil market. Mayer had shaken his head as the short trade was executed on the bank's trading screen. The options, which would guarantee Jafari a sale at a set price, would be worthless or worse if the price of oil continued to rise.

Within several days, however, Iran's delegation at the Organization of Petroleum Exporting Countries in Vienna announced that Iran was seriously considering a temporary withdrawal from OPEC because of critical domestic budgetary needs and that it planned to double its production output over the next few months. The floor fell out from under oil prices as the Islamic Republic, sitting on top of the world's fourth largest reserves, shocked the markets with the possibility of unrestrained production. Jafari's put options soared in value as quickly as the price of crude plummeted, and he tripled his money in short order.

Ten days later, Jafari abruptly did an about-face and started buying call options, which would be profitable only if oil prices reversed their downward plunge. When Iran's OPEC ambassador announced a few days later that Iran had reconsidered its choices and would continue to observe its OPEC quota, the price of oil skyrocketed. Again, within days, Jafari's trading brought stunning profits. It was as if he could predict the future.

A few months passed and Jafari's account remained largely quiet. The oil traders in the bank concluded that these initial trades were flukes. They scoffed that Jafari was having beginner's luck. Nothing more. Moreover, some of Jafari's smaller trades were mediocre to fair, occasionally with some losers. Luck seemed to be evening out, as it usually did.

At least until Jafari suddenly instructed the bank to purchase fifteen million dollars in call options during a relatively quiet time in the oil market. He further leveraged his trade based on his credit at the bank, fully tapping his account. Nothing happened for a while. The traders began to shake their heads and exchange knowing looks. Here was another client whose trades burned brightly for a while and then winked out like a falling star. The day of reckoning was drawing nigh.

A few days later, however, hordes of small fast boats manned by the Islamic Revolutionary Guards Corps roared into the Strait of Hormuz from various Iranian ports and began waylaying oil tankers that had "strayed into Iranian territorial waters." Commerce through the strait came to a standstill as insurance premiums skyrocketed. Because twenty percent of oil traded worldwide passed through the two-mile-wide chokepoint, oil prices rose to levels not seen in recent years and threatened to keep climbing. Just as market commentators and pundits claimed that "oil prices know no limit," Jafari executed his call options like the grim reaper, again making a fortune, and then began to purchase "put" options again.

Jacquard's seasoned Alpine oil traders shook their heads in amusement. This was akin to roller-skating the wrong direction in a buffalo stampede. In short order, however, U.S. Navy ships sent by an American president pledging to keep shipping lanes open arrived to find no sign of IRGC gunboats, which had retreated swiftly back to their bases, hours before the fleet's arrival. Once soaring oil prices now swooned. Jafari made a fortune on the rise and even more on the fall. It was truly a coup. Now, the bank's traders took careful notice of Jafari's trade orders and started to secretly mimic them, soon openly piggybacking on his moves.

Jafari glanced at the wine list for a few moments. Seeing what he wanted, he beckoned the hovering sommelier to their table and said simply, "The Beaune, Bouchard Pere, 'Vigne de L'Enfant Jesus' 2010. Still a bit young but one of my favorite Burgundies, and it goes so smoothly with your Veal Zurichoise."

After the wine was opened and carefully decanted, the sommelier poured a small amount into Jafari's sparkling Riedel goblet. Jafari swirled it, sniffed, swirled it once more and then slowly sipped the brilliant red wine. It was a masculine and powerful wine with cherry and cassis notes, a flowery nose and a faint earthiness present only in fine Burgundies, the aftertaste of which lingered on the palate for thirty seconds. Pure harmony, pure bliss.

"Ah perfection," Jafari murmured. "As the monks in Beaune used to say, 'It goes down the throat as smoothly as baby Jesus in velvet trousers.'"

Mayer momentarily lost his composure and almost choked as he swallowed a bit of the Burgundy. In spite of being thoroughly opportunistic and thoroughly agnostic when it came to religion or politics, an involuntary shiver began at the base of his spine. He thought ever so briefly that there could be times when he probably should not open accounts for some people.

This would have been utter blasphemy to his father, a Swiss banker to his utter core. The old man was known to comment that just as every accused deserves legal representation, every Jacquard client deserves refuge for his money until he is proven to be a criminal. Who were they to judge? Wasn't that a matter for the courts?

He and the bank had also profited handsomely over the past few years from this Iranian gentleman's occasional "hunches." At least that is how Jafari routinely characterized his perceptive insights. And he had claimed that his initial deposit was "just old Persian family money seeking a safe haven from unfair and confiscatory taxes by a regime controlled by enemies." Still, something about this client made Mayer uneasy.

Dr. Mayer lowered his glass, barely tasting the fine Burgundy. He nodded to Jafari and produced the special cell phone that he had been instructed to procure. The phone featured an advanced encryption system developed by cryptomathematicians at the Swiss Federal Technical Institute that would defy cracking by the supercomputers at NSA or any world-class eavesdropping service. Second was its "phone within a phone" or ability to conceal its encrypted system and its precious documents and private links through a special app, innocent in outward appearance and labeled "Call to Prayer" but which opened like a jewel box and appeared when tapped five times in rapid succession.

Finally, it used The Onion Router on the Dark Web to connect covertly to the trading system at Alpine inside of Jacquard. Previously, Jafari had been forced to rely upon foreign travels in order to contact the bank via phone or Internet due to the ubiquitous communications monitoring by his enemies inside Iran. Now, using the encryption and TOR, which had been designed (with other intentions) by the U.S. Navy, he could securely access the bank seven days a week and no one would be the wiser. He could invest whenever he wanted and in complete privacy.

After showing Jafari the phone's primary features and ensuring that it and Mayer's sister phone could securely link, the banker showed his client how to access his account.

"There, that's right. That's your account balance as of yesterday's market close. If I recall, that's at least fifteen times your balance when we first met. If I didn't know better, I would swear you had a magic genie advising you."

"No such luck Dr. Mayer. I'm simply a careful observer of world events and your most admiring student in the fine art of commodities trading," replied Jafari with a note of forced humility as the food arrived with a flourish under gleaming silver covers.

Not one to dwell on small talk, Jafari spent the rest of the meal quizzing Mayer on finer points of advanced trading techniques as well as the latest buzz in the markets. After the lunch dishes were cleared away, he suggested dessert or coffee, perhaps a cognac? No? Well, they would have to do this again soon.

The banker bade him farewell and scuttled away towards his bank like a hermit crab returning to his hidey-hole. Jafari smiled slyly and beckoned the waiter. After seeing that amount in his Swiss account, why not a special treat?

Soon he was indulging in a silver dish of rich vanilla ice cream smothered with melted Sprungli chocolate. The thick, dark sauce ran down the scoops of ice cream like lava, creating luscious swirls of delight. He stared out at the gleaming lake as he spooned the delicious dessert into his mouth and daydreamed of his riches. He had a long trip ahead of him back to Iran. But, home would wait.

CHAPTER 8

◇◇◇

The Riding Dead

Oakland, California

Click, click, swish. Click, click, swish. Click, click, swish.

Darkness swamped the corridor and seemed to amplify the sounds of her black leather boots on the cheap linoleum floor as the large handbag swung from her left shoulder. The tall dark-haired woman with splotches of white face paint and heavy mascara, was forty feet from the motel room when she heard the teenage girl scream shrilly from within. The woman touched a concealed microphone near her throat and barked, "Goddammit, we need back-up now!" This was the fourth time in the last fifteen minutes that she had repeated this procedure, but the wire she was wearing was clearly malfunctioning because there had been no response whatsoever. Technology can be such a bitch.

At almost that same moment, the door opened and the beefy outlaw motorcycle gang leader walked out toward her, obviously bound for the parking lot in order to retrieve something from his bike or maybe just to relieve himself. His group, The Riding Dead, took their name and inspiration from the current mania for zombie movies, and they delighted in dressing (and smelling) accordingly. Having heard some of what she had said into the mike, a dim realization slowly dawned on him, and he growled, "Just what the fuck're you doing?" At the same time, he instinctively pulled a silver handgun from his torn leather jacket.

The woman reached inside her handbag and with incredible celerity withdrew a 1911 Colt Commander 38 Super pistol as she screamed, "FBI! You're under arrest! Drop the gun! Get down!"

The gang leader snorted, "Fuck you bitch!" and brought his gun to bear on the woman who stood some thirty feet away. He fired a wild shot that went over her head. Hers, however, did not miss. The .38 caliber slug hit him in the left shoulder and knocked him back against the wall.

The tall woman screamed again, "FBI! Get down! Drop your weapon! Now!"

Dumbfounded but still very much alive, he tried to train his gun on her again, at which point, with a brief shrug of regret, she raised the Colt higher, took aim with both hands and shot him squarely between the eyes. This resulted in a neat round hole in the front of his head and blew most of the few brains that he had out the back of his skull.

The leader of the Riding Dead was history, now a member of the dead Dead.

Special Agent Lacy Merrill and her partner Chet Clinton were part of an elite FBI undercover squad in Oakland targeting organized crime. They had managed to penetrate The Riding Dead after several months of hard, nasty, distasteful work. As Captain Justin Thibodeaux, a retired senior Louisiana State Police officer and one of her undercover instructors at Quantico, had lectured, "If you gotta go undercover and ride with these dirtbag dipshit outlaw motorcycle gangs, you're gonna do thangs you don't want yo mama to know about."

How true, Captain Thibodeaux. How true.

The gang had gradually accepted Chet and Lacy (Lacy playing Chet's old lady) after the pair had been vouched for by a disaffected Riding Dead member they had flipped. This had been another valued lesson from Captain Thibodeaux – titled, "Running a Rat."

Their full acceptance into the gang had been accelerated by a stage-managed shoot-out at a convenience store hold-up in which Chet had seemingly killed two employees. Both were in fact other FBI agents wearing concealed squibs with Hollywood special effects blood. The members of The Riding Dead who witnessed this bit of legerdemain had been most impressed.

Over the next few months, Lacy and Chet gained a great deal of intelligence on the The Riding Dead and their connections to other motorcycle gangs as well as to some dysfunctional elements of the old Italian mafia whose members were too tired and lazy to do their own dirty work. The real payoff would be coming in a few days, when The Riding Dead took possession of a shipment of fully automatic weapons and high explosives, which they were importing from a slightly smarter Chinese gang. After that, they planned to resell them to a jihadist terrorist cell in the Bay Area. At least that was the steady rumor among The Riding Dead.

Lacy knew that brains, good judgment and common sense tended to dribble downwards in ever decreasing amounts in this dismal little ecosystem.

But things seldom go as planned, especially when the perps come from the very shallow end of the gene pool and are easily distracted by drugs, rumbles, and poontang. The latter proved to be everyone's undoing when four of the members got a seventeen-year-old girl very drunk and took her to this cheap motel for a party. Knowing that this would quickly turn into a gang rape, Lacy and Chet rode with them "to watch the fun." As they arrived, Lacy excused herself to go "buy some beer for the boys" and radio for help. Although it would compromise the entire undercover operation, they couldn't let a young girl be raped. Chet had gone inside with the four thugs while Lacy stayed with their bike.

Now, things were really going to shit, and Lacy stepped over the leader's body and burst into the motel room screaming "FBI!" Ordinarily this little public service announcement has a sobering effect upon a roomful of miscreants, nitwits and lowlifes, but The Riding Dead were riding high on octane and cocaine and low on brain cells, and everyone went for their guns.

Chet had clearly broken cover and tried to protect the teenager. Now, he was being held with a knife at his throat while another Riding Dead with his pants down was about to assault the girl. Going against all of the protocols of her training, which called for her to shoot center-mass, Lacy aimed at Chet's assailant's hand. She shot the knife out of his grip and took off two of his fingers in the process. When the meth-strung biker whipped out a large nickel-plated pistol from his waistband with his good hand, she promptly shot him through the throat. Turning to the would-be rapist, she fired into his crotch as he drew down on her with his little silver .38 caliber snubbie. He fell backwards, blood spraying everywhere and his lust a forever forgotten thought.

Reacting to a sound coming from the bathroom, she swiveled to face the last Riding Dead member present, a ferret-faced fool named "Pops" who should have given up outlaw bike riding two decades earlier. He'd kicked open the bathroom door and was wheeling a sawed-off shotgun toward her. Reflexively, she fired the Colt twice dead-center into his chest ("there's center mass for you," she thought) and the .38 caliber slugs knocked him off his feet as he pulled the trigger.

The partial shotgun blast hit her like a sledgehammer and blew her back several feet onto the floor. Dark descended and she blacked out. When she came to, Chet had called for help and was administering first aid. Fortunately, she'd had a Kevlar vest packed in her motorcycle saddlebag and had donned it under her jacket before coming to the room. Only a few stray pellets had penetrated her skin, including two grazes on the left side of her face and - thank you thank you Jesus - none in her eyes.

Six months and some minor surgery later, the small facial scars were healing. Her hair had been restored to its lustrous strawberry blonde from the hideous raven-black chop job she had sported as a Riding Dead zombie slut. Even the carefully designed bogus tattoos were gone, although she had grown fond of the one that had a skull with two crossed 1911 Colt Commanders on her right forearm and the words "A Girl's Best Friends." That one she might have to get for real.

Bottom line: she felt almost - with a stress on the word "almost"- back to normal.

Now she was working out of a little cubicle at CIA Headquarters on joint assignment to the Agency's Targeting Group in the Counter Proliferation Center. For the last several months, disturbing dreams had haunted her nights – dreams in which the gang leader and his cohorts burst into view, and she tried in vain to shout at them to drop their guns, words sticking in her dry throat. She shot them again and again and again. A Bureau psychologist said she had "a mild case" of post-traumatic stress disorder. Time would help; the nightmares would gradually recede and eventually fade away. Nevertheless, if this was mild, Lacy couldn't imagine a severe case of PTSD.

Her superiors at FBI had thought it wise that she take some time off from undercover work and try her hand at something less intense. She could decompress back in Washington for eighteen months and learn all she could from the CIA and FBI about combating the spread of weapons of mass destruction. After, she would take an onward assignment back in the Bay area as an FBI Agent in the Lab at Lawrence Livermore National Laboratory. Her direct instructions were: "Relate to the scientists. Protect our nuclear secrets. Protect them from doing stupid-ass things. And take it easy, Lacy. Chill."

Well, maybe.

At first, it was hard to live without that familiar undercover adrenalin boost, though she had to admit that the scientists she met in Washington were a fascinating breed, and the things she was learning about nuclear weapons were both interesting and terrifying. She could see why the case officers and Special Agents in the CIA's Counter Proliferation Center and the FBI Weapons of Mass Destruction Directorate were so motivated.

Plus, her CIA assignment in the Targeting Group came with a most pleasant reward. After several months of hard work and excelling in the art of targeting, she was promised a temporary assignment to Geneva to provide intelligence targeting support to the nuclear negotiations with Iran. This might actually beat chasing zombie meth-head bikers. She also had to admit: preventing someone from killing tens of thousands of people in a nuclear fireball or an anthrax attack had its own intrinsic virtue.

Lacy had been raised on a large cattle ranch outside of Midland, Texas. Her daddy, Tommy Merrill, was a wealthy cattleman who had been widowed when Lacy was only five. She had grown up shooting and riding, a tomboy and wild child. Tommy absolutely doted on his only child. Adoring her father and his love of the outdoors, she started competitive pistol and shotgun shooting at nine. He bought her a 28-gauge Beretta over and under shotgun and taught her the essentials, but she was a natural shot and took to it right away.

When introduced to skeet shooting, Lacy blew apart 24 out of 25 clay pigeons in her first set. It seemed as if she knew exactly how far to lead the clay and when to pull the trigger. Mystically, it was as if she willed the pellets into the targets. When Lacy finished shooting, Tommy uttered the word "Shit" under his breath in amazement. He turned to see Lacy with tears welling up in her eyes.

"What's the matter, honey? Why're you crying?"

"Daddy, I just want you to be proud of me. I'm sorry. I, I…I thought I hit all 25. I'm sorry I didn't blow apart that last one but I was sure I hit it. I felt that I hit it."

"You 'felt' that you hit it? What do you mean, sweetie?"

"It just felt like I hit it. I felt all the others in my mind connect, and I felt it too."

Tommy nodded but had no idea what she was talking about. He walked over to where the one clay pigeon had fallen intact. He picked it up and flipped it over to examine it.

On the far side, he saw where two pellets had grazed and chipped but not broken it.

Lacy grew into a tall, beautiful young woman. But when she reached seventeen, instead of a debutante ball, she asked Tommy if she could have a precision-made Italian Perazzi 12-gauge MX12 competition shotgun with screw-in chokes just like Kim Rhode was using in the Olympics and winning gold medals. Tommy agreed, the several thousand-dollar cost notwithstanding. At nineteen, she was destined to be an Olympics skeet contender. Her then-boyfriend, a Marine infantryman in a light armored reconnaissance vehicle, was killed in Iraq on deployment by an IED with an explosively formed penetrating head which had been supplied to the insurgents by the Iranian IRGC.

This changed her world.

Lacy became more serious and finished her studies at Rice University, which she had neglected to an extent during her competition shooting.

She then went onto law school at the University of Texas. From there, she became an assistant district attorney back in Midland, but several years of prosecuting cattle rustlers, credit-card hustlers, small-time gunrunners and meth dealers made her wonder if she was having any real impact in the scheme of things.

One Sunday at the local Presbyterian Church, the pastor, a transplanted Scot with a powerful style of delivery, preached a sermon entitled "Is My Life Significant?" Although she had no doubt that her life mattered to God, she questioned whether her life was significant in other respects. Sending the scum on the cesspool of life to the penitentiary had its moments but it seemed like small potatoes to her. She thought she could do more.

Lacy applied to the FBI. She was accepted and excelled at the FBI Academy at Quantico. Ironically, her one close call was on the Academy's range. Lacy's initial ten rounds with the Glock at 25 yards were so closely grouped that they formed just one big hole in the paper, making the skilled FBI firearms instructors wonder if she had missed the target altogether with most of her rounds. After finding a second close grouping of ten rounds at 30 yards, they became fans. They realized who Lacy was in the world of competition shooting, and the grizzled veterans gathered around her like groupies. Challenged by six of them to a contest, she outshot them all.

There was talk of offering her a spot on a Bureau Hostage Rescue Team as a sniper, but she made it clear that she wanted to do more conventional investigative work as a Special Agent. This led to a criminal squad and then undercover work. The one thing she demanded in her undercover work was to carry the .38 Super 1911 Colt Commander rather than the standard issue .40 caliber Glock 23. She was more comfortable with it. It also fit in better with her undercover role. But the real reason she carried it was that her father had given it to her in honor of her childhood heroes, the Texas Rangers. Their unofficial motto was, "One riot. One ranger."

Ultimately, a few months after the shootout in Oakland, Lacy was awarded the FBI Medal of Valor for an exceptional act of heroism in her undercover work against the Riding Dead. Tommy Merrill's eyes glistened as he watched his only child's medal ceremony. And Lacy cried as he hugged her. To make him proud of her was all she really cared about.

Getting rid of her nightmares was a close second.

CHAPTER 9

◇◇◇

The Bouncing Balloon

Geneva

By the time he met Leopard, Lane Andrews had five field tours as a CIA case officer under his belt, most of them devoted to counterproliferation operations. As a teenager, Lane had read John Hersey's "Hiroshima." He was haunted by the image of the permanently etched shadows of three unfortunates near Ground Zero of that 13 kiloton bomb. They were. And then they were not.

Motivated by Connor McBane's HEU letter from Afghanistan, Lane found himself contemplating recruitment targets in Geneva during a several month period when Iran and the U.S. and other Western powers were locked in another round of negotiations on the nuclear issue. Earlier negotiations had resulted in an agreement barely acceptable to either side, but then this fragile bargain had fallen apart with accusations of bad faith coming from all parties. The current U.S. administration had nudged the Iranians back to the bargaining table, but prospects were bleak.

The U.S. did not dispute Iran's right to peaceful nuclear energy, but wanted ironclad verification that Iran was not secretly building an atomic weapon. There was ample evidence of covert Iranian uranium enrichment efforts at various sites and even nuclear weapons work in the past. Why should Iran be trusted now? Therein was the rub. Neither side wanted to budge.

He first met the rotund Iranian nuclear scientist when both were serving on their respective delegations to the Geneva negotiations. In attendance were several well-known Iranian nuclear scientists and technocrats from the Atomic Energy Organization of Iran. Before the negotiations, CIA targeting officers and analysts had studied their mug shots and files like kids trading baseball cards, then placed them in organizational diagrams. Once each had been fitted into his proper niche, the targeting officers doled out prize targets to the operations officers like candy to eager children. Arguments and even fights occasionally erupted over who got what.

Sadly, not many officers ever approached these "trading cards" in the flesh. In Lane's opinion, the fault lay with operations officers who seemed to lack imagination in engineering an approach to the targets. Such encounters needed to appear innocent - a "bump" to borrow their crude term for it. You had to sidle up next to someone innocently, and then, somehow, get a second meeting, an opportunity for magic to happen. It was possible. Lane had done it often.

In fact, Lane usually had no problem with a pretext bump, and he enjoyed playing the game. It was a routine that changed constantly according to the circumstances, making his work challenging and enjoyable, never boring. He often joked that if the job were easy, they'd have left it to the real diplomats. Still, plenty of operations officers talked about "asset hunting" in theory while waiting for something to fall in their laps, later complaining that their cover was flawed or that the targeting officers never found them accessible worthwhile targets. Their excuses seemed endless, their track records dismal.

It was surely no coincidence that these same officers rarely left the office to work the street and press the flesh, but instead worked their fellow officers and bosses at Headquarters, lining up that next ideal assignment when their ship would certainly come in. Lane suspected that even if targeting officers had lassoed the targets, thrown burlap bags over their heads and delivered them all trussed up to these benighted operations officers, the latter would still find ways to avoid doing the needful.

Lane had read once that the most successful fighter pilots weren't necessarily the best pilots, but instead they were the pilots who engaged the enemy the most. The same could be said for case officers. To succeed, you had to get off your ass, use a bit of imagination and boldness, and bump targets frequently. What he never could have predicted, however, was that he was about to experience a reverse bump in a few days. The wildcard would fall squarely in his lap. And no one would ever need to deal another.

The name of Dr. Ali Javadpour did not appear on any targeting officer's list. He was a complete unknown, and in Lane's business, "if he wasn't on the list, he didn't exist." Certainly, he didn't exist to Headquarters, which showed little patience for case officers who chased after marginal targets – the low-hanging fruit in the business – who had little intelligence value to offer.

Still, Lane noticed the curious little Iranian man on the delegation, or at least on its fringes, whose shabby clothing would have made Lane wonder if he were a member of the hotel custodial staff, except the latter were better dressed. His shirttails were untucked, the back of his trousers shiny from wear, and he bounced along like an untethered balloon with a will of its own.

At one point, Lane even had to stifle a laugh as he watched the bumbling Iranian almost collide with two stylishly dressed female tourists in the hotel lobby and then struggle to keep up with the other Iranian scientists and their two MOIS minders sent to protect them from the likes of Lane and other Western intelligence officers. The rearmost minder roughly strong-armed the little man back into the herd, causing the poor fellow momentarily to lose his perpetual goofy smile.

Lane observed all this from a leather armchair in the hotel lobby, reading his newspaper and nursing an espresso. Amusing. Amusing but sad at the same time. Lane hated bullies.

Later at the U.S. Mission in Geneva, Lane went to his temporary office and looked in his database to see if he could identify the little man. The targeting packages were actually quite impressive, including job descriptions and presumed access, known publications, and photographs, along with anything operationally relevant they knew about the target: attendance at earlier conferences, past approaches, attitude towards Westerners (especially Americans) and where they supposedly fit in the Iranian nuclear hierarchy. There must have been twenty such dossiers in the database, including photos of the two thugs who were the obvious minders, but no roly-poly little Iranian. So, who the hell was he?

"I see you're admiring some of my friends," came a soft voice from his office doorway. A tall woman with long strawberry blonde hair looked down at Lane and smiled. The first thing Lane noticed were her lovely blue eyes, and he promptly lost interest in his search of the Iranian delegation.

"I'm Lacy Merrill," she said. "I helped put these targeting packages together at Headquarters. I just got in from DC this morning to see if I could help during the latest show across town. And you are…?"

Lane introduced himself and invited her into his office. He took the targeting packages, spread them on his desk, and leaned forward, intent on the photos, self-consciously ignoring the attractive woman seated across from him.

"Where's the little chubby guy? Kind of looks like Oliver Hardy? Seems sort of out of it? Like an absent-minded professor?" Lane fanned the targeting packages out, looking for the man.

She looked at him, a bit puzzled. "What little guy? I don't recall anyone like that. Are you sure?"

"I didn't think he was part of their team either at first. I mean the guy seems clueless, but the MOIS minders got him under control when he wandered off."

Lacy's expression softened. "Let me tell you my feelings about this job. We usually have incomplete information at best. We deal with what we have and let you know it. He may well be a last-minute addition to their team. Maybe someone else was sick. Maybe he has special expertise. Maybe he's here for some other reason. If you go after him, at least we'll have something we don't have now."

Lane smiled. "Well, that's a refreshing take."

She smiled. "If you think he's a viable target, my recommendation is go for it. Get his background, get a feel for him. Do your case officer magic." She shrugged. "Hell, now you've got me curious too."

Lane shook his head. "You definitely don't sound like the average Agency targeting officer."

Lacy laughed. "I think you just drew a low card, Lane. I'm not a CIA targeter at all. Just a very curious FBI agent assigned to CIA to assist with targeting WMD scientists. Sorry if I disappointed you."

Lane was far from disappointed.

He put up his hands. "No, not at all. I'm all for FBI-CIA teamwork. It's just that targeters tend to be very smart but also rather dogmatic about who we should pursue. It kind of makes sense that they want us chasing the sure thing – but it's not like I'm gonna meet the head of the delegation, much less turn him."

Lacy laughed again. "That would be priceless. I can picture the Secretary of State and our Chief of Station when you tell them that you just cold-pitched the director of the Atomic Energy Organization of Iran."

"Hey, you give me the goods on these guys and I'll try my best. But seriously, I try to tell the targeters at headquarters that we don't know what we don't know, but it usually falls on deaf ears."

"I guess my philosophy's more like yours. Or maybe I'm swayed by your reputation as a recruiter. I've heard good things about your work. Or at least most of it," she joked.

Lane stacked the targeting packages in the center of his desk and stood. "Well, I could definitely use your help with this. You clearly have an open mind, and I could use a second opinion. In return, maybe I could show you around Geneva? It's a gorgeous city. If you haven't done it already, you need to have lunch down on the Quai Wilson and try a little *filet de perche*. You won't regret it."

Lacy smiled and nodded. "That sounds lovely. Let's do it. We can talk targeting later."

They walked up Quai Wilson and found a table in the café facing the lake. A gentle breeze whispered softly off the water. As they looked at the menus, Lane ordered them each a glass of St. Saphorin, a delicious Swiss white wine. The wine seemed to capture the light in their glasses as it sparkled.

Lacy sighed. "To think that last week I was sitting in CIA Headquarters drinking Starbuck's coffee and noshing on a donut. What was I thinking? This, on the other hand…" She stared out at the rippling water of the lake with the wavering reflections of the mountains.

The waiter soon brought them each a plate of lightly sautéed lake perch in a beurre blanc sauce along with a heaping serving of scrumptious, thin, golden French fries. The alpine air, the view of the soaring Mont Blanc, the scent of their meal and the sunlight sparking golden off of their wine glasses gave them both pause. Neither spoke for a minute or two.

"And to think that they pay us to do this," Lane murmured at last. "I'm not sure I ever want to go home."

"I was thinking the same," replied Lacy.

"So, how did a refined FBI agent like you get into this sordid spy business?" he asked with a mischievous grin.

"Oh my, now aren't you quite the recruiter." Lacy joked back. "Just like they say…"

"One tries his best."

"I'm sure you do." Her smile never faltered. "But if you want to know the truth, I kind of backed into this job. It wasn't something I planned on." She paused for a moment, then continued, "A few months ago, I was riding undercover with a scumbag motorcycle gang a few light years from here. Or it seems that far away now. It was…it was…it was different from here for sure. There were…things that happened." Her voice cracked and she looked away from Lane out over the lake.

"Things were bad and then things got worse. I had to shoot some men… complete vermin…but they were still men, not clay pigeons. They bled and died…all of them…" She looked down at her hands, "Actually, I'm not sure I want to talk about it." She breathed deeply.

"It's OK," Lane said. "Forget I asked." He reached over and took her hand and gave it a squeeze. As she looked up at him, he raised his glass and said, "Here's to Lacy Merrill. An American patriot who serves her country, be it on a bike or in Geneva." They clinked glasses and sipped their wine.

Lacy smiled. “May I also propose a toast?”

He nodded.

“To a fruitful meeting with your absent-minded professor.”

They both laughed.

CHAPTER 10

◇◇◇

The Air Guitar

Zurich

Still enjoying the high from seeing his rapidly increasing Swiss bank account, Jafari took a cab to the Zurich main train station and boarded a first-class compartment on the express to Frankfurt. He relaxed as he sipped a glass of Dezaley "Chemin de Fer" from Luc Massy, one he intended to savor because it would be some time before he would indulge thusly again.

He activated his new phone and instantly established the encrypted link to Jacquard's trading company. He checked his Bloomberg account to see what the markets were doing. Today was a dull day with little movement. No dramatic ups and downs, meaning no opportunities for dramatic profits. Dull, dull, dull. Well, no matter. That would change soon.

Jafari arrived a few hours later at Frankfurt Airport and caught the Emirates Air flight to Dubai. He immediately took a cab to a quiet apartment building in an upscale neighborhood in the gulf city. He let himself into the well-appointed second floor apartment and into the master bedroom. He carefully removed his elegant clothing and hung it all in the large closet where similarly expensive suits, shirts, ties and shoes were stored neatly. He redressed in a much more modest dark suit and plain white shirt, no tie, and an understated pair of simple black shoes. He unhooked the $15,000 Swiss IWC chronograph from his wrist and replaced it with a simple metal Seiko.

Jafari then proceeded to the concealed safe in the apartment's study and entered the combination. The steel drawer slid out smoothly with a soft metal click. He proceeded to swap the passport of Mohammed Ali Jafari for that of Colonel Masud Alborzi, along with his Islamic Revolutionary Guard Corps credentials. His Jafari persona served him well for stashing the proceeds that he siphoned off from various IRGC charities. He felt no guilt at this. Why should he? Some of the proceeds did go to needy causes, and who was to say his cause wasn't needy? After all, didn't charity begin at home?

He had obtained his initial nest egg in a more direct manner in Damascus a few years earlier, when he was just a newly promoted Major in the IRGC Quds Force on a liaison mission in Syria to meet with his Lebanese co-religionists from Hezbollah.

He and his young IRGC adjutant had been under orders to deliver three million dollars in cash to these filthy Arabs along with plans for a new type of improvised explosive device with even greater penetrating power against armor – something referred to as an "explosively formed penetrator" or EFP. All of this so that the Quds Force could project power in Lebanon and help its Shi'ite brothers overcome Sunni and Christian oppression, not to mention provide an irritant to Israel. What did he personally care about these people? Nothing at all.

On that particular day, he thought he could smell the Arabs as they came into the apartment safe house even before he saw them. The leader still had bits of shwarma in his beard, and the other three were even less clean. The tall, thin leader was dressed incongruously in blue jeans, a tee shirt from the New York City Marathon and a New York Yankees baseball cap as well as Oakley shades, obviously radical chic from his stinking slum of a Lebanese neighborhood. His three slouching acolytes were as slovenly attired as their leader, each trying to look nonchalant and super cool. The four ill-dressed morons could have been part of a gangsta' rap group from some U.S. slum rather than members of a paramilitary force allied to Iran in its resistance to Israel. Was it any wonder that these people were going up against the Israelis and regularly getting their sorry asses kicked? More to the point, he wondered, could we pick worse allies? He glanced over at his adjutant and rolled his eyes before he looked back at them, holding his breath lest the rancid mixture of body odor, sweat and garlic overwhelm him.

Alborzi hid his disgust and put on his warmest, most inviting smile. A few more minutes and he would be rid of these stupid vermin. They sat and smoked while he showed them the drawings for the explosive device. They smiled as he explained its expanded deadly properties. Did they understand a word he was saying? Probably not. Did he really care? Absolutely not. But their biggest smiles came when he pulled out the satchel with three million dollars in cash, which his adjutant had carried all the way from Tehran. First, however, would they be so kind as to sign for it? Even the IRGC had its bean counters in Tehran. Alborzi's adjutant produced the receipt from his pocket.

One of the more junior Hezbollah operatives, an overweight little man, signed the proffered form with a flourish and considerable disdain and purposely returned it to Alborzi, ignoring the junior IRGC officer. Their leader snatched the satchel from Alborzi's hands, eagerly looking at its contents. His eyes almost popped out from behind his sunglasses. He caressed the carefully wrapped bundles of genuine one-hundred-dollar bills – not the counterfeit crap printed in the Beka'a Valley – and giggled in a high-pitched tone like a young girl.

He opened the satchel wide to show his three colleagues and then walked over to the apartment window for better light to admire the loot. Flouting all safety protocols, the leader threw back the curtain to see the contents of the satchel in the afternoon sunshine. Alborzi instinctively backed away while the man took a few packets of the crisp notes and slowly riffled them with his dirty thumbnail next to his equally dirty right ear, basking in the sound. He strutted in front of the window, prancing like a rock star, and Alborzi thought he might actually play the air guitar and hum a Stones' melody like "Jumpin' Jack Flash." The Arab chortled like a teenager copping a feel of his girlfriend's tit.

As the Hezbollah squad leader turned back to the room, his hands full of cash, there came a soft crack and a sound like an angry bee from the window. Glass tinkled on the floor, followed about three seconds later by the body of the Arab, the bundles of notes sprayed with blood tumbling out of his hands. His designer sunglasses fell beside his body with a ragged hole through one lens where a bullet had exited his head.

The Iranians and the Arabs stared at that gory scene for an incomprehensible eternity. Then there was another sharp crack and the fat little Hezbollah cadre suddenly grabbed his throat and sank to his knees, bubbling sounds emerging from his mouth, the light already leaving his eyes.

Alborzi's adjutant looked to Alborzi in shock before he too fell victim to the sniper in the apartment across the alley, parts of his brains splattering the faded wallpaper.

Finally, chaos erupted in the room.

Everyone hit the floor, and after a few seconds, the two remaining Hezbollah operatives scrambled from their knees towards the door like cockroaches running for cover in a lit room. Alborzi remained still, flat on the floor, his sidearm already drawn as the others exited and reached the first landing in the stairwell. Not unexpectedly, Alborzi next heard sound-suppressed automatic weapon fire through the open doorway, undoubtedly from Israeli Uzi submachine guns coming up the stairwell. Woodchips flew off of the doorframe as the sharp buzzing continued, and he heard the muffled thump of two bodies falling.

Alborzi lay still, pistol ready. He heard careful footsteps ascending the stairs. A creak, and then another creak on the landing. He made sure the safety was off and shot the first person to pass the doorframe – a hard looking man with long dark hair and a beard not dissimilar to that of the now-dead Arabs, but evidently he was much better at this type of work. Alborzi's shot caught the man in the thigh, and he threw himself back out the door barking something in Hebrew to someone lower down the stairs. There was a scuffling sound, obvious cursing, the sound of stairs being descended and then the slamming of a car door. A car engine roared and tires squealed. Then silence.

Alborzi marveled at the sheer audacity (indeed the Yiddish word "chutzpah" came to mind) of the Israeli assassination team striking in the heart of Syria. Talk about professionalism and balls! Why couldn't Iran have such allies instead of these dead incompetents littering the floor, dressed like ridiculous American rappers. Alborzi was disgusted. Instead of Snoop Dogg, it was Dead Dogg and his band of deadheads.

Alborzi waited only a few seconds and then decided to make his own exit before the Israelis decided to come back and finish the job. He looked at the lifeless eyes of his adjutant and the spilled satchel of money. He stuffed the bills, some stained dark blood red, back in the satchel and made for the doorway.

With the signed receipt safely in his pocket for the IRGC accountants, he decided to put the money to a much better use than these dead, useless Arabs intended.

The Stones' tune cycled in his head as he descended the stairs, and he started to hum to himself, smiling all the while, the guitar chords resonating in his mind, Mick leaping in the background, lips pouting.

Alborzi smiled and strummed the satchel in a circular motion like his own special air guitar. Yeah, Mick, it really was all right now. And it was surely a gas.

God truly helps those who help themselves.

God is great. Allahu Akbar!

He looked at himself obliquely in the mirror of his Dubai apartment and liked what he saw - dark penetrating eyes, well trimmed, slightly greying beard, his strong chin, and his steady countenance. A man of action if ever there was one. A man in charge of his own destiny.

As he exited his apartment and headed for the Port of Dubai, Alborzi thought of the rich irony in choosing "Mohammad Ali Jafari" as his Western alter ego and alias. The expert document forger, a wizened Syrian Jew he had found in Dubai, had not blinked an eye at his choice. Why would he care? He was paid well for creating the travel document, which used a real Iranian passport blank that Alborzi had secured from the IRGC documents department devoted to undercover work by its Quds Force operatives abroad. So Alborzi's joke – using the name of the leader of the entire IRGC – remained a private one.

The Iranian sailor lounging at the foot of the gangplank in a special section of the Port of Dubai snapped to attention as he caught sight of Alborzi approaching his private launch. He stood stock still as the colonel swept past him and proceeded to his cabin.

Minutes later, in his cabin, Alborzi heard the engine roar as the sleek craft pulled away from shore on a course for home. He reflected on several things.

Using Major General Mohammed Ali Jafari's name also had a fringe benefit. If the fools in the Iranian Ministry of Intelligence and Security ever came upon his trail, they would back off quickly. "Ministry of Ignorant Shits" was more like it. The MOIS might have been trained by the Russian KGB, but when they encountered rank and privilege, they still acted like their sniveling predecessors in the Shah's SAVAK intelligence service. And if not? Well, he might profit from a little management shakeup above him – a trick that was becoming a specialty of his. In fact, a bit more headroom could be exactly what he needed.

A thought came to him – one he'd had for a while.

CHAPTER 11

◇◇◇

The Guild

Langley, Virginia

The attractive, immaculately dressed woman in her fifties sat in her seventh-floor office at Langley overlooking the forested grounds below and pondering her discontent. She was at the top of her profession after twenty-five years of unrelenting effort, proving that the world of espionage was not only a man's world. She had ultimately been rewarded with the position of Deputy Director of Operations – the DDO – the top job in the clandestine service. But what did she have to show for it?

She stared at her overflowing inbox filled with personnel actions – almost all unpleasant: reprimands for shoddy performance or lapses of judgment, requests from Chiefs of Station that problem employees be removed as quickly as possible, poor morale in other overseas and domestic stations. The most troubling of all were the ones that involved questions of integrity. Paula Davenport could endure most mistakes and even sub-par performance, but a question of shady ethics in an officer was her personal bête noir – something she found difficult to forgive. Ironically, the very profession of espionage was built on trust, and once that trust was fractured, little remained.

The saddest thing was how little her job involved espionage operations these days. She was now Deputy Director of Operations and where were the operations? When her job did concern operations, it seemed inevitable that she dealt with operational failures. Messes to be cleaned up like someone following the circus elephants as they marched grandly into the Big Top – Paula and her trusty shovel. These ops were just like those big showy elephants, beribboned and trumpeting their grand entrance. They looked great marching into the Director's office, or better yet into the Oval Office. Indeed, "they briefed well," as one cynical friend of hers joked. Lots of derring-do and chest-thumping.

More often than not, they accomplished very little because they were so often run by committees. To make matters worse, the committees typically contained inexperienced or mediocre officers, all of whom had an equal vote regardless of how much or how little they understood the particular issue or operation. This produced not the wisdom of crowds but the idiocy of mobs.

This phenomenon of "operational rot" had begun a decade before, as the Agency found itself drawn inextricably and simultaneously into multiple war zones where espionage was an afterthought, and if it occurred, was conducted at the point of a gun. Traditional espionage became yet one more casualty of the global war on terror, the GWOT, which Paula thought of as the global war on tradecraft. Young officers, bright and courageous all, received a totally erroneous impression of what spying was really about: dealing with human beings over a sustained period and finding their motivations and stress points so that they could be recruited as intelligence sources. Instead, these youngsters raised on the adrenalin pump of the war zone wanted the instant gratification of recruiting their target in only a few meetings.

To be fair, a few meetings could suffice if the recruitment target were truly desperate for contact with U.S. intelligence, but this was rare. Instead, this "warspionage" involved CIA officers recruiting desperate people in dangerous war zones while accompanied by armed bodyguards. Subtlety, sophistication and patience were sacrificed for quick wins and higher body counts. Rather than recruitment, it resembled renting sources by the hour.

When had the last Penkovsky- or Tolkachev-class asset been recruited? Those Cold War Soviet assets had boasted priceless access. They had saved countless lives, even prevented wars. They'd paid the Agency's budget for years. Now, most mid-level managers and even senior managers had little experience at recruiting any human assets much less intelligence treasures.

Granted, Penkovsky and Tolkachev had been volunteers rather than classically recruited, but there were others whose true names even Paula did not know – only code words for deep penetrations of senior levels of foreign adversaries – who had been recruited through persistence, perception, persuasion and the highest order of tradecraft by an exceedingly small cadre of gifted case officers who operated at the pinnacle of the profession.

Those officers were spoken of in hushed tones and informally referred to as "The Guild." These were the elite headhunters consistently assigned to go after the most difficult and most valuable targets – clandestine sources that made a significant difference to U.S. national security. It was often said that twenty percent of the Agency's case officers recruited eighty percent of the sources. But The Guild consisted of the top half-percent, and their recruitments frequently changed the course of history.

Years earlier, well-meaning efforts had been made by a couple of case officers to have The Guild formally recognized by the Directorate of Operations. It was meant as a badge of honor for the small group of elite recruiters, just as the military recognizes elite special forces such as the SEALs or Delta Force. Not surprisingly, it had quickly run up against opposition from senior DO leadership who feared that such recognition would lead to a "poisonous elitism" and be divisive.

Paula suspected that the real reason was that these leaders feared they themselves would not qualify for inclusion. So, it remained an informal designation and Paula concluded it was best that the DO bureaucracy was not involved. They would ruin it with their benighted notions of operational socialism where no case officer was any better at operations than the other case officers, a ludicrous notion if ever there were one. There would be no mention of it in personnel files, no induction ceremonies, no special designations, no elitism. Nothing at all. Still, people knew who was in The Guild.

Paula did not count herself among The Guild, although she had had her moments in the field when she had glimpsed the awesome beauty of bringing an important new source into the fold – one who, but for her efforts, would not have cooperated. The degree of focus required had been draining for her. In so doing, she'd gained an even greater appreciation for The Guild. They neither strained nor labored at their work. No one had taught them their ability. They'd had it from birth. Their recruitments were legend.

Paula had decided early in her tenure as DDO that she would protect and nurture The Guild as much as possible. She did not favor them like spoiled children but tried to the best of her ability to keep others, particularly those who were operationally mediocre or totally bereft of ops talent, out of their way. These others were the operational sludge that gummed up the system and killed creativity, initiative, and stealth. Moreover, it was a time-honored principle that swiftness is the best counterintelligence defense. You get in, you accomplish the mission, you get out, and you protect your people. But woe unto swiftness when these "operational mavens" stuck their clumsy fat fingers into the mix. They hesitated, they fretted, and they asked endless questions and then rarely understood the answers.

This had become a constant struggle, and occasionally she lost out to the unrelenting bureaucratic imperative, which seemed to grind on eternally. In fact, it was seldom productive to confront the naysayers head-on. They were masters of "death by memo" and "the slow roll" and dwelled in the world of ass-covering "what ifs." But there had been times when she was sorely tempted to throw them out of the floor-to-ceiling windows in her office. The grounds crew could probably use them for fertilizer since they were composed mostly of manure.

As tiresome as this could be, her principal challenge was explaining the nuances and greyness of her profession to the political appointee who currently occupied the Director's chair. He had surrounded himself with sycophantic aides from his former position as a successful hedge-fund manager as well as some overly ambitious officers from the Agency. These latter apparatchiki prided themselves on being intelligence professionals, but their counsel to the Director seldom, if ever, ventured into political headwinds or evidenced strong operational creativity. The joke was that there were more dissenting voices in the Standing Committee of the Chinese Politburo than there were currently in the Director's office or entire Senior Staff of the Agency.

But The Guild...The Guild was different.

CHAPTER 12

◇◇◇

Mac the Knife & Cloud Computing

Langley

Paula was reading the latest "DDO's Eyes Only" cable from a field station in East Asia that was running an especially sensitive counterterrorist operation, when her phone rang, and the nasally voice of Roberta, the Director's secretary, came over the line.

"The Director needs you right away. Come here as soon as you can. The senior staff is meeting in the Director's conference room. It's urgent." The phone clicked in her ear.

It was always urgent.

Here we go again, Paula thought as she put the cable in her personal safe, and strode down the hall to the Holy of Holies, the Director's office. This Director had been sworn in only a few months earlier, but it seemed as if he had been there for years. She knew she should feel grateful to him, as it was he who chose her to be his DDO, but she was torn.

To say that CIA Director, Macgregor White, was extremely well connected to the White House was an understatement. "Mac," as he insisted on being called, had worked faithfully for many years as a tireless fundraiser for the President in this and all of her past campaigns for public office. His many connections around the country had proven invaluable to her. She wanted someone trustworthy to run the Agency, (some said to keep it in line), and he did not disappoint in that respect, lack of intelligence background notwithstanding.

Paula nodded to the Director's security detail and they smiled as she passed them on the way to his conference room. A female security officer whom she'd befriended during one of her trips to the White House with the Director even winked in silent solidarity. Mac White smiled broadly and stood as Paula entered. He came around from his chair near the door to usher her to a seat across from him.

Paula reflected upon his smile and could not help thinking of his nickname. The Bobby Darin tune "Mack the Knife" played silently in her head. She also couldn't help thinking of that lyrical predator with the "pretty teeth" and how he flashed them so "pearly white."

The Director held her hand as he showed her to her place. His hand was cold and clammy, and it gave her goose bumps, so she quickly sat and he reluctantly released his grip. He repeated his courtly performance with each of the senior female Agency officers. Eva Gutierrez, head of East Asia Division, sat next to her, caught her eye and arched her left eyebrow. Paula smirked back.

Various officers nodded to her. Every DO Division Chief and Center Director was present, plus the Security senior staff and the Executive Director.

"I want to talk to you about our new cloud computing initiative. The company which won the bid, California Cloud Computing – 3C - was far and away our best choice according to a blue-ribbon panel and my senior Agency IT advisors."

The Director always liked to use personal possessive pronouns when referring to "my people" as if they personally belonged to him. In a way, they did.

"This new capability will store our Agency records securely and allow instant data access by our officers around the globe. Today's intelligence is all about speed. The President is counting on us to be quick." With that, he snapped his fingers three times for emphasis. Two officers whose thoughts had been elsewhere sat up smartly as if they had been whipped.

Paula thought that if this were the primary goal, then Madame President should just turn on CNN. She also wondered what was so damned "urgent" about this meeting to discuss the Agency IT system when she had at least a few real operations with real assets to focus upon.

"This will take us into the 21st century in a big way. And it will save us money to have them store our data on state-of-the-art equipment rather than our aging IT infrastructure, which is both obsolete and inefficient. Just imagine case officers being able to access files from wherever they are on the planet! This is the type of data management and agility which my officers deserve and need." He smiled at Howard Masterson, the Director of IT Security, who smiled back at the pat on the head. Paula thought if he had a tail, he would wag it.

Inwardly, Paula shuddered as she contemplated the immense risk of storing the Agency's most sensitive secrets in one readily accessible database even if it were compartmented according to a need-to-know basis and encrypted with the latest encryption standards that NSA claimed to be unbreakable. The thought still gave her a very uneasy feeling.

Earlier in her career, Paula had been part of an operational team tasked with using cyber means to attack nuclear proliferation networks that also used unbreakable encryption. She knew that cyber defense had to be right 100% of the time while cyber offense was free to try innumerable routes and only one had to work in order to render a cyber defense worthless. And that winning route almost invariably was the human factor. One well-placed insider with access made unbreakable encryption irrelevant.

The Director continued, "Now, I know some of you have reservations about parking our most sensitive information in the cloud even with the most sophisticated encryption standards. I share these concerns, but I'm convinced that the risk is acceptably low. NSA has red-teamed the encryption, which it developed on its own super computers. Breaking it would take many decades and perhaps centuries. Isn't that right, Howie?" the Director asked the IT Security Chief.

"Absolutely, Mr. Director. None of us will be around when that encryption is finally broken."

Paula looked at Howard, thinking that truer words were never spoken. *You'll be nowhere close to this fucking disaster, you dickless wonder, when the system is breached and some poor unfortunate assets are arrested and shot due to your carelessness.*

"Moreover," Howard continued, "We've obtained the latest big data analytical tools to sift through all of our classified and open source information holdings in order to make those critical links which our analysts have been demanding. It will be a major, I repeat major leap forward."

Gag me with a stick, thought Paula. *Big data typically equals big bullshit. How come I've seen so few tangible results in intelligence operations from this so-called wonderful breakthrough? Oh sure, it works for Amazon and Netflix which depend on this for targeted marketing. I guess we could now divine the movie preferences of the strongmen in the Kremlin or the Chinese Politburo. But the really important secrets in the hearts of our enemies will still be available to us only if we recruit spies who can steal the secrets. Technology is to Americans what shiny objects are to magpies. They are fascinated by it. They line their nests with it, and yet it doesn't prevent the clever Russian or Chinese fox from eating their chicks.*

And Americans far prefer technology – digital bits and bytes - to human intelligence, which is messy and squishy and not black and white. Moreover, Americans love to throw money at problems and threats. Look at the billions spent on technology since 9/11. Did that money buy us safety? Paula knew that was a fair question, which wouldn't be resolved until the next colossal intelligence failure.

And it was probably looming like a runaway locomotive as we step gingerly across the tracks, attention on our smart phones.

Bits and bytes do not equal sources of information. And sources are what we need, not more analytical wonders, she thought. *We need sources in the Iranian nuclear program, sources in the Kremlin, sources in the Chinese Politburo, and sources in the dark councils of terrorist groups everywhere.*

"Mr. Director, with all due respect to you and Howard, I'm sure that this encryption is technically unbreakable and the system is agile and an analytical wonder, but my job for more than twenty-five years has been to penetrate governments and steal secrets. This has taught me that systems are only as secure as the people who protect it. What do we know about these people?"

Howard looked towards the Director with a raised eyebrow, as if wondering if they should let Paula in on their little secret. "If I may, Mr. Director?"

The Director nodded, "Please Howie. Proceed."

"We're well aware of how you and other DO officers protect the identities of our covert assets. If you recall, I was a DO case officer at one time." He looked up and down the conference room table as he said this, seeking nods of assurance from the fraternity of case officers present.

Paula nodded politely. Howard had had two rather mediocre tours marked by few accomplishments other than recruitment of some low level marginal sources and a safe-house keeper or two, all of whom were terminated or quit upon his departure from the respective stations. He had been clear-eyed enough, however, to recognize the ascendancy of information technology and the value of recruiting his own senior management at headquarters. He'd shrewdly used his credentials as a former operations officer to bridge the gap with IT between the technicians and the operators - a strategically brilliant path to his current position.

"We have thoroughly vetted all of the 3C employees with access to our information. The 3C Project Manager is Stan Morris, who was one of our best and brightest Agency IT specialists until he resigned a few years ago and went with 3C. Stan and his entire staff have had updated background and security checks, and all have had recent counterintelligence polygraphs, same as mine and yours and everyone else in this room. They're clean and reliable."

Maybe, maybe not, thought Paula. Polygraphs were not lie detectors but stress detectors, and their validity, if validity it was, were only good at a static point in time. It wasn't like an inoculation against betrayal, nor a flu shot against treason.

"That's all well and good," she said, "and I'm sure Stan and his folks are loyal Americans, but there's something about allowing them access to our most closely guarded secrets – the identities of our prize sources – that gives me the willies. Excuse me but it's in my very being." She looked to the Director. "Mr. Director...Mac...I was at Headquarters as a junior officer in the late '80's when we lost ten Russian assets to Aldrich Ames's treachery and betrayal. One of my best friends recruited one of the Russian assets who were betrayed by our own colleague and then was shot in the Lubyanka. My friend wept when he told me of this loss. He wept, Mac. Protection of our sources is our most sacred duty, and I don't think we should outsource it to a third party. It rubs a raw nerve with me."

"Thank you for the fine sentiment, but if you think that I have less regard for our sources than you, then you'd better..."

Mac White interrupted Howard with a flash of his pearly whites and a commanding tone, "Howie, I'm sure that Paula did not mean that at all. It's simply an emotional subject for you case officers, right?"

Paula felt her face flush as she struggled to maintain her composure. *Emotional subject, my ass. If you think 'this little lady' is about to get emotional, you haven't fucking seen emotional yet.*

She started to rise from her chair and leave the room in disgust when across the table, Pat McCabe, Chief of the Near Eastern Division put his hand up as if he were in third grade and spoke only when Mac gestured to him.

"I have a compromise solution to offer. Why don't we put a subsection of my Division's information on the 3C cloud as a pilot program for six months to a year, and if it works well, we can progressively expand it. My CI officers will watch this like hawks."

Paula was hardly reassured. McCabe had a reputation as a fair-to-middling operations officer but he was also enormously ambitious and arrogant – and some said without much to be arrogant about.

"In light of Paula's concerns," McCabe said, "I propose that we place Iranian operations, which are now rightfully part of Near Eastern Division once again, in this test category. We're moving ahead smartly with these ops again after..." He hesitated briefly. "After some distraction."

The "distraction" McCabe was referring to was the reabsorption of Iranian Ops into his Division. That and some severe operational reversals. The reversals sometimes meant...Paula shivered.

"We're having to merge their databases back with ours in any event, so the partitioning already exists and we can keep Iranian operations separate. We can monitor it closely for irregularities and any breaches. We should catch anything wrong quickly, especially with Howard's new big-data tools."

Howard, looking as if he had just been thrown a bone, smiled at McCabe, his new best friend.

Paula's anxieties were hardly mollified by Pat's throwing oil on the water to calm the waves, but some of the division chiefs nodded, considering Iran's MOIS an unsophisticated player compared to the Russian FSB or the Chinese MSS. Paula, however, recalled reporting of Russian-Iranian intelligence cooperation, and she knew the Persians should not be underestimated.

Sensing the mood of the room and knowing that this was a losing battle – yet one more loss of HUMINT to technology – Paula nevertheless asked for a vote on the issue. She would be damned if she would just throw in the towel. She wanted accountability. The others looked at her as if she had been brazen enough to ask for a vote in Stalin's Politburo. This was just not done. Assumed consensus was the norm.

Fuck that boys. Mess with my assets, then put your balls on the line.

Mac White looked steadily at Paula and said tersely, "Fine. Let's vote then. Those in favor of the pilot program with 3C?"

Twelve hands went up – several so quickly they almost wrenched their arms out of their sockets.

"Opposed?"

Three hands went up: Paula's, that of Eva Gutierrez, and, interestingly, that of Arlo McReedie, the Director of Counterproliferation Operations. Arlo was an analyst and not a case officer, but he surely knew the value and rarity of his human assets, and he was a man of integrity as well as possessed of a keen instinct.

As they left the conference room, Arlo muttered under his breath to Paula, "We're doomed."

CHAPTER 13

◇◇◇

The Bump

Geneva

Several days later, after his lunch with Lacy, Lane sat in his car in the hotel garage after pulling out of his parking spot and adjusted his cell phone to read an incoming text message. Suddenly, he felt a crunch as something rear-ended his rental car. A bit annoyed at being disturbed, he stepped out of the vehicle to inspect the damage. He approached the other car and saw the chubby little Iranian emerge from his vehicle with a look of panic on his face.

Lane asked, "What happened? Are you okay?"

In barely accented English, the man said, "Oh my God. I'm so sorry! I didn't see you. I'm such a scatterbrain. Are you hurt? I hope not."

Lane replied, "No, not really. You're not hurt, are you? Maybe I shouldn't have been just sitting there reading text messages like an idiot." Glancing at both cars, he continued, "It doesn't look like any real harm to either car – barely a scratch on mine. You can only see it if you squint your eyes." As he said this, Lane screwed up his eyes in a funny squint, making the Iranian smile slightly in spite of his distress. "And yours looks okay. I doubt the rental car companies will even notice. How about we just forget it?"

The Iranian looked at the cars and nodded. "I think you're right. Thank you for being so understanding. This could've caused me great problems."

Lane reached in his pocket and retrieved a business card listing him as First Secretary at the U.S. Mission. He started to hand it to the little man and then hesitated. "Maybe this would also cause you a problem…considering the unfortunate relations between our countries."

The Iranian took the card, read it. "Mr. Andrews. Thank you. You are very considerate, but I have no problem with Americans. I like them. I studied there in the 70's when times were better. I've never forgotten the kindness of your people." He handed Lane a card of his own. It read "Dr. Ali Javadpour, Delegate, Islamic Republic of Iran."

Lane thanked him and pocketed the card. His mind had been on Lacy just before the tap on his rear bumper, and he was now somewhat disoriented. Though he was at a loss for words, the Iranian was not.

"Please allow me to buy you a coffee as a gesture of thanks for not making a fuss over my gross negligence. Or perhaps you would prefer a gelato at the Moevenpick Restaurant at the end of the block?"

"Are you sure that would be wise being seen with an American – a devoted disciple of the Great Satan?" He laced the last part with an ironic chuckle.

Javadpour also laughed. "You're being considerate of my position, and I thank you, but my babysitters are sleeping late today because there are no sessions until this afternoon. I can safely afford an hour or so without their company. Please, this would be my pleasure."

The two men walked to the nearby restaurant and chose a small table in the back, well away from casual observers. Within a few minutes they were both enjoying small dishes of delicious, sweet ice cream and listening to the soft background jazz music coming from the establishment's speakers overhead. With closed eyes and a soft smile, Javadpour said, "Ah perfection. Swiss chocolate ice cream and Miles Davis's "Kind of Blue" album. Brings back nice memories from my time in the States."

Though Lane could play the conversationalist, he decided to shut up and listen. He knew you don't recruit people when you are in "send mode."

"As I recall, Bill Evans co-wrote this with Davis, and they were joined by some of the greatest jazz musicians of all time: Cannonball Adderly, the great John Coltrane, Paul Chambers and I think…yes, Jimmy Cobb on drums. How could I forget?" Javadpour smiled and moved his head with the music. "In fact, it was Jimmy Cobb who said this album must have been made in heaven. And I agree. Do you believe in heaven Mr. Andrews?" asked Javadpour in a lowered voice.

Lane simply nodded and closed his own eyes to listen to the sublime music. He could easily imagine six angels playing this music, not a note out of order, everything ethereal, everything perfect.

"It's a pity it's so difficult to get this music in my country. I'm a man of simple tastes except when it comes to music - and then I demand perfection. *This* is perfection," he murmured.

"I won't argue that," agreed Lane. "Perhaps our countries should hold a joint jazz festival to ease tensions or at least have something we can agree upon. Kind of like ping pong diplomacy between China and the U.S. in the '70's."

"I like how you think," replied Javadpour. "When I was at Berkeley, I had my own little international jazz combo of other grad students in the physics department. We had a pianist from China, a black saxophonist from New Orleans, an Algerian drummer from France, a Jew from Brooklyn on bass, and myself on trumpet. We never once let politics or religion interfere. Not that any of us were especially political or religious in any event. It was so relaxing to play with them. I miss that so much."

"I can only imagine," said Lane. "Unlike you, I have no musical talent whatsoever. I do, however, share your love of listening to it." They listened to the music as they finished their ice cream.

"Hey," said Lane, "how would you like to join me this Saturday night at 'Le Chat Noir' – a nice little jazz club in the Old Town of Geneva? They get some good local groups and occasionally some out of town talent. Sometimes they even get artists who've played at the Montreux jazz festival up the lake. It could be our own small effort at a joint jazz summit. Maybe around nine o'clock?"

Javadpour hesitated only for a moment, then eagerly agreed by saying that his babysitters typically left him alone on the weekend. They shook hands and went their separate ways.

During the week, Lane spotted Dr. Javadpour a few times, but the Iranian barely acknowledged him, nothing but a slight smile and once a quick wink when they were only a few feet apart. Lane did not try to approach him or give any sign of recognition lest the two security goons suspect a relationship.

In fact, there wasn't much of a relationship…yet. But Lane felt the personal chemistry with Dr. Javadpour was positive. This was an important first step.

Additionally, Lane genuinely liked him. And that helped.

He also liked Lacy. Maybe more than liked.

CHAPTER 14

La Perle du Lac

Geneva

The silvery disc hung in the sky, and moonshine shadows were cast on the manicured bank of Lake Geneva with a gorgeous view of Mont Blanc and the French Alps across the lake. The periodic 200-foot fountain of water of the Jet D'Eau in the lake only added to the atmosphere. She could see it splashing light from the moon like drops of quicksilver in the lake. The effect was breathtaking.

Lacy walked down the treed path to the restaurant, La Perle du Lac, Lane at her side. She held his hand as they walked from his car and thought about what this evening might mean. She was dressed in a striking black dress that she thought accentuated her figure. Skipping lunch, she felt incredibly lucky to find a flattering little black dress in less than an hour. This decision was driven after she found out where Lane intended to take her for dinner – according to him, "just to discuss business in a more relaxed atmosphere so we can plan our strategy." The guidebook she consulted said the restaurant had a well-deserved reputation as one of the finest in Switzerland.

She thought there might be more to his invitation, however, than a business strategy session.

Lane was a really nice guy but often so quiet. Indeed, for a case officer with his remarkable recruitment record, he seemed a bit shy. There was an underlying intensity to him, however, that intrigued her. He was an excellent listener, and she had enjoyed their conversations about tradecraft. He was passionate about operations and she admired passion. She hoped that this dinner would give her greater insights into him.

The maître 'd warmly welcomed them, "Ah, Monsieur Andrews what a pleasure to see you again!"

Lane returned his greeting, and the maître 'd showed them to their table situated strategically next to a window with a stunning view of the lake. Soft music was playing in the background as their waiter, again acknowledging Lane by name as a returning guest, brought them their menus and the extensive wine list.

Lacy said, "So, I take it you come here frequently from the way the staff welcomed you. All business I'm sure."

He laughed, "Of course. And as another Texan used to say, it's excellent for strategerie. I hope you'll like it."

"I love it. I'm quite sure that I've never before been in a restaurant this beautiful. How did you find it?"

"Oh it was a long time ago – way back on my first tour as a case officer when I was stationed about three hours from here by train. This place brings back memories. Good memories." He looked out on the lake, his thoughts obviously far away.

"Of some woman, no doubt," Lacy concluded with a mischievous grin.

"Actually yes, but not what you might imagine. In fact, it was work-related. But I don't want to bore you."

"No, far from it. Tell me about it. Please."

He continued to stare out on the lake and the moon's reflection on the water for a couple of moments. Finally, he turned to her and said, "When I arrived in Switzerland, I had a difficult first year with no recruitments and none in sight. Typically, your first tour can make or break your career as a case officer, and if there are no recruitments, then probably there'll be no career." A moment later, he added, "Unless of course if you slither into management, and then the sky's the limit."

He shrugged and Lacy nodded sadly.

"I was watching my career slowly but surely founder. I'd look at myself in the mirror in the mornings and wonder when I'd get some traction. It was horribly frustrating."

"Then I got a break. I was able to pose as a businessman and commercially recruit a significant Middle Eastern female asset with wide access to senior policymakers in her country. After accepting my offer of a consultancy, she proceeded to inform me of some very sensitive plans for an upcoming round of international negotiations: key players, plans, and intentions. Not only had she agreed to the deal and accepted money, she provided some classified intelligence as evidence of her recruitment."

"So, you scored. I bet that made you happy."

"I was ecstatic. I dashed off a touchdown cable to Headquarters along with three intelligence reports. The next morning, congratulations arrived with words to the effect that this was the first recruitment in Europe of a person with such key access in her country in a very long dry spell and that all three reports would be graded excellent. I was overjoyed. I shot from the depths of despair to the summit of success in a few short weeks."

"So, you jumped the recruitment hurdle and cleared it by a substantial margin. Good for you." Lacy smiled.

"Sadly, my joy was short-lived."

Lacy looked at him quizzically. "Why's that?"

"My Chief invited me to his office and said that he and the big bosses were absolutely delighted with my recruitment, but there was a big catch. He said I had to return to Geneva and inform her that she was really working for the CIA."

Lacy said, "You're kidding. Whatever for?"

"The Chief said there was no way they could securely handle her in a commercial pretext once she returned home. And, they had a lot of questions about intelligence issues to which she had access but which had very little or no commercial relevance. Finally, to prove her bona fides and help dismiss any concerns from the counterintelligence section, she would need to take a polygraph test. This would also be difficult or impossible to explain in a commercial context."

Lacy nodded, "Well, I guess that makes sense but how did you react? I mean that's a pretty abrupt about-face with your cover. One day a businessman and then 007 the next."

"I was completely bummed out. I told the boss that she'd never go along with this. And you know what he said?"

"What?"

"He said that he knew I could do it. But I was convinced that it would be a complete fiasco. And it was. I still recall the look of horror on her face as I revealed my true identity to her. She blanched and started shaking her head. 'They'll catch me, torture me and execute me. I'm not capable of treason. I quit.' Those were her exact words, and I didn't try to argue with her because I could see her fear. I could feel it. Besides, I was already convinced that this was the inevitable outcome. I went back to the office and told the Chief that the relationship was now over. Just as I predicted. My career was officially back in the toilet. *Sic transit gloria*." He shook his head.

Lacy leaned forward. "So that's not the end of the story is it?"

"It would've been, but my Chief wasn't convinced that it was the end of the story. Instead, he asked me, 'Lane what did I say the first time that you didn't understand? I told you that senior managers at Headquarters and I are cheering your recent score. And now you want to take the score off the scoreboard? I don't believe you do. I know you can recruit her. So, go do it.'"

"Nothing like a little pressure, right?" said Lacy with a grin.

"You're telling me. Frankly, I wasn't sure what to do. This lady was about to return home and would soon be gone forever. So, I contacted her and asked her if we could have a farewell dinner the following Friday at La Perle du Lac. She said that would be nice but kept her voice quite neutral. At least she didn't hang up on me.

"I gave considerable thought over the next two days as to what clever arguments I might use to change her mind. First it was one thing and then another. They all seemed so brilliant in my dreams and so hollow in the light of day. By Friday, I was no closer to a solution, but I still had the three hour train trip to Geneva that afternoon. I thought surely I could come up with just the right words to persuade her to get back on board."

"And I suppose you did, you who are so good with words," teased Lacy.

"In a word, no. I didn't. When I got off of the train in Geneva, I didn't have a clue. So, I trudged through the train station towards my hotel and passed a small gift shop. Thinking that the decent thing to do was to buy her a going away present, I purchased a small Imari vase that was quite delicate and only fifty Swiss francs. I had it giftwrapped and continued to my hotel to await the inevitable rejection at dinner."

"You must've been pretty discouraged."

"Yeah, I was. I arrived at the restaurant with a feeling of resignation. I chose La Perle du Lac only because it's one of my favorites, and I thought she might enjoy it.

"I should add at this point that I think that women from her country are really gorgeous women, lovely complexion, beautiful hair, flashing eyes, and always stylishly dressed like Parisians. Female perfection."

He paused for dramatic effect, and then continued, "She wasn't."

Lacy laughed and said, "You're terrible!"

He continued, "She was really sweet but like that woman you get a blind date with in college; it was her sense of humor and sweet nature that were her most endearing qualities.

"Dinner came and went, and I had no idea how to persuade her to work for us, so I didn't even try. We simply talked about our families, our dreams, and our hopes. I was going to call it a night when I felt a plastic bag at my feet and remembered my small gift to her. So, I bent over and retrieved it and removed the gift-wrapped vase and placed it in front of her. She looked quizzically at it. I said, 'Just open it.'

"She opened it and placed the small delicate vase in front of her. I told her that it was something for her to take home, and that I hoped she would take it to her ministry and place it on her desk, and whenever she saw it to think of me."

At this point, Lacy knew instinctively where he was going with his story.

"I thought that was the end, but she sat there and just looked intently at the vase and didn't say anything. Then I noticed a tear roll slowly down her cheek, then another. I realized she was crying and I wondered if I had said something to upset her. I heard her say something low, but her voice was hitching and it wasn't clear. So, I leaned forward, and she took a breath and repeated, 'I can do this.'

"I said, 'Pardon me, but what did you say?'

"Again, she repeated, 'I can do this.'

"I said 'I know you can do this, but I don't want you to do this unless you really want to do it.' I meant that with all my heart."

Lacy was struck by the depth of his feeling and the fact that he would sacrifice the recruitment if necessary.

Lane continued, "She said again, 'I can do this.' And she really could. We polygraphed her and trained her in covert communications and sent her home. She didn't disappoint us one bit. In fact, I'm told that Headquarters had trouble keeping up with her production. That made me very happy.

"The other thing I didn't mention earlier was her position. She was not an ordinary diplomat but an executive secretary and very talented. She was rotated among the senior leadership of her country, she was that good. They adored her because she was so efficient and discreet, or so they believed. So, everything they saw, she saw and we saw."

Lacy said, "It's amazing what persistence can do. Whatever happened to her?"

"A few years after her recruitment, a CI disaster occurred when quite a few of our sensitive assets in her country were compromised somehow, rounded up and thrown in prison. All of them were tortured. Several were shot. She wasn't among them, thank God."

Lacy looked out across the rippling lake water reflecting the lights from the restaurant and the stars and moon, then back at Lane. "You manipulated her with something other than words. In fact, I think words would have been useless. But I can sense a deep empathy in you for people. You genuinely care about them and they can sense that deep down. Sure, there was possibly some kind of romantic fantasy on her part, or possibly just deep loneliness or maybe a need for some male attention. But you really cared about her and she knew it."

She paused, then added, "I'm told that a few case officers also claim to have a metaphysical link with their targets. I'm even told that some envision it as an invisible physical hook between themselves and the mind of the person they're recruiting. The target relaxes completely in almost a trance-like state. Like having your brain relax in a warm waterbed. I'm not sure how true all of that is, but I suspect you have that talent. When you look at people, you look intently, and they seem to be the total object of your attention. Who wouldn't like that? A lot of people pay therapists good money for that kind of undivided attention. But you do it because you're genuinely interested in people. People love that." She shrugged, "Maybe your talent is like my ability to shoot. I don't just aim and shoot. Instead, there's some kind of link I feel between me and where I want to put the bullet into the target. I can feel the connection in my head." She looked at him, almost embarrassed.

Lacy broke her gaze and laughed. Lane's hand slipped over hers and she squeezed it.

CHAPTER 15

◇◇◇

Critical Mass and the Wannabe

Geneva

A French quartet was playing some jazz standards on Saturday as Lane entered Le Chat Noir a few minutes before nine. He was pleased to see Dr. Javadpour beaming at him from a table to the right of the players. The doctor was almost entirely concealed in the shadows, displaying good sense on his part about his personal security.

He rose from his seat as Lane approached and grasped his hand with both of his.

"I decided to come early and just absorb the music a bit before your arrival. They've been playing some Bill Evans. It's lovely. Reminds me of California."

"Did you ever consider staying?" asked Lane casually.

"In California? Oh, sure. The thought occurred to me many times. I truly loved my life there and only returned to Iran in the early 80's because my family needed me at home. Things could have been so different otherwise. Maybe I would have become a jazz trumpeter for real instead of a wannabe." He laughed.

"Ah, a Persian Miles Davis," said Lane. "Something tells me that you could have been the real thing. You seem to have the passion and soul for it. Music without passion or soul is just a collection of notes, right?"

This brought a big smile to Dr. Javadpour's face. "Well you've never heard me play, but I agree that music, real music, requires both passion and soul. It's the expression of your soul."

"Not that it's any of my business, and you can tell me just that if you wish, but why did your family need you back home?"

"Ah, it's a sad story. My older brother was killed in a car accident in late 1981. I was then the oldest son and responsible for my widowed mother and younger siblings. Family obligations are sacred in Iran, so I gave up my California dreaming and returned home. It was the right thing to do. Or at least I thought so at the time. Always the dutiful son. Sometimes I wonder though…"

"Dr. Javadpour…" began Lane.

"Please, just call me Ali," Javadpour interjected.

"Okay. Dr. Ali," Lane corrected himself.

"No, just plain Ali," Javadpour insisted.

"Ali…what exactly is your specialty and your doctorate in? Or will I even understand it?"

Ali chuckled. "It's not so difficult. I'm a criticality safety engineer."

Lane nodded. "I'm not sure what that is exactly, but I think safety is one thing that we can all agree upon, especially as it relates to nuclear technology."

Ali explained that criticality safety referred to ensuring that fissile material not 'go critical' and cause the atoms to fission prematurely.

"It's another application of the Goldilocks Principle," said Ali. "We want the nuclear reaction to happen so that we can heat up water, create steam and power a turbine, but under proper controls. Not too fast, not too slow. It needs to be just right.

"A criticality accident can occur if two smaller subcritical masses are inadvertently brought together into a critical mass and then hell breaks loose. This happened in a Japanese nuclear plant a few years ago when some technicians carelessly added too much of one nuclear solution to another. Several of them were exposed and one died."

"So, in essence, you keep the lid on the nuclear cook pot from blowing off."

Ali laughed and said, “I guess you could describe it like that, although usually it’s not an explosion but a deadly release of radiation. Some describe it as a blue flash. Something you definitely don’t want to see.”

“And if you don’t mind my asking, does this ‘criticality safety’ apply to nuclear weapons too?” asked Lane in a low voice.

Ali glanced around and replied in an equally quiet voice, “Yes, it does, but I can assure you that my country does not want nuclear weapons, and I personally don’t want nuclear weapons. We just want our rights to peaceful nuclear energy as guaranteed by the Nuclear Nonproliferation Treaty. That’s all, and that’s why I’m here in Geneva.”

“Then I guess we’re in complete agreement. Maybe you and I should just shake hands and we can all go home,” joked Lane.

“Were it not for this nice jazz and sharing the moment with you, I would agree wholeheartedly!” said Ali. “I love this place.”

The doctor closed his eyes and tapped his left foot in time with the music as the notes of “Take the ‘A’ Train” began.

CHAPTER 16

◇◇◇

Crack Patterns

Geneva

In the coming days, Lacy's research found that the good Dr. Javadpour was indeed an expert in criticality safety. She printed some of his published research papers and gave them to Lane. She explained the virtually unfettered access that criticality safety engineers have to nuclear facilities, be they peaceful nuclear power plants or nuclear weapons production facilities.

As Lane was studying one of the papers, Charlie Grable, the blustery Chief of Operations for the local station, popped into his office to nose around. He rested his beefy right arm on the front of Lane's desk and propped his chubby legs on Lane's other guest chair.

"What's the latest?" he asked Lane.

"Well, I've met a very interesting target on the Iranian delegation – Dr. Ali Javadpour. He's a criticality safety engineer," Lane indicated the paper in front of him.

Charlie, who had very few real recruitments to his name, scoffed, "Safety! Why would we care about their safety? They sure as hell don't! Where are the weapons designers? Bring me the bomb designers! Go after the crown jewels. Recruit their asses off!"

Lane outranked Charlie and believed him to be a buffoon, though a mostly harmless one. Rather than pick a fight with a fool, he said, "Charlie, I can see where you might think that. I did too at first, but we're both wrong.

Criticality safety engineers have unrestricted access in nuclear facilities, at least in the U.S. Lacy and I bet it's not much different in Iran. This guy has golden access, those crown jewels you and I want. He could be the perfect agent. I can feel it. You're always advising us to 'go for the red meat,' and frankly I can smell the blood."

Actually, Lane hated Charlie's trite red-meat expression since this clown could be slapped with a three-pound Porterhouse steak and not know what had hit him. But Charlie loved to have "his officers" quote his favorite aphorisms back to him, as if he were the fount of all operational knowledge.

Charlie nodded, started to say something, thought better of it, and left the office.

Later that day, Lane's mentor, Gary Scott, a retired senior operations officer back on contract dropped by his office. Gary was a skilled Farsi language speaker as well as an expert on all things Iranian and most things operational. Younger officers teased that Gary had been working the Iranian account since Cyrus the Great but everyone treated him with great deference and the respect he was due. He had earned his spurs repeatedly and had been decorated on numerous occasions for courage and spectacular operational achievements. He was a founding Guild member, in whatever unofficial capacity the group existed.

He was also the winner of the Distinguished Intelligence Cross and Intelligence Star, the CIA's highest awards for valor and equivalent to the Medal of Honor and Silver Star but bestowed by the Director. He also was a recipient of the Donovan Award, which is the highest award granted by the DDO. Of course, he never spoke about any of it.

Gary sat and asked Lane about his latest target, and the younger man described Javadpour and his potential access to Iran's nuclear program.

Gary listened carefully, then asked, "Where are the cracks?" In short, where were Javadpour's vulnerabilities or handles upon which Lane could base a recruitment pitch. What motivated him? Where are the stress points that Lane could relieve? As Gary had explained on more than one occasion, the target was the patient and Lane the therapist. How could Lane relieve his stress?

"I don't see any cracks yet. Just a very nice guy who likes good jazz and is not a rabid Islamist. He does have an interesting job, as I said. Great access but not a whole lot else to work with. Just smooth rock so far. But I'm trying to be patient."

The latter was a reference to rock climbing. In his youth, Gary had been one of the best free climbers in Colorado. He emphasized that one cannot climb smooth, featureless rock. You follow crack patterns and stress fractures in the rock, in which you place your fingers and the toes of your climbing boots. Only then can you traverse the rock, hopefully with skill and grace if you are good, but always following the crack patterns. Significantly, a climber cannot see the tiny crack patterns from a long way off.

People are the same. You can't see the cracks from a distance, nor in a brief amount of time, unless you're incredibly lucky. Over time, however, you can always find the cracks in people. And unlike rock which can be totally smooth, people always have stress patterns, although they're not always obvious or constant. They change over time and sometimes abruptly.

Lane said, "He likes Americans and loves American jazz. He spent his student years at Berkeley. The guy thinks fondly of those days. He even told me he would've stayed had his brother not died in an accident in Iran. Plus, I have a gut feeling he's a rule-breaker."

Gary seized upon those as positive signs. He said, "You know you can recruit this guy. It's just a matter of time. I have complete faith in you."

He took Lane's right hand and shook it slowly while looking into his eyes, as if he were transferring his own confidence to the younger man. Lane certainly felt infused with new energy and hope.

No wonder the guy was a first-class recruiter. His positive energy was infectious.

CHAPTER 17

◇◇◇

The Very Thought of You

Geneva

The jazz outings with Ali Javadpour became a regular thing over the next few weeks – usually on the weekends but sometimes on a weeknight. As Ali gradually let his hair down, Lane got more hints that the Iranian was not a regime supporter. The scientist complained about some of the mullahs' stupid restrictions on freedom of expression in the arts and politics. He was offended by the necessity to show "appropriate revolutionary fervor" when seeking professional advancement or tenure. By his account, Javadpour, refused to play such games. Fortunately for him, there was not an abundance of criticality safety engineers in Iran, which thus allowed him a modicum of freedom to be himself and not toe the mullahs' line – at least up to a point.

"As much as I would like to think that I'm untouchable because of my skills, I know that I have to watch out too." Javadpour rolled his eyes and shook his head sadly. He looked about the room to be sure they were not being observed.

Lane brought Lacy along on some of the jazz evenings, and the Iranian was charmed by her warm nature, pretty smile, and sly sense of humor. On one such occasion, Lane arranged for the quartet playing at Le Chat Noir to lend Javadpour an extra trumpet and they invited him to jam with them on stage. At first a bit reluctant to go up on stage, Lacy gently goaded him to take the leap for her…to honor Miles Davis.

Finally, Ali nodded, stepped onto the stage and tentatively picked up the extra trumpet. He admired the horn briefly, wiped the mouthpiece with a deliberate, loving motion. As he brought the horn to his lips, a metamorphosis swiftly took place before their eyes. He tapped his feet and swung into the rhythm of the piece within a couple of beats, playing with command and assurance as if he had been part of the little group for years. The other members looked at each other as they heard him accompany them with verve and nodded with knowing smiles.

The trumpet's bright and airy notes soared as the now-quintet played a mellow and joyous sound not heard in many years in Le Chat Noir. The players moved smoothly in and out of different pieces and styles with abandon and not a care in the world. Towards the end of the set, "Round Midnight" brought waves of enthusiastic applause from the audience. Then, at one point, the others motioned and Ali stepped forward and did a long solo of "The Very Thought of You" as they deferred to his obvious skill on the horn. He played the piece with a soulful focus on the mellifluent notes, which flowed like honey from the trumpet. Though Lane had heard this haunting composition before, he thought there was something timeless and personal about this version. Pure sweetness, which spoke of better times in the past.

When Ali concluded, the room cried, "Encore, encore!" Ali hesitated at first, then looked over at Lane and Lacy, and upon seeing their encouragement, conferred briefly with the quartet's pianist. Then Ali spoke softly into the microphone and said simply, "For Mia, with love."

The pianist looked at Ali, nodded and led with several soft chords. Then Ali returned the horn to his lips to play a piece not ordinarily associated with the trumpet or with jazz clubs. The music was ethereal and haunting. At first Lane wasn't exactly sure what he was hearing, but then it struck him. Something inside of Lane stirred as he heard the hymn from his childhood. It was "Amazing Grace." Ali played with passion and his whole heart as he struck those high notes, his eyes closed, the spotlights highlighting his glistening skin and the uplifted silver trumpet. He concluded as softly as he had begun, with fabulous tonal quality.

The players joined the patrons in the club at the conclusion of the set with a standing ovation. The Iranian, however, seemed melancholy as he rejoined Lane and Lacy. He sat there for a while, not saying a word, his jawline rigid, and a single tear coursed slowly down his right cheek. Lane and Lacy let him be.

Finally, Lane reached over and patted him affectionately on the back and said, “Well done, Ali. Very well done.” Ali just nodded and smiled slightly but did not look up at them.

CHAPTER 18

◇◇◇

Succession Planning

Iran

Colonel Alborzi's IRGC unit, a counterintelligence and counterterrorist brigade, was devoted to rooting out enemies of the Islamic Revolution, disrupting and destroying them. Officially called Ettalaat-e-Pasdaran (the Intelligence Office of the IRGC), they vied with the feckless fools of the MOIS to catch traitors and terrorists. They had been successful at this, although Alborzi's critics claimed this was due more to the ineptitude of poorly organized criminals than to Alborzi's own intelligence skills. The fools knew nothing.

Alborzi knew that it was his own creativity and ruthless devotion to hunting these miscreants down that explained his group's excellent record. He was on a roll and necks continued to be stretched at the Evin Prison gallows on a regular basis. He fancied that he could smell treachery a mile away, maybe because it had such a familiar, sickly sweet odor.

This skill did not translate, however, into a rapid promotion for Colonel Masud Alborzi. A few other officers, who simply had outmaneuvered him on the way up the IRGC ladder, had passed him in rank, much to his chagrin. Chief among these Islamic suck-ups was Brigadier General Hussein Lavassani, who never failed to detect which way the wind was blowing among senior Iranian leaders. Son of a senior and highly venerated ayatollah who had been martyred by terrorists, Lavassani would hold his peace until he saw the obvious direction of senior sentiment and then he would weigh in with typical bombast in his deep bass voice. He also seemed to believe that a statement uttered at twice natural volume had twice the import and twice the revolutionary commitment.

The grinning fool certainly had no original thoughts of his own but parroted what he heard certain key leaders say, especially the Supreme Leader and his retinue of nitwits, the Assembly of Experts. Alborzi wondered at what these fools were truly expert? Fucking up the country? Did Lavassani really think that the leadership was so stupid as to fall for his blatantly obsequious behavior? Sadly, they evidently were that stupid. Lavassani soared in rank and passed Alborzi as if he were standing still. A better group name would have been the Assembly of Morons.

In times like this, Alborzi thought a man must take his destiny in his own hands and shape his own future. And so he did.

On that particular day, he left IRGC headquarters dressed in his well-pressed khakis and got into his armored Mercedes with his uncle, the Grand Ayatollah Mohammad Alborzi. That pompous idiot Lavassani was riding in the car two vehicles behind him, and the black turbaned Supreme Leader was in the trailing VIP vehicle, a large shiny black Mercedes, three cars behind Alborzi's own automobile, the entire motorcade en route to a ceremony to commemorate some ridiculously glorious holiday of the Islamic Revolution. Such bosh! But it led to an opportunity.

Beside Alborzi in the back seat, his uncle who fretting about some obtuse piece of Shia religious dogma and fingering his worry beads. Click, click, click. More muttering, more clicking of the beads. It was rapidly getting on Alborzi's nerves, and he had to restrain a powerful urge to reach over and use his uncle's prayer beads to strangle the old fool. It also distracted Alborzi from focusing on the task at hand, which involved the precise timing of his own little palace coup.

As the motorcade slowed to take a long curve around a Tehran city park, Alborzi spied the large trash receptacles on either side of the broad tree-lined boulevard, as well as the manhole cover ahead. He fingers closed around the cell phone in his pocket with the pre-set phone number as his uncle continued to blather on about some religious inanity. *Shut up, shut up, shut up*, he thought to himself. He really needed to concentrate now.

As he gauged his own vehicle's speed, he prepared to press the "send" button at the precise moment when he calculated their car would be safely past the kill zone. At that moment, the motorcade ground to a sudden halt because of a large trash truck momentarily stalled in the road ahead. Thrown slightly forward by the momentum, Alborzi's thumb involuntarily depressed the button at least a few seconds and thirty yards before he'd intended.

There was a tremendous bright white flash, a huge deafening roar, and the sound of tearing metal and shattering glass as a hundred kilograms of high explosive concealed in each of the trashcans and under the manhole cover simultaneously detonated. The shockwave proceeded at supersonic speed in all directions. Alborzi's own car lifted in the air and flipped on its back like a large toy. He briefly blacked out. When he regained consciousness, he heard nothing for what seemed like an eternity and only felt blood seeping down the back of his neck. He groggily lifted his head and scanned his body for injuries. He decided that his scalp wounds were superficial, but it had been close, much too close. A few seconds slower in the blast zone, and he would have died. Not exactly what he was planning on.

Finally, sound returned and his ears were filled with screaming and police sirens. He heard his uncle groaning beneath him. He rolled jerkily off of his uncle, and burrowed with considerable difficulty from the inverted car through its shattered right rear window. His uncle's arms were moving spasmodically, and his hand grasped Alborzi's foot as he exited the car. He was moaning. Alborzi started to kick out at the stupid fool, then reconsidered as people rapidly converged on the wreckage. Instead, he grabbed both of his uncle's arms and slowly pulled his fat carcass through the window and out of the upside down car and onto the smoldering and blood spattered street.

Alborzi stood slowly, still groggy from the explosion and looked around. Chaos began to come slowly into focus. Pieces of mangled steel, detached human limbs and melted detritus littered the street in a macabre landscape as far as he could see. The three trailing VIP vehicles were tossed together in a jumble, and he could see several unmoving bodies in the street between the cars. Most of the accompanying motorcycle escorts were likewise devastated.

He stepped gingerly over an IRGC motorcyclist's eviscerated form next to the car, glanced down and saw his uncle's body curled up beneath him, moving ever so slightly.

Alborzi had a flash of inspiration and fingering the blood on the back of his neck, he leaned over out of sight and drew the bloodied fingers down his face beneath his eyes. Then, smelling gasoline, he partially lifted his uncle from the ground and dragged him to the far sidewalk, reaching it as his vehicle's gas tank exploded with a loud "whoomfff!" He felt the heat and pressure bathe him from behind.

He started walking slowly through the corpse-strewn street behind his mangled car. Spying what appeared to be a prostrate form in black turban and white robes splayed about nearest the wreck of the Supreme Leader's vehicle, he headed in that direction with determination, his uncle now standing but still held firmly, his own head held deliberately high, eyes straight ahead.

A bystander with a smart phone took the iconic photo of Alborzi, with what appeared to be bloody tears streaming down his face, shepherding his injured uncle, mere yards away from their burning vehicle and not far from the mayhem behind them. But if that photo was soon to be famous all over Iran, the next one eclipsed it by far and made the international press.

Alborzi placed his uncle carefully down beside the fallen Supreme Leader's broken body, and placed his uncle's limp right arm on the Imam's left shoulder. With his own body concealing his actions, he took the Supreme Leader's lifeless left hand and placed it on his uncle's head. His uncle continued to babble deliriously. Another photographer rushed up and began snapping photos. Alborzi placed his own head down on the asphalt as in prayer and waited for history.

Hardly anyone seemed to notice that the turbaned head of the Imam was at an awkward impossible angle where his neck had snapped upon impact. Or perhaps it made the scene all the more miraculous. What did it really matter? The photos were accompanied by a caption that simply read, "The dying Imam anoints his successor."

Nearby, Alborzi saw the mangled torso of General Lavassani, identifiable by his tan uniform. Alborzi stepped closer and saw that the general's closely cropped grey-haired head had neatly separated from his body and rolled ignominiously under one of the black Mercedes. Too bad people were so close or he would have kicked the damned thing all the way to Turkey. He bent over as if to embrace the new martyr and covertly slipped the cell phone into the general's tunic and put the now ex-general's hand around it in a death grip. Alborzi kissed his tunic and general's insignia for the sake of the gathering photographers and screamed out "My blood for yours!" He added, "Round up the Zionist dogs who did this and kill them!"

He then placed his head down on the shattered chest of the general and muttered softly to him, "Fry in hell you pig-fucker."

The Assembly of Experts deliberated for only a few hours in the next few days regarding the choice of the martyred Supreme Leader's successor. The choice of Ayatollah Mohammad Alborzi was rather obvious. It helped that the IRGC charitable wing made some strategic contributions to several key members' favorite Islamic charities - themselves. And it was no surprise to hear that Colonel Masud Alborzi, nephew of the new Supreme Leader and a new national hero, had been promoted to the rank of Brigadier General in recognition of his heroism.

In his new office suite, Alborzi envisioned an entirely new future.

I've replaced one doddering old fool with another, but this old fool is mine.

CHAPTER 19

The Crack in the Windshield

Geneva

In spite of the warm friendship and the increasing candor in their relationship, Lane still did not see an inroad to recruiting Ali. And the clock was steadily ticking as this round of the nuclear negotiations wound down – still no breakthroughs in sight, only a mutually agreed-upon deadline that was looming. If neither side made further concessions, then everyone would go home with nothing to show for it.

The deadlock was still over the Western demand that their inspectors have access to certain Iranian military sites where suspect nuclear research had allegedly occurred. They also wanted to interview key Iranian nuclear scientists. Iran balked at this "insult to its sovereignty," and the Iranian Foreign Minister jokingly asked the press if the U.S. was going to allow Iran access to its military bases, especially those in the Middle East, and perhaps the ability to interview American nuclear scientists.

Lane was writing a contact report in his office when Lacy burst in with the news. The Iranian Supreme Leader and a number of senior IRGC officers had been assassinated by a bombing in Tehran. Confusion reigned. The nuclear talks were suspended.

Lane had been scheduled to meet with Ali at Le Chat Noir that evening, but he wasn't sure that he would show up now, given the time of mourning and the likelihood that the delegation would simply head for home. Lane decided he would go in any event and was more than a little surprised to see Ali sitting there in his usual spot at the jazz club, as if nothing had happened.

"I want to offer my condolences on your country's loss."

Ali looked at him for a moment and shook his head. "I appreciate your kind sentiments. You're a friend, but this loss is neither my country's nor mine. It may be treasonous to say, but these mullahs don't have my country's best interests at heart. They have always put their own interests ahead of the country. They replaced a kleptocracy that had pretensions of royalty with an even worse kleptocracy that has pretensions of piety. I find the latter more despicable because it combines kleptocracy with hypocrisy. Call them the klepto-hypocrites. At least with the Shah you had the bloodsucking without the religious giftwrapping."

Lane felt a bit stunned at this revelation of Ali's true feelings. This was the first glimpse of a significant crack pattern in Ali. Should he press forward or let those feelings gel for a bit? A few days earlier, he had managed to get Headquarters' approval to pitch Ali should the opportunity present itself. Lacy had backed him up when he got into a heated discussion with Charlie Grable over Ali's validity as a target.

As the music subsided between sets, Lane began his pitch. He noted that he and Ali wanted the same things for their countries: peace and prosperity and an end to the bickering. Ali nodded. Lane continued that the only solution to the impasse was for Iran to be able to gain America's trust so that the sanctions could end. The two of them could bridge this gap together if Ali would help Lane.

Ali betrayed no sign of his thoughts.

"In times like these, men like us become the ones able to change history. Your insights into Iran's nuclear program would be exactly what we need to verify Iran's commitment to peaceful nuclear energy. You alone hold the way to a peaceful future for all of us. Would you help me in a confidential way?" asked Lane.

Ali sat quietly for a few seconds, then held up his hand. "Lane, look. We're friends. I like you and I trust you, but this kind of arrangement would be morally wrong for me. I see where you're going with this conversation, and I'm no secret agent. The thought is ludicrous. I can't get involved in spy games. Besides, I'm confident that Iran has no nuclear weapons program. You can tell Washington that. For free."

Lane nodded. "You're saying exactly what I want to hear, but we need to hear it from you on a regular basis. We need sources to verify exactly what you're saying. There has been so much deception in the past from your government, concealing the nuclear centrifuge enrichment sites for uranium. And the past work on nuclear designs for ballistic missiles and various experiments carried out at your military sites. How can we trust Iran with that kind of track record of deceit? Our president would be insane to accept your government's word for it, and the Congress would never approve it. I really need your help. I really do. You alone can make a difference, become a hero."

Ali shook his head ever so slightly and said, "Like I said, you're my friend and you're extremely convincing. I grant you that. But I just can't do it. I'm not a hero. I'm just a minor Iranian scientist. A tiny unimportant cog in a big machine. I keep my head down and try to do my job. And, I really don't want to be a dead hero – all for nothing since there aren't any weapons."

"Not that you know of now," Lane countered. "But what if that changed? You know things can change. Just like that." He snapped his fingers.

"Listen, I might even agree to your proposal if I really thought Iran was on a path to a nuclear weapon. I don't want that horror either. I hate the thought of nuclear weapons in the hands of these people. A single idiot with a heavy finger could trigger a catastrophe. On that, I agree with you one hundred percent. And you know I'm no fan of the mullahs who are trying to take my country culturally backwards by centuries. I despise them. But I'm no risk-taker and there's no weapons program as far as I know. So, you'd be wasting your time and I'd be risking my neck, all for nothing – just to prove a negative to your president."

Lane could see that Ali was firm in his position and sincere in his ignorance of any weapons program. It would be fruitless and probably counterproductive to continue to press the pitch at this point. Instead, he nodded and said simply, "Okay. I can see your point. Our friendship is worth enough to me that I won't risk it over this. Especially when we agree that the mullahs shouldn't have access to nuclear weapons. But," he said, "because things can change in a heartbeat, I want you to consider being a tripwire in case they do change. If you suddenly see something that causes you personally to doubt Iran's commitment to peaceful nuclear energy, would you at least try to warn me? I would appreciate that a great deal. It would mean a lot to me. A whole lot." He said the last few words slowly and in a soft voice.

Lane held Ali's gaze and leaned forward in his chair. Nothing else existed in the world but the two of them in this club with a soothing beat in the far distant background. Just a faint sound, some blurry oh-so-soft thing on the verge of consciousness – a trumpet and a drummer playing a slow and lonely duet somewhere out on the edge of reality.

After a moment or two, Ali said softly, "I could probably do that." He straightened up in his chair. "I'd better be getting back to the hotel before they miss me. Most of the delegation has already left, and I'll be flying back to Iran in the next day or two. I just have a few loose ends to tie up. I'll miss you and Lacy and our evenings together. The jazz and the discussions with the two of you have done me a world of good."

"Me too. How about a final drink tomorrow night here, maybe about nine?"

Lane looked deeply into Ali's eyes as the scientist nodded. He was almost there. Lane could feel the link strengthening between them. A half commitment could mature into a full commitment over night. At least the seed had been planted. Lane knew that a tiny crack in a windshield can spider web in a hurry.

The next morning, Lane wrote it up for the record exactly as it occurred – no hype, no mention of their deep connection. He described it as a failed pitch, but with some small hope for a future commitment. In fact, Lane seriously downplayed what he thought was the real potential for Ali. He hated those charlatans like Charlie Grable who existed on hyperbole, hot air, and phantom cases – that and a lot of ass-kissing of his bosses. Let the case speak for itself.

Naturally, Charlie told everyone that he'd known this case would end up like this – a complete failure – which is why he'd urged there be a Senior Review Panel. He never attacked Lane in a frontal assault – no, not Charlie;

not his style - but he was a master of the back stab and the slighting remark. He would toss off something like, "Pity about Lane. He tries hard and I really admire his intensity, but his finesse leaves a bit to be desired. Maybe his luck will improve. I surely hope so for his sake." His camp followers would invariably nod at these pearls of wisdom.

Say what you like, Lane thought, *but at least we have a tripwire now. Before, we had nothing.*

The next evening, Lane found Ali in a somber mood at their usual table. They listened to the music for a few minutes before either spoke. Finally, Lane said, "I saw something downtown and had to get it for you." With that, he handed him a remastered compact disc of Miles Davis's "Kind of Blue" album with some expanded tracks. "Enjoy."

Ali examined it carefully, and simply said, "Thank you. It means a lot. When I play it, I'll think of our time together. Also, I'll call you the next time I'm here. Maybe in a few months when the negotiations resume. Will you be staying at the same hotel?"

Lane handed him a plain white card with a phone number written on it. "Probably, but let's avoid the hotel. You can always reach me at this number, but don't use it unless you're outside of Iran. Also, it would be best if you write it on a piece of paper in your own handwriting and add a few phony digits to the first part. Just phone it and tell the operator that it's 'Gabriel for Miles.' I thought you could remember that little phrase easily enough. The trumpet-playing angel contacting Miles Davis."

Ali smiled at the image.

"Call me, and I'll meet you here at Le Chat Noir three nights after you call – usual time."

Ali took the card, looked at the number and wrote it on a paper napkin with two extra sevens at the beginning, and then handed it back to Lane. He slipped the napkin into his breast pocket.

"Maybe I'll call you even if I have nothing at all, just for an evening of jazz."

"That would be fine too. I certainly hope you will." Lane hesitated and added, "I've been meaning to ask you one other question but maybe it's too personal."

Ali arched an eyebrow at him. "Go on. We're friends."

Lane said, "Who is Mia? Her name at the club the other night…your song dedication."

Ali reflected a moment. "Ah Mia. Sweet, beautiful Mia. She was the real reason I almost stayed in California. A very beautiful and sweet young woman. I loved her…and she loved me. But she was a devout Christian, and I'm a Muslim, if somewhat of a lapsed one. We were both young but thought we could work things out. Unfortunately, my family got into it and it became much too much complicated. Then, as I told you, my older brother died suddenly, and I had to leave in a hurry. I just couldn't lay that burden on top of my mother right after my brother's death." He sighed. "I still think of her a lot. Back then, I even considered converting, but my family would have disowned me. I just couldn't do it. It's still painful. Things could have been very different. The French singer Edith Piaf claimed to regret nothing. But I do. I regret a lot. A whole lot."

Lane nodded and, as both men stood, he gave Ali a warm hug and a pat on the back. "Safe travels, Gabriel. Go with God."

They walked out of the club into the cool Swiss air to the lilting tones of "Take Five" by Dave Brubeck. Tendrils of fog rolling in from the lake muffled the jazz as the men went their separate ways into the night.

PART 2

CHAPTER 1

◇◇◇

Expert Cherry-Picking

IRGC Compound North Tehran

The massive flat screen television with its ultra-high-definition capability would have been the envy of any American sports fanatic. Indeed, Dr. Dmitri Grishin kept toggling the remote to the DVD player backwards and forwards as if studying slow-motion replays of an American football game. He would watch a few frames, stop the player, reverse it if he thought he had missed a key element, scribble a few notes on a pad of paper in front of him and then resume the video playback. He had a short stack of DVDs beside him on the coffee table, and nothing escaped his attention as he focused on the screen with all of the rapt attention of a snake watching a bird.

Grishin was whip-thin with a steel-grey buzz cut and wore light brown tortoise shell glasses and a dark blue pinstripe suit, a starched white shirt open at the neck and no tie, the latter out of deference to his client. He chain-smoked Gauloise cigarettes as he watched the action on the large screen. In his late sixties, Grishin was still at the top of his game. He had been with the Committee for State Security for more than forty years. He continued to refer to them even now as the KGB, in spite of the new acronyms – the FSB for the Russian internal security service and the SVR for external intelligence. Maybe new names but no real difference. Chekists all. Chekists forever.

The large man currently on the screen had been filmed discreetly, from multiple angles on several occasions. He was the one upon whom Grishin focused most intently after having reviewed hours of clandestine video of multiple subjects. The slightest hint of a smile crossed Grishin's lips. This bumbling oaf was his target. No doubt about it. Smoke curled out of his nostrils as his smile broadened, and his head began to nod just a bit as he watched this moron. He rapidly scribbled more notes on his pad and felt the quickening of his pulse like an angler watching his lure. No doubt at all. He had his man.

While still a KGB officer, Dr. Grishin had built a reputation as the best operational psychologist in the organization. He could assess a group of targets remotely and analyze who was the most susceptible to a recruitment approach or to use as an unwitting dupe in a double-agent operation. There were telltale signs in body language and speech patterns, as well as how they interacted with peers, subordinates and superiors. The mosaic was usually varied with subtle hints, signs and countersigns and shades of grey - a lifting of an eyebrow, a frown or a nervous tic, a downward glance, a rolling of eyes, a drumming of fingers or tapping of feet, a slight speech irregularity, all of which had to be calculated and weighted in a complex formulation of visual and audible clues. Occasionally the signs were so clear and compounding that the prediction was a virtual certainty. Such was the case here. Grishin would bet his entire hefty consulting fee on this one

Having retired a few years before with the rarified rank of Major General, Grishin took considerable satisfaction in having achieved flag rank in the intelligence service while not an operations officer himself. Instead, his uncanny assessment abilities made him a force multiplier. He was rarely wrong, and if there were a mistake, it was almost always in operational execution rather than his professional assessment. He sometimes felt like a high-powered sniper's scope zeroing in on a hapless target. If the bullet missed, it was not because of his assessment but because of bad timing or fumbling operational fingers.

Grishin had pinpointed several key penetrations of Western intelligence, including some spies within the CIA, FBI and British MI-6 and MI-5 as well as in the U.S. Congress and British Houses of Parliament. Upon retiring to his dacha outside of Moscow, he quickly became bored and also discovered that a pensioner's life in the post-Soviet era had considerable material limitations. Combining his love of the sport of hunting humans with a new entrepreneurial spirit, the good doctor hung out his shingle in certain professional circles, some of whom he had traveled in a foreign-intelligence liaison capacity. These circles included senior Cuban, Syrian, North Korean and Iranian intelligence officers. They respected his judgment and paid damned well - and in dollars. Not a bad way to spend one's retirement: – irritating the West and making good money doing it. It was a great combination.

And so it was that one day he received a telephone call from a foreign colleague whom he had met in Tehran a few years earlier and heard that his services were in demand once again. Packing a small suitcase, he arrived in Iran with only a few changes of clothes but more than four decades of human-targeting experience.

The morning after his arrival, there came a knock on his hotel room door and an IRGC officer with piercing eyes and a self-confident air introduced himself as General Masud Alborzi. The two men quickly got down to work. Alborzi described his goal of spotting a fool in the U.S. delegation. He needed someone to whom he could feed crumbs, morsels of intelligence, in order to influence the negotiations. In other words, he wanted the most susceptible target for a double-agent operation.

"An impressionable imbecile is what you want then, dear General?" Grishin nodded in anticipation.

"Yes, that would be perfect," said Alborzi.

Grishin had brought with him several highly sophisticated technical tools of his trade. There was an FSB folding parabolic antenna for remote-listening in open areas, as well as a brand-new concealed camera with a high-powered telephoto lens and new software with artificial intelligence capable of turning images of lip reading into text. Nifty, but they all proved unnecessary. He also placed a few wood blocks with audio devices around known American watering holes, but even those were unnecessary to capture the braying and posturing of his various potential targets, especially that of the particular idiot on the screen. Ultimately, he just sat across the café or bar with a concealed digital video camera and filmed to his heart's content not three tables away from the happy crowd. The only challenge was to refrain from laughing.

Grishin watched and listened to the blowhard on the large screen as he lectured his young charges in a local bar on intelligence tradecraft. Grishin could not believe the nonsense that this lumpy fool was spouting. A man who believed so thoroughly in himself with so little foundation in reality was a rare find. He'd assumed that his old nemesis, the vaunted CIA, had higher standards. But, no, the Agency had produced the pigeon of all pigeons.

This could be Grishin's masterpiece. He should ask for a bonus for this one.

CHAPTER 2

◇◇◇

The Nuclear Wild Card

Tehran

General Alborzi detested visiting his uncle the new Supreme Leader unless it was really important. Although largely recovered from his injuries in the explosion, the old man was clearly a mile or two south of rational, and his nervous habit of fingering his beads incessantly had only worsened. To top it off, his uncle's breath stank. No wonder Iran was under international sanctions. Maybe a bottle of mouthwash and a new toothbrush would bring the Islamic Republic in from the cold.

Business was business, however, so Alborzi made an appointment to see the old fool. This new scheme had come to him in a dream and was nothing short of brilliant. The markets had been all too quiet in the eight weeks since he had given his uncle a career boost. What good was it to own the candy store if you couldn't enjoy the candy? That would end soon.

He was ushered into the Supreme Leader's office, a space decorated with dark furnishings, plush pillows and rich carpets from Tabriz and Shiraz. Portraits of his uncle's predecessors adorned the walls - imams as far as the eye could see.

Alborzi held his breath as he kissed his uncle hello and began by saying he had had a vision that would benefit Iran greatly. The old man gestured for him to sit down. His chief advisor, a beetle-browed cleric, Hojatoeslam Mohsen Khorasani, seated to his right, nodded briefly to Alborzi. From the very early days of Alborzi's uncle's rise in religious stature, Khorasani had attached himself to his uncle like a remora to a shark. Khorasani's religious honorific of "hojatoeslam" denoted that he was a learned Islamic scholar just below the rank of ayatollah.

In fact, Khorasani was exceptionally bright, but he had an unfortunate tendency to stutter when speaking in public or in the classrooms of the Hawza (seminary) in Qom. His written works, however, were so highly regarded that sometimes his stuttering and slurring of words were studied closely as having special religious significance. Still, Khorasani needed a smoother-talking mouthpiece with gravitas and respect, and that mouthpiece had been Alborzi's uncle Mohammad. A symbiosis had resulted to their mutual advantage. The old man had the stature while his sidekick possessed the intellect.

Never one to leave anything to chance, Alborzi feared that Khorasani could pose a threat to his own influence over the ayatollah, so he had taken measures to reduce that risk. Through IRGC "special channels," he'd learned that Khorasani evidently believed, as some American evangelists did, that if God (Allah) truly loved you, then you would materially benefit and His love would be manifest. Accordingly, a certain percentage of the "love gifts" that the ayatollah collected from his followers went into special executive accounts controlled by Khorasani. This largesse supported not only the ayatollah's good works but also his acolyte's heroin habit (to calm his nerves and soothe his stutter) and an occasional indulgence with impressionable young seminarians (those in need of enlightenment).

Wasting no time, Alborzi had sought a private audience with Khorasani to tell him the bad news.

"I've received some disturbing documents and photos," he'd told the cleric, "and I thought perhaps you should see them before my uncle the Ayatollah. Some are bank records, some are these glossy photos."

When he fanned the pictures out before him, Khorasani had immediately blanched, his normal stuttering reduced to pure gibberish. Alborzi briefly wondered if the venerable scholar was going into cardiac arrest.

"Please calm yourself. In fact, I understand your special spiritual needs, considering the tremendous pressure, which you must feel advising the

Imam. He, however, is of an older generation and would probably consider these photos not only obscene but also criminally punishable, most likely by death. He need not see them, however. Indeed, as his beloved nephew, I believe he must have your valuable counsel regardless of your spiritual needs. In return, I only ask that you support my own special needs, which involve the world of politics and those select areas under my purview."

Khorasani had nodded his head in agreement, still unable to utter an intelligible word, and quickly left the room.

Alborzi now recounted his vision to the Imam: "As the spiritual guide of this nation, any vision that I, your nephew, have is in fact your vision. I am just the unworthy vessel of it. In my dream, I saw a dove alight on your head, and you blessed it. Clearly, this was a sign from heaven that it is time for Iran to hold out an olive branch to America by asking for a resumption of the nuclear talks suspended after the tragedy two months ago."

His uncle blinked but said nothing.

"The country needs your bold spiritual leadership, and this is the way. God willing, we will re-engage the Americans, but we will not immediately concede anything. Instead, after some discussion and bargaining, we should offer them access only to selected military sites in return for more American concessions. Once the American side unfreezes our U.S. dollar accounts, ceases all trade sanctions, and increases oil-field investments, we should concede access to all of the military sites. Sanction relief alone will free up 100 billion dollars." And, thought Alborzi, a hefty percentage of that should end up in IRGC investments, and more specifically in his personal investments.

His uncle looked at him vacantly, and asked, "And why would I do that dear nephew? Why should I allow them to see our military sites?"

"Because we'll simply move the currently stalled nuclear weapons program to a much less obvious place. Hiding it in military sites is lunacy in any case. Why didn't we just paint big signs with arrows for their satellites to see that say 'Nuclear Weapons Work Done Here!'

"Instead, we'll move it to an old abandoned sulfur mine deep on the east side of Mount Damavand in Lar National Park. We can transfer the scientists and engineers and technicians to labs we construct inside the largest mine shafts. I have already inspected it, and it looks perfect. Everyone will wear uniforms from the Park Service. No one should ever suspect. Who would ever think to put a nuclear program inside of a national park?" He shrugged as he said this and grinned.

Even his uncle could see where Alborzi was going with this now. Khorasani spoke up and stuttered his own endorsement. *Thank you for the amen chorus,* thought Alborzi. *You are well-compensated for that. Amen, brother.*

"With your blessing, I will select the personnel who will man this project. We shall preserve our nuclear option under your guidance and obtain the necessary concessions from the West to restore our economy. Naturally, it will be your decision as to whether we ultimately execute the nuclear wild card, but you'll have it at your disposal if needed. Consider this a simple insurance policy. The Zionist regime will not have a monopoly on this special option in our region. And, of course, who *knows* what the deviants in Riyadh are up to."

"And wha…wha…what of their spies? If th…th…this wi…wi…wild card leaks?" asked Khorasani.

"We're aware of the American CIA and the Mossad trying to penetrate our nuclear program, and we're taking appropriate countermeasures. We've employed a behavioral psychologist, formerly a General of the Russian KGB. We know that American law firms employ such specialists to study prospective jury candidates who will be most accommodating to their clients' positions. So, in like fashion, we have installed hidden cameras around the U.S. delegation and its habitat, and our expert has been studying the videos to select a suitable dupe – a useful idiot to whom one of our officers can volunteer and become a double-agent. In fact, he's already selected just such a target, a complete moron employed by the CIA.

"Through this person, we'll feed the CIA some useful information and then the precise disinformation we will need for our negotiations to succeed. The Americans will love this. They enjoy simple answers. The White House badly wants this deal to succeed and this will be their confirmation. We will give them what they want and of course what we want. I think in the West, they call this a 'win-win situation.'" He raised a hand before his uncle or Khorasani could ask questions.

"I am *not* relying, however, on this single deception channel. I am launching a major counterintelligence offensive to detect spies and traitors in our own ranks. As the great Soviet spymaster Viktor Cherkashin said, 'It takes a spy to catch a spy.' Well, I intend to recruit a spy within the American camp who will deliver our traitors to us. Our plan is already in motion."

Now was either thumbs-up or thumbs-down. Clearly excited, Khorasani tried to speak but could not quite get the words out. Finally, he bent over and whispered into the old man's ear. His uncle smiled and nodded and offered his blessings to his nephew. Holding his breath, Alborzi kissed the old fool and bade both of them farewell.

Alborzi ordered his driver to return to his office at once. He intended for work to proceed on the nuclear weapon with all possible speed. Time was of the essence, especially when money is at stake.

Time is money, he thought. *Money in my pocket.*

CHAPTER 3

◇◇◇

Technically Sweet

Tehran

Dr. Daoud Tabatabai sat in his office in the Atomic Energy Organization of Iran doodling on a pad of paper and punching buttons on his desktop computer. His pencil point suddenly snapped on his paper as it hit him. He was sure he had it this time, and it was…well, it was beautiful because the formulae fit like perfectly machined gears of a fine Swiss watch. Their simplicity and pure logic appealed to him most of all. He wondered why he had not seen them so clearly before. How oddly the mind works… What now seemed obvious had been previously translucent, barely glimmering on the edge of his awareness. These mysteries had tantalized him ever since his days in graduate school at Sharif University, where he had taken a double PhD in mathematics and physics. Now, they were mysteries no longer. He could hardly wait to tell his brother Majid, who worked as a materials scientist in the laboratory.

Daoud thought it wise, however, to withhold this breakthrough from anyone else in the AEOI, for at least the time being. There were a certain number of small-minded, mean people in the AEOI – people who would gladly hurt him or Majid out of jealousy. All things considered, it was probably best if he not reveal his latest work and the "eureka moment" and instead carried on as if nothing had happened. There was already whispering and catcalls about "the special Tabatabai brothers." Part of this was resentment from the less talented among the staff, but a certain part of it might be due to other "issues" about his private life, which he strongly preferred to keep confidential.

His new approach to nuclear fission could be revolutionary with dramatically improved efficiency. The Little Boy bomb, which the U.S. detonated over Hiroshima in 1945, was a relatively primitive "gun-device" in which two subcritical masses of highly enriched uranium were slammed together with high explosive and the super critical result produced roughly fifteen thousand tons (kilotons) of explosive energy. While horrible, it was terribly inefficient with only 1 to 1.4% of the total mass of HEU fissioning and releasing all of that energy before the device exploded. The Fat Man nuclear bomb a few days later was an implosion device, which improved the fissioning efficiency to 17% and a yield of about 20 kilotons.

After more refinement, there was the Ivy King test in 1952. It was designed by Ted Taylor, a genius weapons designer from Los Alamos National Lab. This enormous yield of 500 kilotons put it on a scale with a thermonuclear weapon, the most powerful of all nuclear weapons (which combines fusion and fission), and yet this was fission alone. Most textbooks cited Ivy King as close to the theoretical limit of a pure fission weapon. Still, Daoud felt far greater efficiency could be achieved. It had been his goal for a long time because it was like a puzzle that people thought could not be solved. But now he had it.

Daoud's new discovery involved a method that he termed "neutron phasing." This dramatically increased the mathematical chances of a speeding neutron hitting another uranium atom and producing yet more neutrons in the chain reaction, hitting more atoms and releasing even more energy. Rather than relying on random collisions of neutrons and other uranium atoms, as current nuclear weapons worked, his formulae reduced the serendipity factor by using a newly developed extension of quantum entanglement to increase the probability of locating the nearest nucleus of another uranium atom and smashing it with the neutron.

This deterministic approach to neutron collisions was a radical step forward and definitely unproven. Nevertheless, the power and logic of it appealed to Daoud. To modify a quote from Einstein, if God were to allow him to play dice with the universe, he wanted to use loaded dice.

Moreover, Daoud's breakthrough combined his new mathematical formulae for greater fission efficiency with his brother Majid's newly designed "tamper" constructed of a super-dense and incredibly strong nanomaterial, which surrounded the core of HEU. This new tamper used a two-dimensional material similar to graphene, which is a hexagonal lattice of carbon atoms, one atom thick, and over 200 times stronger than steel. Instead of carbon, however, Daoud used natural uranium atoms of U238 interlaced with uranium deuteride layers. These alternating super-thin layers of nano-material interwoven in a tight lattice were like a surrounding meta-cocoon designed to reflect speeding neutrons back into the fissile material for more collisions and even greater efficiency. In the end, the U238 and UD3 in the tamper's lattice would fission as well - his "secret sauce" that would further increase yield.

Additionally, this super strong metallic lattice tamper held the weapon assembly together for just a few extra "shakes." The term "shake" was whimsically coined by U.S. weapons designers to measure extremely short intervals of time, jokingly referred to as "two shakes of a little lamb's tale." In reality, a shake specifically is a unit of time equal to ten nanoseconds or ten one-billionths of a second. The chain reaction of fissioning U-235 neutrons proceeds at a rate of one fission generation per shake. So, a new generation of neutrons is created for every shake, and they in turn create exponentially more neutrons and thus more energy. Usually, a chain reaction in an explosion is completed from 50 to 100 shakes before the bomb assembly flies apart in an awesome release of energy. To hold it together for even a few more shakes would further contribute to the bomb's efficiency and ultimate yield in explosive power.

If Daoud's calculations were correct, the new design's super efficiency could easily eclipse Ivy King with a probable explosive yield well in excess of a megaton or million tons of TNT, possibly more – maybe fifty percent more. So, he might even triple Ivy King's yield. This was in the "city buster" range of nuclear weapons and only a very select few countries had access to such awesome weapons: the United States, Russia, China, France and the

United Kingdom. And then there was the question of Israel. Maybe. No… probably.

Pointedly, Daoud told himself that he was not doing this to create a monster weapon. That was irrelevant to him, and in fact abhorrent in reality. Daoud was not a violent person. Far from it. He was doing it to see what was mathematically and physically possible, given certain constraints of known physics. If he could just push closer to the theoretical maximum – the perfect 100 hundred percent conversion of mass to energy – then he would be satisfied that he had found the perfect or near-perfect harmony in nature. The fact that his creation could release destruction on a scale hardly comprehensible to the human mind was secondary in his considerations – almost irrelevant. The goal was to see if his improvements would mimic the asymptote – the line that approaches the curve of perfection but can never quite reach it, at least not in our universe. To approach it was the whole point - and the *only* point as far as Daoud was concerned. Skim the line of perfection…closer, ever closer.

Daoud recalled Robert Oppenheimer's famous quote about this dilemma, "When you see something that is technically sweet, you go ahead and do it and you argue about what to do about it only after you have had your technical success. That is the way it was with the atomic bomb."

Yes, technically sweet.

CHAPTER 4

◇◇◇

Criticality Safety

Tehran

A few days after his return to Tehran, and upon his Director's orders, Ali Javadpour reported to a special section of the Atomic Energy Organization of Iran. He was ushered into a guarded room with a dozen uniformed IRGC officers seated at a large table. They were hard looking men and supposedly the protectors of the revolution. Ali suppressed a shudder as he wondered who would protect the people from their protectors.

A large portrait of the new Supreme Leader stared down upon them all. The intense eyes in the portrait made Ali nervous. At the end of the table, a man with a close-cropped grey beard and dark piercing eyes looked intently at him. The eyes resembled those of the Leader. It was eerie. This man, though he bore no clear rank, was obviously in charge, as the others deferred to him. When he spoke, all eyes turned to him.

"Dr. Javadpour, greetings, sir. May the mercy, peace and blessings of Allah be upon you. I am General Alborzi. We have learned that you have contributed substantially to our negotiations in Geneva. Thank you, Doctor."

Ali nodded. "I am pleased that my humble performance served our country."

General Alborzi continued after a brief pause, "You have been specially selected to participate in a program known as Project Zulfiqar, which is of the greatest importance to the Islamic Republic. It will allow us to defend our borders, our national interests and our faith and preserve the dignity of the Islamic Republic. I assume this would be meaningful to you."

Ali nodded. "But of course, sir. Whatever I may do for the Islamic Republic would be my duty and my honor. As always, I am at its service and yours."

"I've heard that you served our delegation well in Geneva. We've further need of your services. You will start in our Tehran office and, if your work satisfies us, and you are satisfactorily vetted, then you will be promoted and work in another secure location. Let me be very clear: Your promotion will hinge upon the next round of negotiations in Geneva. Your U.S. education, fluency in American dialect and easy interaction with the U.S. negotiators should endear us to them and make our task easier. We need this breakthrough. The sanctions must end."

Ali nodded again, but this line of questioning made him nervous. Why was the IRGC involved in the nuclear negotiations or in peaceful nuclear power production? After a moment of reflection, he concluded that expansion of the IRGC's vast economic interests probably hinged on relaxation of Western sanctions. Perhaps it also planned to have its iron grip on the tap of nuclear power production as well as production of nuclear fuel from the centrifuge plants. Those could be very lucrative investments for the Revolutionary Guard Corps, whose fingers were always in many tills. Knowing the extent of IRGC corruption and their cobweb of investments, this made perfect sense to Ali. It also made perfect sense for him to keep his mouth shut and do as he was told.

"Here are the latest position papers for the next round of negotiations and also a sheaf of documents from your predecessor on the delegation, the other criticality safety engineer, who became…well, ill at the last moment." Alborzi stressed the word 'ill' as if it were a buzzword for something else – as if that illness might be contagious and Ali should be careful.

"The negotiations should recommence in Geneva within a couple of weeks. We need you on the delegation, Dr. Javadpour."

General Alborzi handed him the documents, nodded and walked out of the room, trailed by his faithful IRGC retinue.

Back in his office, Ali flipped through the papers briefly. He saw little of interest until he reached the last page, which looked blank. Something on the blank page, however, caught Ali's eye. Faint impressions, as if someone had written something on the preceding page and then discarded it. Curious, Ali took a pencil and lightly shaded over the impressions. A drawing started to reveal itself as he held it up to the light. He could barely make it out. He stared at it, uncomprehending at first. Then it struck him. He blanched.

The rough drawing was of four canisters, each marked "15 KG 90% HEU," and there were criticality safety calculations with distances marked between the canisters. Ali stared at it for the longest time and then ripped the paper to shreds. His hands trembled.

CHAPTER 5

◇◇◇

Family Matters

San Francisco Bay Area

Stan Morris bit his lower lip as he studied the photo of the unsmiling woman on his Facebook page and muttered, "Bitch!"

He then photo-shopped a pair of horns onto her head and added the caption, "Beware all who venture here. There be dragons." He laughed grimly. How could he have been fooled for so long?

What an exquisite betrayal. Seven years of marriage, their beautiful six-year-old daughter Allison, their lovely five-bedroom home, and this worthless bitch runs off with a guy at her office. That knife cut deep and it hurt.

First, there had been the occasional not-so-gentle pokes at his less than perfect physique. Okay, so he wasn't a body builder like her moron of a father had been, and maybe his midriff had a few extra inches these days, but he was busy building his career in computer network security – first in the Agency and now with California Cloud Computing as Chief Information Security Officer. He reflected on this. He was the CISO with the nation's fastest growing cloud computing company, guarding the nation's most precious defense and national security secrets behind unbreakable encryption using the most advanced algorithms. Even NSA with their supercomputers estimated it would take centuries to crack their convoluted code.

She certainly never taunted him when she saw his monthly paychecks deposited to their account. Couldn't she understand that he was doing this for the whole family and not just for himself?

Then, there was the barely visible mocking smirk on her face when he had experienced a little problem in the bedroom after a particularly tense time at work and maybe a little too much to drink with dinner. How could she expect him to focus on her pleasure and sixteen other things at once at the office?

Finally, three weeks ago, he came home one Friday a bit early and found thc notc on his pillow. It was short and to the point, and the point was barbed and caught in his heart. He had been betrayed.

Ironically, this ultimate heartbreak occurred only a few months after he had sealed the deal with CIA, his former employer, to park some of their sensitive operational data on 3C's secure servers. This had been announced with much fanfare in the industry news. In fact, it was a huge feather in his cap and surely a harbinger of more good things to come. His ship was coming in…but to a bombed-out port in a warzone.

Now, here he was, letting the whole world know how she had abandoned him and his precious Allison. The truth felt good. In fact, he would unlock the goddam access controls on his Facebook page and let the whole fucking world know how this bitch had screwed him royally. The more who saw the truth, the merrier. He hoped her family and all of their friends, indeed the whole world, read it and saw her for what she really was.

"You mess with me…" he muttered, then stopped abruptly as he heard, his daughter's voice calling to him from upstairs.

"Daddy, I need to find my backpack for school. Have you seen it?" asked the little blonde pixie from the head of the stairs.

Stan looked up and said, "I think it's in the kitchen on the counter next to the breakfast table. Are you ready for school, sweetie?"

Stan's entire mood brightened as Allison bounced down the stairs and ran into the kitchen to retrieve her pack. As she scampered back into the den where her father sat with his laptop, now closed, she ran over to him and he hugged her. She put her arms around his neck and looked solemnly in his eyes. "Daddy, I'm still really sad about Mommy. Isn't she coming home? I miss her."

"I know, Allison. I'm sad too. But you and I have to be strong for each other. I'm not sure what Mommy's going to do. She's confused and I…I can't explain it. Maybe she'll come to her senses and maybe not. But you and I have each other. That's what's important. We love each other, and we'll get through this together."

Allison put her head on his shoulders. Stan just held her as she breathed in and out slowly, trying not to cry, trying to be a big girl. He held her tighter and closed his eyes.

Twenty minutes later, as Stan dropped Allison off at her school, she looked at him and said, "Do you remember my scout trip over vacation break? The camping trip? It's coming real soon and I really want you to come with me. I really do. Please say 'Yes,' Daddy."

"Oh, honey, I hadn't thought about it, with everything happening these last few weeks. But let me check with my boss today. I think it might be possible. I mean I really want to, but I just have to ask first. It'd really be a lot of fun."

Allison smiled, her blond bangs swinging across her forehead. "I hope he says yes. Ask him today…tell him pretty please with sugar on top."

"All right sweetie, I will. Now, you study hard and have a good day in school. I love you."

"You too, Daddy." Allison kissed him quickly on the cheek, and ran up the sidewalk to the school entrance, dodging a couple of slower moving children, then looked back once and waved. Stan knew he would do anything for that little girl. Anything at all.

As Stan drove onto 3C's compound secured by guns, gates, and guards, his friends and family were discovering his latest Facebook postings and shaking their heads. Such a shock. Poor, fragile Stan and sweet, little Allison. So sad. A few bold souls posted emoticons in solidarity with Stan but others just looked on as if watching a slow-motion train wreck. And a very few others – two in fact - read it with unusually intense interest.

◇◇◇

Stan was distracted as he looked over the secure servers in the locked area devoted to the CIA and its secrets. The soft hum of the air conditioning and the blinking green lights were mesmerizing. Rack upon rack of computer servers were arrayed in front of him, bathed in soft blue light, with a profusion of brightly color-coded wires running between the machines in an internal logic pattern, while large coolant pipes, also color-coded, ran overhead keeping the guts of U.S. national security cool as a cucumber. Several attentive technicians and network administrators moved among the machines like vigilant shepherds keeping careful watch over their flocks.

Today's maintenance was minimal and routine. In fact, all was secure on today's watch – thankfully. As a highly skilled IT specialist with all of the requisite security clearances from top secret to code word compartments, Stan had a keen appreciation for the unbreakable encryption, the multiple electronic defenses and sophisticated firewalls, the biometric access controls, and armed guards that California Cloud Computing employed twenty-four hours a day. All was secure, keeping his CIA client happy. Yes, all was indeed secure, snug, and serene while his own life was in chaos.

Truth be told, however, the real reason 3C had this sensitive account was because of his own extensive information architecture and security background as a former CIA employee. The fact that senior officers at the Agency knew him and valued his expertise and diligence meant they could trust 3C with their top-secret data. That surely had a significant effect on 3C getting that very lucrative cloud-computing contract a year earlier. Yes, he had gotten a healthy starting salary from 3C compared to his old government salary, but it certainly didn't reflect his true value to the company. In fact, if not for him, this contract would not be 3C's. And what did he really have to show for it? Not a whole hell of a lot.

How ironic. These fucking computers are secure and I'm not.

Later that morning, after screwing up his courage, Stan decided he had to go ask his boss, John Stoddard, for some leave time for his camping trip. Big John scared Stan. His booming voice and beefy 6'6" frame made it easy to believe that Big John had been a football player in his younger days, even if now that athletic frame was rapidly going to seed.

Stan walked slowly down the corridor to Big John's office, heart beating loudly in his chest. He tried the doorknob to Stoddard's office and found it locked. So much for Big John's "Open Door" policy. He knocked softly on the pebbled glass of the door and heard muffled sounds, including a squeal, from within.

About a minute later, a pretty young college intern emerged from the office, her face flushing, her rumpled blouse not quite tucked in the back of her skirt as she strode past Stan. He hesitated slightly, shook his head in disgust, and stepped into the office to find John peeling himself from his visitor's couch and moving behind his massive oak desk. His red face cracked a sly smile like a teenaged boy sharing a smutty joke with a friend, "Come in, Stan, my friend, do come in!"

Stan faced John and noticed the copy of the Ten Commandments on the rear wall next to the framed 3C Vision Statement. "Hey, sorry to interrupt, but I need to ask for a little time off to spend with my daughter on a scout camping trip that's coming up."

John looked at him. "Okay. How much and when?"

"The trip's planned for Thursday through Saturday next week. With Marla gone, Allison really needs me for this."

"Listen, I have every sympathy in the world with the pressure you're under. Believe me my friend, I do. You're in my prayers. But the end of next week is simply impossible. Remember? We've got your Agency buddies coming to visit and check on their babies in your area. Remember, we talked about this, and you've got to be there. You're the face of the program to them."

He nodded. "I realize that's important for the company, but when we scheduled their visit, I wasn't aware of Ally's trip. And, of course, my marriage was still intact. I just need a couple of days of 3C's Family Friendly leave. I'm sure they'll understand."

"Stan, Stan, Stan. I feel your pain, but this is crunch time for 3C. You're the point man with CIA and this contract can succeed or fail depending on you, my friend. If I could help you, I would. You know how important family is to me. I've been praying for you and your family. But you'll have to take your daughter camping another time. It kills me to say it but that's all there is to it." John shook his head sadly as if he'd had to put the family dog to sleep.

Stan saw this conversation going nowhere fast. He stopped himself from telling Big John what he thought of him and his family values as well as 3C. Instead, he nodded and left the office quickly before he lost it completely.

Fuck Big John and fuck 3C.

He walked back to the CIA section of the server farm and permitted his retina to be scanned. He had to do it three times because of tears in his eyes. He then entered his personal pin number and put his right hand on the hand geometry and fingerprint reader. The access light glowed green, and the access door clicked open. Stan walked in. He eased himself down on a short stool and tried to control himself but failed. He shook with fury as tears coursed down his cheeks.

Still in a foul mood two days later, Stan left 3C after work and started to drive home. He did not notice the dark grey late model BMW parked across the street from 3C's entrance, or the fact that it pulled out behind him at a discreet distance as he sped away. The BMW remained several car lengths behind him until he pulled into the parking lot of his local grocery store, then parked close to the exit on to the main road.

Stan pushed his shopping cart down the aisle of the store, gathering the basics for that night's dinner – a collection of prepackaged food and prepared items, nothing too difficult. He was neither in the mood for complexity nor did he have the patience to cook properly. Fortunately, like the good kid that she was, Ally usually didn't complain.

An olive-skinned young woman with light chestnut hair was down the next aisle busily plucking some items from the shelves and putting them in her handheld shopping basket when he passed her. She suddenly lost the stacked items in her arms, and they fell right in front of him.

Without skipping a beat, Stan was bending over to pick them up when he heard her breathe, "Oh, my God," and she dropped her basket with everything else in it, and cans, jars and packages of dried food scattered for several feet. Stan stepped back to see the woman frantically trying to retrieve her purchases and then losing her balance, slipping and falling over, her shapely arms and legs and grocery items toppling in a confused jumble on the floor.

He knelt beside her and said, "Hey, I hope I didn't cause this. If so, I'm very sorry." He found himself looking down at the swell of her tanned breasts in her rather low-cut blue dress and quickly averted his eyes. She really was lovely. The young woman looked up at him, tried to smile and replied, "No. Not at all. I'm just clumsy and it's been a bad day – a very bad day. This just caps it. It wasn't your fault at all."

As Stan helped her to her feet, he said, "Are you sure? I'm having a bad day too. Actually, a bad month. They should hang a sign from my neck that reads 'Walking Disaster – Stand Clear.'"

She laughed, and he saw that, in addition to her groceries, an iPad with a green leather cover lay on the ground at her feet. He retrieved that as well and handed it to her.

The pretty young woman looked steadily at him with her almond-shaped dark-green eyes and said, "Nonsense. It's all my fault. You're just a dear man to help me. Thank you, Mr...."

"Ah, Morris. Stan Morris. No problem at all." He quickly gathered up her other items, placed them in her basket and handed it to her. "Are you okay? You didn't twist your ankle, did you?"

"I think I'm okay. A little shaken up, but fine. I'm just a bit worried about that iPad. It's had some hard knocks lately, and I've got some important things on it. Let's see if it'll turn on." She pushed at the on button but nothing happened. "Damn it! Come on." She poked again at it but the screen remained dark. "Oh, please work, please...."

Stan held out his hand and said, "Let me try." She gave it to him and he gently depressed the button. The iPad blinked on. He handed it back to her with a smile. "Here, I must have the magic touch."

"Oh, thank God! I'm studying computer network security in college and I have some important assignments on it. If that iPad dies, I might as well die too. Thank you soooo much. You're a lifesaver."

Stan smiled. "No problem. No problem at all. Funny, I'm a network security specialist myself. Have you considered backing your work up to the cloud? That's my expertise. Then you don't have to worry about it. Even if the device dies, you've got a copy. Even companies and government agencies do that, and companies like mine safeguard it."

The young woman looked admiringly at him. "You're really my white knight today. May I ask you for some tips on network security? I'm new at this but a fast learner. Maybe at the Starbucks next door for just a few minutes? My treat. I promise not to keep you. Just a few concepts I can't quite master."

Stan slowly nodded his head, unsure if she was serious or not. As pretty as she was, Stan thought she could keep him for as long as she wanted. Ally had her scout meeting after school today, and thoughts of fixing dinner and of that asshole Big John at 3C faded in the background.

"By the way, I'm Leila. Leila Fereydoun, Mr. Morris." She took his hand and shook it. He took it and was reluctant to let go. It was so soft and slender and seemed to send a current up his arm.

"No, please, just 'Stan.' I'm in no particular rush to get home. A coffee sounds good."

As Stan felt the warmth of her hand in his as well as the admiring gaze from those big green eyes, suddenly he thought this wasn't such a bad day after all. Maybe his luck was changing.

CHAPTER 6

◇◇◇

Lift to the Scaffold

Geneva

The commercial jet touched down at Cointrin Airport in Geneva, and several dozen Iranian passengers, including the returning AEOI delegation, filed off, retrieved their luggage and proceeded towards customs and their respective hotels. Ali Javadpour followed the others through the airport and after clearing customs, remarked to another delegate that his stomach was upset by the awful airline food and that he needed to stop in an airport cafe for something to settle it. He would catch up with them that evening. His team member nodded and wished him well. Ali ducked into the nearest airport café and ordered some tea. In truth, his stomach was churning but not from the food.

After waiting twenty minutes, slowly sipping the tea and observing no one he knew, he walked up to a nearby phone booth that worked on an anonymous Swiss phone card. He looked at the scrap of napkin in his hand for a long moment as if he were reading his own death sentence. His hand shook and a drop of perspiration rolled down his face. He hesitated and then phoned the number Lane had given him a couple of months earlier. A pleasant female voice came on the line and said only, “Hello.” He hesitated and could tell he was losing his nerve. He started to hang up when the woman again said, “Hello.”

He swallowed and then responded, “This is Gabriel for Miles.”

Three nights later, Lane was nursing a drink in a dark corner of Le Chat Noir when Ali walked up to him and shyly smiled. In the background, a familiar tune was playing. Lane grinned and said, "I thought it appropriate that the band play something off of Miles Davis's "Milestones" album since tonight is a milestone for us. I asked the guys to play a few cuts. I figured you might like it."

Ali shook Lane's outstretched hand, smiled grimly and said. "Ah, yes. Maybe a very good choice. I do like that album. At least it's not the soundtrack that Davis did for French director Louis Malle's premier film in '58. Do you know that film? Classic film noir. Haunting music. Horrible theme. Makes me a little nervous to think about it, especially now."

Lane was puzzled at the reference. "Afraid you have me on that one. What was it?"

Ali shook his head and sat down. "No, just look it up later. I don't want to think about it now. Not at all." Lane looked at him inquiringly as Ali continued, "Really too depressing. Might make me change my mind. But I could use a drink." He looked over at a waiter and ordered tequila and lime on the rocks.

Ali looked at Lane and spoke softly but clearly, "Things have changed since we last spoke. Or maybe I've just now seen them. I've seen indications that possibly I was wrong about my country's intention not to pursue nuclear weapons. I've seen and heard things that give me serious concern. Great, great concern." He paused. "Frankly, I'm scared, Lane."

Lane leaned over and took Ali's right hand in his, squeezed it and said, "Tell me what you've seen. I'm here. I can help. Please." His low voice soothed Ali and he relaxed.

"First, I learned that the Islamic Revolutionary Guard Corps have responsibility for my section. This could possibly be explained away since they have their tentacles in so much, but the IRGC connection is very troubling to say the least."

"Agreed. Not a good sign."

"Next, the IRGC General in charge is one Masud Alborzi, nephew of the Supreme Leader, and he definitely acts like a serious secret squirrel. He's very intense and his emphasis on security is scary. Says I will move to a new 'secure' location once I've been vetted, whatever the hell that means. Why would we need a new 'secure' location for peaceful nuclear power? And why in the hell is the IRGC involved? Just their typical bloodsucking? Maybe, but I doubt it, not with all the secrecy involved. I knew right away something was wrong, but naturally I acted interested."

"Okay, go on. You've got my full attention."

"But the worst was when I got the papers from my predecessor, and I found a page at the end with impressions from a missing page – a page which indicated four containers totaling 60 kilograms of highly enriched uranium – 90% HEU. Lane, there are only two practical uses for 90% HEU and we don't have a fucking nuclear submarine fleet!"

Lane sat back, shocked. His mind flashed back to the report he had received a couple of months earlier from his friend Conor McBane. It also referred to 60 kilograms of HEU. Although not pure corroboration, the coincidence was striking to Lane, given the identical amount, the timing and destination of the HEU. That, and Lane trusted McBane's instincts and the fact that he was not given to sensationalism. He might be an old fox, but he was a clever one.

"That's enough for a workable nuclear device," said Ali. "Little Boy had about the same amount, enough for almost 15 kilotons yield at Hiroshima."

Lane said, "My God." He looked around him to make sure again that no one was in earshot. He thought of the 140,000 dead at Hiroshima. His worst nightmare. "Okay, we'll have to get to work as a team. I'm calling in some experts, but we've got to maximize our time together over the next few days. Let's discuss when you can slip safely away from the delegation. I want to ensure your security. That comes first."

They spent the next hour deep in conversation and arranged their meetings over the next few days – usually late at night after the minders were asleep. Lane promised a new secure communications method that would minimize the risk of personal meetings.

Both men were near exhaustion by the time they left Le Chat Noir, the jazz only a memory. Lane embraced Ali and said, "We're in this together, as a team. You're doing the right thing."

"I know I am," responded the rotund little Iranian. "I know it, but I'm worried."

Lane could see that Ali was more than worried. He briefly wondered if Ali was up to this challenge. But then he thought Ali might be their only shot at a peek at Iran's cards. And those cards could be devastating.

As soon as Lane arrived at his hotel, he got his iPhone out and looked up Malle's directorial debut in 1958, which used Miles Davis's music. He winced as he read it.

"Lift to the Scaffold."

CHAPTER 7

Dream Lover

The nipple of her left breast brushed lightly against his lips. He exhaled lightly on it and then gently brushed it with his tongue ever so softly in a tease of a darting movement. He did it once again and this time she moaned way down in her throat in ecstasy. He thought that giving her such exquisite pleasure almost exceeded his own level of animal satisfaction and need. Almost, but not quite. He was nearing his limit of restraint and thought he would burst soon if he did not satisfy this raw hunger built up inside. Her lips met his and then continued down his neck and chest as he lay back and surrendered to her silky tongue and dancing fingers which caressed his muscles in his chest and groin as they descended gradually to where he needed her so badly. His own hands kneaded her soft breasts, which further heightened his desire. Her nipples were taut against his palms as she pleasured him and she moaned again as he held her breasts and squeezed with a light touch. And then at last her lips closed around him and he thought he would soon explode as she licked and nibbled; the feeling was so intense and utterly intimate and deliciously smutty at the same time. Instead, he woke up.

His footsteps echoed along the Quai de Cologny on the eastern bank of Lake Geneva in the lonely hour before sunrise. The air was cool and still, the tourists and commuters not yet stirring. His pace was fairly swift. He looked down at his GPS watch and saw he was doing a bit better than a nine-minute mile pace on this eight-mile run. Lane had just reached the turnaround point a few hundred meters past the Geneva Yacht Club and was now on his way back along the lake path to his room at the Hotel Eden. He strained to pick up the pace to a sub-eight-minute mile, which would be possible if he focused. It just required discipline, and that he had in abundance, if the fact that he ran every day of the year but Christmas morning was any indication.

Yes, lots of discipline but not lots of life and certainly not lots of love. It had been a long time since there had been any of that. Maybe he had just hit a dry spell. He wondered if Bedouins in the desert said that about the weather with the same foolish irony. At least they had the occasional oasis for some relief. With that thought, he pictured Lacy dressed provocatively in a harem girl's outfit, her breasts jiggling just behind the diaphanous white top and a "come hither" look on her face, and this sudden notion further stimulated his baser thoughts and other more physical parts.

When Lane awakened from the erotic dream an hour earlier, he had looked about his room in confusion and realized he had once again imagined Lacy in bed with him, but all he had to show for this fantasy was a raging erection and intense frustration. At least in his teens it would have resulted in a wet dream, but he was denied even that pleasure, slight as it may be. Typical of his luck with love these days: to be denied even in dreams. Denial may sharpen one's appetite and raw hunger, but eventually you starve.

Lane reminded himself that recruitment was a lot like seduction. But then why was he so good at the former and so lousy at the latter? Was it that he refused to use his recruitment skills for his sexual conquests? The very word "conquest" was distasteful to him in this context. His cardinal rule of recruitment was to cause the target to want the result as much as he did and possibly even more.

He was strongly attracted to Lacy and sensed she might be attracted to him too. But he had yet to make any real move forward other than a few dinners and jazz evenings, and most of those were in Ali's company anyway. Hardly romantic. Whose fault was this? His own, he admitted miserably to himself. To make matters worse, Lacy had informed him yesterday that she had to leave in a few days for the States to start her job as Agent in the Lab at Livermore. The clock was definitely ticking on their relationship – if they even had a relationship. He wasn't sure of that.

Sure there had been the magic evening at La Perle du Lac when he thought he felt the electricity between them, but it seemed premature to make his move then. Stupid. Maybe he had missed his moment…a depressing thought. Maybe he shouldn't have been overly concerned about using his recruitment magic, if he actually had any.

He was conflicted.

The sun was coming up to his right as he crossed the Pont du Mont Blanc and swung into the homestretch up the Quai du Mont Blanc, now at seven and a half minutes per mile for the last mile home. He was flying at this pace and going into oxygen debt, his lungs beginning to ache, but he reached inside, breathed more deeply, and kept going. He crossed the Rue de Lausanne through light early traffic, like a cheetah swiftly crossing the veldt, and pulled up sharply to the hotel breathing hard. It had been a good workout and dampened some of his frustration and sexual tension.

He still had to write up his meeting with Ali from the night before. He was excited about this development, at least. Headquarters would be happy enough over the fact that the recruitment was now firm and that Ali would willingly accept covert communications. But they would go crazy over his report of the sixty kilos of ninety percent HEU, the move to a "new secure location" and senior IRGC involvement and emphasis on secrecy. This was a recipe for a dynamite report and was the reason Lane loved being a case officer – to get the scoop on new intelligence that had a major impact on U.S. national security. It didn't get any better than that.

Lane ran up the four flights of stairs in the circular stairway that surrounded the hotel elevator and let himself into his room. He went into the bathroom and tried to start the shower but no water came out. Crap! What was going on? He stalked out of the bathroom towards his room phone when he noticed the slip of paper on the floor that he had overlooked as he came through the door. It said that unfortunately the water would be turned off on his floor for another hour for emergency plumbing repairs. The management regretted any inconvenience. He gathered up a towel and some clean clothes and headed down the stairs to demand an empty room with a shower so he could get ready for work.

Unfortunately, the front desk clerk informed him that the hotel was full and he would simply have to wait until the repairs on his floor were completed in an hour. The clerk offered his apologies and as compensation a voucher good for a free bottle of wine with dinner that evening. Lane took it, somewhat mollified, but he still needed to get to work so that he could send his message to Washington. He started back up the stairs towards his room, walking a bit dejectedly this time rather than running, when he almost bumped head on into Lacy as she was descending the stairs towards the breakfast room.

"What's the look for and why are you carrying a towel and your clothes?" she asked.

"The water's off on my floor for plumbing repairs and I've got to cool my jets for an hour until they're finished. I'm just pissed because the meeting with our friend last night went extremely well and I've got to get into the office and send out a cable with some great stuff. Stuff that you and they are going to absolutely love. But now I can't take a damned shower, first."

Lacy shrugged. "The water's working fine on my floor, so why don't you take a shower in my room? Just ignore the mess in my bathroom."

"Are you sure? I'd hate to inconvenience you."

"Sure. No problem. It'll save you an hour. It's the very least I can do after you've had a great night with our friend."

"Thank you so much! You're the best, Lacy. I appreciate it."

Lane turned on the shower and blessedly hot water came out in a strong flow. He stepped in and began to soap himself off while mentally composing the operational message and intelligence report he planned to send to Langley first thing. He was so deep in thought that he didn't hear the bathroom door open nor hear the shower curtain be drawn back slowly behind him.

His first awareness of her presence was when he felt Lacy's breasts against his wet, soapy back and her hands massaging his shoulders. He didn't turn around, but shut his eyes and inhaled sharply. The feeling of her stiff nipples circling against his back was erotic beyond belief. He felt himself stiffen almost immediately. Her hands left his shoulders and went gradually down his sides and around his front, through his pubic hair and then she held him in her fingers as she whispered in his ear, "I had such a nasty dream last night about you. It made me so hot I couldn't stand it any longer. You can use my shower any time you want. Any time."

He slowly turned his head and looked into her deep blue eyes, "You had that dream too? Are we dreaming now?"

"You tell me. But if we are, let's not wake up." Having said that, she slowly sank to her knees and indescribable pleasure commenced, her hands and mouth busy with him. The dream had become reality and the thin membrane between this world and the dreamer's world vanished.

CHAPTER 8

◇◇◇

A Turnkey Deal for Chick

Geneva

The tall, distinguished-looking Iranian delegate sat sipping tea in the small café near the location of the nuclear talks after that day's session had concluded, negotiations still deadlocked. He watched the door and slowly drew in his breath as the chubby American delegate took a table thirty feet away and ordered a beer and a bowl of peanuts. The American began to read the sports pages of his newspaper, oblivious to his surroundings, guzzling his beer and munching handfuls of nuts. Foam from his beer stuck to his upper lip and errant peanuts fell from his hand onto the floor and scattered. Disgusting smacking and crunching noises and an occasional belch came from the American's table. It was almost painful to watch and certainly to hear. The Iranian was reminded of the American expression, "Like a pig at a trough."

The Iranian bided his time for a few minutes, then stood and made his way towards the men's room on the far side of the café, a route that would take him directly past the American's table. He palmed the note he had written earlier and discreetly dropped it on the floor next to the American as he passed and coughed so as to signal his action. He continued on to the restroom.

Upon emerging a couple of minutes later, he was distressed to see that this idiot had not noticed the note dropped next to his left shoe. Instead, the heavy American's attention was still completely devoted to his newspaper and gluttony. The Iranian deftly bent and retrieved the note as he passed and sat back at his table. *Amazing. They spend millions trying to recruit us and then ignore our efforts to volunteer.* Well, that was good news for his general and the IRGC counterintelligence forces, but bad news for him. He had a job to do.

The tall Iranian sat back at his table and waited another five minutes. Then, he stood up and walked towards the bar to order another tea. This time, as he passed the American's table, he took no chances and flipped the note directly into the rapidly dwindling bowl of nuts and kicked his shoe. He might as well have blown a bugle and sat in the idiot's lap.

As he walked back to his table with his steaming new cup of tea, he finally caught the eye of the American, who had fished the note out of the bowl and read it. He looked directly at him as he walked by and nodded at the exit. He set his teacup on the table, recovered his coat from the back of his chair and started for the door. He lingered briefly outside about forty yards from the entrance as the American scanned the note again and finally followed him, looking as if he had just won the lottery.

The tall Iranian made sure that the American was in tow and headed deliberately towards a nearby hotel, walking a bit slowly so as not to lose him.

Finally.

Upon entering the hotel's bar area, the Iranian sat in a dark corner and waited for the American's arrival. This did not take long because by this time the American was almost running and was out of breath as he sat down heavily next to him. The two men looked at one another for a few seconds before the Iranian spoke.

"Good evening, sir. Permit me to introduce myself. I'm Alireza Kazemi. I'm Chief of Staff to His Excellency the Director of the Atomic Energy Organization of Iran Dr. Shirazi. As you surely know, he is head of our AEOI delegation to these negotiations, and I want to make a deal with you. I know you're part of the American team because I've seen you at the talks with your colleagues. You are…?"

The American blurted out, "I'm Ch…um…Chick, Chick Baker."

"And I assume you're CIA?"

"Why would you assume that?" asked the American nervously.

"Because a State Department Officer or someone from your Department of Energy would have walked away after looking at my note. Instead, you followed me like a hound chasing a bitch in heat. Am I right...Chick?"

"Maybe so, maybe not." The American gave him a wary look.

The Iranian looked closely at him and asked in a low voice, "Are you interested in talking or is this just a waste of my time? I can leave right now, if you wish." He pushed his chair back and started to stand up.

The American started. "Hell yes, I'm interested. I read your note. What've you got exactly and what do you want?" His voice took on a slight higher note of anxiety.

"Quite simply, I'm prepared to trade you all of the information you need for successful nuclear negotiations for a...um, how do I put this? – let's say a realistic fee. Basically, I've got complete access to my country's negotiating positions and its strategy. And I do mean complete access. I have our basic positions and our fallback positions – the concessions we are willing to make. Everything you need to make a deal; well, I've got it. I see it every day before giving it to my Director. And I'm willing to let you have it in advance of each negotiating session."

"Okay, like I said, I'm interested. Go on. Tell me more." The American was sweating profusely.

"Further, I'm prepared to supply you with more information after the agreement, which will verify whether my country complies or not. Let's call it a 'turnkey deal.' But it will cost you money. A fairly large amount of money. I believe the technical term you use is 'a shitload of money?'" The Iranian grinned as he whispered the last words slowly.

"And why should we trust you?"

"Ah, you don't have to trust me. You can have a sample in advance. Actually, two samples in advance. I think you refer to these as 'freebies.' If you like them, then you'll pay as you go. Today, I'll give you exactly what you need for the next negotiating session, which occurs in a few days. I have here the positions we will take. I've included both the Farsi originals and my translations. These are ready-made intelligence reports." The Iranian reached into his coat pocket and retrieved a sheaf of papers and handed them to the American, who fanned them open. His eyes nearly bugged out as he read the first couple of pages. The Iranian nodded with satisfaction.

"If this material is no good, then don't come back. Just forget this entire conversation. It didn't cost you a dime. But you'll quickly learn that these papers are pure gold, and each time I'll give you exactly the same advantage. Also, I'm handing you an insight into a few of our military research sites – some you may not know about. They should be inspected by the International Atomic Energy Agency once the agreement is concluded. Consider it further proof of my access."

"Okay, fine, fine. I'm very interested, but what do you want?" The American had worked himself into a state of visible anxiety. The veins were popping out on his temples and his left knee was bobbing up and down like a sewing machine.

"Ah, the bottom line. Yes, Americans always want to know the price. I admire you for that. 'Cash and carry' is what you call it, correct? Well, I want $500,000 in cash by the next meeting and $100,000 per month thereafter."

The American's jaw dropped. "You're out of your mind."

"Not at all, my friend, Chick. You and I know what this information is worth to your government. We're talking about pocket change. To conclude these negotiations quickly is entirely within your grasp. And the information is priceless."

"I'm…I'm gonna need some time. That's a hell of a lot of money."

"Well, just don't take too long or my next visit will be with your British cousins or French allies. I know they have vision, and they move very quickly. Or perhaps with the Chinese or Russians. They'd love to emerge as the winners and saviors of these negotiations, not to mention what it would do for their investments in Iran. There might even be a Nobel Peace Prize for one of their leaders and that would be embarrassing as hell to the White House. And let's not forget the dear Germans. Ah yes, the Germans. *Deutschland, Deutschland Uber Alles.* Truth be told, they supplied us with most of our nuclear enrichment technology in the first place, so I strongly suspect they would love to be the ones to 'redeem' themselves in the world's eyes. It kind of goes full circle if they do the deal; you know what I mean?

And they'd do it in a heartbeat. Euros spend as easily as dollars, but they might even pay in gold."

The American was quickly losing his smile and composure.

The Iranian suddenly bent forward and peered directly into the American's eyes from about a foot away, "Speaking quite frankly, Chick, I'd say I can name my own price. And the more I think about it, the more I think $500,000 is starting much too low. I think my position is referred to as being in the 'catbird seat.' So, let's say one million dollars up front at the next meeting."

"That's fucking impossible!" The American was starting to look sick and panicky.

"No, Chick, I think it's entirely fucking possible. And it will tell me that you're fucking serious. Look at my material and you'll find out that I'm still being reasonable. This is the bargain-basement price. I make a little money and you become a hero. What's not to like?"

"I...I don't know, it's just so much money."

"Well, if that figure's no good, let's try two million dollars. Maybe that figure will suffice. It should catch the attention of Langley. Otherwise, I'm going, going, gone." The Iranian snapped his fingers and shrugged.

At this point, the American, quite pale by now, looked completely devastated. "You just said a million dollars up front and that'll be hard enough. Give me a fuckin' break...please," he pleaded in a small voice.

"Ah Chick, you do drive a hard bargain. Tell you what. You consult Langley, then bring the million in cash. One-hundred-dollar bills, the new ones, would be fine, although 1000-Swiss-Franc notes would take up ninety percent less room and be easier to carry in a valise. I wouldn't want you to strain your arms. Shall we meet a week from today, same time? And it'd probably be better for my security if you got a hotel room here, wouldn't it, Chick?"

The American nodded weakly as the Iranian rose from his chair, shook his hand perfunctorily and strode purposely out of the bar. He looked at the papers in his hands and then noticed that he was still wearing his picture badge from his shirt collar. It read "Charles Grable."

Shit. Had the Iranian noticed? Hopefully not. It would not do to mention that slip-up in tradecraft in his cable to headquarters. Besides, hadn't he just bargained the Iranian down from two million to one million? His shrewdness had saved Uncle Sam a million dollars. There could be a promotion to Senior Intelligence Service in this for him. He couldn't wait to write up the recruitment cable and get the intelligence to Headquarters. They were going to love this. Absolutely love it.

CHAPTER 9

◇◇◇

Project Zulfiqar

IRGC Office of Intelligence North Tehran

Drs. Daoud and Majid Tabatabai sat in the anteroom of the IRGC Intelligence office to which they had been brought by special limousine from their labs at the AEOI. They were curious as to what was so urgent that their research should be interrupted so abruptly. Their boss, a competent administrator but inept researcher, only said a serious matter of national security was to be discussed. They contemplated the dull surroundings, plain furniture and unadorned walls, except for a few photos of the Imam and his predecessors, and wondered who had summoned them and why. Neither of them was especially concerned with politics or matters of state, and so they were not overly nervous, but still, they were in the office of the intelligence organ of the guardians of the revolution. This was unlikely to be a summons for tea, sweets and chitchat.

A door opened behind them and a voice boomed out, "Majid, Daoud! How are you, my brothers? It's been far too long! You're both looking well!"

They turned to see Masud Alborzi, whom they had barely seen in twenty-five years except in news broadcasts in the last few months. He was dressed in khakis and a safari jacket as he strode confidently into the room and extended his hand. Both men rose and accepted his hearty greetings.

Alborzi invited them into his office and bade them sit down.

"I understand your scientific work is progressing nicely and I thought it time we had a chat. All of us are still mourning the loss of the late Imam. A national tragedy. We miss his guidance so much." He looked up at the late Imam's portrait with a look of reverence and pulled a handkerchief out of his breast pocket to dab at his eyes.

He bent forward as if to take them into his confidence. "Our investigation into the assassination conspiracy shows not only a Zionist connection but also the cat's paw of the Saudi regime. This shouldn't surprise anyone. Fortunately, it was Allah's will that my uncle survive and take the reins of state for those faithful to the Revolution and to Allah. He has entrusted me with a special program and I know I can count on you to support it." Alborzi looked at both of them with his penetrating gaze. "It has become obvious that your valuable work must continue at all costs as a guarantor of freedom for the Islamic Republic. Mind you, the negotiations in Geneva must succeed so that we can find relief from the Western sanctions. But we must also have a means to defend ourselves from our enemies. The Islamic Republic is in, as they say, 'a tough neighborhood.' The assassination only confirms that. It was outrageous. Right here in the heart of Tehran! Am I right?"

The Tabatabais nodded in agreement.

"Consequently, I've been authorized by my uncle the Supreme Leader to move your research from your current location at the AEOI to a new, much more secure location which will never arouse the attention of the Americans or their allies."

The Tabatabai brothers looked at one another, and Majid asked, "Where, Masud? Our current facility meets all of our research needs and we need access to the lab infrastructure."

"Have no worries about that. I have a generous budget to give you a first-class facility. You will have not only top of the line supercomputers for modeling but also precision machine shops for fabrication with Swiss machining centers and German 3D printers for specialty parts. Additionally, you will have a select team of technicians and other scientists to assist you. In short, you will want for nothing. Not only must your research continue, it must accelerate so that we're never held hostage by the West. I want the two of you to lead this team and report directly to me."

Alborzi continued, "As for the location...well you'll both be pleased. It's hardly ten miles from our old hometown. In Lar National Park on the slope of Mt. Damavand in an abandoned sulfur mine. How's that for a secure underground location? Say, didn't your father work there?" he asked.

They both nodded uneasily. Daoud ventured, "Really, Masud? In that old abandoned sulfur mine? It hardly seems fit for our scientific research."

"Don't worry. You won't be wearing mining helmets. We're constructing an underground, hermetically sealed laboratory of the first rank within the mine. The two of you as project leaders will be allowed to live in our old town. Just hometown boys coming back home. Your research covers will be geophysics and special metallurgy. You could relate it to the recent earth tremors they've been having in the area. The others will be bussed into the facility in special National Park vehicles. The cover is impeccable. Completely innocent research in the national park." Alborzi grinned and looked back and forth between them. "Well, what do you think? Do you accept this honor?"

Both men nodded and Alborzi smiled broadly and clapped his hands and said, "Excellent! I knew that I could count on you! You'll start right away. There is the small matter of acknowledging that your work is top-secret, but I think you're aware of that, right?" He then shoved a form across the table for both of them to sign, which flatly stated that the work they would be engaged in was vital to the national security of the Islamic Republic of Iran and that secrecy violations concerning "Project Zulfiqar" would be punishable by imprisonment or death.

Both men glanced at it briefly and signed their names. They had no real choice.

The Tabatabai brothers rose to leave, but Alborzi said, "Daoud, could I have a brief word with you? Majid, if you'll excuse us, please. Just a word with an old childhood friend. I won't keep him long. Again, I'm so delighted that you're on board!" He slapped Majid on the back as he left the office.

Once the door was closed, the grin fell from Alborzi's face like a veil. He looked somberly at Daoud, who sat impassively and simply looked back at him.

"Daoud, we've known each other since we were boys. Our families have known each other even longer. There is a strongly venerated religious tradition in both. As you know, my uncle had tremendous respect for your great uncle and considered him a mentor of sorts. So, it distresses me all the more to bring up this subject. I think you know what I mean."

Daoud remained quiet, his face composed.

"Very well, I'll be blunt. I've been told by some of our most eminent scientists that you have a mind as great, if not greater, than the great English mathematician Alan Turing. I'm also told by some of my colleagues that you share another unfortunate characteristic with Turing, one that can get you executed in this country. Need I say more?" Alborzi looked at him with raised eyebrows, awaiting a response.

Daoud continued to look at him without flinching.

Alborzi raised his voice. "I am responsible not only for the success of this project but also for its security, and susceptibility to blackmail is something for which I am ever vigilant. Is that clear enough for you?"

Daoud finally spoke with a defiant tone, "Fine. If you already know so much, then how can I be blackmailed?"

Alborzi stood up, anger rushing to his face. "You goddamned fucking fool, listen to me and listen well. What I know about you is irrelevant. Hell, I've known it for a long time. Probably longer than you think. There were always rumors when we were younger. People talk in small towns. And personally, I don't even give a damn who or what you screw. But if it were ever to be made public that the father of our atomic weapon is queer, then we'd have a public-relations nightmare on our hands. My uncle would have you castrated and hanged, and I would lose everything. And I mean fucking everything!" He shouted the last and glared at him until he finally looked away. "Here's how it's going to be. You're going to remain celibate throughout this project. If I ever catch the slightest hint that you are not, I will personally castrate you with a rusty knife and toss your mangy ass into prison until you swing from a gibbet. Is that clear enough for you?"

Daoud nodded and said in a harsh whisper, "Completely clear."

He then rose and left Alborzi's office. He joined his brother outside and together they walked to their waiting car. Daoud's only words to Majid, were, "We have to talk."

Once they were back at the AEOI building, Daoud asked Majid to accompany him for a short walk around the compound.

"He knows about me," Daoud told his brother.

Majid nodded. "Did he threaten you?"

"Oh, he threatened me all right. He said if I didn't stay a good boy throughout the project, he'd cut my balls off himself and then have me hanged for good measure. The shame of having his chief nuclear weapons designer outed as a gay man is just too great for him and this country."

"Damn it! You realize that there's a good chance he'll have you arrested after the project is concluded. That asshole…He was an asshole when we were kids and he's a bigger asshole now!" Majid angrily kicked a large rock twenty feet down the sidewalk.

"I know it. But what should I do? I'm less concerned about me than about you and your family. You've got a wife and kids. This mud will splash wide. You've always been accepting of me. I don't want to bring dishonor or worse to you."

"Daoud, I love you as you are – unconditionally. I told you that fifteen years ago when you told me. I still mean it. We're in this together as brothers."

Daoud turned to Majid and hugged him and said with a tremor in his voice, "Thank you, Majid. You've always been there for me. I love you too."

Majid said, "Look. This is a threat to both of us and we're not going to just lie back and let this fucker walk all over us. Alborzi said they need this weapon as a guarantor of freedom. I'd say we need a guarantor too and for the same reason - freedom. I'm thinking of my old physics professor at Berkeley, Dr. Rand McKeown. He not only taught physics, he was also a nuclear weapons designer at Lawrence Livermore. He's brilliant. And he'll listen to me and know how to help us. I'll take care of it. Don't worry."

CHAPTER 10

◇◇◇

Mind Over Matter

San Francisco Bay Area

Stan found Leila to be a quick learner. Her follow-up questions and the way she listened to him so intently made him feel like he was the only star in her universe. It felt really good. He had never had anyone pay such undivided attention to him before, especially not his ex-wife. Leila, on the other hand, hung on his every word, and the young woman quickly absorbed his explanations of complex network security architecture. Was it that she was so bright or was he a great teacher? Well, what the hell did it matter? He loved it.

Their initial time at Starbucks quickly developed into several meetings a week after work. He timed these with Ally's outside activities so that he would be there when she needed him. Ally was still first in his life, but he came away from the meetings with Leila hardly able to wait for the next one. His anger at Big John Stoddard and 3C had not abated, but it was becoming less relevant to his feeling of well-being and self-respect. In fact, he felt like they were just annoying bugs on the windshield of life, and he would simply wipe them away. Swish, swish, gone.

Four weeks after they met, Leila arrived one Friday afternoon at the Starbucks, ran to Stan, hugged him tightly and squealed, "I aced my exam and all because of you, Stan. My hero. My white knight." She kissed him on the cheek and hugged him harder, her hands against his back rubbing his shoulders very lightly.

Stan felt her breasts pressing against his chest through her dress and smelled her exotic perfume. When was the last time he had been held like this? It was bewitching and for the first time in a very long time he felt aroused.

"Should we celebrate? There's a nice pub down the street if you have time. I should at least buy my white knight a drink." She held his hands in hers and squeezed them, her touch on his palms was electric. Her wide green eyes never left his and seemed to drink him in. He didn't resist. Why should he? Moments like this were far too rare in his miserable life.

"Why the hell not? Let's go, but these drinks are on me. You're my prize student. You worked hard for this victory, and I'm very, very proud of you." Stan kept her left hand in his right and led her out the door and toward the pub. He felt like skipping. When was the last time he had felt this good? Not in a hell of a long while. Maybe never.

CHAPTER 11

◇◇◇

Condor and Leopard

Langley

Paula Davenport felt like singing. Within ten days, the Agency had gone from virtually no reporting on the nuclear negotiations with Iran to two well-placed sources. It was amazing how quickly their fortune had changed…and this bothered her slightly. A little voice inside her head told her that this was too coincidental, too good to be true. She understood that this road could lead to disaster and heartbreak. She wanted to enjoy this feeling if only for a while. Such moments had become increasingly rare in recent years.

Granted, one of the Iranian sources had been "recruited" by that big clown Charlie Grable. Paula knew that Charlie had been a "suck-up" favorite of two of her predecessors, and now he was working with that senior suck-up, Chief of NE Division, Pat McCabe. She thought maybe it took one to know one.

This so-called recruitment of Charlie's smelled more like the source had volunteered, although the congratulatory cable from McCabe to the delegation in Geneva had praised Charlie's "diligent tactics of shrewd persuasion and persistence." Well, not likely, but maybe. Even a blind pig occasionally finds a tasty morsel. This morsel had been encrypted "Condor."

What was incontrovertible, however, was Condor's position and direct access to the highest quality of intelligence. The reports had gone directly to the White House and the negotiating team in the field, and the negotiating sessions had played out exactly as the source predicted. Director Mac White was "deeee-lighted" as he put it. He hadn't even flinched at the million-dollar upfront money for the follow-up meeting, nor the $100,000 monthly retainer. Of course, if you're a billion-dollar hedge fund manager, this was truly small potatoes. His company held office parties that cost more.

The White House echoed Mac's delight with glowing praise from the National Security Advisor. In fact, the National Security Advisor personally noted to Paula that the President was very pleased with the stream of high-quality intelligence which the CIA was producing and which was enabling her goal of a peaceful resolution of the nuclear deadlock with Iran. No mention was made of the fact that the President was about to start her re-election campaign in the next few months.

So, Condor was soaring. And Charlie Grable was flying high with him. And yet… Yes, and yet what?

The second Iranian recruitment had also caused her a few stomach flutters, albeit for different reasons. An AEOI criticality safety engineer had been carefully developed and brought on board and trained in covert communications. He was encrypted "Leopard," and his reporting on the negotiations tracked with Condor's, which was nice corroboration. But he also had provided indications of IRGC involvement in the nuclear program, which was troubling enough. Then the real "bombshell" (a poor choice of images thought Paula) was his story about the etching or impression of four containers of 90% HEU – a total of sixty kilograms. If his intel were true, then Iran already had enough material for a weapon. True, it was only an etching and not firsthand observation, but Leopard's claim made Paula's blood run cold. What if these negotiations were all a sham – a Persian Punch & Judy show for their benefit?

CHAPTER 12

◇◇◇

Peace in Our Time

Geneva

The Secretary of State smiled toothily for the cameras as the television networks filmed him and his Iranian counterpart shaking hands. He stole a glance at the monitors to check his hair and wondered why he had to share this moment, his moment, after all of these many months of hard work with that worthless bitch of a president who was flying to Geneva for the signing tomorrow. Had he prevailed in those Iowa caucuses, it could have been his moment alone. He wondered if the Nobel Committee still considered him a short list candidate for the Peace Prize. And the current occupant of the White House might only be a one-term president. It happened. Not to mention, he was still a relatively young and vital man. At least young enough and plenty vital. Just ask his executive assistant.

Certainly, it had been him and not the president who had proposed the "amnesty" on whatever was found at the Iranian military sites suspected of conducting nuclear research. Of course, he knew it had been his young executive assistant who had come up with that idea when they were languishing in the afterglow of a particularly vigorous session of lovemaking one night in his hotel suite. It was fascinating how fucking could focus the young woman's mind.

The Iranians had finally accepted the proposal a session or two later, after a bit more horse-trading on both sides. These Persians may be sharp in the bazaar but he was one hell of a negotiator himself. And later that night, he intended to inspire his executive assistant once again to flashes of brilliance, come what may or whomever. He smiled at the thought.

The Iranian Foreign Minister was also smiling, and almost for the same reasons, albeit from a slightly different perspective. He and he alone had utterly convinced the American side to relax sanctions on Iran in a phased but complete manner in return for International Atomic Energy Agency inspections of their nuclear facilities -- inspections that would show that Iran was sincere in its commitment to peaceful and only peaceful nuclear power. Granted, their last-minute concessions had ultimately included some military sites, which previously had been off-limits in earlier sessions but they also had the amnesty for any past "misdeeds," which he had characterized as "defensive research."

Wisdom had prevailed in Tehran, however, and the Supreme Leader had made a wise decision to bare all in return for even more American concessions, including some badly needed high technology, which would bolster their sagging economy and their relatively antiquated military. Why use shabby Russian or Chinese weapons systems when one could buy American? And God forbid they would have to buy any more crappy North Korean weapons from that fat moron with the bad hair in Pyongyang.

Some leading American aviation and defense firms, plus a host of those from Silicon Valley and the energy sector, had already sent representatives to Geneva in anticipation of this result, and some really ambitious ones had already called upon him, eager to sign some letters of commitment. Once he signed the letters of intent, he was to send the list of companies immediately to the Supreme Leader's nephew IRGC General Alborzi for security vetting.

Standing next to them, also shaking hands, were the Director of the Atomic Energy Organization of Iran Dr. Hamid Shirazi and his American counterpart and Secretary of Energy, Dr. Manuel "Manny" Alvarez, who was an eminent nuclear physicist and former lab director from Los Alamos

National Lab. Shirazi was an owlish looking man who looked as if he would have been much more comfortable in a university classroom rather than in front of the throng of reporters. He actually was quite outgoing and smiled bravely for the cameras. Dr. Shirazi had gotten his M.S. and Ph.D. in physics at the University of Texas, and he still spoke English with a disconcerting Texas accent and local phrases ("y'alls" and "howdies" and an occasional off-color joke about U.T.'s college rival - the Texas Aggies).

Additionally, and to the secret delight of Dr. Alvarez and some of the other American and Iranian delegates, Dr. Shirazi knew how to get under the skin of the Harvard-educated, usually imperturbable Brahmin U.S. Secretary of State with his sporadic and well-timed use of some rich Texas profanity. The most notable occasion had been at one particular impasse in the negotiations when Dr. Shirazi leaned forward, and affecting his best John Wayne imitation drawled in the Secretary's face, "Well, fuck you and the horse you rode in on." It actually broke the ice as the other delegates, including the Americans, laughed even as it annoyed the shocked Secretary to no end.

On top of that, Dr. Shirazi liked to needle the Secretary in other ways as well. One of his more memorable barbs was when he asked the Secretary, "Please remind me when the last time Harvard beat U.T. Oh, I forgot, they've never beaten them, have they? Pity."

Once, the Secretary tried to turn the tables on Dr. Shirazi and attempted to tell a joke about the Longhorns and the Texas Aggies but his comedic timing was off and he muffed the punch line so badly that only his pretty executive assistant laughed.

Today, unlike the other Iranian delegates who almost religiously hewed to the "no necktie rule" of the Islamic revolution, Dr. Shirazi was wearing a tailored black leather jacket, a powder blue cowboy shirt and a bolo tie with a silver Lone Star clasp. He was also sporting a pair of highly polished handmade black crocodile Lucchese cowboy boots. He joked a bit with the reporters and laughingly asked them just to call him "Tex."

Yes, smiles were in abundance. Champagne flowed, although the Iranian delegation politely demurred and took mineral water. They would drink later privately. Glasses were clinked.

The American Secretary of Energy tried to force a smile, but he had an uneasy feeling about this agreement. Something didn't seem quite right, especially towards the end. The negotiations, which had been tough as nails for many months, had gone almost too easily after a certain point. This coincided with the new streams of intelligence, which their CIA liaison officer had provided. The intelligence presented remarkable insights into what the Iranians planned to do and what they wanted. The Iranian side acted precisely as the reports predicted, to the point that things seemed scripted. Like most scientists, Dr. Alvarez was a student of logic, and he thought that this was illogical, considering the fallibility of human intelligence. How could it be that perfect?

It bothered him so much that at one point a few weeks earlier, he'd brought it up with the Secretary of State during one of their regular strategy sessions.

"Don't you think these recent breakthroughs are a bit much? I mean things were deadlocked or moving slower than molasses. Almost zero progress and suddenly it seems like we're all ready to sing 'Kumbayah' around the campfire?"

The Secretary of State screwed up his face and looked at him with disbelief. "So, let me get this straight, Manny. You'd be happier if they were more obstinate, dragging this out, continually objecting to everything? Don't you remember? It was like fucking pulling teeth! The fact that things are going smoothly now is a result of our being fair and empathetic. And frankly some superior negotiating skills – on my part, your part and, and...." A brief pause. Then almost as a grudging afterthought, "And of course some good intelligence. What is there about this that you don't find to our advantage?"

"I didn't say it wasn't to our advantage that they are being more compliant, but it just seems like a sea-change in their posture and I wonder why. Doesn't this seem the least bit strange to you?"

In a tone of exasperation, he replied, "Christ, I don't know. Maybe common sense has prevailed at long last in Tehran. Maybe they realize that being a friend, or at least a non-adversary, of the U.S. is to their advantage.

Maybe the new Supreme Leader has more smarts than the last one. Who knows and who really cares? Frankly I don't give a rat's ass as long as these negotiations succeed."

"And what if they already have sufficient fissile material for a bomb or two and this agreement is meaningless to them? You saw that intelligence report about the sixty kilos of HEU."

"No, Manny, I saw a report that described a faint impression on a piece of paper of a sketch of 60 kilos of HEU. A friggin' impression of a sketch? And that's supposed to be intelligence? Give me a break. I was shocked that the Agency would even disseminate such a poorly sourced report. If you read it carefully, it had so many caveats that it should be taken with a grain of salt."

"And what about the letter that I showed you from my friend Conor McBane? It mentioned the same amount – sixty kilos of HEU from Russia – in the same timeframe. And, I must emphasize, several more shipments to follow."

"I realize that, but I also know that his letter was never disseminated as intelligence and rightly so, especially after the embarrassment of the first report based solely on an impression of a goddamned sketch. Like our other source, your reporter friend never saw the material firsthand. Instead, he's repeated hearsay from an Armenian smuggler, who's now conveniently dead. With all due respect, I don't think McBane's exactly a reliable or well-placed source."

"With all due respect to you Mr. Secretary, my friend Conor almost became a dead source. His attacker in his hotel room in Baku turned out to be a former Russian Spetsnaz operative, according to the Azerbaijani officials. Two others were killed. Conor was lucky that he got out alive."

The Secretary of State maintained his composure but looked at Alvarez as if he were a child and spoke slowly. "I have no doubt that your friend Conor met up with some desperate criminal elements, but that part of the world is rife with them. They could have been smuggling guns, gold, women, anything and he would have become a target. It's a dangerous beat he covers."

Alvarez said nothing but was seething inside. He felt that there was more to this than that. He knew that Conor McBane was not given to sensationalism. That his letter mentioned the same amount of HEU as the CIA report was more than coincidence.

"To your point about loose material," said the Secretary. "When I was in Moscow recently, I asked Russian Foreign Minister Petrov if Russia were missing a sizable quantity of HEU. Mind you, I didn't specify an exact amount but I said 'several tens of kilos.' Nick was frankly astonished by my question and assured me that all of their material is accounted for and 100% secure. He was very sincere. He trusts me and I trust him. I accept his word; if he's not worried, let's not worry about it."

But Alvarez was worried about it and wondered if the Secretary knew what his good buddy "Nick" Petrov had said about him behind his back in Moscow. Although Alvarez was not on the limited distribution list for a sensitive report from CIA, he'd seen a bootleg copy of the report provided by a good friend at the Agency. In the report, which was from a source in the Kremlin, Petrov laughingly described the Secretary as "a vainglorious ass-kissing cocksucking fool." Alvarez's respect for the Russian Foreign Minister's character judgment had increased immeasurably. As had his concern.

CHAPTER 13

◇◇◇

Anything at All

California Bay Area

Stan Morris looked at himself in the mirror and grinned slyly, then turned serious and narrowed his eyes in imitation of some movie star's unblinking stare. This was "Steely Eyed Stan." He mugged a bit more with self-satisfaction, looking at his profile from various angles. This past three months had been the happiest time of his life. Things were finally going his way. And God was he happy.

He looked in the mirror over his shoulder and saw Leila sleeping sweetly in bed, only a thin sheet covering her curvaceous body, the contour of one soft breast peeking out at him. Every sexual fantasy he had ever had was coming true, including some he hadn't previously imagined. She allowed and even encouraged all of his dreams and extended them to become new realities. Her sensuous body, her soft knowing touch, her sultry voice, her pouting lips and her sinuous movements pushed him beyond what he thought was possible in the realm of human desire. He had heard about someone metaphorically fucking his or her brains out but this was coming true. Leila had taken him to heights of pleasure he'd never even envisioned with Marla.

Not only was he fucking Leila on a regular basis, but also he was fucking 3C and Big John Stoddard. It was almost debatable as to which was more satisfying. Plus, he was making good money as a consultant for Leila's Uncle Abbas, who was a crypto-mathematician with his own computer networking business. His consulting consisted of him providing Abbas with some of 3C's basic commercial algorithms, which were proprietary technologies, but Stan had devised most of them, so he considered them to be his own intellectual property. If 3C didn't appreciate him, Uncle Abbas and Leila certainly did. And they paid cash.

Leila called to him softly from the bed. God, what would he not do for her? He couldn't think of a thing.

"Stan, I need your help on something," she whispered as she took hold of him with her delicate fingers, lightly caressing his scrotum with her nails, just a touch here and a touch there.

"Sure, sweetheart. Anything. Anything at all." Stan lay beside her, his erection and desire for her so fierce it almost hurt.

Leila whispered in his ear, "I need your help but first, I want you to do all those nasty things to me that you do so well. I need you so badly! God, I just can't stand it! I'm dying to feel you inside of me." She brushed her breasts against him and then whispered, "You're still my white knight, you know."

With that, she rolled on her back and brought him between her legs to her moistness. She wrapped her legs around his torso and brought his hands to her breasts. Once more, he entered his living Technicolor fantasy. Nothing else in the world existed.

Twenty minutes later, as they lay together, spooned up, spent and exhausted, she spoke softly. "Darling, I do need to ask you something."

"Um. Yeah, what?"

"Uncle Abbas has a huge contract coming up. This is the one that'll make or break his company. But I'm…I'm afraid to ask you. Afraid you'll say no."

"Hey, now, you can ask me anything. Any time." He cupped her left breast.

"It's a big favor and I wouldn't dare ask except that I owe him so much – bringing me here from Iran when I was a child, paying for my college education, helping me get started in my career. I wouldn't be here but for him. I don't want to let him down after all that."

"You just name it. We won't let him down."

"Well, this new contract would be for a defense company, and the network security design requires a much more sophisticated encryption algorithm than he's previously used. The company's so afraid of Chinese hackers stealing their designs that their security requirements are on a par with the CIA. They're *that* paranoid."

"Mm," he murmured in her ear. "And they should be."

"Exactly. And Uncle Abbas thinks the only person who can help him is someone as sharp as you. He told me how pleased he's been with your other work."

"I'd be happy to help. What's he want?"

"He says he needs the top-of-the-line algorithm that you told me about a few weeks ago…the one which you said is so unbreakable because of its complexity. You said something about it coming from, ahhh…what did you call it? Oh, yes, 'the Fort.' That's what he needs."

Upon hearing that, Stan sat up in bed. "But, babe that…that…that's impossible. I can't give him that. It's highly classified. I could lose my job or go to jail. The other stuff was all unclassified algorithms for commercial protection. Ask me anything else. Please."

Leila looked at him and a tear streaked down her cheek. "I told him that already, but….oh, forget it. I'll just tell him that we can't help him. I'll…I'll… God, I don't know what I'll do. Maybe I should just go back to Iran, where life is simpler, so I don't have to face him. I owe him so much!" She turned over in the bed away from him, softly weeping.

Stan looked at her dismally, silent for a minute. "This contract is for a U.S. defense company?"

Leila turned back to him slowly and wiped her eyes. "Of course. I wouldn't ask you if it weren't. He just needs a copy of that one key algorithm. Nothing else. He already has a clearance, and he just needs a little kick-start to design his own algorithm. It won't look anything like yours by the time he modifies it."

She slowly stroked him. He realized his heart was racing.

"But if you don't think you can do it," she said, "it's OK. I'll…I'll do something else. Somehow. I just…I just thought we could help him…that's all. You know I wouldn't want to ever do anything that would hurt you." She sniffed.

"No, no, I don't think that would hurt anything. We're just talking about protecting an American defense company. It's all for national security, right?"

She squeezed him and her voice broke. "Oh Stan, you're truly a hero. My hero. Thank you, thank you, thank you."

And with that, she slid her hands around his thighs and drew him in.

CHAPTER 14

◇◇◇

Gabriel to Miles

CIA Headquarters

Leopard Message # 12

Hello Friends, Things continue to get weirder and weirder here. In my previous messages, I mentioned that I have been asked to do criticality calculations for highly enriched uranium in quantities far exceeding research amounts but not yet in quantities for a weapon. Please note that I haven't yet physically seen the sixty kilos of HEU that I had originally reported, but I continue to see things, which tell me that this is not purely peaceful nuclear energy research. For one thing, I heard that the Tabatabai brothers are involved. You probably don't know them, but they are a genius nuclear physicist and a very talented materials scientist.

Daoud Tabatabai, is a math and physics prodigy who stunned his professors at Sharif University of Technology (our best technical school) with his amazing abilities. Some say he is another Einstein or Hawking, only smarter than both of them put together. His older brother, Majid, also is brilliant and has pioneered new applications of nanotechnology for super strong materials. Both are involved in this classified program, about which I have heard only whispers and inferences. Why would we need these two specialized scientists for regular centrifuge uranium enrichment and peaceful nuclear power production? Those are fairly straightforward concepts already well developed, and we've imported (bought or stolen) most of the technology from the Pakistanis and the Russians.

Secondly, security is extremely tight and closely guarded by IRGC cadre. These are mean motherfuckers, if you know what I mean. Their boss General Alborzi is a royal asshole who is utterly ruthless. He is also the nephew of the Supreme Leader and is completely ego driven. I have heard that you never want to be on his bad side. I never intend to be there, that's for damn sure. He scares me and everyone else.

As far as I can tell, and consistent with my earlier reports, we have completely abandoned all of our old AEOI research sites and even the previously off-limits military sites. I believe I sent you a list of those sites – at least the ones I know about. My prediction: Search as they may, the IAEA inspectors will find nothing or next to nothing. They will then issue us a clean bill of health. Sounds good if you accept that result at face value. I don't. You can be sure that the first time I have hard evidence of duplicity that you will know as soon as possible. I think this is inevitable.

Here's a tidbit for you. I have heard that we are transferring soon to a new secure site – maybe forty or fifty miles from here. Someone said to bring warm clothing. And a mining helmet. Why do we need a new secure site if everything is aboveboard and declared openly? Why the new classified program at a secure site? For nuclear energy production? I don't think so.

I'm playing "Kind of Blue" here as I type this. Mellow. Very mellow. Wish you were here to hear it with me. Better yet, I wish I were there with you and our lady friend at Le Chat Noir. Many thanks again for the generous gift. I think of you every single day.

Best wishes to Miles from Gabriel

Leopard's weekly clandestine messages filled Lane with both satisfaction and concern. Satisfaction because his excellent reporting was being validated for the most part by reporting from Condor, another source. Although the two assets' reporting tracked closely regarding objective facts on the ground, there were differences in perspective, which was to be expected from separate sources, and a complete difference in tone.

The latter concerned Lane enough that he decided to phone Lacy on her secure line at Lawrence Livermore to discuss it. Since Geneva, the two had seen each other as often as an East Coast-West Coast romance would permit, which wasn't a lot, but they phoned and texted each other almost daily from their personal cell phones. This secure call, however, would have to remain purely professional because it could be monitored. Lane felt no need to conceal his relationship with Lacy, but this matter was purely business and he wanted her advice. Although it might sound sexist, he firmly believed that a woman could pick up nuance better than a man in communications.

And Lacy also knew Leopard better than anyone other than himself.

After some innocuous chit chat, Lane asked, "Have you seen Leopard's latest reporting? And have you compared it to Condor's? Do you see a difference?"

"Well, yeah, I do. They seem to track with one another but…but there's a definite difference in tone. Is that what you mean?"

"Exactly. Condor's reporting is almost always a dry, matter of fact description of how Iran is adhering to the nuclear agreement. Sure, he sometimes adds some humorous asides, but they always support the conclusion that Iran is not violating the various protocols it signed. And sometimes, he throws in a little tidbit about earlier Iranian efforts to bypass sanctions in order to acquire embargoed nuclear technology, but they're all historical – interesting but not earth shattering.

"Leopard's reporting, on the other hand, is crammed with his doubts and suspicions about Iran's real intentions, plus there are his biting criticisms of the mullahs and their supporters."

Lacy said, "I think I see where you're going with this. I've noticed a big difference in the raw covert communications that we've gotten from Leopard and the finished intel product."

Lane said, "Right. It really pisses me off because few of Leopard's doubts and none of his colorful and derogatory witticisms make it into the finished intelligence reports that are disseminated to the Intelligence Community and the White House. But our Chief of CP Reports, Belinda Ballard, favors a dry 'just the facts' approach, not what she calls 'colorful opinions and rank speculation.' Frankly, I think this is a huge mistake."

Lacy agreed. "The intel is being bleached and all of the color removed. That's not smart."

Lane laughed with a bitter note in his voice. "Not only is it not smart, it could be disastrous."

CHAPTER 15

◇◇◇

IAEA Inspections

Military Compound, Northern Iran

The six men in the lab coats of the Atomic Energy Organization of Iran watched impassively as the ten IAEA inspectors completed their inspection of the previously off-limits military site a few miles northwest of Tehran. The inspectors had scraped and wiped and prodded all day long and found little to report. In addition to radiation counters, they had little plastic sacks of soil samples, which looked remarkably like bags of dog poop, as if they'd all just been walking their dogs in a city park. After two weeks in Iran, they were tired and frustrated and frankly impatient to get back to their Tehran hotel for dinner even if there was no liquor.

Only one of the six Iranian AEOI observers was in fact a real scientist. The rest were IRGC intelligence officers assigned to monitor these IAEA inspectors and ensure that nothing – absolutely nothing – gave the slightest hint of Project Zulfiqar. So far, so good. The IAEA inspectors, who were the United Nations' nuclear police, bumbled about like the Keystone Cops, found squat, and clocked out promptly at five pm.

The IAEA team leader, an acerbic Japanese nuclear engineer who took his job seriously but who was sick of this country and this inspection, signaled to the one legitimate AEOI scientist that they were satisfied, and they prepared to leave in their little white minibus. Something bothered the team leader about this two-week series of inspections, but he couldn't quite put his finger on it. Things seemed stage-managed like a movie set. The Iranians had left nothing glaringly obvious on site, and the inspector knew that their samples and swipes would prove unremarkable.

And what to make of the five goons in AEOI coats who clearly couldn't tell a Roentgen from a Rottweiler? Oh well. Another day for world peace and no nuclear weapons. He'd be on a plane for Tokyo tomorrow in Business Class, and he thought of the glass or two (or three) of champagne he would have as soon as they left Iranian airspace. God, he hated it here.

As the little white minibus pulled out of the compound, the five IRGC officers looked at one another and laughed. Back at the reception building locker room, they changed into their Lar National Park uniforms and returned to their real jobs at the intelligence and security office of the Zulfiqar facility on the northeast side of Mt. Damavand. They joked about the feckless nature of the inspections and the mounting frustration of the inspection team at finding nothing amiss. They were all agreed, however, that the attractive thirty-five-year-old female French nuclear inspector with the large breasts was someone they would all like to inspect privately.

The leader, a forty-two-year-old IRGC major, who had visited Yellowstone National Park as a child, put on his park ranger garb, lowered his voice an octave or two, and in a fair imitation of Smokey Bear, said, "Remember kids, only you can prevent nuclear weapons!"

They all laughed when the Major explained the American context of the joke, but a young Captain nervously cautioned that he did not think General Alborzi had a sense of humor and maybe they should tread lightly. The Major snorted and said, "Ah, fuck him if he can't take a joke!"

CHAPTER 16

◇◇◇

Mullah Madness

IRGC Security Office, Project Zulfiqar

"Yes, fuck me indeed!" General Alborzi sat back from the large flat screen TV monitor with its remote surveillance camera and audio feed. He thought that perhaps he should teach the major a lesson in humor. He then resumed playing the computer game on his iPad Pro and laughed uproariously at the images on his high-resolution screen. Now, who didn't have a sense of humor? Come on. Really, this was too much!

The game, "Mullah Madness," depicted various long-bearded mullahs in turbans and on prayer rugs running across the screen while Alborzi manipulated the cursor and tried to zap them with lightning bolts from Allah. When struck, their turbans and prayer beads flew, their beards fell out, and they squealed like baby pigs as they fell in a writhing heap. The object was to see how many of the little fuckers you could zap in a given time period. It was addictive as hell. One of the little shits actually resembled his uncle – vacant stare and all. Alborzi particularly enjoyed zapping him. Zap, zap, zap!

He had received this contraband as a result of a Basij raid on the University of Tehran's computer club. The Basij was renowned for being a paramilitary voluntary militia subordinate to the IRGC. They originally drew their fame from the fanatical way members would form human-wave attacks against entrenched Iraqi enemy positions, often unarmed and suffering tens of thousands of casualties in the '80s during the Iran-Iraq War.

That and they were used to clear minefields for the regular army by walking hand to hand across them. Either was a rapid path to instant martyrdom. Nowadays, however, they were more likely to be used to suppress student riots or demonstrations and to enforce public morality and piety.

This was all a crock of shit in most people's opinion. In Alborzi's view, the Basij were royal pains in the ass, but they could be useful from time to time if channeled properly. Even if you couldn't send them across minefields, thereby ridding Iran simultaneously of Basij and mines, they occasionally stumbled upon something useful.

In this case, they brought him this amusing little piece of blasphemy.

Alborzi made sure that the Basij had also arrested the computer game's creator, a hapless twenty-five-year-old student, and ordered him held in Evin Prison. He also made sure that he had the source code to the game in order to prevent its replication inside Iran, for "public morality purposes." Instead, he intended to contact a computer game producer in Taiwan to mass-produce the game. Demand was evidently quite heavy around university and high school campuses, and the game could command a high premium in other quarters as well – probably in parts of the Iranian Majlis or parliament and certainly down in the bazaar. This could be an amusing little gold mine.

Alborzi also intended to have a GPS device built into the game in case geo-locating its owners proved useful in the long run. Using that feature, one could make money on the front end and the back end -- a virtuous cycle with Alborzi the winner at each turn.

Although Alborzi had briefly considered employing the imprisoned game creator as his production engineer, this idea turned out to be as short-lived as the game creator himself. Oh well, there are always more computer specialists around. Alborzi contented himself with zapping his uncle's stupid looking avatar another dozen times.

CHAPTER 17

◇◇◇

Ali's Sword

Leopard Message # 28

Hello Friends, The pace is picking up around here with a lot to report. As I predicted, the IAEA inspectors found nothing of consequence, which had not already been declared by Iran. Did you really think it would be otherwise? They only found what we wanted them to find. It was kind of like the Easter egg hunt on the White House lawn. What they did not find was the location of my new facility, which is the location of Project Zulfiqar. (Quick lesson for you in Shi'a symbolism: Zulfiqar was the double-bladed sword that Muhammad gave to his cousin Ali and therefore is of special significance to Shi'a Muslims.)

General Alborzi, our project head, is a devious son of a bitch, but I must hand it to him. In picking the new location of our facility, he has truly outdone himself. You would never suspect or find this place in a hundred years. I could keep you in suspense and tease you with hints but I won't do that. So, curtain number three please, Monty! Ha!

Project Zulfiqar is in Lar National Park on the eastern slope of Mt. Damavand, about forty-five miles from Tehran. It's a national symbol of Iran, so I guess the location is fitting. The truly clever thing is that he located our facility inside an abandoned sulfur mine, deep underground. I cannot give you the precise GPS coordinates of the entrance because we are searched before and after work on a random basis, but we are housed in a special dormitory during the week. It is located in a small village called Gazaneh just off of the Haraz Road (Highway 77) which comes from Tehran and skirts the eastern edge of the park and goes north all the way to the Caspian Sea. Our dorm is less than a fifteen-minute drive from the entrance of the facility. I seriously doubt that your overhead systems could spot it because of the trees and foliage near the mine entrance, so I will try to get a more precise location for you.

I have met the Tabatabai brothers and frankly I like them. They are extremely bright, as I had heard, but also genuinely modest in their interactions with the rest of the technical staff and pleasant to be around. I cannot fathom why they would work for Alborzi. Majid, the older brother, actually did graduate school at U.C. Berkeley, but we didn't overlap and my field was different. Still, it's kind of bizarre that two scientists in the Iranian nuclear program are Berkeley alums. Go Cal! The brothers are rather quiet and we don't discuss work because everything here is on a "strict need to know basis." And as far as they are concerned, I guess I don't need to know. But I do need to know, and I will find out.

You are probably wondering why I have not yet disclosed the purpose of Project Zulfiqar. That's because I still don't know, although I strongly suspect it is nuclear weapons related. Just a hunch. Why this much secrecy otherwise? And why the Tabatabai brothers? I just do my criticality calculations, which still seem rather routine and have not yet seen any reference to the 60Kg of HEU, but I remain alert.

Oh, I almost forgot to mention something kind of strange about General Alborzi. The last few times I have walked into his office, I've noticed him softly humming and nodding his head to the beat of an old rock and roll tune and grinning ear to ear. I haven't recognized the tune yet, but I have a phonographic memory. I'll let you know when I figure it out. It could be nothing at all.

I burned several of my Miles Davis CD's to an iPod and have been listening to them at night in my dorm room. Currently, I'm listening to the "Milestones" album, but I'm back at home in Tehran. I thought it appropriate, considering our last night in Geneva. I'm grooving on "Two Bass Hit" as

I type this message. Don't worry about my security. I only send you messages when I'm home on weekends in Tehran.

Best wishes to Miles from Gabriel

CHAPTER 18

◇◇◇

Who will Guard the Guardians?

California Cloud Computing

Lights blinked but the only sound was that of the ever-present air conditioner hum. Stan stood in front of the server bank with the small thumb drive Leila had given him clutched tightly in his fist. He fingered its plastic surface and polished steel end and thought of her and what she meant to him: everything. He looked at the strategically mounted cameras monitoring the space 24 hours a day, seven days a week. They would have made him nervous, except that he had programmed them and controlled them. What they recorded could be changed to fit whatever reality he wanted, their time stamps suitably altered. So, that didn't bother him. But something did. He couldn't quite put his finger on it. This really should be okay. He had reasoned this out and it was fine…wasn't it?

For some reason, a small voice in the back of his head, from his Latin class in 11th grade, intoned the Roman poet Juvenal's crucial question: *Quis custodiet ipsos custodes?* Who will guard the guardians themselves?

How else should he respond to Big John and his hypocrisy. What an asshole. Screwing little college interns and screwing Stan out of his family-friendly leave. Not paying him what he was worth when it was his efforts that had brought them the Agency account. As far as he was concerned, it was time to even the accounts with a little covert compensation. It was his due. This betrayal was John's betrayal. Fuck him. Fuck them all.

Not that that what he was doing was wrong. He was simply copying one algorithm. Just one. For a cleared U.S. defense contractor. And it meant so much to Leila. What else really mattered in life? Sweet Leila. Sweet sensual Leila. Sweet sensual sexy Leila.

The small cautionary voice inside Stan went silent, and he pushed the thumb drive into the now unblocked receptacle and began the download.

CHAPTER 19

◇◇◇

Ivy King 11/16/1952

University of California, Berkeley

The subject of the email caught his attention. Otherwise, he would have probably deleted it without opening. Dr. Rand McKeown received about three or four dozen emails a day from his physics students, other faculty, and of course the ever-loving administration, not to mention a fair number from colleagues in other physics labs domestic and abroad. That, however, was just the tip of the iceberg. On top of that were many dozens more from professional associations and publications, headhunters, hucksters, touts and just plain commercial spam. He was getting tired of filtering through the ninety percent in his inbox that was pure rubbish, and his finger almost systematically hit the delete button on most. But this one was different. The subject simply read "Ivy King 11/16/52."

To most people, that would be gibberish. But not to Dr. McKeown. He had spent the early years of his career at Lawrence Livermore National Laboratory's renowned B Division working on designing nuclear weapon "primaries" -- the first stage of a multi-stage thermonuclear weapon. In essence, you needed a nuclear bomb to set off a more powerful nuclear bomb. Primaries typically consisted of highly enriched uranium, plutonium or a mixture of the two, and while terribly powerful and destructive by themselves (they are nuclear bombs after all), they're eclipsed by the secondary and sometimes tertiary stages, which are triggered by the intense x-ray energy of the primary. The resulting thermonuclear explosion could be well in excess of a thousand times more powerful than the primary yield of the initial nuclear explosion. One could therefore consider the primary to be a nasty but necessary explosive fuse that opened the gate to Hell itself.

As a designer of primaries, Dr. McKeown was well acquainted with the Ivy King nuclear test, which was exploded on November 16, 1952 at Enewetak Atoll in the South Pacific. It was the largest pure HEU fission device ever detonated, producing more than 500 kilotons upon detonation. It was also the date he was born, which made it even more significant to McKeown. Maybe that's why he had gone into nuclear weapons work. At least that's what he told his graduate students in the seminars, which he had taught at Berkeley since the mid-'80's on a part time basis and now full time after retirement from the Lab.

McKeown opened the email and read its few lines.

"Greetings Dr. McKeown, I hope this note finds you well and that you are continuing your wonderful teaching at Berkeley as well as your important work at LLNL. I have some most important information to convey to you but am sensitive to your equities as well as my own. Therefore, I have taken the liberty of encrypting the attachment and the key is to be found in our hobby at position M12, which I recall stood as the largest such number for more than 75 years. I believe this will be as clear to you as it was to Lucas. Plug that number in as the variable in the formula from your lesson on April 22, 1987. Best wishes, Your Devoted Admirer"

McKeown reflected briefly on this and set it aside. He went on in his inbox to an email marked "Urgent" from the chairman of the department. He could not recall the last time he had received an email from this man that was not marked "urgent" or "most urgent" or (horrors!) "terribly urgent." Even as he read the chairman's note, however, he considered the puzzle from the other email, his mind processing it subconsciously as he read the chairman's latest pontificating drivel. When he could stand it no more, he went back to the mystery note.

He looked at the last two lines and its clues. He thought about this for only a second or two because it was so obvious. Since the early 1980's, one of McKeown's hobbies had been working on finding Mersenne prime numbers – a rare hobby that he shared with a few of his graduate students. This esoteric pass-time among physicists and mathematicians deals with a special category of prime numbers. Currently, there are only 49 known Mersenne primes including the largest known prime number, which has more than twenty-two million digits. Nowadays, math geniuses searched for ever-larger Mersenne primes, using sophisticated computers for the calculations.

Referring to a chart he had in his desk, he found M12, which is the 12th smallest Mersenne prime, which was 2 to the 127th power minus 1. The result was a prime number 39 digits long discovered by French mathematician Edouard Lucas in 1876. Amazingly, this number had stood as the largest Mersenne prime until 1952 – again the year of McKeown's birth.

Intrigued now, McKeown quickly did the math on his computer and recorded the 39 digit number of the Mersenne prime. He then looked at his old daybooks on his shelf and found his lesson plan for April 22, 1987. He saw the formula, which they had discussed that day and entered the entire numerical expression along with M12 as the variable into the encryption key of the attachment. He pressed "Enter." *Voila!* The attachment opened. McKeown smiled in satisfaction as the words appeared. He felt like a codebreaker.

He stopped smiling as he read the decrypted contents.

Hello Dr. McKeown, If you are reading this document then I know that not only did my subject line catch your attention but also my hints regarding its encryption. The subject line came to me as I remembered your comment one day in a lecture about your birth date being identical to the date of the Ivy King test. Plus, I recalled your affinity for Mersenne primes and figured you would easily crack the code.

I was one of your graduate students from 1984-88 but you will pardon me if I am a bit coy regarding my identity because what I am about to tell you could sign my death warrant were I to be discovered. It would also mean a noose for my brother. You can easily find my name among your graduate students. Even though there were four or five of us from Iran in your department in those years, I was the only one who shared your passion for Mersenne primes. I celebrated with you and a couple of other post-docs on January 29, 1988, when Mersenne prime number M29 was discovered.

You may recall that I specialized in solid-state physics and materials science. Obviously, this field has advanced greatly since the mid to late 1980's, even here in Iran. I currently specialize in nanomaterials. You once said that I was a math prodigy, a gracious comment which I feasted upon like a rich dessert for days afterward. But my younger brother is much more talented than I am. In addition to being an exceptional mathematician, my brother is a specialist in nuclear physics and would surely win a Nobel Prize were his work known in the west. I am writing on behalf of both of us and I ask you to treat this information with extreme discretion. You may share it with people who need the information, but please be careful.

I will not beat around the bush any further. My brother and I and a few other Iranian specialists have designed a nuclear weapon, which employs only fission as Ivy King did, but which is two to three times more powerful. Yes, this nuclear weapon has a projected yield of one to 1.5 megatons but has approximately the same sixty kilograms of HEU as Ivy King had. You may think that this is impossible to have this degree of extreme fission efficiency or that such an advanced nuclear weapon could be designed in Iran, but I can assure you that my brother's calculations are probably correct.

I must confess that I personally do not understand my brother's concept of neutron phasing and how it utilizes an advanced extension of quantum entanglement except on the most superficial level. My own contribution was limited to the design of the tamper, which provides extra yield due to its density and the extreme strength of its uranium nanostructure lattice. But the increase is only a token amount compared to his revolutionary concept that produces most of the yield. I have attached a summary of his papers and design calculations as well as my tamper design so that you and your colleagues at Lawrence Livermore may see for yourselves.

Now, you may ask why I am telling you this. It is because the new man in charge of this Project Zulfiqar is IRGC General Masud Alborzi. If his surname sounds familiar, it is because he is the nephew of our new

Supreme Leader. My brother and I have known him since childhood and he is extremely charismatic and completely ruthless. He is an opportunist of the first rank. Since he was a child, Alborzi has ridden his uncle's coattails. Now, that his uncle is Supreme Leader, his ambition and arrogance know no limits.

General Alborzi uses religion only for his own ends. He has threatened my brother because he is gay. Not that Alborzi abhors homosexuality but simply as a matter of blackmail. We are certain that he will arrest my brother once he knows the weapon is completed so as to prevent any embarrassment to the project and Alborzi personally. We have not yet told him or the other scientists what the true expected yield of the Zulfiqar device is. We have led them to believe that this design is a simple improvement on the design we obtained from the Pakistanis, which would be on the order of 15 kilotons, similar to Little Boy in 1945. Instead, as I noted above, my brother believes it will be as much as a hundred times greater because of its efficiency. Why the deception? Because we do not believe we can trust such a powerful weapon to a man – a demon – such as Alborzi. Frankly, he should not control a nuclear weapon with any yield, much less one equivalent to a sizable thermonuclear bomb.

So, why did we develop such a devastating weapon in the first place? My brother and I began designing this weapon in order to stretch the scientific boundaries of the possible. We had no intention ever to use it. Admittedly, we were tremendously naïve, indeed foolish. Nevertheless, we might still be devoted to our work were it not for the appointment of General Alborzi as head of Project Zulfiqar. We are patriotic Iranians, but Alborzi is no patriot. We fear not only for our lives but also for the lives of many others if he thinks it in his interests to use this nuclear device. He must be stopped.

Unfortunately, the computer-aided design work is completed and has already been submitted to the engineering staff to refine and construct. I don't believe that we can safely alter the design at this point, but it will likely take the engineers close to a year to produce it. We can occasionally introduce delays, but we must tread carefully because there are other smart scientists involved in the project.

Our secret lab is located in Lar National Park inside a refurbished, abandoned sulfur mine on the side of Mount Damavand, about 45 miles northeast of Tehran. Ironically, our father used to work in this mine. This covert location has the advantage of being underground and with the cover of the national park. There are no visible guns, gates and guards to tip off foreign intelligence services or leave telltale signs for their satellites. Nevertheless, the site is highly secure.

I have heard that we have sufficient HEU for four such weapons, and I understand that there may be more HEU available. I'm not sure of its origin but suspect it was Russian. Iran's agreement with the West to limit our centrifuge enrichment program was quite simply a ruse to end sanctions. In fact, we don't need the indigenous highly enriched uranium produced from those centrifuges.

I'm sure you have many questions and we will try to answer whatever we can. It is imperative that General Alborzi be stopped. You may communicate with me at this email address, which is routed through several proxy servers outside of Iran, but I implore you to use encryption. My suggestion for your response is an algorithm involving M13 and the formula used to decrypt this email. After that, we can develop other means to securely encrypt our messages.

Best wishes, Your Student

Dr. McKeown looked up from the decrypted email and took his glasses off. He leaned back in his desk chair and gazed at the ceiling, deep in thought for more than a minute. His hand trembled slightly as he reached for an old list of graduate students from the mid-'80's, but he already knew who his anonymous correspondent was. How could he ever forget the brilliant Majid Tabatabai? Because of this, he knew this email had the distinct ring of a terrible truth. He also knew that he must contact Livermore's B Division with all possible speed.

CHAPTER 20

◇◇◇

Drop Shields!

IRGC Office of Intelligence North Tehran

Dr. Dmitri Grishin sat to the left of General Alborzi in the General's "War Room" and watched the monitor closely on the large screen digital receiver. He smiled with satisfaction as Alborzi described the efforts of his agents in California: the patience in selecting the target by sifting through social media, the long careful development, the dangling of the bait, the playing of the fish, setting the hook, and finally the landing.

Grishin nodded. "Colonel Cherkashin, would be so proud of you, my dear General. You have learned his lessons well."

Alborzi laughed too and said he was grateful for the Russian service's technical assistance on this joint project. The thumb drive his operative used as the Trojan horse had a specially designed Russian payload, which was injected into 3C's compartmented sectors at the moment their target deployed it. It would worm its way into the kernel at the core of the operating system and could not be overwritten or deleted. This was the ultimate backdoor -- or maybe it was more of a front door. Either way, the only way for 3C to get rid of it would be to yank every CPU out of the server farm and dump them all in a landfill. Until then, Tehran and Moscow could remotely and covertly access everything inside of 3C, which Grishin now jokingly referred to as 'Chekist Cloud Computing," the Russian word "Cheka" being the acronym of the original name for Soviet intelligence.

Alborzi redirected his attention to the large flat screen television monitor. "I believe our technicians and yours have just made contact with their system."

On the screen were streams of random seeming letters and digits, pure encryption. Nothing intelligible. Alborzi asked Grishin if he wished to have the pleasure. Grishin responded no, that Alborzi should have the honor, as it was his agents who made it possible. "We helped technically but your people took the risk and got the job done. Please, be my guest."

Alborzi nodded, sat up straight and, mimicking the old television series "Star Trek," he pushed the button on the controller in his hand at the same time he said, "Drop shields."

Immediately, plain-text files of classified CIA cables filled the screen. The two intelligence officers sat mesmerized.

PART 3

CHAPTER 1

◇◇◇

McKeown and the Muskrats

B Division, Lawrence Livermore National Laboratory

Dr. McKeown's normal commute from Berkeley to Lawrence Livermore would have taken him a little under an hour without traffic. Today, however, he was speeding along in his Tesla, his one indulgence, and he reached the Lab in only forty minutes. This might have been a new land speed record on I-580 but he truly didn't care. He called several B Division colleagues in route and noted that it was imperative that they see him immediately to discuss something sensitive. Fortunately, he still had a Lawrence Livermore badge and all of his security clearances were intact so that he could do some occasional consulting for the lab. He breezed in through West Gate, pausing only long enough for the guard to touch his badge and wish him a good day. All six physicists were waiting for him in the secure conference room when he jogged in from the parking lot, breathing hard not from exertion but excitement and concern.

In a most unscholarly fashion, McKeown made a quick summary presentation of the communication he had just received from Iran as well as Majid's background, and then he lay Majid's brother's calculations and formulae before them. The six weapons designers looked at one another and then at the papers before them, which they handled gingerly.

Dr. Peter Muskie, who was the B Division project leader on Livermore's latest design submission to the Department of Energy and who was every bit as arrogant as his professional reputation allowed, was openly skeptical. "Rand, my learned friend, this frankly sounds like so much bullshit from this...this Iranian. 'Neutron phasing' sounds like voodoo – I've never heard of it and I think I would have! Sounds like something from a bad 'Star Trek' episode. And to mix this up with 'quantum entanglement' from quantum mechanics turns the voodoo into, well, doodoo, if you ask me."

Two of the other younger designers, who worked for Muskie, laughed.

Even physicists have their lickspittles, thought McKeown.

"Majid said it was an 'advanced extension of quantum entanglement' not quantum entanglement as we know it, and he invited us to run the calculations ourselves," said McKeown, a bit defensively. Dueling mentally with Muskie in front of an audience of other designers was like dancing in mud. Any way you looked at it, you were going to get muck and slime on you.

Muskie, smelling an opportunity to act like the brilliant prick that he was in front of a captive audience, quickly rejoined, "Look, I know you were this man's advisor thirty years ago, and he may be brilliant, but his country is utterly incapable of producing a pure fission weapon that is two or three times more powerful than the one Ted Taylor designed in 1952. With only 60kg of HEU, you know that Ivy King is pretty much the limit for a pure fission weapon. Maybe we could get a bit more out of it today, but Iran? Come on! That claim of his is crap and I can't believe you've bought into it. According to the intel I've seen, not only don't they have the 60kg of HEU, I seriously doubt they could produce a yield that is one percent of Ivy King's even if they did. You're talking about a level of sophistication in weapons design that they simply don't have. Finito. End of story."

McKeown shook his head. "The chances of this design being right may be remote; maybe it's a crock of shit. But let's not forget that there were plenty of disputed scientific theories like a sun-centric solar system, a round Earth, evolution, black holes etc that turned out to be 100% true."

Muskie said, "Yes, we always like to cite poor Galileo as a scientist wronged. Of course that was, let's see...I think maybe four centuries ago. And your other examples go back centuries or many decades. This is the 21st Century, for cryin' out loud."

McKeown refused to back off. "You want a much more recent example? OK, remember how Linus Pauling and a bunch of other eminent scientists ridiculed Dan Shechtman, who discovered quasicrystals. That poor guy went through living hell. Finally, Shechtman was vindicated with the Nobel Prize in 2011."

Dr. Robert Carlton, a talented weapons designer from Texas, who still wore cowboy boots daily to the lab, interjected in a conciliatory manner, "I don't see how it would hurt to run these formulae on Sequoia. The Persians were a much further advanced civilization than ours at one time. They were conquering most of the known world while we still wearing animal skins and living in mud huts. Who's to say who'll make breakthroughs? Frankly, I tend to share your skepticism, but Sequoia will help us sort this out."

Livermore's Sequoia was the world's third fastest supercomputer and capable of the intricate calculations required for advanced nuclear weapons design and simulation. Getting time allotted on Sequoia, however, was not a simple matter. Sometimes the queue could be months long.

Muskie shrugged and said, "If you want to waste your computer time, please proceed. I've got far better things to do with my precious time."

Carlton responded, "Actually, Rand has piqued my curiosity and I want to probe this a bit. I do have some time reserved on Sequoia in the next week, and I'd be happy to help Rand run some of these. Maybe they'll teach some old weapons designers some new tricks. You never know."

Rand looked gratefully at Carlton and nodded his thanks. Muskie, trailed by his two acolytes, known in B Division as the "Muskrats," all made their exit, shaking their heads in synch as if controlled by a single puppeteer. The other two weapons designers hung around and poked through the papers a little, eyes carefully averted. They had studiously avoided getting drawn into the verbal jousting because Muskie was a project leader and had his fingers in their funding. Clearly, though, they thought the material seemed interesting.

"Whatever comes of this," said Carlton, "I'd suggest we drop by the Counterintelligence Office and also call on our new FBI Special Agent in the Lab, Lacy Merrill. I don't think you've met her yet, but you'll like her. She's just arrived from some special duty assignment at the nuclear negotiations in Geneva."

Rand agreed. "I was thinking the same thing. Even if the design is flawed, Majid's an incredible source, and I could use some guidance on how to respond. Let's go."

His warm hands described a slow sensuous curve down the sides of her neck, barely touching her at times, descending lightly between her breasts in a teasing gesture ever so lightly flicking his nails against her nipples, then past her belly and gently brushing the soft inner surface of her thighs, barely whisking against the fine down almost like a butterfly flirting with a flower. His fingers danced along her skin with a deliberate almost languorous rhythm. It was ecstasy as they brushed like a feather against her with that easy sure touch. Her breath came in sharp intakes. Lane was one of those rare men whose sense of pleasure derived as much or more from her delight than his own. That slow caress, that easy touch....

Suddenly, a sharp knock on the door brought Lacy out of her reverie. She opened her eyes and managed weakly, "Yes, just a minute please." She stood up, her face flushed with the thoughts of what Lane had been doing in her fantasy, which had been all so real only a few months earlier in Geneva. She had to compose herself in short order and welcome her guests. The Bureau was not paying her to indulge in daydreams.

Dr. Robert Carlton came in with a pleasant looking man in his mid to late sixties whom he identified as Dr. Rand McKeown from B Division. They showed her the communications from Iran and McKeown explained the background. The part about the IRGC jumped out at her and her attention was riveted. McKeown told her about Majid Tabatabai and tried to explain the so-called new weapons design to the best of his ability but stressed that this part of the message was controversial.

"We're going to run some calculations on Sequoia next week but it may take us a while to see if these have real merit or not," added Carlton. "We have some real doubts but the interesting part is that they claim to have sufficient HEU for four weapons and are working on a weapon design in a secret facility. This flies straight in the face of what we have been hearing in the intel."

As she reviewed the details, Lacy immediately thought of her friend and mentor Bette DiSanti at FBI headquarters. Bette was the senior analyst in the WMD Directorate and a great source of both knowledge and wisdom (there was a difference as Lacy discovered) about Bureau ways and about WMD. The Special Agents who worked with Bette only half-jokingly said that when she came into the room, the average IQ went up fifty points. She awed them and kind of scared them. They might be packing Glocks but Bette was packing Bette – a sharp mind and a sharper tongue. And no bulletproof vest would stop her.

Lacy decided to send the information at once via secure fax to Bette. She would know what to do. And she'd be willing to cut through any Bureau bullshit that got in the way. Like a hot knife through butter. In fact, Bette's nickname in the Bureau was "Bette the Blade." Actually, that was the polite nickname. Others called her "Bette the Bitch" and "Bette the Ballbuster," although not within earshot. Not that it mattered to her. Bette had been heard to say that she didn't give a shit how you referred to her as long as you knew how to spell and pronounce "Bette" correctly. She claimed that she and Bette Midler (same pronunciation, please), to whom she bore some passing resemblance, at least in temperament, had the same cross to bear, living among dimwits.

When Bette received the information from Lacy, she was noshing on reheated linguine with meatballs in homemade marinara sauce for lunch in her office at FBI HQS. She glanced at the fax casually as she ate but her attention was focused more on how she planned to "fix" an errant Supervisory Special Agent's attitude about trying to reduce her WMD analytical budget once again in spite of her having explained to him in very small words and very simple terms that even an imbecile such as he could understand that her budget, which dealt with WEAPONS OF MASS DESTRUCTION, could not fucking be further reduced without endangering the country. End of story. What about that couldn't his little pea brain understand?

Bette went back to the secure fax from Lacy and the accompanying description of her meeting with Drs. Carlton and McKeown. She felt that there was something to this. She had immense respect for Lacy, whom she considered a hero from the Riding Dead shoot-out. But she was also tremendously impressed with the two Livermore scientists, whom she had met on a couple of occasions when she sought expertise on cases of attempted illicit nuclear technology acquisitions in the U.S. by foreign powers through cut-outs and subterfuge. She always found their guidance on-the-mark and neither alarmist nor dismissive. This message from McKeown's former graduate student sounded serious, and the fact that these two Livermore weapons designers did not laugh at it gave her further pause.

Accordingly, she put her thoughts of what she planned to do to the nitwit SSA messing with her budget in her mental file drawer marked "Fools to be Dealt With." This file had unfortunately been growing at a prodigious rate as of late.

So many fools, so little time.

Bette knew she needed to contact the counterproliferation experts at CIA who followed the Iranian nuclear program. They had much greater depth in these nuclear matters than the Bureau and if this case were to go forward, the Agency would have to be brought in as a partner in a joint operation due to the scientists' location in Iran. She dialed the secure phone of Lacy's boss, the Special Agent in Charge in San Francisco, and then she phoned Lacy. Everyone agreed that Lacy and the Livermore designers should hop on the next flight to Washington

CHAPTER 2

◇◇◇

Serious Shit

Leopard Message # 31

Hello Friends, Hold onto your hats but I have a news flash! I'm sorry I could not transmit this sooner but I am only now back in my flat in Tehran over the weekend. Five days ago, I was brought new designs to calculate criticality safety, and I can now say without reservation that Project Zulfiqar involves nuclear weapons. Factors such as the shape of the material, its size and mass, reflectivity of surrounding materials, and naturally the degree of enrichment has to be presented to me so that I can do my work properly or a criticality accident could easily occur. That would be disastrous and the resulting radiation could kill people even if a nuclear detonation did not occur. I guess my security vetting either has promoted me to the inner circle of trust or they've reached a stage of design and testing where they can't proceed without my assistance. Probably it's the latter. Fear of being lethally irradiated and having their hair fall out and their balls shrivel up may have focused their minds and caused them to accelerate my vetting. I'll take whatever I can get.

In any case, I can now tell you without fear of contradiction that the goal of Project Zulfiqar is a nuclear weapon. No one has said "nuclear weapons" to me explicitly, but the designs I've seen are unambiguous. Bear in mind that I'm not a nuclear weapons designer, but I sure as hell know what these damn things look like from my studies in graduate school and the open literature depictions of the geometries of the fissile material, which make up the physics package. You don't keep 90 percent HEU in these amounts and shapes for peaceful nuclear power production. This conclusion scares the hell out of me. Also, it reinforces my reasons for working with you. I have no regrets. This is serious shit.

I was taken yesterday to the fissile material vault, which is guarded by some of the meanest looking motherfuckers you'll ever encounter – obviously IRGC knuckle-draggers. What assholes! I had to do some calculations for various amounts of HEU to be stored there and ensure that each mass was properly separated from the others, again for criticality safety.

From what I saw and calculated, they anticipate at least 240KG to 280KG of 90 to 92% HEU in there, and that's just the start. There are several more identical rooms in the vault. This is madness! No wonder they capitulated in the nuclear discussions and restricted our centrifuge enrichment program. They don't need it.

Obviously, our Persian bazaaris snookered your negotiators. They got sanctions lifted and have, or will have soon, several nukes in the bargain. Such a deal. I should feel proud of them, but now I'm on your team. They're out of their fucking minds.

I have seen the Tabatabai brothers again and they do not look happy. Both look distracted and the younger brother, Daoud, looks even thinner than before and really haggard as if he's under a lot of pressure. Something's up with them. Something bad. I speak to them on occasion but I don't want to act overly curious.

The only other thing happening, and it's hardly worth mentioning, but we have been experiencing minor little earthquakes and tremors lately. I guess that's not surprising given the frequent geophysical activity in the area.

Oh, you may recall that I was puzzling over a rock and roll tune that General Alborzi has been humming lately. A few days ago, I heard him doing it again and I realized what the song was: "Get off of My Cloud" by the Rolling Stones. Odd, huh? An IRGC general humming a tune by the Stones? I wonder if Mick and the boys know how popular they are with the

RevGuard in the bowels of Mt. Damavand. Maybe they'll do a free concert at Evin prison, like Johnny Cash did at Folsom.

Best wishes to Miles from Gabriel

Lane read the message from Leopard in his office at CIA Headquarters and felt thrilled but horrified at the same time. This was the smoking gun he had been looking for. He was still upset that Headquarters had not disseminated Conor McBane's report on the 60 kilos of Russian HEU smuggled through Azerbaijan, especially when the amount tracked with the criticality sketch that Leopard had seen. But Belinda Ballard, the Chief of Reports in the Counterproliferation Center, had shaken her head and said that Conor never saw anything himself. It was fragmentary intelligence at best – "not worth publishing and panicking people downtown." Lane had argued that the amounts of HEU from the two sources tracked, but Belinda said maybe that Leopard's report should not have been disseminated either. That it had arrived while she was on vacation, and wouldn't have met her professional threshold for publication as a report. End of discussion.

Except it wasn't. Not by a long shot.

In spite of their disagreement, Lane actually felt sorry for Belinda, a middle-aged bureaucrat with a perpetually furrowed brow. She was evidently under considerable pressure from above not to repeat the "Curveball" disaster, in which an Iraqi intelligence fabricator helped push the U.S. into a war in Iraq based on spurious reports of WMD. Add to this other hyped reports about so-called centrifuge equipment for Iraq, which turned out to be for conventional aluminum rocket tubes, and selective cherry-picking of intelligence by certain bellicose elements in the U.S. administration, and pretty soon one had a colossal intelligence failure, or as Lane's friends in the British intelligence service had described it, "a massive cock-up."

To be sure, there had been human failures in both collection and analysis in that situation. These shortcomings had supposedly been corrected by new regulations and controls as well as creation of the Office of the Director of National Intelligence. All of these remedies had their purported virtues, were well intentioned and staffed by intelligent people, but Lane thought they largely ignored the intricacies and ambiguities of the human element. In some ways, the situation was the same as before, and in many ways it was worse. Systematizing intelligence assumed you could systemize human beings and their nearly infinite shades of grey. Lane wondered if he was about to witness yet another WMD cock-up, simply in reverse. Ironically, this time the WMD *did* exist and no one wanted to believe it.

Except now, Lane was holding onto proof.

As he was contemplating walking into Belinda's office with his latest intel from Leopard, his secure line rang. He was delighted to hear Lacy's voice.

"Hey, I'm at the Hoover Building. Just got in on the red eye from San Francisco and am about to make a beeline over to see you."

"Just can't stay away from me, huh?"

She laughed. "Right. You're thinking with your little head instead of your big head."

"Could be."

"Listen, I've some really hot intel to share with you right away. This is going to knock your socks off."

"Funny. I was about to call you at Livermore and tell you I've got some interesting intel as well. This from our jazz-playing friend. And if mine knocks your socks off too, maybe we can play footsies right here in my office."

Lacy chuckled. "Okay, lover, but keep your socks on 'til tonight. I'll be there in less than an hour. Stay put."

When Lacy walked into his office an hour later, her eyes were sparkling, transcontinental flight notwithstanding. She was clearly excited to see him but even more pumped up from adrenalin. She gave him a quick hug, and he showed her Leopard's message as she stood next to his desk. She drummed her fingers a bit as she read and then muttered, "My God," as she sat down in one of his guest chairs. This is dynamite. Leopard's right in the thick of it, and he's not the type who sees ghosts where there are none."

"I know. They've gotta put this out quickly."

Lacy nodded. "Now check out this email. It was sent to a Livermore nuclear weapons designer yesterday from one of his former Iranian graduate students. When you read it in conjunction with the Leopard report…well, you'll see."

She unlocked the classified information lock-bag she had been carrying and handed him the printed email. His eyes widened as he read it. He reread it twice more and made a few notes.

Finally, he looked up. "These two reports are a one-two knockout punch. Amazing. Let's see what Gary Scott thinks."

Lane and Lacy found Gary Scott eating his lunch and reading classical Persian poetry, which he claimed relaxed him immensely. The guy lived and breathed this stuff. Was it any wonder that he was an operational expert on Iran? Gary had the quality Lane most admired in top-notch case officers: passion.

"We hate to break into your lunch," said Lane, "but would you look at this latest message from Leopard? Then check out this separate email Lacy got from one of her Livermore scientists."

A broad smile broke out on Gary's face as he read Leopard's message. "Man, this is good stuff. He's giving you the keys to the kingdom." He pointed at the printout Lacy had given him, "And this is great corroboration."

"Yeah, but they fly in the face of those Condor reports that the NSC and the White House are drooling over. These'll be like two turds in the punchbowl at a state dinner at the White House." Lane shook his head but arched his eyebrows and smiled wryly because he didn't care who it upset.

The older case officer looked at Lane for a long moment. "Let me tell you something: I'd rather have one Leopard than a whole flock of shit-eating Condors."

They walked over to Belinda's office but she wasn't in. Lane left Leopard's message and the Iranian email on her desk chair and a note that read, "What you were awaiting. Please see me, Lane."

Lane and Lacy then returned to his office, which had an unobstructed view of Belinda's open door about fifty feet away. They waited quietly, chatting about next operational steps with Leopard, and in ten minutes the Chief of Reports returned to her office and closed her door, a common occurrence of late for the beleaguered woman.

Lane looked at his watch and after about ninety seconds, he started counting down from ten like a missile launch at Cape Kennedy. Precisely after he reached one and said "Ignition, blast off!" her door flew open and Belinda emerged looking as if she had seen the dead. Her eyes were wide and unblinking and she clutched the Leopard message and Lacy's email to her chest.

CHAPTER 3

◇◇◇

McBane Sends

Baku

There's no fool like an old fool thought Conor McBane as his Lufthansa flight touched down at Baku's modernistic Heydar Aliyev International Airport. Anyone with half a brain wouldn't be returning to a place where he had almost been assassinated, but the temptation to pursue the HEU-smuggling leads proved too great for McBane.

Initially, McBane had felt frustrated that his letters to Energy Secretary Alvarez and Lane Andrews had not provoked a more forward-leaning response than polite thank you notes from both. Two weeks afterward in separate private meetings with the men, however, he got the distinct impression that they shared his frustration and that he was a hair's breadth away from something important. Neither had encouraged him to chase after the loose threads in this scheme nor had they elaborated on why they were frustrated, but he could read it in their faces.

Lane had been especially appreciative. He had squeezed McBane's hand as he thanked him again and had said, "I can tell you that your info ties into some other things we know. But these guys are dangerous. I've had some firsthand experience with them. It'd be better if you just backed away from it."

Backing away, however, had never been in McBane's DNA. And shortly thereafter he'd received an anonymous phone tip from a Russian-accented voice saying that there was more help for him in Baku. Then the caller had hung up.

Like a red flag in front of a bull thought McBane. *And an old bull at that.*

An hour after landing, McBane was once again ensconced in a comfortable suite at The Four Seasons. He started making a few phone calls to beat the bush with some of his sources in the police department and in less upstanding circles. This simple ploy was like sending up smoke signals in Baku, and within a day there was a polite knock on his door. It was the private security man whom McBane had prudently hired to screen his visitors.

The bodyguard ushered in a couple of visitors who had apparently passed his inspection. One was an older man, possibly in his mid-sixties, and the other was a younger man in his late twenties. Both were dressed in dark, well-tailored suits, and the older man removed his hat, held it to his chest in a deferential manner and turned towards his companion. The younger man spoke in cultured but slightly Russian-accented English.

"Dr. McBane, my father and I would like a private word with you. Would you mind if we came in for a few minutes?"

McBane asked the guard to remain in the hallway and gestured to them to enter and have a seat in his suite's spacious living area. The younger man's facial features and jet-black hair reminded McBane of his dead Armenian source from a few months previous. It turned out that the resemblance was more than coincidental.

The younger nodded toward the older man and said, "Our family owes you a debt of gratitude for avenging the death of my younger brother. The police matched the fingerprints of the man you killed in this hotel to some found in the room in which my brother was murdered. We are...are grateful. My father is a powerful man and would like to satisfy part of this debt with some information which should be of interest to you."

McBane acknowledged his gratitude with a curt nod and motioned for him to continue.

"Within a few weeks of my brother's death, some of our best men and I visited the other family that had unwisely become involved in this uranium trafficking. They were connected with the Russian killer and his cohorts. It is safe to say that they will never traffic in this material -- or anything else for that matter -- ever again." He smiled grimly. "Unfortunately, as we were leaving their stronghold, we found evidence of three further shipments of uranium to Iran from the same supplier."

The older man clearly understood a fair amount of English. He had been following his son's words closely and at this point he nodded and removed a manila envelope from inside his jacket and proffered it to McBane.

McBane opened it and saw a sheaf of glossy photographs of grey cylinders with Cyrillic lettering on them and the international sign for radiation. There were also official technical papers attesting to their degree of enrichment. McBane, who could read Russian, examined these papers carefully. He inhaled sharply when he saw that the HEU was at the ninety to ninety-two percent level and that each of the three shipments totaled at least sixty kilos.

He felt a sudden swell of intense and conflicting emotions. Here in a single swoop, he had achieved the investigative reporting coup of a lifetime. But at the same time, he had burst through the gates of Hell and now gazed upon Oppenheimer's "destroyer of worlds."

He tucked the papers and photos back in the envelope. "Thank you. This is...is very important. I appreciate it a lot. I'll see that it's put to good use."

The older man spoke to his son in Russian, and though McBane caught most of it, the younger man translated so that there would be no mistake.

"My father sincerely hopes that you and your friends can put a stop to this madness. He also wishes you to know that if you ever need anything, especially here, just to let us know. Anything at all. We will arrange it. We are forever in your debt."

McBane started to protest that they had done enough already, but the older man stepped forward, embraced him and kissed him on both cheeks. In English, the old man murmured "Thank you." His son shook McBane's hand and they left. McBane watched the two walk slowly towards the elevators. The older man turned at one point, smiled and gave him a thumbs-up.

McBane sat before the fireplace and started to compose a second set of letters to Lane Andrews and Manny Alvarez. He had to get the letters and these documents and photos to the U.S. Embassy immediately. Then he thought better of this plan. Why should he insert these into U.S. government channels and suffer the interminable time lag involved? He wasn't exactly impecunious, and this was damned important – in fact, it was probably the most important thing he had ever done.

He phoned Lufthansa and booked the next flight to Frankfurt and then through to Washington. If he made his connection, he would be there in less than 30 hours. He reluctantly settled for business class since first was booked. He would treat himself to some better champagne upon landing. The sacrifices we make for God and country....

A few minutes later, he sent an email both to Lane and to Secretary Alvarez:

"Have someone meet me at Washington Dulles. Arriving on Wednesday LH flight from Frankfurt at 1500 with convincing evidence. World peace depends. McBane sends."

CHAPTER 4

The Enigma Dilemma

IRGC Office of Intelligence North Tehran

The CIA files flickered on the large screen in front of General Alborzi as he reviewed the hacked take from the computer penetration of 3C. They had hit a goldmine of information on CIA activities against Iran, but he knew he must be selective in how he used it, lest he tip his hands to the Americans. This was akin to the problem the British had during World War Two when Alan Turing and his team defeated the German encryption device, the Enigma machine. The Allies had to be very discriminating on how they used that priceless intelligence or the Nazis would have suspected that their codes were being broken. So, occasionally, the Allies would sacrifice convoys to German U Boats and suffer other deadly failures in order to keep the Germans in the dark about their code breaking capability.

To Alborzi's delight, his success against California Cloud Computing far eclipsed the sporadic defeat of the Enigma machine by the British. To be frank, he could read everything. To put it in plain American English – every fucking word. By getting on the inside of their cyber defense perimeter with a human spy, he did not have to worry about them changing keys or erecting new cyber defenses. They could erect all they wanted to their heart's content and to their greedy contractors' delight, and it would be an electronic Maginot Line that he would end-run around exactly as the Germans outflanked French fortifications by going around them through neutral Belgium. This was child's play and so far it had cost him only a few thousand dollars in expenses for his team in California. Who knew that espionage could be so much fun?

Now, to be fair, he was limited to that information which the CIA had placed on the cloud, but luck had been with him so far. And that luck was the fact that the CIA had placed all of their Iranian operations in the ever-loving and promiscuous embrace of 3C. He even benefited from the fact that the CIA had also seen fit to park a large portion, if not all, of their Iranian ops information from other intelligence partners and foreign liaison there too. So, he had a clear view of what the Brits, French, Germans, Israelis etc. had shared with the Americans concerning their clandestine activities in Iran. Certainly not all of their information was there, but he had enough to keep his counterespionage squads busy for years. There would be so much blood flowing in Evin prison in the coming months and years that he even pondered buying stock in several companies that made torture implements. Or gibbets. Or possibly coffins. Hmmm. He would have to think of an angle.

Dr. Dmitri Grishin had been delighted with the results even if they were currently limited to Iran. Grishin knew that this was only temporary. He was positively salivating at the prospect of an unlimited view of CIA operations worldwide. The boys back at the FSB's 16th Center in Moscow would be all over that. Soon, the CIA would grow to trust the cloud even more, provided nothing led them to the conclusion that the cloud was nothing but wispy vapor and just as effective at concealing their secrets. For this reason, Grishin insisted that General Alborzi limit his arrests to only the most pressing cases and to arrange plausible alternate reasons for their seizure.

Alborzi said he had no problem with that constraint. If he arrested a few at first, it would look like his own excellent CI work, and the others could be explained away as derivative from some of the earlier arrests, since cases were frequently connected. In either event, his CI squads and he, their leader, would look like fucking geniuses, which of course was true…about him at least.

So, Alborzi set about personally acting upon only the most damaging and/or most irritating cases. There was an ayatollah, a rival of his uncle, whose spokesman had been providing sensitive Supreme National Security Council documents to the CIA. That one was easy since it got rid of a spy and damaged the rival in the bargain – a twofer, as the Americans called it. Then there was a junior Majlis deputy who was a real pain in the butt who had also buddied up to the CIA and given them parliamentary internal documents on military expenditures. A clear case of necessity. He might even lead the firing squad on that one personally.

Alborzi found another jewel in an IRGC colonel who had been embezzling large sums for gambling and who had gone to the CIA to cover his losses, and was providing classified documents in exchange. The IRGC spy had a bank account at a bank in Zurich just down the street from Jacquard Privat Bank. Interesting. This could help cover his own tracks to Switzerland. He might hold that one in reserve as an insurance policy. He also found a senior MOIS officer whose salary could not cover his three mistresses and family and who had agreed to spy for the French DGSE. Naughty, naughty. But of course the French understood about sex.

And finally, he found a chubby little criticality safety engineer in his own Project Zulfiqar. Tsk, tsk. Now *that* one was a potential problem because he wanted zero light shed on the project and zero shit splashed on him personally for allowing this little worm to penetrate his prize apple. He would have to handle this one most delicately and discreetly. Fortunately, he'd had the foresight to have some special holding cells constructed at Project Zulfiqar's facility. They could hold either HEU or traitors.

Ali Javadpour sat in front of his laptop computer in his apartment in Tehran to compose his latest covert communication to CIA Headquarters. He was eager to start his next message because this one would knock Lane's socks off. At long last, he'd had a good conversation with the Tabatabai brothers, who had confided in him that Project Zulfiqar was aimed at producing a nuclear weapon. Moreover, he had finally laid eyes on the shipments of HEU, and it was just as he predicted in his previous messages. Now, he had the undeniable proof. Not only was he going to throw a monkey wrench into

General Alborzi's insane quest for a nuclear weapon, but he would prove his worth to Lane and Lacy. That's what mattered most of all to Ali.

He prepared the special protocol he had been taught in order to encrypt the message and send it on its roundabout path to Langley and to Lane's desktop. He felt a special kinship with Lane whenever he did this, as if they were chatting face to face or listening to jazz together at Le Chat Noir. He could always tell from the personalized responses that Lane drafted the messages and did not delegate the duty to someone else. He took extra care to make him feel like a vital part of the team. For the first time in a long time, Ali felt needed and valued, as well as respected.

He would draft this message with special relish at the thought of their delight and pleasure with him. But first, he decided to put on his digitally remastered "Birth of the Cool" album. He never tired of it. He placed it in his CD player and adjusted his headphones so he could listen as he typed his message to Washington. The soft music carried him along as he typed his message. He described his findings in detail and added some color about General Alborzi being "such a flaming ass-hat."

He did not notice for the longest time that four burly IRGC goons were standing behind him or that General Alborzi himself was reading over his shoulder as he typed. In fact, he might have gone on for considerably more time except that the album's last track, "Darn that Dream," ended and he heard someone shift their weight on his dining room floor and a floorboard creak. He whipped around in shock, then resignation as Alborzi ripped the headphones from his head.

"In the name of Allah, I hereby arrest you for treason against the Islamic Republic!" screamed Alborzi as he backhanded him.

After Ali reeled backwards from the slap, he sat forward and said, "My General. What an unexpected surprise! Had I known you were dropping by, I would have made us a nice pot of hot tea and some homemade scones with clotted cream. Please do sit down."

Alborzi did indeed sit down and spun the laptop around to where he could finish reading Javadpour's draft message to Washington. "'A flaming ass-hat.' Hmmm. I must remember that colorful English expression. Rich and pithy. It always pays to build one's vocabulary."

The IRGC goons then frog-marched Ali from his apartment to a waiting vehicle. He was tossed in the car, not gently.

PART 4

CHAPTER 1

◇◇◇

What is Truth?

DDO's Office Langley

Arlo McReedie, Chief of Counterproliferation Ops at CIA, sat across from Paula Davenport and looked decidedly ill. He drummed his fingers nervously on his chair before he spoke. "Paula, I just heard you're not invited to the big meeting today with the Bureau regarding our Iranian sources. Something tells me that Mac wants everyone to be on message. I don't like this."

She nodded. "Yeah, I think he wants just his A-team players with him. I'm in the doghouse for saying I've got misgivings about Condor's reporting. But what else can I say in light of recent reporting from Leopard and the two new FBI Iranian nuclear sources on serious HEU smuggling from Russia to Iran? And oh, by the way, this was backed up by an American investigative reporter, who's a friend of Lane Andrews." She shook her head in disgust. "It gives me the heebie-jeebies vouching for Condor's reporting without considerable caveats and a rebalancing of the reporting."

"I know what you mean. I saw those new intels. They're consistent in refuting Condor's 'all things are A-OK in Iran' reports. Frankly, I've got a sick feeling in my stomach about this too. I'm also uncomfortable attending this meeting without you."

"No, I really think you should go. There needs to be a voice of reason there. You're the analytical expert, and they need your advice."

"Maybe so, but I'm feeling guilty for playing along with Mac's bandwagon. I feel like a traitor to the truth. I've even thought about resigning, but I'm only a few months shy of retirement. Isn't that pathetic? And I...I guess I'm too chicken-shit to ask for reassignment."

Paula saw the look of self-loathing on his face, and that he couldn't hold her gaze. She sat there quietly. There wasn't much she could say.

Arlo finally spoke, "This is terrible, but I feel like a typical analyst weenie. My dad once told me that I should never stay in a job when I couldn't look myself in the mirror in the morning. Well Paula, I'm there. I'm so much there! I look at myself, and I see...lies. This was my dream job, and now I'm living a lie by just being there, helping Mac pander to the White House."

Paula looked at him with compassion. "I can see your predicament, but you need to hang on a bit longer until the various strands of reporting from Iran make a more coherent picture. Yours is the one sane senior voice that could save us from another WMD debacle. I'm not sure we could survive that."

Arlo looked at her. "What can I possibly do?"

"Just remember what's carved in our entry hall from the Book of John: 'And ye shall know the truth and the truth shall make you free.'"

Arlo returned Paula's serve with his own quotation from the Book of John: "'What is truth?' retorted Pilate."

And with that, he left, shaking his head sadly.

CHAPTER 2

◇◇◇

Your Witness

FBI Director's Conference Room

A tap came on the conference room door, and the FBI Director's secretary ushered in CIA Director Mac White and his retinue, composed of an uncomfortable looking Arlo McReedie, who ran CIA's counterproliferation operations, Belinda Ballard, Chief of CP Reports, who looked weary and guarded, and a statuesque young blonde woman whom Mac introduced as his senior DO Special Assistant, Miss Ashley Taylor. Mac smiled broadly as he worked the room, making introductions and pumping hands as if it were a corporate board he was trying to influence.

Or perhaps this was his last visit under a flag of truce prior to the commencement of hostilities. The FBI Director knew from White House sources that Mac had been whispering steadily in the president's ear that the CIA should absorb all domestic intelligence collection from the FBI and relegate the latter strictly to law enforcement. Moreover, he had his eye on DIA collection as well. As Mac had put it, "Let the intelligence pros handle this part of national security." So far, the president had resisted Mac's entreaties, but the FBI Director also knew Mac White was devious and persistent. He was not about to give up on his idea of a hostile takeover of FBI and DIA intelligence collection. Corporate takeovers were in his blood.

The FBI Director had a great measure of respect for the Agency's ability to obtain foreign intelligence both at home and abroad. Yet, he was troubled by Mac's plan to unite these various intelligence collection capabilities into a monolithic super intelligence agency under his "enlightened" leadership. There was a great deal to be said for diverse collection. It was also preferable to keep intelligence from being potentially politicized under a CIA Director who served a term appointed by the president. The FBI directorship was a fixed ten-year term, which helped insulate the office from the political whims of the White House. Naturally, nothing was perfect, and although the FBI Director respected the president, he didn't feel beholden to her.

Mac and his team sat across from the FBI Director and his staff, and he opened the bidding by saying, "Always a pleasure to visit the brave men and women of the Federal Bureau of Investigation. You may not be aware of it but I actually considered applying to be a Special Agent after I finished business school, but life kind of got in the way. Otherwise, I might be seated where you are." Mac gave his most magnanimous Mac the Knife smile as if to imply he was merely one of them.

The FBI Director thought that it was more likely that the lure of money got in Mac's way, and he involuntarily shuddered to think of Mac as an FBI Special Agent.

Mac continued, "It appears we're all providing the White House with some exciting and complex intel about Iran these days. Very exciting. Some of it's consistent with earlier reporting, but some...some sure as hell isn't. In fact, I'd say some of it's dead wrong. Probably faulty analysis, or more likely, disinformation. Gotta stay vigilant against fabrication. It got us into a war once. We don't want to field any more Curveballs, now do we?" He gave everyone a big wink as if he were letting them all in on a sure-fire investment in his hedge fund.

Bette looked over at the FBI Director, who motioned for her to take the lead. Never one to shy from a fight, Bette jumped in feet first.

She smiled at Mac White as she said, "I think we're in violent agreement, Mr. Director. Some of this intel has to be dead wrong. We'd definitely agree that a substantial portion of the recent reporting going to the president is sheer fabrication. Complete hogwash. No doubt about it. We just regret that it's come to this point."

Mac White grinned at what he thought was a complete capitulation of the Bureau. He honestly had not expected it would be this easy. If they were such pussies, taking over their intelligence functions would be a cakewalk.

"With all due respect, Director White, your reporting from Condor is the fabrication to which I'm referring."

Mac White's smile only flickered for a beat after her words finally sunk in. He composed himself for a moment and then said through gritted teeth, "Say that again Ms....is it Ms. DiSanti? I don't think I heard you correctly."

"Maybe I was unclear, sir. We believe Condor is your Curveball. He's only telling us what the Iranians want us to hear. We have seen several new streams of credible reporting that cause us to believe he's bad."

Mac wagged his finger at her as if to a naughty child. "Okay my dear, let's look at the overwhelming asset validation we have of Condor."

Bette raised her eyebrows and opened her hands wide in a "please proceed" manner.

Mac then asked Belinda to review Condor's reporting. Belinda, appearing as if she was in desperate need of an Alka Selzer, locked eyes with Mac White, avoiding the gaze of others, and dutifully related how Condor's reporting had been verified and validated through a successful conclusion of the nuclear negotiations, by complete agreement with on-site IAEA inspections, by confirmation of his revelations of the hitherto-secret military nuclear sites through subsequent IAEA visits, and of course by corroboration from Leopard. She noted that one must add to this asset's ledger the fact that Condor had successfully passed an ops test designed by his recruiter, Charlie Grable.

The FBI Director, who had cross-examined numerous witnesses during his days as a prosecutor, could tell when a witness had been rehearsed by opposing counsel and was simply reciting from a memorized script rather than testifying truthfully. Their words were too precise and stilted, the account would flow smoothly from start to finish with no reversals or corrections or hesitation, and their eyes would shift and try to remain fixed on their attorney or the ceiling and definitely not on him.

Belinda had all of these signs in spades. She was in wretched shape. He doubted he could ask her name without her referring the question to Mac and her script.

"What kind of ops test?" asked the FBI Director.

Belinda looked nervously at Mac White, who shrugged and gestured for her to respond.

"Charlie gave Condor a trapped laptop on a pretext and then asked him to return it a few weeks later. There were no signs of intrusion. The traps… the traps were intact." Belinda looked away as she said this.

Bette recalled a lecture that Lane Andrews had given at the FBI once entitled "Stupid Ops Tests" which he equated to David Letterman's "Stupid Pet Tricks," and chief among them were worthless, irrelevant tests such as trapped letters and laptops rather than testing for the one thing which would cause you nightmares about a case. Lane had concluded that stupid ops tests revealed far more about careless case officers than about their assets.

"And what did that test prove?" interjected Bette.

"Reliability."

"Reliability? Meaning he reliably doesn't break into laptops given him by CIA officers? How about whether he's reliably telling us the truth?" There was laughter on the FBI side of the table. "I'm sorry but I fail to see how that test proves his reporting reliability."

"Well, it's just part of our normal asset validation procedure. We plan other tests."

"Such as?"

"We've a polygraph planned in a few weeks. Charlie, his case officer, has already had a sit down with him and thoroughly discussed various CI aspects of the case. Charlie assesses that Condor is telling the truth. The polygraph will help establish that."

Bette chewed silently on those tasty morsels for a moment and reflected briefly to herself on the fact that Charlie Grable's reputation for buffoonery and hot air was well known beyond the halls of Langley. She wondered just who was testing whom. She decided, however, to focus on the polygraph test.

"I realize that you folks in the Agency put a lot of credence in polygraph tests, but they're not lie detectors – just stress detectors. It's not a definitive test for veracity by any means. If Condor is a non-reactor like a sociopath or pure narcissist or even from a culture where lying to protect one's clan is not *haram*, he may show no signs of deception and yet, be lying his ass off."

Belinda said, "It's just a tool in the tool chest – that's all."

Mac White nodded his head vigorously and said, "Amen, Belinda. Just a good tool – one of many we have."

"We agree it's just a tool," said Bette. "Unfortunately, from what I've observed, it's a tool that's frequently relied upon at the expense of all others, including common sense sometimes." Bette looked directly at Belinda and saw her squirm. She decided to end this sideshow on a more conciliatory note, however, and not get into a fight just yet. That would come soon enough.

"Listen, I grant you that a polygraph test could be revelatory of Condor's validity, especially if the polygrapher is a good judge of deception and has the instincts of a psychologist, as the best ones do. Those observations are infinitely more telling than squiggles on a graph. And it probably beats the handwriting analysis you used to do. What did you call it? 'Holography'?" Bette thought "whole lot of shit" is what it really was, but she said nothing else. She threw the bones in Belinda's direction and looked over at the FBI Director to signal that she was finished with this poor excuse for a witness.

Belinda looked relieved to be dismissed.

Throughout her soliloquy, Arlo McReedie, Belinda's direct boss looked on the point of some sort of intestinal episode. He hung his head and doodled on a notepad.

Mac White turned to Arlo and asked him, "Arlo, do you have anything to add to Belinda's splendid briefing on Condor?"

Arlo looked up from his doodling and muttered something softly under his breath, which Bette, sitting across from him, thought she caught as the words, "Oh fuck me." She glanced at his scribbling and thought she saw a scaffold and a body suspended from it, swinging back and forth. Mac asked him to speak up.

Arlo cleared his throat and looked at Mac. "No sir. I think…uh, I think she just about covered all your…I mean *our* talking points about Condor. As you said earlier, it's complex. Really complex. Gotta look at it from all angles." He was silent for a moment and added, "I mean there *is* some room for argument…"

At this point, Mac cut him off. "So true, so very true, Arlo. We're looking hard at *all* the angles, aren't we? That's why I've appointed Charlie Grable to be head of Iranian Ops at the Agency and asked him to personally conduct a counterintelligence review of all of the Iran nuke reporting. He's given me the results." Mac pointed to some papers in front of him. "He's an expert and I've got complete confidence in his judgment."

Mac spoke as if this were the end of the argument. Bette thought that appointing an imbecile like Charlie Grable to be head of Iran Ops at CIA must be the ayatollahs' dream come true. And having him conduct the CI review was the ultimate self-licking ice cream cone.

Adjusting his reading glasses, Mac referred to the papers in front of him. "For example, Leopard's new reporting is a sudden about-face. How do we explain that? Do I smell the hand of Israeli Mossad in this? I wonder how they got to him."

Bette protested, "We've seen no signs of that!"

Mac White chuckled and shook his head as if Bette and her FBI colleagues were terribly naïve. "I'll return to that possibility in a moment, but may I remind you that he hasn't seen any actual fissile material, only drawings and calculations. And his judgment that the shapes are indicative of a nuclear weapon is hardly worth anything because he isn't a weapons designer." Mac paused for effect and then added, "But it's clever, I grant you that."

"And what do you mean exactly by 'clever'?" asked Bette.

"I mean the way this little charade's been presented to us in various acts. They're not hitting us over the head with a smoking gun all at once, which might alert us to its artifice. But they're letting us hear the shot, smell the gunpowder and eventually, they'll show us the body. I've got to give'em credit for the packaging. They get an A+ for subtlety and staging. I'm sorely tempted to call Mossad's Director and tell him he just won the Academy Award for Best Director of a Carefully Staged Intel Hoax."

With hardly a pause, Mac pushed forward on the attack, "Next, the award for special effects, the photos of supposed Russian HEU containers sent by the American investigative reporter. What garbage! Hell, anyone could've gotten hold of such photos or faked them, and again he hasn't seen anything in person."

"Mr. Director, DOE and Secretary Alvarez are at least of the preliminary opinion that these are bona fide, and they're worried sick," countered Bette.

"My dear, DOE and Secretary Alvarez hardly qualify as intelligence experts regardless of their scientific expertise. And, in any event, we all know that the Russian nuclear establishment has Jews who emigrate to Israel every year. Would've been easy to take those pics abroad."

Bette could see this was going nowhere but refused to concede any ground. "And our latest reporting, what's your assessment?"

"Finally, your two new internal Iranian sources in this so-called Project Zulfiqar. Seriously, how can we trust folks we've never met? A retired physicist gets an email with outlandish claims and we're supposed to change our intelligence estimates and maybe go to war over it? Come on! These emails could've easily been drafted by the Israelis. Most probably were. They'd love for us to think that the Iranians are cheating on our agreement and stir up another little Middle Eastern war and let us do the heavy lifting. Just what we all need. This whole smear of Condor is probably a carefully orchestrated disinformation campaign coming from Tel Aviv. They're relentless, I must admit."

Bette interrupted Mac's little rant and said, "Wait Mr. Director, we know that Dr. Majid Tabatabai exists because he was a graduate student of Dr. Rand McKeown at Berkeley and he cited certain facts that only he could..."

Mac cut her off. "That may well be but how do we know that the Israelis aren't running dear Dr. Taba....Taba... oh Christ, whatever the hell his name is? That cock and bull story about 'new physics' and new formulae developed by his genius brother who is gay. Give me a break! It sounds like a new Netflix series."

Mac shook his head. “Only the Israelis could come up with such a paranoid little fantasy. And our nuclear weapons sources at Livermore - yes, my dear, we have some too – our sources claim this is all a load of horse-hockey. These physics don’t exist in this universe. They’re scare tactics pure and simple. Anybody can see that.”

Bette shot Mac White a withering stare, but before she could speak, the FBI Director held up his hands and took control of the room. “Look, I suggest we form a joint CIA-FBI WMD squad for the new internal Iranian case of the Tabatabai brothers.”

Mac nodded agreement. “Splendid idea - in the interests of mutual Agency-Bureau equities. The Bureau can work with whomever they please at CIA.”

Bette quickly asked, “Mr. Director, could Lane Andrews be assigned to the joint CIA-FBI team?”

Mac, looking as if he had just been given the opportunity to jettison excess and troublesome baggage, never blinked. “Sure. Take him. Be my guest. Please keep us informed.”

With that settled, Mac White rose to his feet, gathered his minions and evaporated in a cloud of pricey cologne.

CHAPTER 3

◇◇◇

An Espionage Hat Trick

IRGC Office of Intelligence North Tehran

Alireza Kazemi sat across from General Alborzi and summarized his latest meeting with his CIA handler Charlie Grable. "So, lard-ass is flying high thanks to me. He's now is in charge of Iranian ops worldwide, or so he bragged. Can you believe that? Absolutely fucking amazing. I had a higher opinion of the CIA until I heard that. But this, this is an unintended bonus for us. We feed them bullshit, we get paid well for it and now we find out that this idiot has been put in charge of all CIA ops against us. Kind of like an espionage hat trick."

Alborzi chuckled. "Go on, Major Kazemi," referring to his double agent by his IRGC rank. "I'm rather enjoying this."

"He let slip that my codename is Condor. I kind of like that. Makes me feel like I'm in that movie 'Three Days of the Condor.'"

Alborzi gestured impatiently for him to continue. "Okay. I don't have all day."

"So, he tried having a little heart-to-heart CI talk with me at the last meeting. Or, I believe that was the purpose. It was most curious. It must be part of their vetting routine, although what it accomplishes is beyond me. Anyhow, he asked me some questions from a few sheets of paper but seemed happy with my answers. In fact, if I hesitated, he'd jump in and answer for me and ask if that's what I meant, and I would quickly agree. He seemed quite eager for me to pass and overjoyed at the results. Honestly, I don't think I could have made him happier if I'd been a jelly donut."

This made Alborzi laugh.

"He doesn't know that I taped the whole thing so that Dr. Grishin might analyze it for use in future dangle ops. Once we know their vetting procedures, we should be able to run more of us with 'damaged goods' at them."

"Very good. I'm sure Grishin will enjoy it. And did he pay you the $300,000 for the last three months?" asked Alborzi.

"Of course, or I would've quit on the spot." said Kazemi indignantly, handing over the envelope filled with crisp 1000 Swiss Franc notes

Alborzi fanned them briefly, withdrew about ten of them and pushed them across the table to Kazemi, commenting, "Good job. For expenses." He placed the remainder in his briefcase. At the same time, he brought out several papers and handed them to Kazemi. "It's high time we ask for another bonus for extra special material. Let's say five million dollars for this information I'm giving you. Americans love paying for this shit, and the more they pay, the more they like it. Expensive intel has got to be good stuff, right?"

Kazemi nodded and grinned.

"What we have here Major are 'sensitive internal IRGC documents' which reveal two more covert military sites which they can demand for inspection. I'll have a little lightly enriched uranium sprinkled about the sites to give it some added believability. Kind of how the fraudsters would drop a bit of gold dust around a 'mother lode' for prospective investors. Same trick, different set of idiots." He shook his head. "Had I known that we could get so much money for these worthless places, I would have stretched this dangle out further. I may still come up with a few more sites for them to find and pay us for. It also endears you to them, Condor. Or should I just call you Big Bird?"

Kazemi laughed.

"I also included information on a high technology smuggling network in the U.S. that supplied us with some material for the nuclear program in the past. Lately, however, because of the stronger dollar their goods have been more expensive compared to what we can obtain in Europe – primarily

Germany. The Pakistanis, Chinese and the Russians are also making noises that they can supply us with anything we need at bargain basement prices. I honestly think there'll be a bidding war for our business." Alborzi shrugged. "So, this network's superfluous. Plus, we owe them some old invoices. Let'em try to collect…after they're arrested by the FBI."

Kazemi nodded. 'A brilliant plan."

Alborzi sighed. "I know it's brilliant but don't pander to me. Just get the five million from this blithering idiot. Actually, let's make it six. Get that money Major." Alborzi dismissed him with a wave of his hand.

"Yes, sir."

As Kazemi slinked away like a scolded dog, he wondered where all this CIA money was going.

CHAPTER 4

I Will Write Again Soon

Leopard Message # 36

Hello Friends, I have hesitated to write you this message because I am so ashamed and I know you'll be mad. I have really messed up and botched all the signals I've been seeing. Maybe my hatred for the Islamic Republic blinded me to the truth but I must now try and make amends for my past mistakes. There is no nuclear weapons program. It's that simple. I was seeing ghosts and phantoms when in fact there is nothing. I discovered it was all a huge practical joke – not a very funny one – which my colleagues played on me. The criticality calculations were especially embarrassing because of the fact that I overlooked some clues, which should have tipped me off to the fact that the amounts were grossly exaggerated by two orders of magnitude.

My apologies for being so stupid and falling for this prank.

All is well. Nothing is really going on here but some research. I admit that my boredom probably played to my paranoia, but time moves so slowly here. And yet it moves…

I will write again soon.

Best wishes to Miles from Gabriel

In spite of his nausea, Lane scanned Leopard's latest message closely. He knew that all was lost and that Ali was now under the Iranians' control. Not only was the next to last line composed of only five words, which clearly indicated that he was writing under duress, but Leopard had cleverly slipped in one other clue that his recantation was false. Lane knew that the insertion of the phrase "time moves so slowly" was only an opening for Leopard to logically insert the words attributed to Galileo: "And yet it moves." Thus, Galileo stubbornly referred to the Earth moving about the Sun after he had ostensibly recanted his belief in such a scientific fact before the Inquisition. Whether Galileo truly uttered these words or not was irrelevant. This was Leopard's effort to tell Lane that he did not truly recant. The brave little Iranian continued to spit in the mullahs' eyes.

Lane felt gutted. He'd never lost a source before. The security of his sources had always been his highest priority, and he'd prided himself on keeping them safe. And yet, somehow Leopard had been compromised and now could be in a cell being subjected to excruciating torture. He might already be dead. How could this betrayal have happened? Had Lane done something wrong?

In the past few months, both Condor and Leopard had been granted "PL-110" status by Director Mac White. Essentially, this gave them a resettlement guarantee in the U.S., provided they served an agreed upon time within Iran reporting on the nuclear program. Of course, this status was completely worthless if they were in an Iranian prison or dead.

Lane walked the message over to Lacy. She was back at CIA Headquarters as part of the joint CIA-FBI task force that Bette had formed. He murmured, "Only five words in the next to last line."

She read it in disbelief and then looked up at him, tears welling up in her eyes. "Does this mean what I think it means? Oh, Christ, please don't tell me that, Lane, please don't! Leopard is such a sweet man. He...he trusted us."

After another few seconds, the tears streaming down her cheeks turned into quiet sobs. Lane tried to comfort her, but his own voice cracked and he was on the verge of tears himself. Instead, he patted her arm and sat on the edge of her desk, staring vacantly into space like a victim of shellshock. He barely regained control just as Gary Scott walked by Lacy's desk.

Seeing the two of them in this state of distress immediately triggered Gary's case officer instincts and, without saying a word, he came over and retrieved Leopard's message, which had fallen on the floor next to Lacy. After looking at it briefly, he muttered, "And now...."

Lane looked at him, "And now, what? Please tell me, now what?"

Lacy wiped away tears and looked at him.

Gary gave each of them a hug and, after a few seconds, said, "And now, we go to war."

Gary took them back to his cubicle, grabbed his coffee and said, "Let's walk around the compound. I've got a story to tell you.

"When I was on my fourth tour, I recruited an Iranian MOIS officer in early '85 in Rome. My guy was fairly junior and very pro-American and he loved the CIA, and I guess me as an extension of CIA. His family was fairly prominent in Iran and not especially pro-Shah, so they'd weathered the Iranian Revolution in the late '70's rather well. His devotion to us was due to the fact that in the late '60's, his older brother had been swimming in a remote lake in Iran near a U.S. military facility. His brother began to have difficulty due to cramping. A passing American GI spotted him drowning and saved his life. He said that after that he decided he would do anything for America. For four years, he reported faithfully to us and passed along a considerable amount of info on their operations. I saw him from time to time during his travels outside of Iran. I really liked him.

"All seemed to be going well until one day it was announced that most of our internal Iranian sources had been rolled up, interrogated, tortured and imprisoned, awaiting execution. My friend was one of these poor devils. I wanted to mount a rescue mission but was told that this was impossible, which it probably was.

"Headquarters circled up the wagons and there was never any proper accountability for this fucking disaster, but I swore that I would never, ever lose another source through such ineptitude... and I never did. But I still lie awake some nights, thinking of poor Parviz. He died because of us. Because we fucked up.

"Now, I want to help the two of you figure out a way to get Leopard out of there. Somehow, there must be a way. And we need to figure out how he got fucked. I'm figuring something went wrong with his commo, just like with Parviz. And I bet dollars to donuts it's our fault. Any thoughts? Anything strange or unusual lately in his messages?"

Lane shook his head, finding it difficult to focus on the past messages, but Lacy looked at him and asked, "Lane, I've been thinking about this for quite a while, but what was that strange reference to General Alborzi humming 'Get off of my Cloud' by The Rolling Stones in the message a short while ago? Leopard thought it strange, or he wouldn't have mentioned it twice. Why was an IRGC general humming that song and smiling so much?"

Gary looked at her and said only, "Oh shit! I think I know."

CHAPTER 5

◇◇◇

A Cold Test

University of California, Berkeley, Present

Hello Dr. McKeown,

We received your latest message advising that you had contacted the appropriate people in the U.S. and that they take our information seriously. That is good because it is very dangerous what is going on here at Project Zulfiqar. The work on the first nuclear weapon is nearing completion, and three more are in the works. Although we've tried to slow things down, there is only so much we can do without drawing suspicion on ourselves.

My brother Daoud has insisted that we perform a cold (or subcritical) test in one of the remote facility caverns to determine in principle the neutron count and performance of the device. In essence, we would construct an exact duplicate of our weapon but would use depleted uranium rather than HEU. Therefore, there would be no nuclear yield – just a contained blast from the high explosives in the weapon. It will give us a very good approximation of the performance without an actual nuclear detonation. This cold test is virtually mandatory in these devices in order to reduce doubt, so we were not surprised when General Alborzi quickly approved the proposal. Preparations for this test could take two or three months or possibly a bit more. We still don't know when the test will occur.

They have arrested Dr. Ali Javadpour, our criticality safety engineer, on charges of espionage. We heard that he is being held in a special cell here in the Lar National Park underground facility near the HEU vault. General Alborzi refers to him as a traitor, but he is keeping him here on the facility so that he can force Dr. Javadpour to continue to work for us. It also minimizes publicity about Project Zulfiqar that would inevitably arise if his arrest were made public.

I would say that Dr. Javadpour's lifespan can now be measured by the timing of our cold test. Once that is completed, his life is forfeit, and my brother and I fear that we will suffer the same fate. General Alborzi will no longer need us and we become loose threads to be clipped. We are virtually certain that this will happen.

This brings me to my proposal. We would like to ask for asylum in the U.S. In exchange for this: we will try to sabotage the four nuclear weapons soon to be in our inventory. We have not yet figured out how to do this, but Daoud said that if he can design one, then surely he should be able to figure a way to destroy one or more. Additionally, Daoud is working on a cyber logic bomb, which we can deploy in the Project Zulfiqar computer system to completely wipe clean all of the design data so that no one can ever replicate our work after we are gone. Daoud has already surreptitiously gained super-user status on the Project Zulfiqar computers, so this should not be too difficult. As I said before, he is a genius.

Again, all we ask is for asylum in America. Besides the two of us, it would include my wife Miriam and our two young sons, Reza and Ali. My wife and the boys can travel to Turkey to visit her sister's family in Istanbul without raising suspicion. The trick will be for Daoud and myself to escape because we are closely watched, but I'm working on a plan. What I need from you is the commitment that you will help us. Our proposed date of departure should coincide with the cold test. To wait longer would be suicidal.

As further proof of my seriousness in this matter, I am attaching photos of our four devices, which are contained on our computer systems as well as more design data, which Daoud thought you might find useful. He added that he would be happy to consult with U.S. nuclear scientists on these designs once we are in the States.

We have been experiencing periodic earth tremors and the venting of hot sulfurous gases from fumaroles on the far western high slopes of Mt.

Damavand, not far from the adit where the cold test will occur. It smells terrible, like rotten eggs. Some of our more superstitious colleagues, especially some of the technicians, are joking that Damavand, "the shackled white giant" from the poem of our great poet laureate Mohammad-Taqi Bahar, is awakening after seven thousand years of slumber. That was the last time it erupted. But it is still considered an active volcano. It's actually a little scary thinking about it, but maybe I'm being foolish like the technicians.

As you can see from this email, I have elected not to accept your proposal for the special CIA communications system, which you mentioned in your last email. I am willing to gamble our lives on this system using Mersenne primes and algorithms and formulae you taught me but not on a system over which I have no control. My apologies to your CIA friends, but I trust you because I know you. They can use this method to communicate.

Best regards, your colleague Majid

Lane read Majid's message twice and handed it back to Lacy, shaking his head. "Well, this confirms our fears about Leopard's arrest but it also tells us where he is. At least, we know he's alive…for now. As Gary said, there's gotta be a way to get him…out of there." His voice broke slightly on the last three words.

Lacy nodded gravely and took Lane's hands in hers. "Agreed. 100%. I'm with you."

CHAPTER 6

◇◇◇

Big Cats and Big Birds

CIA Headquarters Langley

Lane and Lacy's spirits were considerably buoyed by Gary's steely resolve. They knew that if anyone could help them with the Leopard crisis, he could. The three of them began focusing entirely on enabling his escape and met in Lane's office to plan strategy.

Lane looked at the others with renewed resolve. "First, we need to determine how Leopard was compromised. I think Gary's theory that it was a communication system failure is probably right. I was thinking about his intuitive leap that "Get off of My Cloud" could refer to the cloud computing company that some idiot in higher management has decided should host Agency data. I did some checking and guess what? It's starting with Iranian ops."

Gary laughed. "Surprise, surprise. And if the Iranians have penetrated the company, then even the most sophisticated encryption would be useless. But how do we prove it?"

Lacy interjected, "I just learned from an Agency press release that the company involved, California Cloud Computing, known as 3C, has its server farm in the Oakland area. I need to return to Livermore in a couple of days to brief my colleague who'll take my place as Agent in the Lab while I'm on the joint task force here. Fortunately, our Oakland FBI office has pretty good relations with most of the national security contractors in the area. A visit with the 3C chief of security can easily be arranged."

The three of them decided their next move should be to drive downtown and meet Bette Disanti at FBI Headquarters to plan out their next few weeks.

WMD Directorate, FBI Headquarters

Bette began the meeting by stressing the FBI Director's enthusiasm for the case and his approval for how Lacy had been handling the Livermore scientists. Lacy blushed slightly as the older woman praised her, but clearly she was pleased that it was going well and that the Director and Bette were happy with her.

Bette said, "I hear from my sources that there's growing concern and disdain in senior elements of the CIA for this new reporting stream which goes counter to administration policy with Iran. Hell, they're as nervous as a cat in a room full of rocking chairs! Arlo McReedie positively looked like he wanted to crawl under a rock and die when I saw him in a meeting at the Hoover Building a couple of days ago."

She shook her head. "If the public finds out that we've been snookered, heads will roll throughout this administration. The upcoming election makes this even more critical for them."

Lacy rolled her eyes at this, but Bette patted her hand and said, "Welcome to my world dear heart. Fortunately, your teammates Lane and Gary here are seeking the truth. I'm not so sure about the rest. Mac White appears to be cooking the books and scared that he'll lose the mandate of heaven. Or have his ass kicked by the president, whichever comes first."

Gary laughed out loud.

Bette said, "Let's discuss the various Leopard messages. I'm sure you've noticed how his reporting dovetailed nicely with the Tabatabai reporting up until his last message written when he was clearly under arrest and duress, poor man. I'd also like to mention Conor McBane's information on the smuggled HEU and how the amounts coincide with Leopard's reporting and now that of the Tabatabais."

Lacy said, "As of this morning, the Livermore scientists haven't yet been able to verify the Tabatabai brothers' claim of having designed a nuclear weapon with double to triple the yield of Ivy King. But neither have they disproved it. It might be nearly impossible to fully establish the truth."

She explained, "Drs. McKeown and Carlton say that the physics are so far out there that this'll require much more time than they originally envisioned. Then there's no way to really test the principles except computer simulation, and the programming may prove very difficult if not impossible. They said that it's a bit like asking someone to prove concepts…concepts that are still years in the future with even the interim steps unclear. If the Tabatabai brothers were here in person, we'd have a shot at it, but Daoud is intuiting things, which simply aren't things we grasp. But they do admit the concepts are intriguing."

"So, they think he's right?" asked Lane.

"They're just not sure. Again, it's hard to program the computer when we don't really understand some of the leaps he's made. And his design is radically different from anything ever tried at Livermore, or at Los Alamos, for that matter. Oh, they also send their apologies for not meeting directly with us, but they're spending lots of time on our supercomputer Sequoia to try to prove these concepts. The DOE Secretary is keenly interested."

"It sounds promising," said Bette.

"Now," Lacy said, "let me tell you the negative. There's a whole other school of thought out at Livermore that this neutron phase design is a load of crap. Dr. Peter Muskie, who is quite senior in B Division where they design primaries, is trashing the idea whenever and wherever he can. From my own limited interactions with him, he seems a bit of a prima donna but definitely brilliant. McKeown and Carlton said that he's made special trips to Los Alamos to talk to his counterparts there so that he can disprove this 'nonsense.'" She made air quotes. "I never knew nuclear weapons designers could be so cutthroat. It makes things at the Bureau seem like child's play."

"Regardless of the design itself," interjected Bette, "The other information from the Tabatabai brothers *is* earthshattering. We now have photos of the four nuclear weapons and more design information as well as their intention to conduct a subcritical underground test. This sounds pretty damn serious and the clock is ticking away."

"One problem we've got," said Lane, "is that I'm not sure if we can get Director White to agree to resettlement assistance, what we call 'PL110 status,' for the Tabatabai brothers under the current atmosphere. I understand he's not a fan of their reporting."

Gary and Lacy nodded in agreement.

"I'm not overly concerned about that because our Director has other strings he can pull in the Justice Department and with Homeland Security. And if he has to put a little pressure on Mac White, I don't see him hesitating for these guys," said Bette.

The conversation switched to operational handling.

Gary said, "I read that Majid Tabatabai insisted on keeping the existing commo method of the encrypted emails through Dr. McKeown. Frankly, this is probably wise. We suspect that Leopard's compromise may be due to a botched commo system. I speculated that General Alborzi's constant humming of "Get Off of My Cloud" within earshot of Leopard could have been an oblique reference to his scorn for the cloud computing company hosting Agency data, which currently is limited to Iranian operations."

"Until we check 3C out further, I'd prefer you to keep communications with the Tabatabai brothers in your established channel, and I'll insist on keeping their reports out of our data banks," said Lane. "I have a very bad feeling that Gary's right. Also, I should mention that we've encrypted the Tabatabai brothers so we don't have to refer to them by their true names. Daoud is 'Panther' and Majid is 'Jaguar.'"

Bette chuckled. "Great crypts: Leopard. Panther. Jaguar. They're all big cats and big cats eat big birds like a Condor."

Although he did not say so, Lane feared he would have a fight on his hands with Charlie Grable and Iranian Ops to keep Panther and Jaguar's reporting out of their data system, but he was damned if he was going to lose another Iranian source (or two) because of pigheadedness or sloppiness. He would appeal directly to DDO Paula Davenport.

Gary's right. Lane thought. *Now, we go to war. And lots of it will be internal.*

CHAPTER 7

◇◇◇

The Train Has Left the Station

DDO's Office Langley

Paula Davenport was extremely frustrated. She knew that the intelligence community's Iran nuclear reporting was under intense scrutiny, which was completely understandable. But it was also being twisted and pinched and pulled by various parties without much regard for accuracy or U.S. national security interests, and this was 100% unacceptable.

Condor's most recent reports about two more previously unknown military nuclear sites in Iran and a U.S.-based proliferation network had only excited his supporters more. This was the vindication they needed of the Iranian nuclear agreement, which was beset by opposition in several quarters, especially in the Congress and the press. Leopard's repudiation of his own reporting added further support to Condor, the possible indication of duress notwithstanding. And Panther and Jaguar's reporting only muddied the picture because of considerable technical skepticism, indeed ridicule, from some influential national lab scientists led by Lawrence Livermore's Dr. Peter Muskie. Plus, there was Charlie Grable and NE Division's recent CI conclusion that they were likely controlled Israeli sources aiming to scuttle the agreement.

The analytical community was more divided in their support, but the prevailing sentiment in senior IC echelons seemed to be gelling around the CIA Director's perspective. Skeptics were starting to hear that "the train has left the station" and most were falling into line or asking for comfy seats in the observation car. As for Paula? Not so much. She still had her own doubts about Condor, and she not about to join a collectivist mentality.

Undeniably, however, Condor's reporting was being verified. With Condor's information from the Agency, the IAEA had quickly challenged the new sites, which appeared to be abandoned. But they confirmed the presence of miniscule trace amounts of HEU and some early generation centrifuges and an older mass spectrometer, which could still conceivably be used to measure enrichment levels of the HEU.

The FBI had rolled up the U.S. proliferation network and found evidence of prior shipments of proscribed nuclear technology through offshore cutouts to known Iranian front companies. The three members of the network, two of whom were nuclear scientists who had been fired from the U.S. National Lab complex for various violations of DOE policy and some alleged integrity issues, panicked and turned on one another in a heartbeat, providing ample evidence to the FBI of wrongdoing. The local Special Agent in Charge, in an unguarded moment of candor, confessed to FBI Headquarters that it was almost embarrassing the way the culprits had ratted each other out once they were confronted. He said he had seen thieves, murderers and even a few pedophiles with more honor and dignity.

All well and good and... so why did she sense they were all being played?

Condor's evidence flew in the face of Panther and Jaguar's reporting as well as Leopard's – up until his compromise. When Lane Andrews had informed her that the Iranians had discovered him, Paula had to groan internally. When you lose a source, you question *everything*. She resolved to get to the bottom of this. And like Gary, Paula believed in starting with Agency commo.

And in this case, all roads lead to 3C.

CHAPTER 8

◇◇◇

The Old Man and the CI

DDO's Office Langley

Brian Bannock, a veteran counterintelligence officer, settled himself on a couch in the DDO's office suite, awaiting his appointment with Paula Davenport, and thoughtfully stroked his lush silver beard, a source of justifiable pride to the man. Brian was the spitting image of Ernest Hemingway in his prime, a resemblance he reveled in and played to. He once noted with a chuckle that his autobiography would be entitled "The Old Man and the CI."

Brian understood the nuances and intricacies of CI in all its many forms and permutations and liked to call himself "a practitioner of the art of CI." He knew that this realm seldom offered black and white answers – at least not until it was too late. It was a world of ambiguity and greyness.

He took a holistic look at cases and offered informed and balanced opinions on both the plusses and minuses, unlike many of his CI colleagues who seemed to delight in poking holes in cases while ignoring their strengths. In fact, many were clueless in this regard, since so few had the depth of operational experience as Brian did. And experience was everything. It required more than a textbook answer. It required the truth. And the truth was ever so elusive.

He was at the top of his game and had but one regret. In a small dark corner of his heart was the single disappointment of having been repeatedly passed over for promotion to the Senior Intelligence Service, though this was the fate of almost all CI officers, regardless of ability. It was doubtless due to the fact that the Agency liked to pay lip service to CI, but it was a pain in the ass to most senior officers and they controlled the promotion panels. As one senior officer in charge of CI once remarked, "I live in a world of heartache." This was so true. CI officers rarely brought good news. It was their job to sniff out betrayals and intelligence failures. This aura of deception and breach of trust by Agency sources (and sometimes by treasonous Agency officers), colored their careers in shades of gloom and darkness, making them about as popular as morticians in life insurance companies. Brian had come to terms with this reality, and he had packed it away in a mental box that was seldom opened.

Instead, Brian mastered the dark arts of CI, probing motivations and layers of treachery and deception. Like thin, translucent layers of a psychological onion few of them were obvious or systematic. The Agency's Source Reliability System, referred to as SRS, had been developed years before after a massive CI failure. Brian was disdainful of the SRS, asserting that anything systematic was prone to manipulation and rigid box-checking and ignored the human element with all of its infinite complexities. It also did not account for the element of time, which shifts and erodes people and alliances in unpredictable ways. How can you systematize that?

The SRS was designed to prevent CI disasters, to seal cases within watertight doors of validation just as the Titanic had been designed to be unsinkable. But somewhere out there lurked massive CI icebergs, mostly concealed with jagged edges of lies and deceit beneath the surface that would rip apart trust like a razor to a soft white underbelly.

Brian's CI analysis relied on metaphysical instincts in the same way that Lane Andrews did in recruiting. Some folks referred to it as "gut instinct" and maybe it was. He laughingly referred to himself as "an analog guy in a digital age." The bottom line was the SRS used static quantitative methods, where Brian's were qualitative and fluid. His process stemmed from years of experience and feel – the glimmer of deception in an otherwise airtight case or the fuzzy feeling of truth when others saw lies. And often he couldn't explain it, which drew contempt and skepticism from the bureaucratic CI simpletons who hoped their precious system would mechanically spit out the answers. Brian scoffed at their jejune approach to CI but knew he could not prove his method either. But the instinct was there. Always there.

Paula poked her head out of her office and smiled at him. "Brian, I'm sure you're busy, but I've got a hot one for you. Please come in."

"Anything for you. The CI doctor is in." His eyes twinkled as he gently tugged on his beard and followed her into her inner office.

She laughed. "As you may know, there's a lot of crap flying around about our Iranian nuclear sources. I need a completely objective appraisal of our four sources, and you're the one I want to do it."

"Sounds interesting."

"Great. I've authorized complete access to the files for you. We've got a critical meeting on this issue next week, and I want you prepared to discuss the cases. I just caught wind of the meeting and that's why I asked to see you on such short notice. I plan on attending the meeting personally."

Brian, who had immense respect for Paula (and felt she did for him as well), said, "Consider it done."

Brian relished the challenge and dived right in, immersing himself in the files. About two days later, he got a phone call from Roberta, Mac White's Executive Assistant, asking him to come to the Director's office. This was highly unusual. Brian barely knew the Director. Meetings with His Pearly Whiteness, as Brian referred to Mac, were almost always reserved for the head of the CI Center or other DO luminaries, not the working stiffs. He sensed, however, that this sudden meeting had something to do with his file reviews.

He was taken aback therefore when Mac greeted him as if he were an old friend and asked him to take a seat on his couch near the window overlooking the Potomac. Mac quickly poured him a cup of richly brewed Jamaica Blue Mountain coffee ("I brought it back from my last Caribbean trip!"), and the two sat together, gazing out at the river, like this little chin-chin occurred every day. Two good buddies sharing java and fellowship.

Mac had a piece of paper in his left hand and after a few seconds he looked up from it in a conspiratorial manner and asked, "Brian, you know what I have here, buddy?"

"No sir. No idea."

"This, my friend, is the list of officers being promoted into the Senior Intelligence Service during the next promotion cycle. A very impressive list. But personally I think your name should be on there too. You're a first-class CI officer whose skills have long been overlooked. But no longer, my friend. No longer." Mac smiled broadly.

Brian was stunned. Was he dreaming? He felt like pinching himself.

"I'm looking carefully at those officers who've been outstanding team players but neglected by the system. I'm seeking those guys and gals who're hitting way above their weight class. And I want you to know Brian that you're highest on my list."

"Why...why thank you sir. I...I don't know quite what to say," he managed at last.

Mac leaned over and clinked his cup against Brian's and said, "I want you as part of my close advisory team on CI issues. I know I can trust your judgment and discretion."

"It would be an honor sir. I'm...I'm just at a loss for words," stammered Brian.

Mac filled the next few minutes with some personal anecdotes about working with the president and shared a few inside Agency jokes with Brian, as if he were a long-trusted member of Mac's inner circle. They talked about their common Scottish heritage, and Mac showed Brian a photo of his family tartan, the MacGregors from his mother's side and from whence he had been "blessed" with his given name.

Finally, Mac held out his hand and shook Brian's as if they were best friends. He ushered Brian to the door. He shook his hand again and then just before releasing it, almost as an afterthought, said, "Oh, there is one other thing."

"Yes, sir?"

"Now that you're going to be part of my A-team and an SIS officer, I need you to look more broadly than before at the critical CI issues that impact our great country. You have to take into consideration many aspects of our national security. Think of the international accords that have made our great country secure and prosperous. We all need a reliable peace, I'm sure you'll agree. No room for war-mongering and rumor-chasing, right?"

Brian nodded. "Of course not."

"Excellent. I knew you'd agree. I want that CI Review you're working on to recognize the truth and come down on the right side of history. No more ghosts and conspiracy theories being put forth by our so-called Israeli allies. We're tired of fighting their wars and demonizing the Iranians. I mean I don't care for the mullahs at all - horrible little people - but let's be realistic. Right? Am I right?"

Brian stood there silent, his heart sinking.

"Let's put a stake in the heart of this sucker. As an about-to-be-promoted flag rank officer, I want you to make a bold statement in favor of this fragile peace and defuse any lingering doubts anyone has about Condor. Condor has proved himself time and time again. Coming from you, this will have great impact. I know you can do it."

With that, Mac White patted Brian affectionately on the shoulder and gently closed his door.

Brian drifted back to his office, his head spinning. Everything was a blur. The promotion to SIS would mean not only a sizable salary increase but also the peer recognition and respect that came with it. He thought of his daughter's looming college tuition bills – she had been accepted at a prestigious and very costly Ivy League school - and the cost of elder care for his aging parents. His Dad was suffering from early Alzheimer's. He thought of the fifteen-year-old clunker he was driving with almost two hundred thousand miles on the odometer.

And he thought of that little box in his heart where he had locked away his disappointment at not being promoted. He pondered all of this as he walked down to his file-strewn office, chaotic but ordered by its own internal logic. If he looked at this decision objectively like he looked at his CI cases, what choice did he really have? It seemed obvious.

By the time he reached his desk, he had made up his mind. He had to phone Roberta immediately before he had second thoughts.

He picked up the phone and dialed. "Hi, Roberta, this is Brian Bannock. I was just with the Director. Yes, that's the one. Would you please pass the following message to the Director? Please tell him that I respectfully decline his generous offer. And tell him that Brian Bannock cannot be bought. That's right. You've got it. Thanks. Bye."

He hung up quickly, before he could add, "And tell him to go fuck himself."

Yes, he craved respect but he craved self-respect more.

CHAPTER 9

◇◇◇

The Kid

Directorate of Operations Conference Room Langley

Lane looked at the assembled crowd of senior officers and straphangers, and he smelled trouble. It was a combination of sour faces and quickly exchanged glances between certain participants, producing that acrid odor of jealousy mixed with conniving and raw ambition, seasoned with more than a mere soupcon of arrogance, spelling stormy seas ahead.

Brian Bannock was seated at Paula Davenport's right hand and began the discussion of each case. He went through the Leopard case and noted Lane's careful development. He listed the reporting, which corroborated Condor's reports to a large extent, but then noted the dramatic swing away from Condor's perspective. Brian emphasized that Leopard had concluded that Iran did have a nuclear weapons program.

"And what about his retraction and disavowal of that position in his last message?" asked Pat McCabe, who as Chief of NE Division, headed up their contingent.

"He clearly indicated he was under duress, which makes his retraction spurious. Not only was the freedom-from-duress protocol blatantly violated, but he included the quote from Galileo to indicate the same. I'm in agreement that he has been caught but also that his prior reporting was valid."

"How much was he paid?" asked McCabe, not willing to concede much, if anything.

"Nothing. His motivation for cooperation was his fear of a nuclear-armed Iran and his hatred of the mullahs. This was pretty consistent throughout and well documented. I'm satisfied that he served us well and honorably. And we need to get him sprung if at all possible." This was a nod to Lane, Lacy and Gary, who sat nearby.

Thank you, Brian, thought Lane.

Brian went on to Panther and Jaguar. This case was much more complicated because of lack of human contact, but Brian noted that substantial portions of their reporting were corroborated by Leopard. Also, recent overhead photography seemed to indicate an adit or mine opening on the northeast side of Mount Damavand that could conceivably be the mineshaft housing the covert nuclear complex. A search of old records showed that a sulfur mine had been in the area. One particularly revealing recent satellite photo showed a couple of white buses moving along a mountain road in the park and disappearing from view as they entered a cavern.

Pat McCabe again jumped in. "How much are you paying *these* guys?"

"According to the file, nothing. They're motivated because they hate General Alborzi, the IRGC commander in charge of the project, and fear him controlling a nuclear weapon. One of them is gay and rightfully fears arrest and execution after the bomb is built. Alborzi has basically threatened him. His brother feels they'll *both* be disposed of once their work is completed."

"And this nuke they've developed. I understand we can't prove that it works. Or that's what I hear from Livermore and Los Alamos."

"That's correct, but neither can we disprove it. And we have separate reporting of substantial quantities of HEU moving to Iran. The quantities match up. The weapons formulae are 'interesting' according to some of our national lab experts, but you're right. No proof they'll work. The photos of the nuclear weapons appear legitimate, but again we can't prove it. We hope to be able to get readouts of the cold test from the brother scientists, although they want to defect before then."

"And we've never met these guys, correct?" asked McCabe.

"That's correct. That bothers me, but we've dealt with write-ins before who've proven to be extremely valuable. As I recall, Near East Division has benefited from quite a few of those."

A few heads nodded in agreement. Several of their best sources had initially contacted the Agency this way. It beat throwing a note wrapped around a brick over the Embassy wall.

Brian continued, "They've confirmed Leopard's arrest and that General Masud Alborzi is the head of Project Zulfiqar. We have collateral reporting that he's indeed the nephew of the Supreme Leader but not much else about him. There was a news photo, which got a lot of circulation back when he rescued his uncle after the former Supreme Leader was assassinated. He's evidently a mover and a shaker now in the RevGuards and is on his way up, riding his uncle's coattails, or robes, as the case may be. Ruthless SOB and an opportunist from all accounts."

Lane thought, *Much like several of you in this room.*

Paula said, "I intend to sign off on the PL-110 request to the Director for them to be resettled, providing they continue to work for us on the inside until the cold test. Hopefully they can exfil that data which will tell us a great deal. I'm thinking we can make a remote uplink for them to get it to us even after they've escaped."

Brian added, "And maybe they can figure a way to spring Leopard from his holding cell in the facility."

Lane saw doubtful faces around the table.

"So, we'll tell two untested sources that Leopard's our guy? How wise is that?" asked McCabe.

"He's already a dead man sitting in that holding cell. Unless you want to mount a helicopter rescue, I think it may be our only shot. Actually, 'shot' is probably a bad word to use in this context."

Everybody but Lane laughed as this broke some of the tension in the room. Lane winced.

Turning back to Leopard's arrest, McCabe asked "Why, if Leopard was in fact compromised by a penetration of the cloud computing company, as I've heard from a few folks, were no others compromised? Why are we not seeing massive arrests in Iran? Seems strange to me."

"Probably for the same reason that they've been able to systematically detect your asset networks in Iran for years. They're clever and they're thorough and they're patient. They're waiting for the right moment. As for

Panther and Jaguar, their intel's never been on the cloud network, nor will it be. The DDO has authorized their reporting to be kept off of the cloud and in memo format with extremely limited dissemination." Brian looked briefly at Paula, who nodded in agreement. "I've heard of some other assets disappearing or going silent in recent weeks, however. I understand you haven't heard recently from a senior MOIS officer and a couple of others. I think one is a Majlis deputy; another is a senior military officer, I believe. This may be more widespread than you think. Correct?"

McCabe looked chagrined and uncomfortable as he nodded reluctantly.

"If we're through with the big cats, let's turn to Condor. I've read all the Condor reports and must say that the report evaluations are uniformly superb. I see a large number are graded 'Excellent' and 'Outstanding.' Policymakers have raved about his accuracy in predicting the direction of the nuclear talks and how he has provided a virtual roadmap of verification. Several of the principals say there may not have been a deal without his reports, although I also understand that our dear SecState continues to regard the success as a tribute to his own masterful diplomacy."

Widespread laughter erupted all about the room.

"And I see that a large percentage of his reports have made the President's Daily Brief. Kudos to Charlie, who has actually briefed the president. That must've been a thrill."

Charlie Grable, sitting to McCabe's right, swelled up like a puffer fish and beamed. His acolytes grinned, and two actually applauded.

Brian dropped his bombshell. "So, we were talking about arrests in Iran. Strange, however, that Condor still reports. And he's on the cloud. One has to wonder."

"One has to wonder what?" asked McCabe in a sharp tone.

"One has to wonder if they want him to report."

"Meaning…?"

"Meaning that none of his reporting has ever been counter to Iranian interests. If you look at these reports you can easily conclude that these facilitated the nuclear agreement, which is clearly in their interest. Sanctions got relieved, their economy comes out of the crapper."

"And the secret military sites and the recent report on the U.S. proliferation network?" asked McCabe.

"All well and good, but how did that change anything? The military sites were abandoned and get amnesty thanks to our magnanimous SecState. The network…well that was almost a year ago. Nothing recent. What's damaging? What's incompatible with Iran's interests?"

The NE Division side of the table bristled, but Brian stood his ground. "Look, I'm not saying he's bad, but I am saying that if he's 100 percent Iranian-controlled, his reporting would be no different."

A shifting of chairs and grumbling came from the NE side.

Brian continued in an appeasing tone, "All right. Let's look at the history of the case, okay, folks? I could find no evidence in the file of how Charlie met and developed this guy prior to his recruitment. That's an important element, so Charlie, maybe you can enlighten us?"

Charlie twitched, as if he had been goosed. "Uh, well we saw each other in our respective delegations. Then I hung out at some known Iranian watering holes. It was inevitable that we'd meet. It's an old tactic."

"Hanging out? That's an old tactic?"

"Well, yeah. You know. Staking the place out and waiting for the big game. Being ready to pounce." Charlie bared his teeth and made his fingers look like claws for the benefit of his backbench admirers. They tittered appreciatively.

"So, he comes in the bar and I recognize him from our targeting lists and from several of the negotiating sessions when he was seated next to his big boss, the head of the AEOI. He sees me and then he proceeds to leave. Maybe I spooked him, but I wasn't going to let him get away that easily. I always tell my folks that these guys don't fall in our laps. You need to pursue'em. So, I chased him to a nearby hotel lobby. I immediately pitched him to work for us."

"And you just decided on the spur of the moment to cold pitch the assistant to the head of the AEOI?" asked Brian incredulously. "What gave you any idea that he'd agree? Was this authorized and planned? I'm losing the thread here, Charlie."

"Well, I had, uh…I just had a feeling he'd agree from the way I was reading his body language. Good case officers can do that you know." Charlie said the last defensively, and several of his minions nodded their heads in synch.

"You cold pitched him because of his body language? What was he -- down on his knees begging?" This got some laughs from Brian's side of the table. "Again, was this pitch planned and authorized?"

Pat McCabe interrupted testily, "Let's not badger Charlie, Brian. He did what any good case officer would do to seize the initiative. The result was an outstanding recruitment, which has benefited the U.S. immensely. And I've personally spoken to the Chief of Station, who was as delighted with the recruitment as I was then and *still am*."

Charlie looked with relief at his patron. He had started to sweat when Brian bore down on him.

"I'm not trying to badger Charlie, but it makes a big difference CI-wise if Charlie pitched him or if Condor volunteered. With a lack of any developmental work or documentation, it's unclear. And there's nothing shameful about it if he did offer his services. We get lots of good volunteers and a good case officer must know how to handle one. Good for you, Charlie! But it makes a hell of a difference in looking at it from a CI point of view. So, which was it?"

Charlie avoided looking at Brian and said slowly, "I recruited him. I chased him from one damn bar to another and I persuaded him to sign on with us. I got him to cut his demands by a million dollars. He gave me high quality stuff from the get-go. What more do you want?" The question came out in a whine.

"Stuff." Brian shook his head.

Charlie's lying and this is a charade, thought Lane.

Pat added, "The Director and the White House love Condor's reporting. What's wrong with this picture, Brian? Hasn't this train left the station?"

"Left the station, approaching the station, parked at the station. I really don't give a goddamn. I want the truth. If you say he recruited him, fine. Then I'll note that. As for the Director and the White House, their loving his reporting, hating his reporting or having him whisper sweet nothings up their wazoo has nothing to do with my analysis. Are we straight on that?"

Pat stared at him as the silence in the room became oppressive. "Yes, I think we are."

Paula broke in, "I think we're done here. I'm sending the PL-110 paperwork on Panther and Jaguar forward to the Director. I've asked Brian to continue to monitor all of these cases and keep me advised. I'm also going to be looking closer at compromised Iranian cases to see if there's any connection, but right now the nexus with 3C stands out as suspicious. As a precaution, I'm going to have our Iranian ops data removed from 3C until this is resolved."

Pat looked at Paula with a barely veiled look of condescension. "Sure, let's play it safe. Why not?" He turned to his NE officers and said, "Let's get back to work," as if they had just wasted time at a karaoke bar. He patted Charlie's back. Charlie grinned.

Everyone rose to leave. Lane looked at Brian and winked. Brian winked back.

That was masterful. Lane knew who he'd want in his corner in his next fight.

As they exited the conference room, Brian hung back. Paula also hesitated.

When everyone else had left, he shook his head and looked at her with his grimmest face and said, "We should polygraph that son of a bitch."

She replied, "Condor?"

"No, Charlie. He'd blow ink all over the wall. Damn liar."

She laughed. "I got that vibe too. Thanks for the quick and objective analysis. And for leading that discussion. I thought it might degenerate into a firefight a couple of times. But you made your points loud and clear."

Brian smiled, then held up his hands with his thumbs and forefingers extended like handguns, blew on the fingers and said with a wink, "They shoulda known better than to mess with the Kid!"

CHAPTER 10

◇◇◇

Damned and Lost

San Francisco Bay Area

Stan Morris's heart was in his mouth as he rested his arms on the checkered tablecloth. In the late afternoon, he had walked past Big John Stoddard's office just as Big John was welcoming two visitors. He overheard the nattily dressed man and the tall blonde woman, with small scars on her left cheek, introduce themselves as FBI Special Agents as they offered their credentials. Big John nervously shut his door behind them as he asked them to "come into his happy home."

Happy, my ass, thought Stan. *They should arrest him for crimes against happiness, morality and families.*

But Stan felt a cold stab of fear and wondered what occasioned this federal house call. He had briefly thought that he might in fact know what caused it, but he dismissed it as unjustified guilt at violating a minor technical rule or two. Of course, as the head of Network Security, he had made the friggin' rules. And what harm could possibly come of his technical consulting for a defense contractor like Leila's uncle?

Still..., if they were interested in him, how in the hell did they find out? He controlled the system logs, cameras and monitoring system and they were as clean as a hound's tooth. All evidence of the very brief thumb drive insertion was long gone months ago. Since then, he had done it twice more at Leila's request, but again he erased all evidence. He had super-user status for a reason and he used it. No harm, no foul.

There could be a thousand reasons why Big John was hosting those two FBI agents. *Maybe the FBI wants us to host their data. Maybe we can help them in a cyber investigation.*

Maybe, maybe, maybe…and just maybe there was also one really bad reason that would ruin his career and his life.

Shit.

He sat at his favorite table in his neighborhood Italian restaurant, awaiting Leila. For once, neither her body nor the delicious food and wine were on his mind. In fact, his stomach felt so sour that he began to get sick, and he barely made it to the men's room in time. He sat there for a while on the john, his head in his hands, his thoughts swirling. He groaned involuntarily.

Another patron washing his hands heard him and asked, "You okay in there?"

"Yeah," Stan managed, "I'll be fine. Thanks."

He heard the restroom door open and shut as the other man left. He sat for a few more minutes and left the stall, feeling not much better. He walked to the washbasin and splashed cold water on his face and combed his disheveled hair. He looked at his drawn reflection in the mirror. His skin was ashen. He had to get control of himself or he might just melt into the floor, a pool of liquid humanity.

He drew himself up to his full height and growled, "Get a grip, Stan. They weren't looking for you or they would have already arrested you. It's been months and nothing has happened. Nada. Absolutely zero."

Until now.

"Oh, Christ," he whimpered.

"Stop!" He suddenly slapped himself hard in the face, and the pain of the blow caused him to focus again. He felt a little better.

He emerged from the men's room, still a bit shaky, and saw Leila already at their table with her back to him. She was chatting on her cell phone as he approached. Something caused him to slow his pace, and he hung back as he heard her say, "Tell the general not to worry. He's putty in my hands. He's like a child – a man-child I guess." She giggled and said something in

Farsi, laughed again, and said, "He'll do whatever I ask. He'll bring the drive. Believe me. I've got control of him. Completely."

Stan felt weak and sat down at a nearby table for a moment. After much effort, he regained some of his composure, rose to his feet and strolled noisily over to their table, so as not to startle her. By this time, Leila was concluding her phone call and looked up cheerily at him as she said, "Ciao dear" and hung up. She said it was an old girlfriend and gave him her warmest, sexiest smile.

Stan said he was feeling sick and his head was spinning. She looked at him, an expression of concern on her face, though he was sure it was more concern that he might have overheard her phone conversation than about his health. He excused himself and said he had to go home. Leila didn't argue with him but reminded him of their meeting with Abbas, next Wednesday, when Stan was to bring the fourth thumb drive with the newest algorithms as they changed periodically.

He nodded dumbly and walked out of the restaurant. After about forty feet, he started crying. What was happening? Everything was gone.

The world was black and he was lost. Damned and lost.

Or was he?

If he could only think rationally, maybe there was something he could do.

CHAPTER 11

◇◇◇

Congenital Buffoonery

Department of Energy, Forrestal Building, Washington

The latest report from Lawrence Livermore scientists McKeown and Carlton sat on Secretary of Energy Alvarez's desk, along with the sensitive source reporting from FBI/CIA joint sources Panther and Jaguar. He skimmed both and then re-read them much more slowly. His hands trembled slightly as he digested the reports and his anger grew – anger at the Iranians for gulling them, anger at their dumbass Secretary of State for insisting that they be gulled, and finally anger at himself for not speaking up more when he knew they were being gulled.

Damn it, damn it, damn it.

The latest computer simulations at Livermore on Sequoia showed that there was at least a 75% chance that Panther's calculations and his concept of neutron phasing were feasible. Alvarez shook his head sadly. Months earlier, his own instincts and the mounting evidence of Iranian duplicity had made it clear that he needed to act, but he had been too cowardly to do so. He had told himself that he was just a scientist and not a politician. But he was also an American official and he expected more of himself. He had been party either to congenital buffoonery or to a charade, the pretense of which had gradually dawned on him, leaving him feeling queasy and depleted.

Such a pity. His wife had grown quite fond of those glittering White House dinners and the fine evening gowns. He loved her very much. Yes,

Washington was quite a change from boring academia and the slower pace at the Lab. Well, she would have to readjust to barbecues and tumbleweeds “up on the mesa” in New Mexico. He had only one choice now, one he should have taken earlier.

She’d understand. She always did.

CHAPTER 12

◇◇◇

An Abomination

Project Zulfiqar, Lar National Park

His slender fingers danced slowly across the ultra-shiny surface of the oblong metallic container. He could see the elongated reflection of his face in the mirror-like surface and he could even make out the tears on his cheeks. He stared for a few minutes, trying to make sense of the problem he had created. How could he have been so foolish? His nose was starting to run, glistening in the lights of the room and reflecting back at him.

He wondered if his soul was gone. Why in God's name had he designed this horror other than for pure vanity? Sure, he was intellectually curious, but why couldn't he have been curious about something else? Maybe gravitational waves or dark matter. But this was madness. He looked at it as a parent might look upon a beloved child or pet that committed murder and mayhem. This was an abomination. A 1.5 megaton abomination. An equivalence of 1.5 million tons of TNT. Not only could it injure and kill millions, it would also spark a war that would cause many millions more to die. And it was his creation. His fault. He had to stop it. He had to kill it.

Three other identical silvery shapes lay on holding cradles in close proximity. But not too close. If they were too close, that would be a real disaster, although it might solve his dilemma. And in the adjoining room was yet one more of these polished monstrosities – or at least it was identical in appearance and weight, if not in content. That sparked his thinking.

Suddenly, Daoud had a plan.

CHAPTER 13

◇◇◇

Just Before Nowruz

University of California, Berkeley, 21 February

Hello Dr. McKeown,

We hope you are well. We are fine for the moment, but the timing of our departure is now accelerated because the cold test is set for a month from now on the day before Nowruz, our Persian New Year, on 21 March. We must now insist upon an escape plan from you or we are surely lost. Actually, we have the plan to exit Iran but we must be met by boat in the Caspian Sea. We have cousins in the town of Nur, which is located on the coast of the Caspian in Mazandaran Province. It is about two hours from our housing in Gazaneh northwards on Highway 77 to the coastal road Highway 22. Our cousins own a small pleasure boat, which we can borrow and rendezvous with you about fifteen miles north of the town out at sea at GPS coordinates, which I will provide to you. I would suggest that we then proceed with all dispatch to Azerbaijan, probably the southernmost coastal town of Astara, just across the border from the Iranian town of the same name.

Daoud hopes that his stolen super-user privileges on our cyber system will allow him to liberate Dr. Javadpour from his cell so he can accompany us in the confusion. Daoud will create a distraction with the computers, alarm systems, lighting, HVAC system, sprinkler system and automatic doors. In essence, he will create the illusion that a fire has broken out near the HEU holding area and the vault with the live weapons. He believes that he can create so much confusion and panic that it will greatly complicate General Alborzi's ability to pursue us once he notices we are gone.

Daoud believes that he can sever communications with the outside world and lock the dear General and his security staff inside the underground facility after the cold test for at least three or four hours, allowing us time to be well out to sea and at the rendezvous point. The preparation of the Nowruz festivities in surrounding communities will only compound the chaos. Nowruz will also serve as an excellent pretext for my wife and children to slip away a few days in advance to Istanbul to see her sister.

Once the cold test is concluded, Daoud will trigger the fake fire, excuse himself to look into the emergency and slip away. His pre-programmed cyber commands will open Javadpour's cell door and he will accompany him to a nearby emergency shaft from where they can exit and join me in the parking lot. As you may recall, Daoud and I have been allowed "the privilege" of staying apart from the others near our old home and thus I have my own car.

Per our agreement, the cyber commands will also send the cold test data to a satellite uplink and erase all of the weapons design data from the systems. He has also designed special permission action links for the four live weapons. They will be programmed to scramble their encrypted contents in a random fashion and render the weapons locked and inert. He has not yet succeeded in devising a way to destroy the HEU inside the weapons short of a real fire, but he is pondering this. Uranium is flammable at 300 to 350F, so there may be a way. At least we believe that they will not have the ability to trigger these specific weapons nor have the designs to replicate them. There are no guarantees in life and this plan may be flawed, but we have tried our best and see no alternative.

We have kept our end of the bargain and are content that we are working for peace. It is imperative that someone from America meets us at the rendezvous point. Otherwise, we are doomed. Again, I will transmit shortly the GPS coordinates as well as the radio frequency we will be using from our boat.

With our sincere best wishes from your Persian team, Majid and Daoud

◇◇◇

Lacy and Lane read the incoming message from Jaguar and Panther and then took it to Gary.

Lane waited until Gary had read it and said, “I think it’s kind of obvious what we have to do. This is our one chance to save all three.”

Lacy nodded. “I’m in. There are promises to keep.”

Gary smiled. “Yes, there are. Besides, I always wanted to go yachting in the Caspian.”

CHAPTER 14

◇◇◇

Atonement

San Francisco Bay Area, 11 March

Stan sat in the booth of the coffee shop where they had arranged to meet and contemplated the café mocha he had mechanically bought as he waited for Leila and Abbas. The perky little blonde barista had cheerily asked him if he wanted whipped cream on his mocha and he had replied, "Sure. Why not? You only live once!"

Except that he wasn't living anymore at all. Just existing and barely, at that.

The whipped cream was beginning to melt as he sat there, exactly like his dreams and his life and everything else. Dripping slowly down the side of the dark blue porcelain cup in big glops. So sad. The thumb drive in his pants pocket seemed to burn his thigh. He wasn't sure if he could go through with this or not. But he had to.

He sat there glumly and thought of all the other options he didn't have. *So, just do it.* If only he could get through his self-loathing and act like a man…well, that was what he had to do. He steeled himself for the meeting.

Abbas and Leila showed up on time. That was something at least. They sat across from him and smiled like they were all old friends. He thought of his daughter Allison and managed a weak smile back. He had to go through with this for his daughter.

"Hello, Stan. Always good to see you." He had met Abbas on a couple of earlier occasions. He was in his late forties and of average height, rather slim and had a bushy black moustache. For some reason, he dressed casually, a little like a tennis pro. His sporting attire, his gold Rolex watch, his slightly mussed hair and his lightly tanned skin could cause one to think he had just played a couple of sets at the club.

Leila wore a light green blouse and a turquoise and gold Hermes scarf that wrapped about her slender neck and highlighted her emerald eyes. She had a matching mint green Phillip Lim leather bucket bag at her side. She blew Stan a kiss from across the table. He almost recoiled at this but managed to keep control. Nothing could look amiss.

"Did you bring it?" she asked, then glanced at Abbas, as if showing off her star pupil to the principal.

"Oh yeah. I brought it." He looked past them at the young couple seated at a nearby table but tried not to stare. He had to make the deal go down. He reached in his pocket and retrieved the thumb drive. He put it in his napkin and pushed it slowly across the table to Abbas, who palmed it with a smooth motion.

"Good man," said Abbas. "You're a real life-saver." He put the thumb drive in his pocket.

Yeah, Stan thought, *But the life I save may be my own – or at least my integrity. What a disaster!* His thoughts felt chaotic. He wondered if he were going into psychic shock.

Then all hell broke loose.

The athletic looking young man from the nearby table and his companion, a slim young woman with strawberry blonde hair and small facial scars, quickly approached Abbas and Leila from behind, moved to either side of them and shouted "FBI! You're under arrest!" At least four other patrons from tables adjoining them did likewise. The world became a blur of images and sounds swimming and swirling around him.

Leila stood quickly and swung her bag at the male FBI agent and knocked his credentials across the café. As the FBI agent went off-balance, she used her free hand to retrieve something shiny from her bag. Stan stared in horror as she swung the shiny object toward the tall female agent. "No!"

He fell onto Leila and briefly heard the sound of thunder. All he could register was a cold stab in the stomach and the most excruciating pain. He saw the female agent, whom he knew as Lacy, bringing her own gun to bear and saw a red stain blossom on Leila's immaculate blouse as she cartwheeled backwards from the shock of the blast, her beautiful hair spinning about her.

Stan staggered toward the fallen Leila and saw the light fading from her lovely eyes. As he lost consciousness, Stan saw them handcuffing Abbas and attending to Leila who lay on the ground, unmoving.

When he awoke in the ambulance, Lacy was holding his hand. She told him that he had done well and that all would be fine. She asked him to hold on.

Stan looked up at her, blinked and said, "Tell Allison…tell Allison that I love her. I tried…I…I tried to make it right. I'm sorry I messed up."

Lacy assured him that he had done the right thing by coming to the FBI with his account of the Iranian espionage. She said she understood that he was trying to atone for his mistake and she thanked him for saving her life at the café. He squeezed her hand and looked up at her, a tear coursing down his cheek. Then he closed his eyes. His hand relaxed and loosened. His breathing slowed and finally he let go.

Lacy sat there and her eyes glistened.

CHAPTER 15

◇◇◇

A Sacred Obligation

CIA Director's Office Langley, 19 March

Paula Davenport had been summoned to Mac White's office ten minutes earlier and she was hardly surprised. She sat across from him, firm in her resolve.

He played a bit with his glasses, then looked at her with some sadness.

"Paula, I understand you dispatched a team of three officers to Azerbaijan to effect a rescue of those three Iranian assets – the ones I have considerable doubts about. Why didn't you consult me about this?"

She replied quietly, "With all due respect sir, I did it on my authority as DDO, as a fulfillment of our commitments to these men. I didn't think I had to consult you on what I knew was the right thing to do and within my area of responsibility."

"'The right thing to do.' I see." Mac stared at her. "But didn't it occur to you that the right thing to do is not to endanger our officers, including a female FBI agent, for three very questionable sources – sources who've been contradicted by our primary source – a source who has made the Iran nuclear deal possible?"

"Mr. Director, I have considerable doubts about Condor and have come to the conclusion that---"

Mac interrupted her and shouted, "Oh to hell with your doubts and all of those whimpering handwringing analysts in the Counterproliferation

Center. I might expect backsliding like this from that pussy Arlo McReedie but Christ-almighty, Paula, you're better than that." He wrung his hands and continued, "Your doubts play right into the hands of the Israelis and the warmongering faction in Congress. We've verified and re-verified Condor's information. He's been the key to our success. We've got an agreement! What more do you want?"

She looked steadily at him, unmoved by his outburst. "The truth. All I want is the truth, Mac. And I don't think it's coming from Condor."

Mac lowered his voice and spoke as if to a child. "We all want the truth, but the truth is such a fragile concept. History will show us you are wrong and that the truth is perishable. What we needed to do was cut our losses with these three loser assets and close the books. My company would've cut its losses long ago with these assets who are in fact liabilities."

Paula could barely control her desire to leap across Mac's desk and shove his pearly white teeth down his throat. She managed to speak through gritted teeth. "Mr. Director, we may call our sources 'assets' but they're flesh and blood men and women who have placed their allegiance with us and are risking their very lives by working with us. They are not simply pen and ink entries to be written off of a damned balance sheet when we feel like it. My highest commitment is to the security of our sources. It's a sacred obligation that I will not forsake."

"Don't you preach to me," Mac shot back. "As long as I'm the Director, we're doing it my way. I hereby order you to recall that team of three from this wild goose chase. I have already stopped the shipment of the boat to Baku, the one that you had requisitioned from Maritime Branch. It's over. Get our people back. That's the end of the discussion."

She said in a steady, quiet voice, "That's impossible, sir. I sent them in black and ordered them to destroy their encrypted commo gear the moment they arrived so that they would be carrying nothing incriminating. No spy gear whatsoever. They have emergency re-contact plans, but it's one way from them to us. Lane Andrews is in charge. I have full faith in him. He'll bring them back."

Before Mac could speak, Paula added, "I've also prepared my resignation, which I'm hereby giving to you. I'm tired of living a lie for all these months. I have to live with my conscience. You can run the whole goddamn shooting match from now on. And that is the definite end of the discussion. Good luck to you."

With that, she shoved a folded piece of paper across his desk, stood up and walked out with her head held high.

CHAPTER 16

◇◇◇

A True PAL

Project Zulfiqar, 19 March

Watching figures flash across the screen of his encrypted smartphone linked to his Zurich investment account, General Alborzi saw only the same old numbers – a little up, a little down. Boring, boring, boring. The only thing more boring would be watching his uncle, the Supreme Vacuity and his equally dull Assembly of Morons. He needed to liven things up. Shake the roots of assumptions. You don't make profits in smooth markets. Fortunes were made when others panicked, which meant that stability was not his friend. He needed an unexpected dramatic event to sharply rattle the markets. Then his pre-positioned call and put options would make him a fortune beyond belief.

Kazemi was due back any day now with the six million dollars he had scammed the CIA in exchange for the latest "sensitive nuclear information." That money would only add to the payout. Alborzi was turning bullshit into gold like the alchemists of lore. And the CIA was paying off like a rigged slot machine.

A knock came at the door of the vault in which he's been waiting. A moment later, two guards led in Daoud Tabatabai, who had been brought to review the procedures for the impending cold test.

"So, how are we looking?" Alborzi asked the scientist without preamble.

Daoud shrugged slightly. "This test will be the best indicator of reliability we can employ, short of an actual test explosion. But we really don't need that. Once I've verified the neutron-count after the inert weapon has been detonated, I'll have all the data I need."

Alborzi pointed at the device seated in the cradle in front of him. "So, the only difference between this weapon for the cold test and the four sitting next door in the weapons vault is the fact that this one has depleted uranium with very little U235?" asked Alborzi.

"Correct, but the neutron count should be very similar. That will be the litmus test of the weapon's reliability and characteristics."

"Amazing. But it looks identical to the others."

"It is...with the exception of the substitution of the depleted uranium for the HEU. Otherwise, they're clones."

"Well, I certainly hope you'll be using the one with depleted uranium. We wouldn't want a hot nuke going off by mistake, would we? What did you say it would yield? Ten kilotons?" Alborzi looked over at the other room where the four real weapons lay in their movable cradles.

"That's right...about ten kilotons, maybe a bit more. The cold test weapon here has only a few kilograms of high explosive in the firing set. Sure, it'll collapse the test adit ceiling very shortly after the data is transmitted electronically to us in the control center. But that's about it. A real nuclear explosion, though...that would be equivalent to ten thousand tons of high explosive and create a crater on the western slope of Mt. Damavand along with a mushroom cloud because it'll be less than a hundred and fifty feet below the surface."

"Really? How large a crater?"

Daoud continued as if lecturing his physics students at Sharif University, "Well, Sedan Crater at the U.S. Nevada Test Site was created by a 104 kiloton weapon in 1962. It was 635 feet below the desert and created a crater 1280 feet across and more than 320 feet deep. I've seen photos of it in U.S. Department of Energy publications. Let me pull it up on the Internet for you." Daoud made a quick entry in his laptop and soon both men were staring at the impressive manmade crater, complete with its own viewing stand for tourists to gaze at it.

Alborzi was shocked, “That’s one big fuckin’ hole!”

“Of course, that weapon was ten times the yield of our weapons, but our crater would likely be comparable in size because of the shallower depth of the explosion. It wouldn’t hurt us at this distance on the far side of the mountain but it would definitely get people’s attention…something none of us really want!” He laughed.

Alborzi reflected upon this for a moment and filed it away mentally.

Alborzi returned to his initial question, “Visibly, how can you tell the difference between them – I mean the cold test weapon and the real thing? They look the same. Again, we don’t want mistakes, do we?”

“Of course not. See that little coupling on the side with the digital readout? It’s blinking green at the moment. That’s a permissive action link, or PAL. It’s a use-control for security purposes. I needed to brief you on this PAL in any case because you and I are the only ones currently with authority to cause the weapon to go “hot” and ready for detonation. Here is the matching transmitter in this black laptop. This is kind of like “the football” which the American president carries. It has the nuclear codes, which are encrypted and sent to commanders in case of a nuclear war.”

“And why do you have this authority in addition to me?” Alborzi asked a bit indignantly.

“Because, General, I had to devise the algorithms for the use controls and program it. But don’t worry; you and I have unique codes for accountability. They’re indicated on the laptop screen with your name and mine. See right here?” he indicated the proper area on the screen. “We each will have unique passwords and then nothing can go wrong.”

“Show me.”

Daoud took the laptop, clicked on his name and then entered his new password. The blinking light suddenly flashed red. “The weapon is now armed, but don’t worry. We’re not near the control panel and there are a couple more steps for detonation, so we’re safe. Each PAL is unique to a specific weapon. You also have the option of removing the PAL if you wish, but I don’t know why you would do so unless it malfunctions, and then you swap it for another.” He entered another command and the light returned to green.

"Daoud, thank you. This is absolutely sheer genius. You've performed a great service for the Islamic Republic. My uncle will hear of your work." Alborzi stood and shook Daoud's hand as he left the room.

And a great service for me, thought Alborzi.

Later, in his private office, Alborzi reviewed the video recorded from several angles in the vault where he and Daoud had met that morning. It didn't take long for him to get the correct camera, which after some magnification clearly showed the keystrokes that Daoud had entered for his password. He walked back to the weapons vault and entered those on the black laptop. He then walked into the adjoining room and with gloved hands wheeled in a real weapon with more than a little bit of strain. *Shit, these fuckers are heavy!* He could pull a frigging hernia doing this. But no gain without pain.

It looked identical to its inert cousin. After some more data entry, Alborzi removed and swapped the two PALs and then wheeled the inert weapon back in the weapons vault from whence the real one had emerged. Soon, he would light this little ten-kiloton firecracker off the far western slope of the snow-clad mountain. The world would sit up and take notice. It would also rival what that fat little fuck in Pyongyang had done to date. He and that Hezbollah scum in Lebanon could take a hike. He didn't need their help.

Yes, soon he would loose the furies and shake the world and the markets. He expected to multiply his fortune in Zurich by at least a factor of ten as gutless investors panicked and ran for shelter. This would be his masterpiece.

And Daoud would be the one held responsible in the end. Poor, pitiful Daoud. Ah well, he wasn't long for this world in any event. Any way you look at it, he loses.

CHAPTER 17

◇◇◇

In Bentley's Bar

Baku, March 20

The reflection of the man in the mirrors of Bentley's Bar in the Four Seasons Hotel revealed a pensive face on someone who was not especially interested in his glass of red wine. He lingered over it and swirled it occasionally but didn't drink it. Instead, he was distracted by the front-page story in the morning *International New York Times* which was headlined: "CIA and DOE Lose Senior Officials."

The story read in part:

"The sudden resignation of a CIA Senior Official, the DDO who runs worldwide CIA clandestine operations, and the Secretary of Energy within twenty-four hours of one another seems strangely intertwined. Both cited "personal reasons" for their respective resignations, but sources within both organizations cited fundamental differences they each had over the Administration's Iranian nuclear policy. A senior intelligence official, who asked for anonymity because he was not authorized to speak, said that Paula Davenport abruptly resigned yesterday afternoon as CIA DDO because she felt she could no longer carry out her duties effectively. Sources within the Department of Energy said that Secretary Manuel Alvarez submitted his resignation to the President earlier that morning on a 'matter of principle' and that he abruptly walked out of DOE Headquarters with a smile on his face. Neither official could be reached for comment."

Lane Andrews re-read the article for the third time. He realized now why the promised boat from Maritime Branch, along with the expected team of Agency paramilitary officers had not shown up on schedule. In fact, he knew it would never show up and that he, Gary and Lacy were officially up shit creek without a boat or paddle. Worse yet, Leopard, Panther and Jaguar were now dead men walking.

He pushed the wine glass away and stared off into space.

Gary and Lacy were in their rooms awaiting his decision on what to do next. He had explained that the DDO's order that they destroy their encrypted communications gear before arrival in Baku was probably so they could not be recalled. After reading the news article, he was sure of it. Paula had launched them on a rescue mission and then resigned rather than be overruled. He didn't feel abandoned by her. Not at all. She had done what she thought was right, and in fact it was right. But he knew the system was probably still trying to contact them in order to get them to stand down. *Let them.* They had already tried once that day – and failed.

A thin-faced young man with a mop of blonde hair approached Lane as he was leaving the marina that morning, having checked one more time to see if their boat had finally arrived. He'd little hope it had, but it was his only choice. Nothing. As he walked away from the dock, he heard his name. He turned and a young Agency officer whom he knew was posted to the area approached him from behind. Lane looked briefly at him but kept walking, ignoring his pleas to stop. Finally, the young officer ran and overtook him.

"Mr. Andrews, Lane, we need to talk."

"No, I don't think so. Get lost." Lane did not break stride. Obviously the kid had been informed by HQS that Lane hoped to meet the Agency boat at the marina and he had staked out the place.

"You gotta listen to me. Washington has asked me to tell you to stand down. You and the others, you've gotta leave," insisted the young man with an officious tone in his voice, now almost out of breath.

"I don't have to do anything unless I hear it directly from the DDO," snarled Lane.

"I'm serious. This comes from the Director himself. You and the others need to stop, pack and go home. The operation is no longer sanctioned. You're off the books if you proceed," whined the young man.

"Then I guess we're off the books. Unless the DDO says directly to me to stand down, I'm sticking to my plan. Now, if you'll excuse me, fuck off." Lane turned and walked swiftly away, hopping into a taxi as the young officer begged him to stop. Lane didn't look back as they drove off.

Lane had canvassed his team later that day after informing them about the third consecutive no-show of the boat and of the young officer's attempt to stop them.

"I feel more than a little bit like Colonel Travis at the Alamo, considering the desperate state of our situation. We're outnumbered and besieged from all sides. We have the Iranians in front of us and Washington to our rear and I'm not sure which is more hostile. We have nothing but right on our side. Therefore, I have to ask both of you to consider your personal situation. I'll be blunt with you: Sticking to our plan will probably end your career in addition to being damned dangerous. I won't draw a line in the sand as Travis did, but if you want to leave, no one, especially me, will think ill of you." He looked at each of them in turn.

Lacy nodded, "Count me in. I'm a Texan, Fighting hopeless battles like the Alamo is in my blood. I'm not deserting Ali and the others."

Gary Scott smiled, "You don't even have to ask. My career is long over, but this one…this one's for Parviz. Maybe I couldn't save him, but I'll certainly try to save these guys if I can. Fuck the IRGC and fuck Headquarters. Let's do it."

*What a remarkable team…*But, sadly, he was leading them nowhere. The rendezvous was less than 24 hours from now out in the Caspian Sea and he had no way to get them there. To make matters worse, Paula had resigned. Talk about having no top cover and no backup…The Agency was probably out looking for him and his team as he swirled his wine. He looked deeply into his glass, feeling resigned, when someone sat down heavily next to him. He heard a familiar gravelly voice.

"New in town, sailor?"

He looked at the speaker, who was grinning from ear to ear.

"McBane."

The investigative journalist sat there next to him, beatific in all of his rumpled glory. "I am but your humble servant, my boy."

"How in the hell did you know I was here?"

"Ah, sources and methods, you know. Sources and methods."

Lane had to laugh. "I thought that was supposed to be my line."

"Well, let's just say I've rented a few local Azerbaijanis and they keep me informed. I heard that a group of three Americans were in town and it wasn't about oil and gas business. So, I figured I'd check out the best hotel in town...and le voila!"

"Not too shabby. Maybe you should've been a case officer."

"Maybe so." McBane cocked his head, staring at Lane. "Why so glum? Your gal dump you for some other stud?" McBane smoothed a few strands of loose hair over his bald spot, squared his shoulders. "Maybe she prefers older men, eh? More gravitas, mayhaps." He winked.

"I wish that were the problem."

McBane chuckled, then turned serious. "So, what's the matter?"

Lane shook his head. "Nothing that a good boat won't fix."

"Ask and ye shall receive saith the Lord, or in this case, saith McBane."

"Wait, you have a boat? A fast boat?" asked Lane incredulously.

"Oh, I probably have one of the fastest boats within several hundred miles of this busy little metropolis."

"How in the--"

"Let's just say that I've got a very powerful friend who owes me a favor...a debt of honor. I know that he and his family use fast boats in their commerce and I can get one."

"What kind of commerce?" asked Lane skeptically.

"I think you'd describe it as import-export."

"Uh huh...and what pray tell do they import and export?"

"Well they import what people want and I suspect they export dollars to safer havens shall we say."

"And why the need for speed?"

"Well, time is money and I suppose some of their commerce might be extra-legal – so swiftness is a virtue if one needs to stay a few steps ahead of those pesky revenuers."

"Okay, McBane. Enough joking. Do you really have a boat? A fast boat?" Lane emphasized the word "fast."

"I do. The fastest around. But there's one small string attached to my offering it to you."

"And what's that?"

"That I accompany you as skipper of said vessel."

"Are you out of your mind? You could get killed! It's out of the question. No. Nyet. Verboten."

McBane shook his head. "No tickee, no laundry. No Skipper McBane, no fast boatee."

Lane stared at him but said nothing.

"Listen son, I'm on my last great adventure. All I've done up until now is to write about HEU smuggling and proliferation from the sidelines. I'm tired of just being an observer. I got a taste of intrigue and danger when I got you those HEU smuggling reports – the ones you said were so good. Well, I decided I like that feeling and I want more. I want to make a real difference."

Lane started shaking his head and muttering, "No, no, no…"

McBane then added pointedly, "Besides, I'm sure my powerful friend will only loan his boat to me for my personal use. I'm also probably the most qualified skipper you know in this little burg. I'll have you know I lettered on the Princeton yachting team and have been running cigarette boats off of Martha's Vineyard since well before you were but a gleam in your daddy's eye."

Lane knew he was defeated. More than that – he realized he needed the older man's help. "Ah hell, why not? They're going to fire me for disregarding orders from the Director anyway. Why not go down in flames, right?"

"That's the ticket," exclaimed McBane. "But you're wrong. They're not gonna fire you. You'll be a hero!"

"No, you're right. They won't fire me. They'll send me to prison instead for endangering a civilian's as well as my own officers' lives and using a smuggler's boat in the bargain. I might only get five years if I'm lucky."

"Oh, cheer up. This'll be fun. We can leave at once. But first, let me order you a real glass of wine instead of that dreadful plonk you're pretending to drink." McBane signaled the bartender. "Barkeep, give me a bottle of your best French Bordeaux, a St. Emilion or Pomerol, if possible, for my new best friend and me. We're celebrating a new adventure."

CHAPTER 18

◇◇◇

A Delicious Gipfeli

Bern, Switzerland

The tall, thin man sat on the grand terrace of the majestic Bellevue Palace Hotel in Bern and gently stirred a small dollop of Swiss cream into his morning espresso, breathed in its delicious aroma, sipped it carefully. He then slowly munched the buttery flaky Swiss pastry – a gipfeli – on the plate in front of him with some raspberry jam as he gazed out over the Aare River at the snow-clad Berner Oberland. It was his third gipfeli, but he wasn't in a particular hurry this morning, and he felt rested and resolved in his course of action. And the gipfeli tasted so good.

As he chewed, he thought about his now-former boss and how the SOB had been claiming all the credit and all the profit from the series of highly lucrative transactions he had conducted at great personal risk. In fact, his boss deserved zero credit or profit from any of it, especially in light of how he had treated him in their last meeting – one in which he should have been congratulated and not chastised like a common servant.

Well, screw him.

The thin man lingered a few more minutes over his breakfast, consulted his map and decided to walk to his destination, which was only a leisurely twelve minutes away. He retrieved the large black leather bag at his feet. It was a bit heavy, but he didn't mind the weight considering its contents. Moreover, he had spied a small, discreet Swiss private bank about half way on his walking route where he could hopefully rent a safe deposit box and stash the contents, no difficult questions asked. He rose from the table and strolled swiftly out of the hotel into the bright sunshine and cool mountain air, a spring in his steps.

Indeed, the Swiss bank threw no curves at him, and within short order he had a sufficiently large safe deposit box with a one-year contract. After storing the bag's contents, he continued his trip up Sulgeneckstrasse to number 19 and saw the modern-looking office building behind the security fence. He read the sign at the front: Embassy of the United States of America.

The thin man proceeded to the entrance, where he met a sharply dressed Marine guard behind thick green protective glass who asked him politely to state his business.

"I would like to see a CIA officer because I have information of vital importance to the United States."

The young corporal's eyes widened, and he asked to see a passport. The thin man gave him his passport along with a brief letter of explanation, which the Marine hurriedly read. He asked him to wait for a couple of minutes while the Marine picked up the phone and had a quick conversation. Within a few minutes, he was ushered inside after passing through a metal detector. Here he was met by an earnest young man who introduced himself as "Roy," which may or may not have been his name but was sufficient. They entered a small private room near the entrance and the young man closed the door and asked him to take a seat.

The thin man introduced himself. "I am Major Alireza Kazemi of the Islamic Revolutionary Guard Corps of Iran and I wish to defect. You may check with your colleagues in Langley, where I am codenamed 'Condor.' I have information of great interest to your country and have already been promised asylum."

The earnest young man wrote all of this down and handed Kazemi's passport back after he had photocopied it. The young man asked him, "How pressing is this information? Is there an imminent threat to the United States or its allies?"

"I don't believe there is an imminent threat but I wouldn't waste any time getting someone to chat with me because this involves the secret Iranian nuclear weapons program."

Roy looked up at him abruptly from his pad of paper with a look of alarm. "Say that again, please. Did you say 'nuclear weapons' program?"

"Yes, you heard me correctly. Your country has been completely misled. I have detailed evidence of a covert nuclear weapons program codenamed 'Project Zulfiqar,' and I must go as soon as possible to the United States, where I will explain everything to the CIA. Run my name or the name 'Condor' past them and you'll get an immediate response. In the meantime, you can reach me at the Bellevue Palace Hotel," said Kazemi, writing down the room number on the young man's pad. He then got up and said, "I wouldn't linger on this if I were you. Time is tight. Now I wish to return to my hotel. Have a good day."

Kazemi started to leave but added, "Oh, and tell them I refuse to meet with that idiot Charlie Grable."

As he started back up Sulgeneckstrasse, Kazemi laughed quietly to himself. Alborzi had been right that the new information was worth its weight in gold and that the Americans wouldn't even blink at six million dollars. But what Alborzi had not figured was that they wouldn't blink at ten million dollars either. And that nifty sum in crisp 1000 Swiss Franc notes now sat securely in his new safe deposit box. He wondered how large a house he could buy in Carmel or Santa Barbara. Maybe he'd take up surfing and even start his own vineyard. And buy a Ferrari. Or a Tesla. Or a Ferrari *and* a Tesla…

CHAPTER 19

◇◇◇

For Ali

Control Room, Project Zulfiqar, 21 March

General Alborzi sat before the control panel for the cold test, looking at the bright red button, contemplating the investment decisions he had sent earlier that day via his encrypted cell phone to Dr. Hans-Ruedi Mayer at Jacquard Privat Bank in Zurich. He had wagered most of his now-considerable fortune on the fact that the price of oil was going to go through the roof in the next few hours and that shares in certain Western companies pushing for Iranian contracts would collapse once the red button was pushed. Ah, the glories of puts and calls. Money would be made by the bushel full. He could retire in Switzerland.

Of course, he would have had even more to invest had that weasel Kazemi shown up in time with his six million dollars. His subordinate was now overdue by several days and had better have a damned good excuse or else Alborzi would soon be looking for a new double agent and the IRGC would be short one Major.

Alborzi looked about the room and invited Daoud to come have the honor of pushing the button for the test. Of course, Alborzi had earlier secretly entered Daoud's password in order to arm the PAL. Now, with Daoud's password registered as arming the weapon and with him pushing the button, any fool, including his uncle and his merry band of mullah morons, would conclude that Daoud had either gone off the reservation, was a Zionist spy or had made a mistake.

A fatal mistake.

Daoud approached Alborzi and asked if he was ready for the test. He noted that all the systems and diagnostics were active and in place. Alborzi nodded and sat back so that the technicians in the room could observe Daoud push the button. Nothing better than a few witnesses.

Daoud said quietly, "For Ali" and put his forefinger and middle finger together like a pair of scissors to push the button. Everyone else in the room thought that he was making the sign of the legendary twin-bladed sword of Zulfiqar, which Ali had received from his cousin Muhammad at the battle of Uhud.

Not quite. In point of fact, Daoud was thinking of Dr. Ali Javadpour in his cell and praying that this would free him -- as well as Majid and himself.

Daoud pressed the button. Nothing happened.

Then a lot happened. A whole lot.

PART 5

CHAPTER 1

◇◇◇

A Demon Free From its Chains

Western Slope of Mt. Damavand, Test Adit, 21 March

"I am going to take off your muzzle
If they tear me into pieces.

I will send a flame from my inside fire
That would burn that muzzle.

This is what I am going to do, hoping
That it would please you.

You would become liberated and roar
Like a demon free from its chains.

Your roaring would shake the earth
From Nishapour to Nahavand,

From the sparks of your inside furnace
Rays of light would flood the distance from Alborz to Alvand.

Attack like a poisonous dragon
And roar like an enraged, furious lion.

Make a matchless concoction
Put together an unparalleled mixture.

Send a cloud made of fire's blaze, Hell's flame, gas & ill-smelling fumes
From smoke, hot gas, rotten rocks,

All wrapped in the scorching sighs of the oppressed people,
And the threatening fire of God's punishment."

Mohammad-Taqi Bahar, Iranian Poet, "Ode to Damavand"

The first few thousand neutrons entered the specially designed pit of the weapon. These few thousand impacted U235 atoms, which liberated many more neutrons and they in turn crashed into others freeing even more. Within an extremely short timescale, not comprehensible to the human mind, the few became many and the many became many many more. The chain reaction was well underway.

The weapon's innovative and dense nanostructure shell surrounding the reactions held together for a few extra shakes of time measured in nanoseconds, barely containing the rapidly expanding ball of energy, which was superheated plasma and x-rays and pure explosive fury from hell. But those few extra nanoseconds ensured that at least another few generations of U-235 atoms fissioned, releasing even more enormous amounts of energy. Then it failed spectacularly and the fireball's thermal energy quickly reached 100 million degrees Celsius – the same as the interior of the Sun – and the fireball grew at a rate that would exceed 6000 feet in diameter after only ten seconds.

It consumed or displaced millions of tons of earth in the blink of an eye as the mushroom cloud erupted off of the western slope of Mt. Damavand. In fact, a sizeable portion of the entire western side of the mountain was now gone, far eclipsing the depth of Sedan Crater in Nevada, which in comparison might have been a gopher hole.

After about fifty seconds, the blast wave was already twelve miles ahead and traveling over 780 miles per hour, racing west over the virtually empty Lar National Park, destroying everything in its path. There were several small villages in Mazandaran Province to the north and northwest about ten to twenty miles away from the explosion, but they were largely situated in valleys and sheltered to a degree from the initial shockwave. Nonetheless, there were still several hundred casualties among people outside exposed to the superheated blast wave and from collapsed buildings.

But this was only the beginning.

The semi-dormant volcano had been building up pressure for quite some time since its last eruption seven millennia before, and the 1.5 megaton explosion managed to crack the lava dome underneath the western slope, dramatically affecting other parts of Mt. Damavand. Magma that had been straining to break the surface now erupted violently and lava flowed freely down Damavand's western and northern slopes, turning snow into scalding steam and incinerating all in its path. Other veins of magma were likewise shattered and blew an immense portion of the top of Damavand sky high.

In short order, a substantial part of the mountain resembled Dante's inferno as swiftly moving currents of pyroclastic flow moved in various directions at speeds approaching 450 miles per hour. The villages not obliterated by the first nuclear shockwave were now hit by swift seas of molten rock and superheated gas. Plumes of burning ash and radioactive debris soared miles into the air and were visible in Tehran and further. The ski resorts on the mountain were primarily on the southern slope away from the initial explosion, and snow had been somewhat lighter than usual that season. Their location notwithstanding, between catastrophic avalanches, intense seismic activity and pyroclastic flow, several hundred heretofore happy skiers, hoping for a pleasant Nowruz ski vacation, were either crushed, asphyxiated, irradiated, or burned to death. And the dead were the lucky ones.

Geophysicists and volcanologists would debate for decades whether the nuclear explosion actually triggered Damavand's eruption or was just a less significant and almost coincidental occurrence in a series of preordained seismic events. Academic papers would be written and numerous doctoral theses submitted, taking all sides. There was virtually no debate, however, over the fact that the nuclear weapon turned an already terrible event into one that was truly horrific.

The sky was rapidly turning black. Day had become night.

Damavand had awakened.

Daoud, General Alborzi and the others in the Project Zulfiqar control room felt the explosion before they heard the deep rumbling and roaring in the bowels of the earth. It rippled across the floor like an earthquake and two of the technicians actually lost their balance and fell down. Almost simultaneous with the explosion and eruption was Daoud's pre-scheduled cyber disruption, which triggered fire alarms in the HEU vault and area where the remaining weapons were stored. The "Whoop, Whoop, Whoop" resounded shrilly throughout the room, compounding the confusion and fear.

Daoud, who thought he knew what had just occurred, said, "General, I have to get to the HEU vault right away. I think a fire may have broken out."

Alborzi replied, "Of course. See to it now and report back to me immediately." Not a man given easily to fear, he was shaken by the sheer magnitude of the physical aftermath of what should have been a 10-kiloton explosion on the other side of the mountain. Perhaps he was even slightly in shock. *Is this what 10 kilotons feels like?* The room still shook and in fact the tremors were increasing and the temperature was climbing.

A new louder cracking sound surrounded them and the pungent smell of sulfur pervaded the air. The control room ceiling bulged and some support beams gave way, one of them striking Alborzi a glancing blow that sent him reeling. He lay still on the floor, and all the others decided it was time to leave.

Daoud didn't hesitate but beat a quick retreat from the control room and started running for the HEU vault as various technicians sprinted past him in the other direction, trying to get out of the Zulfiqar facility as quickly as possible. He entered the cipher combination to the HEU vault and then released Ali Javadpour, whose eyes were wide with fear as the floor continued to vibrate violently. No one paid them any attention.

Daoud said, "Come with me quickly if you want to live. The mountain is erupting. There's little time."

Javadpour did not press for explanations. "I'm with you. Let's go!"

As they left the holding cell, Daoud looked briefly in the portion of the HEU vault where the three remaining weapons and the inert cold test weapon lay and saw that the fire alarm was not exactly false because the temperature was rising rapidly and the floor had been split in half by a jagged crevasse that threatened to engulf the weapons altogether. He saw that there were possibly only minutes remaining before they rolled into the yawning gap and disappeared forever into the maw of Damavand. Two IRGC enlisted men who were guarding the nuclear weapons suddenly rushed into the vault from a side door, their automatic machine pistols leveled at Daoud, but their advance was halted by yet a further cracking in the floor which zigzagged across the room underneath them and swallowed them whole. Their screams lasted only a couple of seconds.

Steam and sulfurous fumes wafted out of the pit, which emitted an ominous glow. He thought he could sense a primordial presence beneath, but he pushed it from his mind. He quickly closed the door and rejoined Javadpour and advised him to run for his life. Javadpour needed no further urging, and the rotund little Iranian took off at surprising speed with Daoud at his heels.

They sprinted down the corridor towards the emergency exit. Daoud pulled at the lever on the massive steel door, but it was hot to the touch.

And jammed.

CHAPTER 2

◇◇◇

The Wrong Racehorse

Office of the Chief Near Eastern Division, DO, Langley

"Shit, shit, shit," was about as profound a value statement as Pat McCabe was capable of uttering as he read the incoming cable describing Condor's debriefing in Europe. He had bet all of his money on a racehorse only to discover that his horse was no Seabiscuit, but rather a broken down fat-ass nag. He looked up from this litany of woe to stare across his desk at said nag. Charlie Grable stared back at him, a worried look on his face.

"This fuck-up has already caused a shit-storm on the 7th floor. Rumor has it that Mac is trying to circle the wagons but there aren't that many to circle. Rats are jumping off of this sinking ship as fast as possible. And I know that I'm going to have to retire over this fucking fiasco," growled McCabe looking intently at the source of his misery.

Charlie squirmed under McCabe's stern glare and finally managed to whine, "Jeez Pat, how was I to know that Condor would double-cross us? I did all of the Source Reliability System requirements: the ops test, the CI talk and assessment. Everything by the book. He even passed his poly. And what he gave us was constantly verified. I mean you yourself and the Director… you guys thought he was good. Remember? Better than good. Great even. You loved him. Remember, Pat? Remember?" The last word little more than a squeak.

McCabe shook his head, bit his lip. Then he snapped a pencil he had been holding, which caused Charlie to sit up, startled. McCabe looked off in the distance at his career going down the drain.

All he could say was "We're really fucked. Royally and truly fucked."

Charlie asked in a low voice, "I know it's an awkward time, but what about that promotion? Remember, you promised."

McCabe looked at him incredulously. He barely refrained from leaping across the desk and strangling Charlie. It would almost be worth going to prison for. He could feel his fingers on his fat neck. Instead, he spit out, "Charlie, shut the fuck up! You'll be lucky if they don't demote you three grades and put you doing name traces on the Yugoslav desk.

Charlie looked confused. "But Yugoslavia doesn't exist anymore, Pat."

McCabe retorted, "Exactly."

CHAPTER 3

◇◇◇

A Win-Win Situation

Counterintelligence Center, Langley

The incoming Condor debriefing cable had shaken most of the CIA Headquarters building like a 9.9 earthquake on the Richter scale, but the office of Brian Bannock was an oasis of calm. He had directly led the debriefing the day before via secure video link and now reviewed the station write-up as he stroked his beard, a warm feeling of vindication and satisfaction suffusing his very being. His only regret was that Paula Davenport wasn't there to share this exquisite feeling. He would raise a glass to her tonight and one to Lane and his team, as well as to Leopard, Panther and Jaguar. He prayed they would all be safe soon.

Condor had come clean and confirmed his IRGC double agent status and the fact that there really was a covert Iranian nuclear weapons program codenamed "Zulfiqar" located in Lar National Park – GPS coordinates provided.

Condor stated, "Virtually all the information I gave you was in fact true. But I didn't give you everything – only that which we wanted you to have. Naturally, we wanted you to succeed at the nuclear talks, so we gave you our positions. Your President and the administration won a big victory and so did we. I think this is what you call a win-win situation." He laughed.

"And why are you telling us now?"

"Suffice it to say that I've had a major difference with senior management; specifically, an asshole named General Masud Alborzi who heads up Project Zulfiqar. He's the nephew of the Supreme Leader and he's deceived and used us all." He shrugged. "Turnabout is fair play."

"And what can you tell us now? Is there an imminent threat to the U.S. or its allies?"

"Not at this very moment, but it's coming. Alborzi's a driven man, but everything's about him – not about Iran or you or even Israel. He could care less. In that respect, he's exceedingly dangerous. To help you stop him, I've brought all of the project plans, weapons data, the location and quantity of the HEU and its origin, how we deceived the IAEA, and a complete Zulfiqar personnel list and their last whereabouts. I believe I've squared accounts with you with what I've brought with me."

Finally, Brian asked the loaded question, "What do you want?"

Condor hadn't blinked an eye. "Ah, what I want, dear sir. We now cut to the chase. I like that in you Americans. Well, I don't need your money, but I do want the fulfillment of your original commitment to me for asylum in the U.S. I'm thinking maybe Santa Barbara. Something with sun and an ocean view. Maybe a vineyard in my backyard."

CHAPTER 4

◇◇◇

Turning the Other Cheek

Oval Office White House 21 March

The large flat screen TV in the Oval Office showed a CNN journalist in Tehran with a breaking news bulletin on a huge eruption of Mt. Damavand, which had so far resulted in at least several thousand deaths as well as widespread destruction and chaos in northern Iran. Film images of what was occurring only forty-five miles northeast of the Iranian capital showed an apocalyptic landscape of massive obliteration of civilization as if it had been scoured from the land by a giant scalpel. Dark clouds of ash and smoke and rivers of lava only added to the misery. The newscaster also mentioned the numerous reports of an intense flash of light and massive explosion on Damavand's west slope, which had been seen and heard by thousands only minutes before the eruption. There were also reports that substantial portions of the ash were radioactive and warnings that civilians should remain inside.

The National Security Advisor turned to the President and said, "Madam President, our overhead systems focused on Iran also reported a brilliant flash on the western slope of Damavand moments before the eruption. Our seismic detection systems in the region confirm that a nuclear weapon was detonated beneath the surface of Damavand this morning. And our airborne assets in the region have detected numerous fission byproducts of a nuclear explosion. Between the seismic data and the radiochemistry of the byproducts, we estimate that a nuclear device of about 1.3 to 1.5 megatons was detonated today."

The President, who had coasted into the White House largely on a family-values platform, let loose a stream of colorful profanity that would have done a longshoreman proud. The National Security Advisor and two of the President's closest aides shrank from her.

"Those goddam fools," she growled. "I'll have their fucking guts for garters!"

Meaning not the Iranians but the CIA, and especially Mac White. The President wished to castrate him personally with a dull knife. The Secretary of State would be next, but she wanted to scalp him and remove that oh-so-perfect hair.

After another minute or two of the Presidential tantrum, the National Security Advisor said, "I think I see a way to salvage some of our public image here."

The President looked at him as if he were insane. "Do tell."

"We should order immediate relief and aid for the people of Iran with a huge disaster-assistance program of food, medical aid, supplies, anything they need. If we orchestrate this quickly, your magnanimous humanitarian gesture to a former adversary now in dire straits will far outweigh the public-relations damage of having been duped in the negotiations. It will be seen as the ultimate gesture of turning the other cheek and taking the high road. In essence, you can still turn this to our advantage."

He sat back, warily awaiting her response.

She remained still for a moment, her head in her hands. When at last she looked up, she said, "What the fuck. Let's do it. Not much of a choice, is there?"

CHAPTER 5

◇◇◇

Speed

Astara, Azerbaijan 21 October

The soft silvery light of the moon was glinting off of the black water of the Caspian Sea a short time before sunrise in Astara, directly across the border from its larger Iranian sister city. Lane stood on the dock drinking coffee and waiting for Conor McBane to fetch their boat from the nearby marina. Gary and Lacy sat in their rental car, enjoying a light breakfast. After Lane had reluctantly agreed to take McBane with them on their rescue mission, explaining that he had no real choice, all four of them had driven the four and a half hours from Baku to Astara and gotten hotel rooms near the harbor. They had managed a few hours of sleep before the big day. Everyone was understandably nervous.

Everyone that is, except for McBane, who'd been bouncing around like an ebullient child.

Now, Lane only wanted to get to the rendezvous point, which was about 200 miles away in the Caspian and about twenty miles north of Nur, Iran, where Panther and Jaguar's cousins lived. He hoped that the three Iranians' exit from the Zulfiqar facility was proceeding as planned.

Suddenly, he heard a deep-throated rumbling sound that resembled a group of Harley-Davidson chopper engines revving as one. He realized that it was McBane bringing the fast boat around to the dock. He stepped back.

God, what a boat! It was a sleek, midnight black V hull powerboat that looked as if it were racing even standing still in the water. Its beam was less than nine feet and it was about forty-three feet long, like a long black stiletto. McBane, sporting a jaunty captain's hat, was grinning ear to ear as he swung the craft alongside the pier. Lane signaled the others and they all boarded the craft.

"What the hell *is* this?"

McBane grinned. "This my dear boy, this *is* your salvation. It's a Donzi 43R and is 'the ultimate in hydrodynamic efficiency and handling,' as they say in the trade. It has a pair of Teague Custom Marine 975 horsepower engines and can do zero to 76 miles per hour in twenty seconds or less. Its top end exceeds 110 miles per hour, making it surely the fastest damn boat in the entire Caspian Sea. It can carry ten passengers in complete comfort and has a fuel capacity of 314 gallons plus some spares I brought along. I think we're going to do just fine." He smirked as he said the last.

Lane shook his head. "Your friends sure know how to pick a boat."

McBane nodded. "My boy, in their business, speed is more than a virtue, it's everything. Speed means profit, speed means freedom. Now, if everyone's comfortable, I suggest we move out smartly. We've a bit less than four hours to our rendezvous point if I keep it only at half throttle. No sense attracting the gendarmes until we have to. So, let's see what this baby can do."

As they pulled away from the dock and cleared the harbor, McBane revved the engines and gripped the wheel in perfect assurance of what he was doing. He looked back at Lane. Then he smiled, gave them all a thumbs-up and they shot forward like a stone from a slingshot. They skimmed across the water. The wind blew in Lane's hair. He looked at Lacy and she winked and smiled and blew him a kiss while Gary laughed at McBane's wild-man howls.

Lane knew he had made the right decision.

CHAPTER 6

◇◇◇

Mercy on Us All

Project Zulfiqar Facility

Daoud's fingers were still burning from the emergency exit door when he realized that all of the people streaming in full panic meant that they could just join the masses and flow outside unnoticed. He reached inside his jacket and handed Ali a pair of sunglasses and a baseball cap with the New York Yankees logo on it.

"Put these on. It's not much of a disguise but in this madness, no one will be too inquisitive."

Ali looked at them, then back to Daoud. "At least you could've given me a San Francisco Giants cap."

Daoud looked at him in disbelief until Ali laughed and donned the cap, then the pair melted into the hurrying crowds and headed for the main exit and the parking lot where Majid was waiting. The parking lot was in mass confusion, but it beat being underground in a collapsing facility.

Terrified employees and IRGC cadres were mobbing the buses. Men beat on the doors and several were run over as the buses careened out of the small parking area. Daoud spotted Majid waving beside his Toyota; he'd never been happier to see him. He wondered why no one had attempted to commandeer Majid's car until he came closer and saw the large caliber revolver in his brother's right hand, held against his thigh.

Daoud and Ali jumped in. Majid sped out of the parking lot, dodging the fleeing Zulfiqar employees who were fleeing on foot down the small twisty mountain road toward highway 77, about three miles away.

"What the hell happened?" asked Majid after they were about a mile down the road.

"Hell happened." Daoud muttered as he stared straight ahead.

"What? What do you mean? It looks like the end of the world out there."

"For a lot of people, it is. That lunatic Alborzi must have swapped a live weapon for the inert cold test one and you can see the fucking result. Absolute madness! We're at least lucky that the explosion took place on the far side of Damavand and it seems that most of the volcanic activity is also there, but for how long? I have no idea. I don't want to even think about this horror we created. This makes me sick."

"Don't beat yourself up over it. It was Alborzi who did it, not you. We're doing the right thing by destroying them."

"I keep trying to tell myself that, but I'm also thinking I should've stuck to theoretical physics. The worst that would've happened would have been chalk dust all over my fingers instead of blood. May Allah have mercy on us all."

Masud Alborzi slowly opened his eyes and felt thick dust all over him. There was blood on the side of his head as he rubbed his face like a drunk recovering from a bender. He was disoriented and confused at first but then he sat up and his head cleared, although it still hurt like hell. He looked at his watch and figured he had been unconscious for about twenty minutes. He slowly got to his feet and noticed that he was alone. Those goddamned rats had fled without him! He would see them all hang for desertion.

He went to the control panel and noticed they were on emergency backup power. That would suffice. He switched on the monitor of the HEU and weapons vault and saw through the grey steam only a huge hole in the floor where once his babies had rested.

Shit!

He backed up the recording by twenty minutes to see what Daoud had done with respect to the fire alarms. It was then that he saw the queer traitor release the fat traitor and fail to return as he had been ordered.

They would hang first.

Alborzi picked up the control room phone, which mercifully was still functioning, and dialed the IRGC base about thirty miles away. After a minute or two, he was speaking to the IRGC base commander, a man he had personally selected for the job. He ordered the Tabatabai brothers and Javadpour to be arrested and taken to his Tehran office. The IRGC commander hesitated and then asked if General Alborzi was aware that Mt. Damavand had just erupted. The blue profanity which Alborzi used in response was surprising only that it did not melt the phone lines.

"My general," said the commander timidly, "do you know their whereabouts or destination?"

Alborzi almost bit his tongue in two as he clenched his teeth. "Look idiot, they're either headed north or south on Highway 77. There are only two directions, moron, so you've got a 50/50 chance. If I were to guess, oh let me see, oh my, I'd say fucking north to the Caspian Sea where they will try to escape abroad, probably by water. I want them seized as soon as possible. Do you get that or shall I get more specific? I want roadblocks set up now and the water routes covered."

"But the traffic due to the eruption, sir...."

"I don't give a shit about the fucking traffic. I want them dead or alive and I don't care which!" With that, he slammed the phone down.

Alborzi decided there was no more to be accomplished there, so he made sure he had his encrypted cell phone and headed for the exit door. He opened it and that is when the flash wave of intensely hot air hit him full in the face like a blast furnace. He recoiled back into the room, his face reddened and blistered. His vision was blurred from the heat and pain but he saw a river of molten lava rolling forward down the hallway. His screaming sounded throughout the complex and continued for some time. Then there was silence.

CHAPTER 7

◇◇◇

The Right Moment

Haraz Road Highway 77, Northern Iran 21 March

After two hours of slow driving through heavy traffic fleeing north away from Mt. Damavand on the Haraz Road towards the Caspian, Majid spotted trouble ahead as he rounded a curve just south of the village of Haloomsar. He considered alternate routes as he realized it was a roadblock. Unfortunately, there were no alternates in this narrow mountain valley. They would have to brazen it out. He put his revolver under his jacket and drove slowly forward, warning Daoud and Ali to remain calm. They would think of something.

A young IRGC enlisted man stepped forward when it was their turn to be questioned. He looked to be about twenty-three years old and possibly was a student at Shomal University on the south side of town. He asked for their national ID cards and his eyes widened in alarm as he compared their names and photos to the papers on his clipboard. He nervously removed his sidearm, leveled it at them with some shakiness and with a little stuttering asked them to accompany him to a nearby building, normally used by road maintenance crews, which his unit had appropriated for this roadblock command post. He marched the three of them into the small building, which had only two other occupants: another IRGC enlisted man and a junior grade officer drinking tea.

As Majid and Daoud walked ahead of Ali and the young IRGC man into the office, Majid said in a low voice in English, "Wait for the right moment."

Daoud nodded. It came sooner than expected.

They stood, arms raised in front of the three IRGC men when yet another loud boom sounded from Mt. Damavand -- obviously a follow-on eruption. The young IRGC enlisted man with the gun trained on them turned his head instinctively towards the sound from the mountain. When he did so, Daoud lashed out with his foot and kicked him in the crotch as hard as he could. His days of soccer playing might have been long past, but he was still in remarkable physical condition and could kick like a mule. The young man dropped his weapon and collapsed to the floor. Majid whipped out his revolver and put it to the officer's head. The other IRGC man fell backwards out of his chair and spilled tea all over his crotch. Or at least that's what he told his colleagues later.

Less than ten minutes later, the traffic on Highway 77 passed three IRGC officers, one substantially rounder and shorter than the other two, emerging from the metal building and hopping in an IRGC official AWD vehicle. The vehicle with its flashing red light breezed easily through two more roadblocks with friendly waves and big smiles, before arriving at Nur on the coast of the Caspian Sea in a little more than an hour.

CHAPTER 8

◇◇◇

At Maximum Throttle

In the Caspian Sea, ten miles north of Nur, Iran

The small fishing boat motored north with Majid at the wheel, sailing at twenty miles per hour, slow but steady and only ten miles from the rendezvous point with the Americans. It was going to be close.

The bound and gagged IRGC men had probably been found by now in that small metal building – mad as hell and in their underwear – and a search for a sea escape no doubt launched.

Confirmation of this came when Ali saw two small helicopters buzzing far on the horizon, crisscrossing the sea several miles away, less than 300 feet off the water, forced to hang low because of the ash cloud ceiling from the volcano. These small copters were steadily narrowing their search pattern and would soon find them, well before they got to their friends.

At Majid's request, Ali picked up the boat's radio handset, pre-set to the frequency Majid had advised the CIA and pushed to transmit, "Miles, Miles, this is Gabriel. I repeat this is Gabriel. Please come in. "

The radio crackled for a few seconds and then he heard, "Gabriel, this is Miles. Good to hear from you! I think I can see you on our radar system, about ten miles from our position but make a sharp turn to starboard and let me confirm."

After Majid executed the maneuver, the radio crackled again, "Yes, I see you! Are you all okay?"

Ali smiled at Majid and Daoud and said, "Oh, we're all okay, but the bloodhounds from hell are out and soon it'll be our blood on the water. Aerial and probably maritime pursuit is underway. If we're now ten miles from you, I seriously doubt we can reach you before we're detected."

"Can you get any more speed? I see at least one vessel pursuing you on my radar – maybe more than five miles back. They're closing at high speed – maybe 60 miles per hour. Possibly six minutes until they engage you."

"I'm not surprised. No, we're at maximum throttle and she's straining at that. It's going to be real rough, my friend. Be alert. Stay safe and don't come any closer. If we can make it, we will. Inshallah."

There was a hesitation, and then Ali's voice trembled, "Miles, thank you. You've kept your word. It's all I could ask. God bless America. Gabriel out."

CHAPTER 9

◇◇◇

Better Buckle Up

In the Caspian Sea, twenty miles north of Nur, Iran

Lane told the others what he'd learned.

"Our friends are hanging on but they're not going to survive the next half hour if we just sit here. That patrol boat will overtake them in less than six minutes. I've seen other blips farther out but converging rapidly on them. We've got decisions to make. My orders were not to approach closer than twenty miles to the Iranian coast. But I can tell you now that that won't cut it. It's this simple: If we don't go get them, they'll be seized or die. I'm for getting them but this will be dangerous. I need your agreement."

The other three all gave him a thumbs-up. He shook their hands and hugged and kissed Lacy.

I love this team, thought Lane.

Conor McBane said, "We do have a few little extras on this tub to help us. First, next to the radar, there's a police scanner that'll also pick up IRGC freqs. Tune it in, Gary."

Gary fiddled with it and soon they heard a jumble of words, which sounded like gibberish. "Damn it, it's encrypted."

"Not for long. Look at the little black box next to it. Push the red button." Suddenly clear voices in Farsi emerged from the speaker, which Gary could translate.

Lane shook his head in amazement. *This is a nifty little SIGINT collector.*

Wearing headphones, Gary listened for a minute or two. "All of those radar blips are IRGC patrol craft and definitely in hot pursuit and have focused on our friends' boat. Their orders are to take them dead or alive."

Lane looked at McBane. "Set a course directly for our friends at high speed. We might get there in time if you put the pedal to the metal."

McBane nodded solemnly. "We're gonna need a little help. Lacy, would you please reach under that seat and press that slightly discolored spot one inch from the end closest to you?"

Lacy did so and a hidden panel popped open. She reached inside and pulled out a four-foot-long cloth-covered package. She opened it and out popped a wicked-looking black rifle with a long scope and a hollow stock. She looked at it with admiration. "A Dragunov sniper rifle with special PSO-1 optical sight. I've read about them but never used one. They were standard Warsaw Pact issue with an effective range of about a half-mile, if I recall correctly. It's semi-automatic and can fire roughly thirty rounds a minute."

She reached deeper into the cavity under the leather upholstered bench and withdrew a metal box with eight curved ten-round magazines. She loaded one of the magazines into the rifle and set the others close at hand. She looked at Conor and Lane. "Well, I'm loaded for bear. What are the rules of engagement?"

"If they shoot at our friends or at us," said Lane, "Kill the sons of bitches!"

Lacy nodded and returned to adjusting her weapon.

McBane said in a low growl, "Better buckle up. We're going to blow their balls off." He pushed the throttle forward to maximum. The boat shot forward and threw them back in their seats, G forces pushing on them. He kept nudging it faster.

Lane and the others had never been on anything this fast on the water. *If there were a Warp Speed eight on this craft, they were doing it now.*

McBane cackled wildly with sheer delight. The boat was a black streak on the blue water with foam churning far, high and white behind it.

CHAPTER 10

Dead or Alive

In the Caspian Sea, thirteen miles north of Nur, Iran

The IRGC Peykaap class patrol boat was at full throttle in pursuit of the fugitives and the young bearded IRGC navy skipper in the lead boat was eager to make contact. His North Korean-designed boat was equipped with a twin barrel 324-millimeter torpedo launcher and a 12.7-millimeter machine gun. He was hoping to close on the prize first and sink her. His orders were "dead or alive" and dead would be so much easier. He had never engaged in real combat and was far from the occasional action down in the Persian Gulf where some of his friends served. The Caspian had proven to be immensely boring, at least until now.

He spotted the little fishing boat four thousand yards ahead and ordered his coxswain to close on her. When he was within sufficient range, he ordered the IRGC sailor manning the torpedo tubes to fire them sequentially at twenty-second intervals.

Daoud saw the approaching patrol boat through his binoculars and knew their luck had run out. There was still no sign of the Americans. He suddenly noticed the twin torpedo tube launcher on the lead patrol boat and saw both torpedoes fired in turn. They streaked just below the surface of the water towards their craft, cutting a foamy line in the water towards him. He screamed at Majid to take evasive action by turning 45 degrees. The boat swung violently to starboard. That maneuver worked…for a moment.

The first fish passed them at high speed, missing by about five yards, and exploded sixty yards beyond. A few seconds later, Daoud spotted the second one closing quickly, this time dead-on. Without further reflection, he rushed at Majid and Ali and pushed them into the water on the far side of the boat, yelling "dive." They plunged deeply underwater, cushioned from the detonation as the boat exploded moments later, lifting out of the water and splitting in half like a child's toy. The three Iranian scientists were shaken badly, but not injured. They resurfaced near the broken front half of the boat on the far side away from the approaching patrol boat. They clung to it on the flotsam-filled surface.

Daoud dared to look around the broken hull and saw that the IRGC skipper must have ordered the coxswain to close on the debris field and search for any survivors. He may have seen them jump just seconds before torpedo impact. The patrol boat poked through the floating remains of the shattered fishing boat and started to round the broken front half. They were only seconds from being spotted and shot.

Daoud suddenly heard a harsh low-pitched rumble over his shoulder in the distance as if a pack of Hell's Angels were driving their motorcycles across the surface of the Caspian Sea. He turned and saw something long, black and pointed approaching them at a speed that must have exceeded a hundred miles per hour with enormous rooster tails of white water rising up behind. It was almost surreal. Something told him that the U.S. Cavalry had just crested the hill. He waved to the speeding ship and hoped for the best. *God help us.*

At the same time, the IRGC skipper heard the overwhelming noise approaching from the far side of the capsized target vessel. He turned and saw a sleek black alien spacecraft bearing down on him at considerable speed, skimming across the water as if it were levitating above it, its stiletto nose pointed directly towards him, white water foaming high and wide behind it. He simply stared at it in disbelief as it abruptly decelerated and swung around neatly about eighty yards away, coming to a standstill between him and the fugitives.

Several people were in the boat, but his attention focused on a tall blonde woman who stood up and held a long, black rifle with a scope, clearly intending to interfere with his duties. He recovered from his shock and loudly ordered his subordinate to open fire on them with the boat's heavy machine gun. He was not about to put up with this foolishness, if it was the last thing he did.

It was.

Lacy heard the barked Farsi command and looked at Gary who gave her a warning of what was about to happen. She saw the young sailor trying to train the large machine gun on their boat, but he was slow and she never hesitated. She promptly took aim and shot the sailor in the head before he pulled the trigger. His body flipped backwards off of the boat, describing a clean arc. The skipper, shocked, then began to draw his sidearm, but before he could even clear his holster, his chest blossomed red and his legs buckled. The second enlisted crewman, the coxswain, in an incredibly intelligent move, quickly raised his hands and sank to his knees in surrender.

McBane had begun to maneuver the boat closer to the wreckage, still about a hundred yards away, to retrieve the three Iranians, when one of the two circling IRGC helicopters dived down and started strafing. Little fountains of water rapidly erupted across the sea's surface. The three Iranian scientists began swimming as quickly as possible for the Donzi fast boat.

Lacy aimed her sniper rifle at the swarming helicopters and took several shots, but the bullets bounced off of the armored sides. They were moving too quickly to allow her to get an unimpeded shot at any of the occupants. But her multiple rounds caused them to back off momentarily, giving the three Iranians time to make it alongside the Donzi.

The copters pulled away like angry buzzing hornets about a quarter mile off and crisscrossed the open sea preparing for another attack. Lacy tried to aim at the crews through the choppers' small openings, but their distance and speed made for impossible shots.

The three Iranians were climbing into the Donzi when Lacy turned to Lane and screamed, "They're too far off and too fast for me to get a shot at the crewmen. If they'd hover or were any closer, I'd have a chance. We're sitting ducks here!"

Ali looked at Lacy, then at Lane and the others and said, "I'll get those motherfuckers closer."

He then dived back into the water and started swimming furiously for the floating half of the fishing boat. The others yelled at him to come back.

Ali clambered up onto the shattered hull, snatched the Iranian Islamic Republic flag off its bow, and waved it at one of the passing helicopters, its guns silent as its crew tried to figure out what was happening in this strange pantomime.

They did not have to wait long.

Standing tall, Ali spit on the flag and tossed it into the sea. As if this weren't enough, he flipped the bird at the copter in Persian fashion with thumbs up on both hands as it sailed over and screamed, "Madar Ghahbe!" and then in English, "Motherfuckers!"

"Not exactly subtle, is he?" Gary remarked to Lane.

"No, Ali doesn't leave any doubt as to where he stands."

"I can see that," said Gary. "But I don't think this is going to end well."

As if in response, the copter swung back at the end of its next circuit and this time it started firing its door-mounted machine gun well before it passed over the remains of the fishing boat. Everyone saw the bullets rip across the water, including the one that caught Ali. Blood burst from his chest and he toppled off of the capsized half of the boat.

Several things happened at once. Lacy took a careful bead on the helicopter, now slowly passing their fast boat a hundred yards away, fifty feet above the Ali's body. Thinking back to those clay pigeons her father used to toss, she made the calculations and the mental link she needed. With two quick well-placed shots, she took out the gunner and the pilot through its open doors. The copter kept flying for another few hundred yards and then tumbled out of control into the sea.

Simultaneously, Lane stripped off his shoes and dived into the water, his arms pumping rapidly as he swam to the capsized boat and Ali. His arms swept deep into the water and he pulled and kicked with all his might. He found Ali sinking into the sea and bleeding profusely, the water turning red around him, and started to drag him back to the Donzi.

The second helicopter, which had been circling in the background, sped quickly toward Lane, machine gun blazing as it passed. Its rounds stitched the water all around Lane and his human cargo.

Lacy watched in horror as a spray of blood erupted from Lane's right shoulder, and both he and Ali sank below the waves. She looked about frantically, but then they resurfaced only twenty yards from the Donzi.

The helicopter turned and hovered, preparing to finish off the men in the water. As it moved in for the kill, Lacy adjusted her sight on the Dragunov for an increase in wind and drift of the copter, took a bead on the gunner at two hundred yards, focused all of her attention as if nothing else existed in the world, and led it carefully. Then, as she saw him loom large in her sight, she pulled the trigger, more with a caress than anything else. The link had been made.

The gunner's head blew grey and red matter all over the inside of the copter windshield. The pilot was temporarily distracted by this red mist in the cockpit and turned his head sharply towards the door, then he too took a round in the neck from the Dragunov through the open door, The copter cartwheeled hard into the sea and tore itself apart.

Despite the wound to his shoulder, Lane kept swimming and brought Ali to the boat, handed him up to the others, and pulled himself quickly over the gunwale. Once aboard, he carried Ali into the cabin of the Donzi and laid him gently on the leather bench.

Gary, who had been a medic in the army, grabbed the first aid kit and started to work on him, briefly staunching the bleeding from a sucking chest wound. He also attended to Lane's shoulder wound, a stinging graze from the 30-caliber bullet. A slightly deeper angle would have penetrated his lung or heart.

Lane sat next to Ali and held his right hand. Lacy crouched next to them and held Ali's other hand. Ali looked up at Lane, his eyes searching for something. He blinked twice and then through labored breathing said, "I guess I should've ducked, huh?"

Lane said, "It's okay, buddy, we're going home. Just hang on."

"Couldn't take a joke, so fuck'em." Ali coughed up blood as he tried to laugh and winced from the pain. Gary gave him a shot of morphine, and Ali soon lost consciousness. Lane and Lacy remained on either side of him.

McBane told everyone that it was time to saddle up their ponies. Radar showed that the hornets' nest had been kicked over and swarms of bad news were descending upon them from multiple directions. After consulting the chart, he said he would set a course for Lankaran, Azerbaijan, about twenty-five miles north of where they began in Astara. Fortunately, the aerial ceiling had descended further due to voluminous volcanic ash, and now water pursuit was the only option open to the IRGC.

And with that, they held the aces.

He steadily brought the throttle up to its full position and the boat roared like a medieval dragon and shot forward to its full speed of over 110 miles per hour. It whipped across the water like a banshee from hell and headed north.

CHAPTER 11

◇◇◇

Bring Back Our Heroes

Suburban Fairfax County, Northern Virginia

The headlines in the morning Washington papers screamed, "Purge in the Administration." Paula Davenport read these with her morning coffee and yawned as she ate her toast. She was getting ready to leave for the Job Fair at the CIA's retirement seminar, something that she'd been dreading.

In truth, she would have preferred to go back to bed. Hustling contracts in the intelligence community seemed so demeaning. The Old Girl Spy put up on the auction block for the highest bidder. She could not, would not do that. How tawdry. The idea of doing volunteer work at her church and with local schools as a teacher's aide seemed so much more inviting, and certainly more meaningful.

She looked again at the news article about the sudden sacking of CIA Director Mac White and the Secretary of State the night before and the photos of how both officials looked to be in shock as their armored limousines drove away from the White House. The fallout from the nuclear explosion in Iran was not only literally radioactive but also politically nuclear as well.

Good riddance.

She had put the paper down and was picking up her coffee cup when her cell rang. She picked it up. The female voice on the other end sounded vaguely familiar but when the person identified herself as the President of the United States, Paula laughed and said with a cheery voice, "Yes, and I'm Mary Poppins, how may I help you?"

The voice on the other end erupted with a husky laugh, which Paula thought sounded like someone she had heard on the television. A little less certain now, she asked, "Really, who is this?"

"Um, it really is me calling you from the White House."

"Oh my, Madame President, is that really you?"

"I'm afraid it is. I'm sorry to bother you this early in the morning, but I need to ask you to do something for me. I want you to withdraw your retirement papers and return to your job as DDO at the Agency. But that would only be until my nomination of you as Deputy Director of the CIA is confirmed by the Senate. I've asked the current Deputy Director to serve as acting Director until I can find a suitable replacement for Director White, who has...well who has resigned for personal reasons."

Paula was stunned by the offer.

"I regret not listening to you when I should have," the President continued. "That was my mistake. You have a well-deserved reputation for sound judgment and speaking truth to power. I need people like you in positions of authority at the Agency. May I count on you to accept?"

There was silence on the line, and the President finally asked, "Paula, are you there?"

"Madame President, I would be honored. I'm just in a bit of a daze, is all."

"Understood. I think we all are."

Paula hesitated before saying, "May I ask something of you as well?"

"Please."

"On my own authority, I dispatched a team of three courageous officers to the Middle East on a rescue mission of our three Iranian sources a few days ago, not far from what's happening in Iran, and I'm very concerned that they may have been abandoned. I would like...if possible...a military transport plane directed to Baku to retrieve these brave officers and our Iranian friends and bring them home. Home to America."

"Of course. I'll authorize it. Bring back our heroes. And thank you, Paula."

CHAPTER 12

◇◇◇

Home of the Brave

Caspian Sea, five miles south of Lankaran, Azerbaijan

McBane eased back on the throttle with the port city of Lankaran visible on the northwestern horizon.

As the large engines suddenly quieted, Ali looked up groggily. He coughed up some more blood and then managed in a weak voice, "I tried to be brave for once in my life, but...but it didn't work like I planned."

Lane squeezed his hand. "Yes, it did. Don't you doubt it."

Ali sighed, eyes closed again. "Lane, remember how I was supposed to get American citizenship if I did what was needed? Do you?"

Lane nodded, "Yep, and you certainly will. Soon you'll be paying taxes and bitching about Congress like the rest of us. Don't you worry, Ali."

The boat was motoring into the port and the ride was much smoother now. Gary and Lacy were staring out of the boat at the approaching harbor. They were all exhausted.

Ali coughed blood again. "I don't think that's going to happen. I...I should've done it long ago when I was in California." He coughed again. "I should've been part of the home of the brave a long time ago...but...but I didn't quite make it."

Lane squeezed Ali's hand and said, "No, Ali, you made it."

He smiled and held Lane's hand and then closed his eyes. His breathing grew shallower and after a few minutes stopped altogether. Lane held Lacy.

Neither could speak. Gary pulled the blanket gently over Ali's head and said in Farsi, "Peace be upon you, Ali."

And then in English, "God bless you and God bless America."

CHAPTER 13

At a Loss for Words

Counterintelligence Center, Langley

The phone rang in Brian Bannock's office as he was reviewing the morning's take from around the globe, and the voice summoned him to the DDO's office. He thought it strange that he was being invited to an empty office with Paula gone, but he headed to the seventh floor, his curiosity aroused. The DDO's executive assistant ushered him into the DDO's office, and he was dumbfounded to see Paula behind her old desk, smiling.

"Well, this is a surprise! Or am I dreaming?"

Paula laughed with him. "Oh, it's harder to get rid of this old girl than you think."

"Well, I'm delighted you're back. How can I be of service, madam?" he asked in a deep mellow baritone with a twinkle in his eyes.

"This time it's not an assignment or a task. I just wanted to let you know that one of my first orders of business upon resuming my duties as DDO was to correct an omission -- something long overdue. Your recent work on those complex Iranian cases was superb and extremely predictive. You stuck to your guns under ungodly pressure and never wavered from seeking the truth. I want to let you know that I am hereby promoting you, out of cycle, into the Senior Intelligence Service. Congratulations, Brian!"

For the first time in his entire career, Brian was speechless. He looked up at the ceiling and away from Paula, afraid he might make a fool of himself. So he just nodded dumbly and silently mouthed the words "thank you" to her.

Paula hugged Brian and let him drift in shock back to his office. She smiled to herself, thinking it was a perfect way to start the day. Quickly, she phoned the head of the Counterintelligence Center to let him know what had happened.

By the time Brian re-entered the CI Center, a small crowd had gathered. Colleagues patted him on the back as he entered, everyone taking a chance to shake his hand.

Then the cheering began.

CHAPTER 14

◇◇◇

Going Home

Baku

A gentle tapping sounded on Lane's hotel room door. He opened it and saw the thin-faced young American, whom he'd last seen at the marina, standing there, a deferential look about him.

"Mr. Andrews, I'm sorry to disturb you. I really am. I know you've, uh… you've been through a lot."

"It's okay. I was just trying to rest a bit before going home."

"Of course. Again, I'm sorry, but we've just heard that a U.S. military aircraft will arrive tomorrow to transport your team and the Iranians back to the States."

Lane nodded but was quiet.

"The President herself contacted the Azerbaijani leader and spoke to him. There'll be no difficulties exiting the country. All arrangements have been made with the local authorities, including the embalming of…" He paused. "Of your friend's remains and shipment of his coffin in the aircraft."

"Thank you," said Lane.

"Naturally, the Azerbaijani service would like you and the others out of the country as quietly and as soon the aircraft lands and refuels so as not to…well, overly complicate relations with Iran. You know how it is here."

"Of course."

"Fortunately, the massive U.S. relief efforts currently going to Iran are transiting Baku, and this chaos helps provide good cover for your exit and exfiltration. No one should be the wiser."

"Thank you very much." Lane started to close the door but thought of something – something necessary. "Say, before you go, I do have a request."

"Whatever you need, just ask."

"Can you provide me with an American flag from the Embassy?"

The young man looked puzzled but said, "Sure. Not a problem. I'll bring it by this afternoon."

"Okay. Thanks." Lane hesitated and then asked, "And one other thing, *if* they can arrange it upon our landing in Washington."

He told the young man what he wanted.

"I think they can do that, especially for your group," replied the young man.

He paused and added, "Sir."

He stepped back, hesitated again and then stuck his hand out and wished Lane and his party best of luck and God speed.

CHAPTER 15

◇◇◇

An American Hero

Andrews Air Force Base, Maryland

The U.S. Marine honor guard snapped to attention with crisp precision as the flag-draped coffin was carefully unloaded from the C-17 sitting on the tarmac. A number of dignitaries had emerged from several black limousines and SUVs. Passengers from the airplane had also disembarked and stood alongside the officials, all paying their respect to the deceased. They all stood in silence and then, as one, raised their right hands over their hearts as the coffin rolled slowly toward them, the Stars and Stripes concealing the top and sides of Ali's casket.

It paused, and Lane stepped forward in front of the others. He wasn't sure if he could do this, but he had to try. He breathed in deeply to steady himself. This was so hard.

In a voice barely under control, he said, "I ask you to bow your heads in memory of Ali." After a moment of silence, he concluded, "Greater love hath no man than this; to lay down his life for his friends." His voice almost broke on the last few words.

He walked back over to stand between Lacy and Gary, with McBane to Gary's right. He stared numbly at the flag-draped coffin. Lacy held his hand. He felt a gentle squeeze on his right shoulder and then another on his left. He looked behind him and there stood Paula Davenport and Brian Bannock, a look of compassion on both of their faces.

A trumpeter then struck up the notes of "Amazing Grace."

More than a few of the onlookers had tears in their eyes as the hymn concluded.

Afterwards, a young corporal in the Marine honor detail asked his gunnery sergeant, "Gunny, who was that we just unloaded? Some big-shot general? Sure were lots of important looking folks out there."

The Gunny responded, "I don't really know, corporal. I was just told that he's an American hero. Nothing else."

He added, "But you know, they're all American heroes who come through here, corporal." He paused. "I feel, however, that this one…well this hero was pretty special."

Northern Virginia

"For a voluntary act or acts of extraordinary heroism involving the acceptance of existing dangers with conspicuous fortitude and exemplary courage."

Lane read the inscription on the certificate of his Distinguished Intelligence Cross for at least the tenth time as he listened to his "Kind of Blue" album. He sat there and wondered about the point of it all. What was worth Ali's life? This medal? He thought of Ali's warm smile and his infectious laugh and his love of life and the way he so innocently bounced through life like that untethered balloon. Lane knew that whatever he had done paled in comparison to what his friend had done. He was the bravest of them all.

Lane let the certificate and the medal slip from his fingers as he bent over and put his head in his hands and let his emotions wash over him. Lacy sat up from his bed. She put her arm about him and hugged him and pulled him down to where his head nestled in her arms. She patted his back and held him as he cried into her soft hair.

CHAPTER 16

◇◇◇

The Lesson

Lawrence Livermore National Laboratory

Dr. Rand McKeown felt a bit like a student in advanced calculus who had slept through the first few semesters and was now hopelessly lost. He watched in amazement as the Iranian's fingers danced across the whiteboard, the black marker moving with a speed and grace that stunned the various weapons designers seated in the small auditorium. The formulae seemed to flow from his fingertips with carefree ease as Daoud Tabatabai went from one whiteboard to the next without hesitation, almost as if he were transcribing a musical score long committed to memory.

McKeown saw that among the Department of Energy nuclear scientists watching Daoud, conspicuously absent were Dr. Peter Muskie and most of his acolytes. Normally, this would have had a negative effect on attendance, but also conspicuously absent now from Iranian topography was a huge portion of the top of Mount Damavand. To McKeown's amusement, this resulted in at least one renegade Muskrat attending.

McKeown turned in his seat to Robert Carlton. "Are you following all this?"

"Hell, he lost me two whiteboards ago, but I sense we're seeing genius. And I mean real genius." Carlton never looked away from the numbers and symbols flowing without pause from the Iranian's fingers.

Earlier, there had been some tedious discussion among the more pedantic weaponeers as to whether they should even be discussing nuclear weapons designs or "restricted data" with a foreigner, who was not "Q" cleared. This, until they were reminded by Drs. MeKeown and Carlton that they would all be in "receive" mode rather than "transmit" and that the honored speakers, Drs. Daoud and Majid Tabatabai, were special guests of the former Secretary of Energy, Dr. Manuel Alvarez, seated prominently in the front row with a big grin on his face next to their lab director. That had silenced the doubters quickly.

At the conclusion of his presentation, Daoud described how he had successfully destroyed the designs and technical papers on the Project Zulfiqar computers and how Mount Damavand itself had swallowed the remaining nuclear weapons, which were now surely liquefied.

Earlier, Secretary Alvarez had quietly confided to McKeown, with some satisfaction, that this dramatic, albeit tragic, solution to the nuclear impasse with Iran probably was more effective than their endless jabbering in Geneva.

Majid Tabatabai sat next to his old mentor, Dr. McKeown, smiling proudly. But instead of following his brother's lengthy formulae, his eyes remained fixed on the first whiteboard, where, in Farsi, Daoud had written: "For world peace. For Dr. Ali Javadpour. Peace be upon him."

CHAPTER 17

◇◇◇

Uf Widerluege!

Control Room, Project Zulfiqar Facility

The encrypted cell phone rang shrilly next to the unmoving dust-covered body on the ground. It rang for a few seconds and then quit. A grimy reddened hand lay on top of it. After about two more minutes, it started ringing again and this time it rang long enough so that an automated feature took it to voice mail, which recorded the caller's message, and played it audibly because the speaker had been inadvertently turned on when its owner dropped it almost two days earlier.

"Gruezi, Herr Jafari. Mayer in Zurich here. I hope your day is going well. Just to let you know that your various orders over the last few days have netted you well over a hundred million dollars in profits. Your shrewd investments are again literally right on the money. As always, we stand in awe of your ability to predict the markets. I really don't know how you do this, but it's amazing. Please phone me at your first opportunity. Next time in Zurich, lunch is on me. Good bye! Uf Widerluege!"

The phone went silent. More dust drifted down from the cracked ceiling.

Finally, the index finger on top of the cell phone stirred.

The End

ACKNOWLEDGEMENTS

Once upon a time, there was a CIA operations officer, who truly feared nuclear weapons and how they could affect our world. John Hersey's description of the outline of three shadows seared into the wall at Hiroshima has always haunted me.

The idea for this novel began, like many of my CIA operations, with a "what if" question playing in my mind. In this case, it was a question during a conversation with Rolf Mowatt-Larssen, my best friend, nicknamed "Kurtz" for good reasons while serving in Moscow, who led the Agency's Counterterrorist Center's Weapons of Mass Destruction Department for three years after the dark days of 9/11, and later as Director of the Department of Energy's Office of Intelligence and Counterintelligence. It was in 2016, during the first set of Iranian nuclear negotiations, and my question was what if the Iranians decide to cheat. This was where it all began. Rolf was intrigued and has been one of my biggest cheerleaders. Since our first meeting in Zurich in 1994, he has always been like a brother to me, steadfast in his friendship and loyalty. And like Conrad's Kurtz, he and I have stared into the heart of darkness – in our case an abyss of nuclear annihilation of a high-yield weapon – and uttered, "the horror, the horror."

I had several talented editors of early versions of this novel, notably my daughter, Elizabeth Lawler, and former CIA public spokesman and author, Bill Harlow. Their expertise and suggestions were vital. Likewise, the very talented and courageous senior intelligence operative, John Massie, another national hero whose deeds the American people will never know, saved me from some grievous errors right before publication. Thriller editor, Ed Stackler, essentially gave me a seminar in thriller-writing with his many valuable edits. Ed could get inside my characters' heads just like I did with my recruitment targets.

I owe thanks to my brother-in-law, Tommy Schleier, for his detailed knowledge of pistols and shotguns, and for serving as an inspiration for Texas rancher, Tommy Merrill. My appreciation goes to FBI Supervisory Special Agents Robert Graves and Dal Rae Summers for their valuable advice on FBI procedure. Dr. Larry Logory, a nuclear physicist at Lawrence Livermore National Laboratory, turned me onto the esoteric world of the hunt for Mersenne primes. My lifelong friend since our early teens, Ray Wood, a brilliant geophysicist, advised me on volcanology. Naturally, all mistakes are solely mine.

Other early readers included my friend, neighbor and constant walking companion, Bob Moll, who made a number of excellent suggestions. Marc Cameron, a *New York Times* best-selling thriller-writer, has been unstinting in his efforts on my behalf. Marc has been an inspiring supporter and staunch ally

I also owe a deep debt of gratitude to my former colleague, Jason Matthews, a superb CIA case officer and author of the *Red Sparrow* spy trilogy, for his many detailed emails to me with advice on writing espionage thrillers and for urging me onwards. His recent tragic death affected me deeply.

Dr. David Charney, a distinguished forensic psychiatrist and one of the foremost U.S. experts on the motivations for espionage, provided key validation of my descriptions of spy recruitment. I half-jokingly refer to him as "the pathologist," and to myself as "the disease."

As a first-time author, I found it easier to model some of my characters after friends, especially the good guys. I mean who is going to sue me for being one of the heroes in a story? As for the bad guys...well that's Top Secret.

The good-guy physicists at Lawrence Livermore National Lab, Drs. Robert Carlton and Rand McKeown, were based on my friends, Drs. Robert Canaan and Rand McEachern in Z program. They surely believe that I must have been high on drugs when I described certain nuclear weapon designs in the story such as the fictional concept of "neutron phasing." Well, as someone once said, there's realism, and there's entertainment. Guys, I apologize if I violated the laws of physics. Let's ascribe it to entropy, or the gradual decline into disorder.

The CIA DDO Paula Davenport is based on my dear friend and accomplished senior CIA case officer, Paula Doyle. Brian Bannock, the Chief of Counterintelligence for the Counterproliferation Center, is modeled after Scott Stewart – both wily Scots who are CI experts. Scott was my real CI counterpart and valuable ally in many of my own counterproliferation operations.

Daoud Tabatabai was loosely fashioned after my friend, David Taubenheim, a brilliant engineer. The allusion to Lacy Merrill's Presbyterian pastor, a transplanted Scot with a powerful style of delivery, is based on the distinguished Dr. David Renwick, pastor of National Presbyterian Church.

Conor McBane, the persistent proliferation pursuer, was closely modeled after my friend, Dr. Rens Lee, who sadly did not live to see his avatar in print. His loss is the world's loss.

Gary Scott, who is Lane Andrews's mentor, is based on Gary Schroen, who really was my mentor at The Farm and is a true expert on Iranian operations and culture. He was an early reader and also vetted my Iranian scenes for accuracy and realism. Gary is one of the most decorated CIA officers in recent history (our own Audie Murphy) and author of "First In," in which he described leading the first group of brave CIA officers into Afghanistan within two weeks after 9/11. No finer model for my fictional hero, Gary Scott, exists. I stand in awe of him.

As I wrote this book, I often sat next to a soulcatcher – an amulet carved from the femur of a bear and used by the shaman of the Tsimshian tribe of the Pacific Northwest Coast of British Columbia and Alaska. It was given to me by my business partner, dear friend and former CIA officer, Tracy Smith, on my birthday, two years before his tragic death at a young age. It symbolizes the mystical properties of the metaphysics of recruitment that I describe in my Soulcatcher talk and which is known only to The Guild. Tracy understood this. I miss him dearly.

This story was written in recognition of all of the brave men and women of the CIA and FBI. They are our real heroes, often in the shadows, but silently moving events for a freer, safer world. We are all better off because of them.

And to The Guild. I cannot say any more. You know who you are. Do what you need to do. God bless you and our country.

Finally, I wish to acknowledge the unceasing love and support of my First Reader, my dear wife, Ellen. I could not have done this without her and the love of our children, Elizabeth, Austin and Sarah.